# EVER WINTER

## PETER HACKSHAW

Jo,
Thank you for spreading the word and being amazing!
Peter

**PORTAL** BOOKS

This is the 2nd book I've signed!

*For Laura, Arthur, Violet and Rose.*

# Contents

# Part One

# ONE

## Meat

———————

Henry had only ever laid eyes upon one man who wasn't of his kin, and he'd not been long dead when they found him.

"Meat is meat," Father said, then went about the fellow with a whalebone in the normal fashion, not hurrying the task, but casting a watchful gaze about them as he cut.

The snow had not yet covered the man's tracks and Henry could tell he'd not been killed where he lay. If he had, another human or beast would've done the same as them and taken the primal cuts.

Father held the man's clothing up, revealing a pale, sunken chest. Its skin stretched tight over a ribcage that no longer heaved with the rhythm of the lungs.

"This is where they stuck him," Father said, gesturing toward a slit of a wound between two of the man's ribs. It reminded Henry of an eye, although he didn't say so. The late afternoon sun had started its slow descent and a gust of wind snapped at them, whipping Henry's dull, mouse-colored hair across his face. He gathered it in a gloved hand, tucked it into his hood and pulled the hood as far as he could over his forehead. A scarf covered much of Henry's face and trapped the warmth of his breath within.

"Must've fled and thought he'd got away, but the blood escaped him too quick. Can't bolt from the cold, either." Father

3

held the layers of clothing as if he were counting them. "Weren't dressed too well for it... wearing *man-mades...*"

Henry nodded, still transfixed by the neat hole that no longer bled. The dead man's meager garments were a stark contrast to their own: Father wore the pelt of a Big White with the head still attached, which made it look as if Father's skull was held between its jaws, while Henry's coat was a mélange of furs – a tapestry of arctic fox and the wolverine, the muskox and the sea lion.

Father continued to hack off what pieces he could, poking his tongue out as he always did when concentrating.

"Don't know what he was doing this far out o' Lantic." Their homeland had once been a vast ocean, before the Ever Winter. It stretched for hundreds and hundreds of leagues in every direction. It was one icescape, one color, and it was all that Henry had known.

Still saying nothing, Henry finally moved his gaze from the man's fatal wound as Father pulled innards outward and bagged them in a sealskin. Bile rose in his throat, and he thought for a moment that he might throw up in front of Father. He loosened his face-scarf and took a deep breath of the crisp air.

"Guts are bad eating, but we'll use 'em for bait," Father said.

Henry looked away, only to be drawn this time to the man's face. It was a death-mask, frostbitten in places and set in a final expression of accusation. Henry couldn't help feeling guilty under the corpse's silent scrutiny. He blinked, letting the dead man win their staring game, then scanned the distance for any sign of movement.

"Why don't we drag him, Father? I could fetch the sled."

Henry wanted to get home. He daren't admit it then, but he was worried. He'd always wanted to meet *others*, but this wasn't how he'd ever pictured it.

Father cast him a withering look. The cold formed a mist that appeared to take his words away as he spoke them.

"This dead 'un might have companions. My guess is, they'll be looking to finish the job. They'll want proof of a kill... or the man-meat. Likely both." He pointed the whalebone at the corpse, then cut deep into the leg around the calf muscle, making a large diamond in the flesh, which he stripped and bagged with the innards. Henry knew Father would be cursing that he didn't have his saw, which they'd left beside the ice-hole they'd fished the past month, for when it froze anew.

"Take half a day to get back here with the sled," he continued. "Might take 'em less to find him. If we drag him between us without the sled, his deadweight will be a burden. We'd be slow and asking for trouble with the Big Whites."

Father paused for a second, wiped gems of ice from his beard, then carried on cutting. "We take what we can and we move swiftly on, let the snow cover our tracks, take a long route so it does the job and lets none fathom our desty."

Father gave Henry a pointed glance and Henry realized he was supposed to be helping.

Taking the hint, he checked the man's boots, only to find them useless; old, man-made and long worn. He took the laces, then wrestled the dead man's jacket from him, trying to ignore the corpse's head as it bobbed in resistance to their vulgar robbery. He unzipped the fleece that formed the second layer, while Father took what meat he could.

Henry met the corpse's gaze once more. He pitied the dead man and pondered what kind of person he'd been. Had he deserved his death? It mattered none, but he fancied they might have talked had they found him sooner. They might have learned of the other remnants out there. *People.*

Henry bagged the garments they wanted to keep. The dead man had no sack nor satchel upon him; no food, or spear. He had no means of lasting a single night exposed.

In a hidden trouser pocket, Henry found a slim knife that Father called *Anteek*, which meant it was very old. It had been sharpened and oiled and Henry tried it against the dead man's lower leg. He found it good for stabbing the frozen matter, but not sufficient to hack off a limb. Resigned to the fact they could only strip flesh from the man in crude squares and diamonds, they turned the corpse face down in the snow to get to the easier rump cuts. All the while, the sun set defiantly in a blaze of pinks and oranges that they both ignored.

-

The trek home was the nearest to silence that Henry could remember. There was a tautness in the air as they tramped through the powder snow, Father deep in thought, clutching the sealskin tightly to his chest.

After some time, Henry realized they'd picked up the pace, though he wasn't sure which of them was responsible for the swiftness in their strides. They soon grew weary in the blizzard that met them after the day's light had been extinguished, an hour into their exaggerated route back to their homestead.

"Don't scare the girls none, Henry... nor Martin either. No talk of him being *stuck*. We say the cold got him, which it likely did in the end," said Father. Home was finally in sight; a distant smudge on the otherwise flat and sterile icescape.

"Ain't never seen a man other than you, Pa," Henry uttered. "That dead 'un was taller than me, but he wasn't nearly as big as you."

He wanted to say more, but was unsure what else to say. So, he kept quiet and concentrated on the warmth of the blubber lamp, which would be burning low in the igloo to keep the boy-bairn warm. He imagined there might even be a broth awaiting them, which was a rare treat on account of the baby and the fact that his mother needed her strength for the milk. Henry smiled to himself at the thought of seeing his siblings.

The wire encircled the homestead and protected them from Big Whites and other predators, who would become ensnared in it should they try to cross. It was a tangled ring of items collected over the years; things found in the ice, mostly. Frayed and broken things that hinted of the old world: scraps of metal and plastic, and bones from the animals they'd eliminated, which rattled collectively in the wind. They'd killed a few things that had gotten caught in the wire over the years and found some already dead from the struggle. In a way, the wire was both forcefield and monument, and in rare times of a still, peaceful wind, it became an alarm bell.

Father threw the sealskin over the wire then carefully wrangled through the jagged web. Henry followed, snagging himself on it momentarily until he unhooked himself. Father shook his head as he waited.

Night had fallen. The starry sky lit the icescape below it and the igloo, a perfect disc shape, mimicked the full moon in its elevation.

They passed the ice-hole they'd cut to expose the seawater below and allow them to reach the fish underneath, then they reached the narrow entrance of their home.

-

It was a strange taste; *man-meat*. It was indeed a prize, although raw. They stored most of it, and as they ate the rest, Henry wondered if he could ever bring himself to eat the meat of his kin. He watched them as they all chewed in silence: Mother and Father; his sisters Mary, Hilde and Iris; his brother Martin; and the boy-bairn who was sleeping in Mother's arms. Henry wondered if they all shared the same thought at that moment.

Father broke the silence and said that providing sickness had not taken a body, they should eat, even if it were one of them. Iris, the youngest of the girls, couldn't contain her laughter, but the others kept serious faces.

"It's just meat. 'Tis food," he continued. "You can have mine when the time comes, but not for a few years yet!"

They all laughed then, although Martin seemed bewildered by it all and looked like the littlest thing would make him cry. Martin always had a worried look upon his face. They finished their meal in silence.

A shard of reflective glass hung from a coil of flex in the center of the igloo. It had once been part of a gilded mirror that had been intentionally shattered and the pieces shared amongst families in the time of the Great-Greats. Henry caught glimpses of his siblings in the glass as it turned. Mary, Hilde and Martin all resembled Mother, with their fair hair and blue eyes and the same identical nose that tipped up slightly at the end. Mother's ancestors had come from a place far to the north, but the name of the place had been forgotten over time, though they still knew some of the words the people from that land had spoken.

Henry and Iris had darker hair; mousy in color, almost brown. They shared a constellation of freckles that trailed across their noses, and had fuller cheeks with dimples. Although he was closest in age to Mary, Henry felt more of a connection to his youngest sister, who followed him around whenever he was home. He supposed they took after Father, but it was hard to envisage. Father had long silvery hair and his face had been cloaked with a thick beard for as long as Henry could remember. The skin on Henry's face was smooth, like his sisters', although he'd gotten hair in other places which had seemed to happen overnight. Father's eyes were more green than blue (like Henry's) and he was very tall, with a heavy frame, whereas Henry was skinny beneath the layers that cloaked him. He doubted he'd ever be the size of Father, but even Father had been a boy once.

-

Iris grew tired and laid her head on Henry's lap. Henry entwined a curl of her hair in between his fingers and watched as Mary and Hilde played backgammon on the fine board their mother had once hewn from the bones of a beast long-frozen in the ice. Hilde lost her tokens as she always did and went to bed in a sulk, which was her way.

Unaffected by her sister's actions, Mary carefully unwrapped the plastic bag which protected the family's only book and started to read from where she'd left off the night before. It was a very old, frightening story of a demon that dressed as a clown and murdered children in a world that no longer existed.

Henry had read the book himself more than twenty times. He found it terrifying in places, but lots of the chapters confused him. There were too many words that his family did not know the true meaning of and too many things that were completely alien to him. What was *television*? What was a *storm drain*, or a *pig*, or a *balloon*, or a *cola*? What was a *Batman*? What was a *1958 Red Plymouth Fury*?

The words in the book described what a clown was, but that wasn't enough for Henry to picture one clearly in his mind, or comprehend what its purpose was, other than someone (or something) appearing as something else.

Martin and the bairn clung to Mother, who looked exhausted and ready to let sleep take her. She kissed the bairn on the forehead and smiled at Martin, who was resisting going to sleep himself. His eyelids were heavy and he blinked defiantly, trying to stay awake and repel the inevitable.

Meanwhile, Father sorted through the belongings they'd taken from the man who'd become their meal, discovering a small wind-up torch in another secret pocket which layers had cushioned and concealed when they had frisked the man.

Father pointed at the torch triumphantly in the silence and Henry nodded, as pleased with the find as Father was, but unable to move through fear of stirring his sister or disturbing the others. The torch shone brighter in the igloo than the blubber lamp and the fact that it needed no oil was in itself miraculous. Father continued to play with the torch, drawing ribbons and bows with its light, but careful not to shine it near his family as they slept beneath furs and timeworn blankets. Just as the wire circled the igloo, the family formed a circle within it. They were the hours of the clock and the mirrored glass was the center-point of the dial.

After finally carrying Iris to her bedding, Henry wandered outside beneath the brilliant stars that dotted the nocturnal canvas above him, providing their own light. He gazed out toward the wire and the infinite whiteout beyond it. Henry tried to imagine a place where people lived amongst others; tens of families, maybe hundreds, with children his age. He thought of new conversations and the sounds of new voices. He tried to imagine faces that were unlike those of his family, and pictured unnamed girls that were not his sisters. But the visions in his mind all morphed into one or all of his siblings.

Henry stared at the constellation he loved the most; *Canis Minor*, 'The Little Dog'. It wasn't the brightest, or the most spectacular, and that was why it was special to Henry. He had chosen it as his favorite amongst all others.

After some time lost in a tangle of his own thoughts, Henry went back inside and cocooned himself in his sleeping bag, zipping it up to his neck. He closed his eyes, but his mind was haunted by the face of the man his family had eaten.

Sensing that his brother was awake, Martin whispered from where he lay beside him, "What did the man look like, Henry?" Martin's voice was a higher pitch than Henry's, which emphasized his youth. Henry lay with his back to Martin in the darkness, but he could imagine the exact earnest expression that his brother likely wore.

Henry let the question sink in. He tried not to, but it was impossible. He saw the man's patchy dark beard and sunken cheeks and hollow eyes. He saw cracked hands and black fingernails and crooked teeth in a wide-open mouth, with a tongue that his father had removed for the feast.

Henry tried to think of a clever answer to keep his brother quiet, which was usually no task at all, but he had nothing to offer and so Martin asked again, thinking Henry had not heard him the first time.

"He was just a man, Martin," Henry replied casually, as if it were entirely normal to see a stranger, something that happened every day on Lantic.

Martin wasn't satisfied. He pressed him further, until Henry finally gave up and turned to face his brother.

"He looked about the same age as Father, but he wasn't as big."

Martin seemed pleased with the morsel of information and gave up for the evening. Henry turned to face the igloo wall once more and wondered how old his father truly was. He didn't know how old he was himself, although it was somewhere between ten an' three and ten an' six, according to his mother.

Mary was one younger than him, Hilde one younger than her, Iris was nine or ten and Martin was closer to seven.

That night, Henry dreamed that the man they'd eaten had Father's face. Over and over his mind replayed the cutting of the man's flesh, and each time his father was pulling all kinds of expressions, trying to communicate, although no sound came from him. He knew in the dream that Father was still alive, even as he was cutting and bagging him. Father could not protest, as his tongue was in Henry's pocket.

# TWO

## Whiskers

The day began in the usual way, except the family had meat in their stomachs.

Henry had been checking the integrity of the wire with Martin, while Father sharpened the few weapons the family possessed. Henry made a tight knot where the wire had come loose in the wind. The scraps of old tin cans and other junk found frozen in the ice of Lantic clattered and rattled, whilst Martin wrestled with the shaking wire. Satisfied with their work, the boys trudged back to the igloo, with Martin held in a gentle, brotherly headlock by his eldest sibling.

Hilde sat by the ice-hole, trying to catch fish. She used a net attached to a spiked hook that had once been an anchor for a keel-boat or dinghy and was demonstrating to Iris how it was done. The youngest girl chortled, eager to try for herself, before Hilde told her to hush so as not to frighten the fish away.

Mary prepared a daypack for a hunt and filled sealskin bags with rations of dried fish and water, plus spare clothing and a foil blanket in case anyone fell through the ice into the freezing waters, or were injured and couldn't get back to the homestead in a blizzard.

Mother emerged from the igloo with the bairn swaddled in furs and some of the new *man-mades* they'd acquired the day before. Her hair was braided as it often was and she wore a wide grin as she soothed the child in her arms.

"God Morgon, husband," called Mother. "Why don't *you* take the baby today and let *me* catch our family a big, fat, juicy walrus? Vad tycker du?"

Henry translated Mother's words in his mind quite naturally; *What do you think?* Mother had clung onto the few lexes she remembered her parents speaking, which were unique to where their ancestors had hailed from. She'd passed what she could recall to her own family (feeling it her duty to do so) and they had embedded the phrases in their everyday conversations.

Henry knew that Mother felt stifled whenever she bore a child, spending months cooking it in her stomach and so much more time nurturing it when it was out. She was good with most weapons and had been a better hunter than most men when they'd lived in the Favela, which Father was particularly proud of. Henry could tell she missed the thrill of it and was both restless and bored being confined to the igloo with the baby.

Father approached his wife and child, smiling as he neared them.

"What do I think? I think *ten more moons*, Agneta! Ten more moons, and if the baby survives, you can go out alone if you like and kill something big." He used his arms to illustrate the size of the imagined prey, then they embraced and kissed the bairn together.

"They love each other a lot, don't they?" said Martin, picking up on the conversation between their parents as the boys neared the ice-hole.

"They've known each other since they were younger than you are now, Martin. Probably been lovin' nearly that whole time," Henry replied, releasing the grip on his brother.

"Will you and Mary have a bairn?" asked Martin. Shocked, Henry raised both eyebrows as high as they'd go.

"Mary's our sister. You don't have family with family, you prong!"

"But who else are you going to marry, Henry?"

"Mother says I'm handsome. One daylight I'll find some

people. There'll be girls." It seemed that Henry had thought about the subject already. "An' the way I see it, Father ain't much to eyeball, yet he got Mother to like him. I'll marry one who can hunt better than Mary an' catch fish an' gut them better than Hilde."

Martin looked very serious all of a sudden and reached up to put his hand on his older brother's shoulder.

"I don't want to ever get with a girl, Henry. I don't want bairns of my ownsome," he whispered as they came in earshot of their family.

"I'm sure you'll change your mind when you're a bit older," Henry said.

"No way! That's a big deal," Martin said. Henry laughed until his brother finally joined in.

Later, when they set out, Henry searched for tracks, but he couldn't find evidence of even a muskrat in the vicinity. He eventually realized that Father had no intention of hunting. He was looking for something else entirely, and had taken his son in the direction of where they'd found the frozen corpse the day before.

Henry ceased walking and waited for Father to stop ahead of him. He counted eight deep footprints in the snow between them.

"Mary wanted to come. Why did you make her stay?" Henry asked, then added, "She's a good 'un with the slingshot."

Henry rarely challenged Father, but he didn't entirely feel like a child anymore. He knew he still had a lot to learn and he was mostly obedient. He helped whenever it was requested of him and did the chores that had been assigned to him, but he'd also killed plenty of things to qualify him as a man. Henry felt something stir. A changing. He decided he would start to speak up when he wanted to be heard. When things were important to him and needed to be said.

"I know. She can knock a hawk out of the sky with a shard of ice. I've seen her do it plenty."

"But you—"

"I wanted her home today, to protect the family," Father interrupted, a somber look on his face.

"We're not hunting today, are we?" Henry asked.

"No. Not animals, anyway. I don't want that dead 'un's lot to start venturing close to ours. That'd be bad news for us. *Atomic bad.*" Henry was surprised by his father's honesty. He'd expected to be told to keep quiet, or not to ask too many questions.

"What will you do if we find more people out here, then?"

Father frowned and looked down at the snow. Henry remained where he stood. The gap between them felt further than it was.

"It depends, I suppose. It depends on the number of them. It depends if they look like they'd do us harm if they found the homestead. And it depends if we see them first. Let's hope we see them first."

"Why would they do us harm? We're not bothering them any. We're just a family," Henry said.

The wind picked up and Father had to raise his voice above it to be heard.

"People are cruel. They would harm us because they can. I've never said this afore, but we, *people*, shouldn't have survived."

"What do you mean?"

"The world had a chance without us. The winter came, and betwixt one daylight an' next, it was better. It'd cleansed itself of our cities and our drilling and our warring. The few that survived the first cold, they had *the gift* to start anew, this is what my granddad told me and mine. We could've gotten salvation, but we created suffering, even then. It's what we've always done."

"Not us," Henry said. "We've done nothing to no one."

"I know, lad, but you've not seen it – the evil that exists, and the hatred. We kept you all from it, but it's still out there on the landside. The Favela, once peaceful, is now a place of evil. Mother and I left when my seed took in her belly. You know the fable."

Henry thought about Father's words before giving his reply,

just as the wind softened. In the distance the same wind traveled onward, sweeping the top layer of powder snow up into the air in spirals, like churning clouds.

"I'd like to think we survived for a reason. *People*. We ain't all bad 'uns," Henry said, but he privately wondered if he was a bad 'un, because he'd eaten another human, after all.

Father went to add something, then changed his mind. He looked down at his prints in the snow, then turned and looked in the direction they'd been heading toward, where the wind stirred the thaw as it journeyed away from them and beyond that, a place where lay the remains of the man with the secret pockets.

"We've trekked enough this day. Let's get back. If trouble's coming, it will come no matter what. We need to be watchful, is all. Watchful, then ruthless. Fathom it."

Henry waited as Father retraced his steps and stood level with him, and Henry thought of the long years that lay between them; a gap that seemed smaller as he grew older. "Well? What you waiting for, Henry-son? The end of winter?"

The sun, high above, told them it was a little after midday. Henry looked up at it and wondered about all the things that the sun had ever witnessed; all the warring, all the sickness and death. Even their own robbery of the dead man. The sun knew all but would never tell, and that was just fine with Henry.

When they reached the homestead, the sun had just set, and this time Henry had watched it disappear over the horizon.

There was laughter coming from inside the igloo and it made them both smile. Iris was giggling hysterically and even Hilde could be heard joining in.

Then they heard a man's voice. Henry's heart sank. He looked at Father, but he was already rushing toward the entrance of the igloo.

Inside, the flickering yellow glow of the blubber lamp bled

with the white brilliance of the wind-up torch. The igloo was a cavern and the shadows of the family danced upon its walls.

Where Father usually sat, was a man at least a decade younger than Father. Disheveled auburn hair swept across his forehead, in a wave tucked around one of his ears. The man's pockmarked skin was a few shades darker than Henry's; it cloaked the rings around his eyes. His whiskery beard had flecks of gray in it.

Henry's sisters were staring at the man in awe, as if he was something special; an apparition. Henry felt annoyed as he beheld the intruder sitting in Father's place. It seemed disrespectful somehow and he took an instant disliking to the man who sat there, smirking at them.

Henry couldn't quite believe that his whole life had been spent with his family in isolation and in just over a day he'd seen not one, but two outsiders; two men that weren't his kin. One alive and one dead. *The dead man.* Henry recalled his thought that the sun above had seen all and kept their dark deeds a secret... *Pilfering a corpse's belongings. Hacking pieces off of him to later consume.* As Henry looked around the igloo, he saw that those dark deeds were surfacing before him. He remembered the dead man's garments his father had rifled through the previous night, and realized with a jolt of panic that his siblings each wore something that had belonged to the dead man – a navy blue fleece jumper with *Helly Hansen* stitched upon the breast of it; a long-sleeved cotton undershirt that would once have been white, but seemed now to be every spectrum of beige; thick wool socks; and a pair of padded trousers of a material unknown to Henry that rustled when the wearer moved. There was blood on some of the garments, but the stranger seemed not to have noticed.

The man's eyes had widened as Henry and Father entered their home and removed their outer furs, but he did not move from where he sat, which seemed rude to Henry, although his sisters and Martin still gazed at the man with fascinated smiles.

The silent visitor was also dressed in man-mades, yet his were put together from the rags of other garments. The patterns and materials of the patchwork were mismatched, the colors faded and covered in filth. It was similar to the way Henry's attire had been collaged from different pelts, but the effect was wildly different. Henry thought the man looked like the clown in the book. A demon.

Henry noted his sister's slingshot propped against the wall of the igloo where she bedded down each night. The stranger must have convinced her he meant no harm when he'd crossed the wire. Henry was unsure if the man had surrendered his own weapons, or whether he had them upon him still.

"Daddy, isn't it wonderful? We have a *guest!*" declared Iris, finally breaking the silence, beaming and clapping her hands together gleefully. Martin copied her until he saw Henry's disapproving expression.

Only Mother held a countenance different to all the rest. She was smiling like Henry's siblings, but it wasn't her usual smile. It was painted on.

"He's a *Salvage Man!*" added Hilde.

Mother had told them of the Salvagers in the Favela. They were tough, hardy men who found where the rising waters had covered the *old places*. They would go through the ice and explore the ruin of the citadel, bringing back what they could find. The problem was that the easy things, things found in rooms of buildings still standing near the top of the ice, had been taken. Whatever remained was harder to get, because even the hardiest Salvager couldn't stand the frozen waters or hold their breath long enough to get to the unspoiled bounty.

From what Henry knew about Salvage Men, he couldn't imagine the stranger before him being strong enough in mind or body to go through the ice, even for a meal.

"Bom dia. I'm Ginger Lanner." The man finally stood and extended his hand across the circle of Henry's family to introduce himself. His accent was alien to Henry and although Lanner was taller than Father, his build was wiry. *A good wind would blow him over,* Henry thought, which was something his mother had once said to him.

Henry assumed Father wasn't going to shake the man's hand at first, because he stared at it and left their uninvited guest holding it out in front of him. Finally, though, he reached out and took a firm grip of the stranger's hand.

"*Diga-me*. What's a Salvage Man doing out here? Nothing under the water this far out," said Father.

"Didn't expect a bunch of yourn on top of the ice this far out, *ou*," the man laughed.

"We've never had a guest," Iris chipped in. "Doesn't he talk nice? Do all people talk like that?" No one responded. "Do you have children, Ginger Lanner?" she asked the man, whose hand was yet to be released by Father's grip.

Henry was troubled as he saw the altered expression on Lanner's face as he met Father's gaze. There was something unspoken going on between them which Henry couldn't quite fathom and his sisters were oblivious of. Lanner donned a gap-toothed grin, yet his eyes glinted dangerously. Father wore no expression, but his muscles were taut, and his eyes bored into the intruder's.

After a few seconds, Ginger Lanner broke the stare, which reminded Henry of his own silent battle with the dead man the day before. The intruder chuckled to himself in a high-pitched, childlike manner. His mask had slipped during the exchange, and now when his eyes darted around the tiny, now claustrophobic room, they lingered on the girls longer than they should have. Henry felt rage build inside him and Mother's eyes upon him the whole time.

The mirrored shard twisted from its coil in the center of the igloo, reproducing the faces and expressions of each of them as it turned; Iris, joyful. Martin, wary, Henry, vexed. Mary, tense. Hilde, doubtful. Ginger Lanner, malicious, abnormal. Father, benevolent. Mother, restrained...

Henry thought of how Iris would pull funny faces to make them laugh. Each expression in the mirror was such a contrast to the next, it might have been amusing on any other day.

"Ginger Lanner? Do you have any children?" Iris repeated, and the man's pretense changed once more. His mask was restored, and he turned to Iris with overwrought charm and pretended to steal her nose. She gave a delighted squeal.

"Don't ask him personal things, Iris. Herr Lanner has barely been here one hour," said Mary, as Hilde cast Mary a disapproving look, laced with condemnation and her usual jealousy.

"I don't mind, little dear. It's just a question. *Os filhos?* Sadly, I don't, but I come from a place with many children," he said, and he touched Iris' hair. It was then that Henry noticed Father had readied his knife, though he kept it concealed under his bearskin coat. Only Henry could see it from this angle, but Mother knew her husband too well and shook her head, then gestured discreetly toward their children. Henry understood the gesture well. *Don't kill him in front of the girls and Martin.*

Lanner feigned interest in the backgammon board, tracing his grubby fingers along the lines as if he didn't know what it was.

"Do you have a *wife?*" asked Hilde. She blushed as she said it, like Henry had never witnessed before. Ginger Lanner seemed to enjoy the attention; he seemed giddy on it, sitting back down between Hilde and Mary, like he was the head of the family, or their husband. Henry hated him most of all then, and felt a surge of anger.

"Not yet, Hilde," Lanner said, winking at her. Hilde blushed some more.

"What brings you here, *friend?*" asked Henry's father, making the word *friend* sound like *enemy*. His grip on the knife remained firm under the bearskin, and Lanner's eyes widened, noticing the hidden threat.

"Just wandering. You never know what you'll find out on Lantic." Lanner took a sip of broth from a plastic cup with a picture of a cartoon Mouse on it. "Nice furs, amigo. Why don't you put 'em down and come sit with your family? You must be tired from your own wandering, *si?*"

"That's a Big White! Our father killed it before I was born and it bit off one of his fingers," said Martin proudly.

Ginger Lanner looked at the hand that held the bearskin. He actually seemed impressed by the story. No one ever survived against a Big White on their own.

"I count five fingers. Let's take a look at the other hand." Lanner's smile was a crooked sneer. The girls seemed untroubled by it, but Henry had never seen someone grin in such a wicked way before. It was unnerving, that smirk.

*How did they kill the clown in the book? Wasn't it the slingshot?*

Father put the bearskin down and the knife with it, then held up his other hand, which had only four digits upon it. A beam of light from the mirror caught his hand and lingered on the old wound. A scar ran deep into his palm from where the middle finger was meant to be rooted. Henry knew the story; Father had built a shelter during his ritual. The Ritual was a coming-of-age event that all had to endure, where the survival of the Great-Greats was celebrated by sending each child beyond the safety of the homestead to spend a night out on the ice alone. Father had gone out into the wilderness, assembled a makeshift igloo for the night and woke to find a Big White caving the roof in to get to him. He'd fought savagely to stay alive. Somehow, he managed to kill the Big White after blinding it, but had lost his finger in the battle, which had lasted just seconds. No one had believed him in the Favela and suggested his finger had been taken by something smaller, until they realized that he was wearing its fur. Over the years, his frame had filled the pelt from the inside out; in time, he had become the bear.

"Four! So it is true? What a tale! *Parabens!* Such bravery...I might've heard a tale like that afore," declared the guest, much louder than he needed to be in the small room.

"What brings you to our home?" Henry asked the question and took a seat next to Mother and the baby, strategically placing himself on Lanner's other side, making it difficult for the man to defend himself should things go awry.

Henry could see that Lanner was studying him. The man bit his lip, clearly annoyed with Henry's question. Henry assumed that Lanner was calculating the odds and options available to him. Then the man restored his mask, perhaps for the benefit of the enthralled girls.

"Well, the truth is, I was looking for a friend of mine." Henry felt his pulse race and hoped that it hadn't translated to his face in a shade of crimson. "I haven't seen him for several days."

The children looked at their father and Henry in unison and

Henry could tell that Lanner had noticed it. The man opened his mouth in realization of something and Henry imagined a tiny spark had gone off in Lanner's brain, lining all the pieces together in a neat row as clear all of a sudden, as the moon rising outside. *The fleece, the undershirt, the trousers, the thick woolen socks, the LED torch...*

Henry touched the handle of his own knife, but Father gave him a look this time which said, *'Don't kill him in front of the girls or Martin,'* and Ginger Lanner witnessed that also. Lanner picked up a backgammon counter from the board, studied it, then returned it to the board. *Games.*

"He probably froze to death," Lanner added, without any trace of emotion. "How come you live all the way out here on your own? Don't seem fair on the *filhos* if you ask me. Safest place in the world is wherever there's a big group of like minds..."

"It was our choice. A different choice to most, but..." Father paused for a moment and looked as if he was pinching the words from the air around him. "We do what it takes. Something comes our way hinting danger we deal with it. I reckon we're safe enough."

"You have a lot of possessions between you all," Lanner replied, ignoring the threat. "More than most."

"Some of it belonged to our kin. They're ours now."

The uninvited guest flashed a smile, then erased it just as quickly. *"Entendo.* Tell me your story, *por favor."* Henry guessed Lanner meant the story of how their ancestors had survived the ever winter, or rather, the first weeks of it. People always wanted to know how they came to be and they clung on to what little they had from the old world.

Father sat finally and stroked his beard with the hand that had just four fingers on it. Lanner seemed pleased with the extra time he had given himself to think.

"Mine were from Merika, but lived near the warm pocket. My Great-Greats were both drilling holes under Lantic when they met, afore you could walk upon it. Was just luck they were where they were when the cold came, an' they made to the volcano where the temperature ne'er got too low. That part of the story is the same as most." Father spoke with a coldness that was unlike him.

"And yours, Agneta?" the guest asked Mother, having apparently learned her name when Father and Henry were absent. She painted a smile on her face once more and became *The Good Mother*.

"Mine were from the far, far north. They had a grand yot-boat that they lived on most of the time. They had many possessions. They came down here because they knew the ice was coming. They knew history. This, the ice, it all happened before," Mother replied.

"I heard that. We have some old 'uns and some smart 'uns." Lanner took another sip from the cup with the cartoon mouse upon it. "They say people with possessions didn't last long without them. But you're here, I see. Still got some things. Cold never got you, did it?" Maybe, Mother seemed unsure if it was a compliment or a slight, then she scowled at the guest for the first time. Lanner didn't react. Henry found it curious. He knew how his own family would react to each other's words and actions. But Lanner was not of them. He was an outsider in every way.

"Many didn't know how to survive, but my people knew winter. It was in their blood... it's in *my* blood. No, the cold never got me, or mine. What about you, *Mister Lanner*?" Mother sent her words with spikes upon them.

Lanner scratched at his beard, then cleared his throat. "I was told by my papa that ours were into warring. Paid monies to protect some of those peoples with possessions. When the winter came, monies were no good. Mine had *guns*... guns are real good. Proper possessions! They cut through the shit, pardon my language, *os pequenos*..." Henry wondered what had become of the family Lanner's ancestor had been protecting as Lanner continued, "That part of the story ain't the same as most! My great-great granny was the poorest of the poor. She was used to surviving before there was ever a need to for most. Cold came and she spat in its face. That bucket combo of grit and outright fearlessness is what I like to think keeps me alive today. *Sim.* I'm proud of my peoples. Mine rose up when the time came."

"We lived in a place once, where kin would do kin with cutters to survive the next day. 'Til our eyes were opened wide an' a God paved the way for this next life and we got out. We listened to and bided by his commandments and lived each day since in his debt. I'm proud of my peoples and something in that makes *me* fearless too." Father's tone had changed and Henry felt as if the room was getting smaller and smaller by the second. The air felt thicker than it had been and he silently blamed Lanner for that too; for polluting the homestead. Lanner turned to Iris all of a sudden, got to his feet and put his patchwork hood up. He held a jagged knife in his hand, but kept his arm to his side and the blade pointing toward the floor.

"Now, little dear, will you see me to the door? It's *moito* late and I don't think I'm gonna find my friend out here." He cast a look at Mother, then Father and finally Henry. He took Iris' hand and led her to the door.

Father picked up his bearskin once more and the weapon that lay under it. Everyone else stood and moved to the entrance of the igloo where Lanner was headed. The baby awoke and started to cry. Mary and Hilde looked worried, while Martin seemed bewildered and didn't know where to look or who to focus on.

"Ginger Lanner, will you come back to see us?" Iris asked, unaware of her siblings' anxieties.

"That I might, treasure," he replied, "but for now I'm going to get off. Let us play a little game... I'm going to turn every hundred steps, just to make sure you're still waving. Do you think you could wave until I become a tiny dot, Iris? *No horizonte distante?*" *On the distant horizon.* It was a clever maneuver by Lanner, but before she could answer, Father interrupted. "*Venha comigo.* I will see you to the wire." *Come with me.*

"There's no need," Lanner replied. "Stay in the warm with your good family." He stole Iris' nose a final time with the hand that didn't have a knife in its grasp. "*Adeus*, Iris. *Adeus*, girls. *Adeus*, the family of the bearkiller!" He raised his knife to his brow, saluted the family with it, and started to trek toward the wire alone.

"*Hej hej*, Ginger Lanner! Goodbye! *Boa noite!*" screeched Iris as she waved farewell to the man with the dead friend. Father had drawn his knife and taken a step toward the departing Lanner. Henry was eyeing Mary's slingshot.

"Don't, John! The children... and you, Henry!" Mother whispered urgently.

Lanner took slow, casual steps away from the family and began to whistle a tune that none of them knew.

"It has to be done," Father replied, turning toward her. "He ain't got a good bone in his skin!"

"You do this and more will come looking for him," Mother argued. The baby, sensing the tension, began to scream, but Mother did not try to soothe him.

"Is he a bad 'un?" Martin asked, ignored by all except Hilde, who gave him a look of contempt.

"And you think he'll forget about us? The girls? After all we went through to escape? We need to down him, Agneta," Father said.

"Do you fear him, Pa?" Martin asked, louder than before, which drew everyone's attention except Iris, who stood apart from them as she waved. Henry waited for Father's reply, as did the others.

"I don't fear him none. But I fear there may be others like him. That's never good for any."

Lanner stepped over the wire, stopped, then turned to the family. His voice carried on the wind across the space that divided them. "You can't keep your daughters locked up in the middle of Lantic, Bearkiller!"

The family watched as he turned his back on them once more and continued his unhurried strides from the igloo, as if proving his bravery, or madness. Mother grabbed Father's arm firmly, refusing to break her hold as he pulled away from her. "Let go and take the children inside," he said through gritted teeth.

"John! No!" Mother pleaded, but Father was agitated and finally shook his arm free of Mother's grasp. She grabbed him a second time and pushed her face close to his, frown lines creasing her forehead in a wide *M* shape, which always made Henry think of the way birds spread their wings in flight.

Lanner was fifty steps beyond the wire.

"Agneta, he's a danger to us all! We have to kill him! *I* have to!" Father declared.

"Please don't kill him, Father," Iris said simply, "Mother? Father won't kill Ginger Lanner, will he? He was nice."

Henry could tell Mother was conflicted.

"He's going to stick him," whispered Martin.

"I'll do it." Henry spoke quietly, in that moment believing himself capable of such a thing.

"I doubt it," Hilde snarled.

"No, Iris. He won't," Mother said finally. Father glowered and shook his head.

"Damn you, Agneta," he said before throwing his knife to the floor, where it stuck firm in the ice. Father went inside without another word. Mother looked hurt at first, then composed herself. Everyone except Iris stared at her.

"In," Mother instructed her children, though only Martin did as commanded.

"I need to stay here and wave at Ginger Lanner," Iris argued.

"In," Mother repeated and ushered her inside with a firm prod. Iris hung her head in defeat. Her sisters followed quietly, and the baby filled the silence with piercing cries. Henry was the last to go inside.

"It's a mistake," he said, but no one spoke to him.

Lanner was gone.

# THREE

## The Crudest Refinery

Henry woke earlier than usual, drenched in sweat from a nightmare. He tried to recall what he'd dreamt, but the second he'd opened his eyes his mind had erased itself and only fragments of the feelings he'd experienced from it lingered, leaving him unsettled.

Henry found that Father was gone from his sleeping bag. He found him outside, silently undoing the wire that surrounded the homestead. He knew then that they were going to leave their home and build another, further toward the center of what had been a mighty and deep sea.

Henry didn't question it. Instead, he helped Father in silence as the sun rose in the distance with its tantalizing promise of warmth. Yet, it remained a broken vow, never raising the temperature enough to break the cold spell.

By mid-morning, their long-time family home was empty. They'd managed to pack everything onto their sled, with the man-meat, dried fish and personal effects in sealskins slung from their shoulders. The baby was dressed in extra furs and looked twice his size, like a bear cub. He was swaddled around mother's waist, facing her with his head nestled between her bosoms and he slept much of the time, as the rhythm of the journey lulled him to sleep.

None of the children remonstrated. They all knew Father

wouldn't force them to move without good reason, and Lanner's visit had left everyone, apart from Iris, nervous. The atmosphere was altered and their moods were downcast. Henry couldn't remember it ever feeling that way in the homestead, even when times were hard and food was scarce.

Mother was abnormally quiet. Henry had seen her battle with her own conscience the night before; he knew that if Iris and Martin were a few years older, she wouldn't have hesitated to kill Lanner herself.

Henry, Father and Mary took turns to pull the sled in teams of two, allowing one person to rest their arms and shoulders for a time, before getting back to the long haul.

They traveled for five days, sleeping in makeshift shelters unlike the carefully built home they had long shared. The family moved farther and farther out on the ice, beyond anywhere they had ever ventured before. They finished the man-meat between them, and eventually found a spot they all reckoned upon.

The family set up the wire as they built their new home from hard-snow. Yet no sooner had they started, Henry pointed out a storm in the distance, which crept slowly toward them. They worked in haste, but it still took them five hours to complete their new home and unpack their belongings from the sled. They made it inside just before the weather turned for the worst all around them and the storm intensified

Inside the Igloo, there was an air of relief that they were all no longer exposed to the conditions outside and had secured a safe shelter for the family. But the temperament shifted once more, as the storm moved overhead and the skies rang with thunder and the howling of an ireful wind.

The snow was unceasing and soon dulled the sound of the bluster, as it covered the roof of the igloo. That noise was replaced by the sound of the baby crying, until he eventually succumbed to his tiredness and fell to sleep once more. Father unfurled his sleeping bag and everyone else followed suit.

~

The snow had put more distance between them and the outside and the austere weather confined them to their new home for days. Hunger pain and absence of energy left them subdued. They talked little and the storytelling and games of backgammon to pass time were replaced by silence, or sleep. The endless snow masked the ice all around them and made it impossible to breach. The family couldn't fish the waters less than a meter below. Father suggested breaking the ice floor within the igloo to reach the bounty beneath them, but it was too dangerous, in case they fell under the ice, or the structure around them fell in as they penetrated the floor below. As the days went on, the expression on his father's face became ever more serious and his temper increasingly short. The family argued in those moments, but none had the energy to sustain it and the awkward silence returned, broken only when the baby cried.

Henry had had another brother once, but that one had not survived long enough to gain a name. "It's harder to lose something once you've named it," Father had said. So, they waited until it was strong enough to eat food proper. The boy-bairn wasn't old enough yet to secure a name and they had still worried about it with the cold.

Stuck in the igloo, without food, Henry worried about his youngest sibling the most in their current predicament. The thought of death remained as he sat in silence watching Mother with him. He'd suggested once going out to see if there was anything to hunt, but Father told him simply, they'd be snow-blind and would be at greater risk of being prey to another creature than victor. In all likelihood, they'd just get lost and freeze to death without shelter. They were frustrated, but had no choice but to wait it out.

The comforting warmth of the blubber lamp died out when the last of the oil was burned. They huddled together for warmth, instead of in their usual circle; no longer the hours of the sundial clock. Twice, Father and Henry had to dig out the entrance when the snow threatened to encase them within.

Finally, the heavy snowfall ceased and the temperature rose slightly. The wind howled less and a calm fell within the igloo as well, although the immediate hunger remained. Henry caught Mother giving a huge sigh of relief, marking the moment they all left the igloo. She kissed the baby on his forehead.

Henry saw how the snow had built up around the igloo and obscured its shape.

There was no time to waste to get food. Any longer confined to the igloo would have been perilous.

Father clapped his hands loud, getting everyone's attention.

"We've all got jobs today," He said. "I'm going to smash the ice so we can fish. Hilde, Iris and Martin, I want you to set a second wire, a way past the first. Before the storm, as we trekked this way, I saw signs of a Big White. It was just half a day from here an' that's too chummy for me just now. Keep a lookout for each other. We ain't got no claim on this icescape yet."

The children nodded, glad to leave the igloo finally. Even Martin seemed pleased despite the danger.

"What about me and Hen?" Mary asked, already holding her slingshot.

"You won't need that, Mary-daughter," Father replied, "but you'll need this." He handed her a whalebone pick. "Take the sled. Be watchful. You an' Henry are gonna fetch us a seal or two. We need the oil and we need the meat, but the oil is important 'case the temperature drops quick."

Mary's face lit up. She looked at her brother and sprinted to the sled. Henry put on his boots and hurried after her.

The rarest thing on Earth was wood, which is why food was often eaten raw and use of the blubber lamps restricted to a minimum.

It wasn't always that way, according to Father. Wood came from trees, which grew everywhere on land once upon a time. The family had seen some old pieces of it, frozen or stuck beneath the ice crust they walked upon. Mostly they were rotten and crumbled easily, but some bits the children kept. Father said they weren't good for anything, unless they were burned. If they were burned, then they were gone for good. Wood was rare and wood was pointless. Oil was wondrous and it came from seals.

Henry and Mary both knew that a harp seal pup was fairly easy to kill. They were most common since the world had frozen over. There was a month during the year when the premature seal pups were fair pickings; they'd die on their own and the family did not need to kill any single one of them. They'd simply arrive with their sled and take what they could, then store it. They'd not go back and forth to get more, and Father gave two reasons for that.

First, dragging meat around for leagues left them exposed to Big Whites and other things that might also want the prize. One trip was considered enough, for the prize would last a good time if the family was careful with it. Mother said that *'greed was downfall to every man that wore it,'* and that stuck with Henry for a long time.

The second reason for just taking one load was that dead pups were food for lots of other creatures the family might feed on; snow leopards, white wolves, birds of prey or muskrats; some small and not much nourishing, some fat and fierce. By leaving the premature pups behind, the family was helping others eat, and that was important.

But this month wasn't the early month, which meant they'd have to kill a pup. Henry didn't enjoy killing pups. He liked the look of the seals and thought their eyes were sad. They looked human somehow.

The way to get a seal was to find one of its breathing holes. The seals would make them in the ice at intervals, so they could come up for air. Some would be iced over, but with enough air in them underneath that the seals did not need to break through. Others would be fresh and broken, exposed to the air and the hunter's pick.

The siblings trekked all morning, taking turns to drag the sled, although it weighed nothing with just their weapons upon it.

"That man. Ginger Lanner. Would you have gone with him to the Favela?" Henry asked, surprising himself when the words came out. None had mentioned the visitor for some time, especially by name, although Martin had nightmares most nights since their encounter with the outsider and was even more timid than usual in the daylight.

"No. Maybe, at first. I wanted to go someplace. Just for a while." Mary paused for breath. "I couldn't leave you all, Hen. It'd be too much not to see Iris' grin every day, or Father's scowl. I'd even miss yourn ugly face. I belong with you and mine. If that man comes back, I'll free his soul for him and put him under the ice. Ain't seen anyone with cruel eyes like that afore. It makes me shiver more than the cold itself."

"Do you think the Favela is an evil place? I mean, none of us have seen it, have we?"

"Mother and Father said it is, so it must be," she replied.

"But they were saved by the fable, Penhaligon!" Henry spoke of the man who had helped his parents escape their plight many years before the family had even existed. Back then, they had just been John and Agneta. Two young people in love, in a place where it was dangerous to dream of such things. Penhaligon had concealed them and protected them, then helped them escape with the critical items and wares they needed in order to survive the cold.

"What if...what if we're the bad 'uns? What if..."

"I've known you my whole lifelong. Only thing bad about you, Henry-brother, is your smell. Fathom it."

They proceeded in silence until Mary abruptly stopped and blocked Henry's path with her arm. A few feet ahead of them was a ring in the ice, about a meter across, which they would've walked straight into had they not been paying attention. The top layer of ice had been shattered and shards of it floated on the water. Henry bent a knee beside it and watched his reflection move in the pieces that drifted. One of the pieces was shaped like a lightning bolt and it reminded him of the mirror in their old igloo. He realized that the ice pieces were moving because the surface of it had only recently been broken.

Henry leaped to his feet and confirmed that Mary had found a hole that a seal would use. They scanned the horizon and Mary signaled again when she saw a speck a few hundred yards to the west of them. It appeared for a moment, then submerged.

They took the weapons from the sled, leaving it where it lay, and began to run toward the place where the seal had been. They could tell it was long gone but sped across the recent snow with urgency, as they knew that the seal would always leave scratches at the side of the hole with its front flippers, which was a hint at the direction to the next haven where it could come up for air. Father had told them that seals had a sixth sense and that they felt things about the Earth — which humans could never understand – but the scratch marks always worked for the hunters.

The children had little energy without food in their bellies, but their hunger gave them a new strength. Henry had been the last to pull the sled, but felt renewed power in his legs as he ran with his heart pumping beneath all the layers he was wearing. Mary overtook him, whooping as she passed. Her hood slid down and her hair flew wildly in the breeze. Henry ran faster so he could get ahead of his sister once more and they raced like they had done so many times when they were small children, but not much since. Their hunger drove them forth. Adrenaline surged through them and the thought of eating their catch was uncontainable.

The seal popped up from the hole in front of them; they were closer than they had been when they'd last seen it, but still too far from the next hole to catch it in time. The seal went under. Henry got there a short sprint later and noted the claw marks aiming north.

This time, the duo ran harder than they'd ever run before. It was as if the days they'd spent cooped up in the igloo during the blizzard had made their bodies and minds ravenous for exercise, as well as food. Their breaths were thick and fast and the picks felt heavy in their arms, but they did not stop. Mary pulled ahead of her brother once more and when she got to the next hole, she signaled that the seal had not appeared.

Henry realized their prey was somewhere below the ice and they'd beaten it to the breathing hole.

Henry arrived at his sister's side and all was silent apart from the sound of the two of them trying to catch their breath from the sprint.

"Be still," Mary said in a whisper. Henry raised his pick high above his head.

The claw marks at the side of the ice showed that the seal's next refuge was further north still, but they knew that they would not let it reach the next one, for they needed oil to keep the bairn warm, long enough so they could name him.

Henry wondered if the seal had heard them thundering above it. Had it slowed, or turned course in panic? As Henry got lost in that thought with the pick held above him, the seal leaped from the water suddenly and Henry brought the pick down upon the creature's head before it could give either of them the stare which Henry had a weakness for; the sad look behind bulging childlike eyes.

The pick made a noise like ice breaking as it met the top of the seal's head, followed by a slosh as yolk matter within the skull debased.

The seal itself made no sound. Henry's pick had driven so deep into its skull that the creature couldn't have known what had been done to it. Henry suddenly found himself in trouble as the dead weight of the seal became heavy on the pick and began to pull him down into the depths of the sub-zero waters. Henry imagined a soul leaving the creature, but saw only blood pour from the place where his pick was lodged. He feared that the seal would simply slide off the pick, back into the water, but the angle had the creature hooked and their only choices were to either let go of the pick and lose both tool and creature, or hold on.

Mary held on to her brother and they fought with all their strength to stay firm upon their feet so as not to be dragged through the ice. They dug their heels into the slush by the edge of the pool. Pain ran through Henry's arms and legs as his muscles burned, stretched taut under the strain of the creature as they lifted it. Mary wrapped her arms around her brother's waist and pulled, using her entire weight to anchor them. Together, they let out a cry which rang across the icescape as one sound. Henry's arms shook and his legs began to wobble as he scraped and dug his heels.

With a sudden rush, the dead seal came free from the water. They dragged it onto the ice, where they let it fall before collapsing beside it, exhausted from the ordeal.

After a time, breathing hard and sweating from the exertion, Mary spoke.

"That weren't no tiddler pup. That's a big ol' fat 'un," she said, laughing.

"I nearly shitted my trousers hauling that blubber in," Henry admitted.

"You think they go to the light when they die? Seals and pups?"

"Like us? We will never fathom it. Maybe they swim to the light and they too go to a whole new place."

When they were able to stand, Henry fetched the sled and together they dragged home their prize. Once more, they had oil for the blubber lamp and food for the family to survive on.

"The chook will live. We did well," Henry professed.

"We did, Hen," agreed Mary, proud of what they'd accomplished. Henry was looking forward to breaking the news to the rest of the family.

# FOUR

## A
## Relic

It had been weeks since they'd moved further onto Lantic. The family had settled into a routine and grown accustomed to what had been unfamiliar territory in the vicinity around them. The oil from the seal had kept the igloo warm and there was fish aplenty. The name Ginger Lanner had been erased from their conversations and the boy-bairn was starting to thrive. Hope had returned. Even Father appeared calm and didn't spend half as much time scanning the horizon as he had done.

Henry, Mary and Father hunted in ever-widening circles to discover what lay around the homestead. Henry and Mary reluctantly took turns to stay at home protecting the family, but one night, Father was unwell with a sweating fever and the siblings insisted that he rest when the day broke. Henry and Mary hunted together for the first time since their adventure with the seal and set out early to prove to Father that they were proficient hunters, despite their youth.

The early morning had not been fruitful, but they stumbled upon fresh tracks in the snow and followed them north-east. They thought the tracks were from a muskrat at first, but they differed in size, which indicated they were following more than one animal.

"Might be wolves, Hen. We should head back," Mary worried.

"You ain't seen a wolf afore and neither have I," Henry replied without looking at his sister.

"I know that," Mary spat defiantly.

Henry crouched and studied the prints in the snow. He felt a chill as he stopped moving. It was far colder than they'd ever experienced as they ventured further on Lantic still. Father had said it was because the wind had nowhere to go. Landside, it wasn't so flat and there were bumps on the terrain (and even mountains) that took all the force that any wind could give.

"Don't think there are any wolves anymore. They're just stories, like Santa's reindeers, or sea monkeys."

"Well, if it ain't wolves, what is it?" Mary asked.

"Looks like three different sets of tracks. They weave in and out of each other. See how the little ones criss-cross the bigger 'uns? It's a bairn of some kind, following its parents." Henry shrugged. "That's my bet, anyway." Mary didn't respond. She ignored the animal tracks and gazed ahead of them, tilting her head to the side and squinting as if it would draw whatever she was looking at closer. She looked puzzled.

"What is it, Mare?" Henry asked, trying to visualize what his sister was seeing ahead of them. "Mare?"

"I'm not...It's probably nothing...but..." Mary shook her head. Still squinting, she used her hand to shade her eyes from the sun. "Something up there...can you see?"

It took Henry a while to spot what had caught his sister's eye. Ahead of them, the white panorama harmonized with a pallid sky. But it was imperfect; a raised plateau above the rest of the terrain, which must have been fifty feet in height, stretched for a few hundred yards, on an otherwise flat icescape.

"Ain't no sky towers out here. What is it?" Before Henry could answer, Mary started to jog toward the object. Henry tried to catch up with his sister, but she'd already broken into a run.

"It's a relic," Henry said to himself as they neared it.

The object lay at an angle as if it had once been diving, or rolling into the ice. Smaller cubic shapes lay indiscriminately around it, where they'd spilled from its sloping deck. The siblings marveled at the sight before them. As they drew closer, they saw that it wasn't entirely covered in snow due to its shape, and some of the hull glistened where ice crystals and stalactites had formed. It gave it a pearlescent look up-close and the scale of it made it look otherworldly and majestic.

The rusting steel of the structure was visible in places and the name of the container ship presented itself before them.

"MV Greyhound," Mary pronounced slowly. "It must be one of the yot-boats that mother's Great-Great-Great-Greats had!"

The funnel of the ship had once been torn from the boat. Now it lay beneath several feet of snow beside the vessel and had become a cylindrical run up to the angled deck of the ship, from the icescape. There was a raised area to the deck. It was a superstructure, thirty feet in height, that hinted of portholes beneath the rime. It reminded Henry of Ginger Lanner's pockmarks.

"You could fit a million people inside it," Henry said. Drawing his eyes from the hull of the vessel, Henry spotted that one of the containers nearby was open. "Look!"

Mary reached the container first. The outside of it was covered in lichens. Daylight trespassed into the darkness where rust had finally breached a gaping hole in the roof, revealing a bounty within that the ship had never delivered. Mary shuddered when she saw what was inside.

"What is it?" Henry asked.

Some of the old boxes at the side of the container were intact, but those in the middle had turned to mush, leaving their contents strewn on the floor. Mary picked one of the items up. It was a plastic doll; one of hundreds that formed a mountain of limbs with the same identical faces and the same identical stare. Again, Henry thought of the corpse he'd found with Father. He wondered if he'd ever forget that face and the moment that gave it prominence.

"Possessions," Mary said. "I thought they were... they're horrid, atomic bad," she added, before tossing the doll back in the pile amongst its brethren. It was instantly lost within the duplicate ranks. "These are..." Mary tried to remember the word, then spoke it. "*Dolls*. What do you think's in the others?".

"Hopefully not more of those. Wouldn't fetch one for Iris. She'd freak," Henry replied.

"Martin would be worse."

They moved away from the container, and above them, on the precipice of another unit, was a stocky, short-legged creature with small ears and a short muzzle. They stopped laughing and froze on the spot. The snow leopard hissed and snaked its long tail as it studied them. Mary reached for her slingshot.

"Don't. It's the bairn. You hit it and the other two will be on us. We can't fend against three," Henry muttered under his breath, careful not to alarm the creature, or move too suddenly.

"Where are the other two?" Mary said. She seemed too scared to turn her head in case the animal took exception to the movement, or if it attacked when her eyes were no longer upon it.

"They won't be far. When they find us, we're food. We need to get inside the yot-boat. I'm guessing the entrance will be up top." Henry thought for a moment and took a breath that turned to fog when it met the air once more. The animal looked intrigued and cocked its head to the side, the same way Mary had when she'd first spotted the ship in the distance. "Back up. Don't run from it until we get around the other side of where the... *dolls* are. The thing looks fast, even if it is the bairn."

Even as he spoke, Henry saw a second snow leopard, twice the size of the one before them, atop the deck of the container ship near the bow. The bairn turned and mewed to its parent, who caught sight of Henry and Mary, then instantly changed its stance and bared its teeth. Even from a distance, Henry could see the creature's ears stand on end as it heightened its senses ready for the hunt, just like they had with the seal. Henry thought briefly of the sad, childlike look of the seal, then of dragging and cutting it, refining it, then eating and boiling its oil for warmth. He looked at Mary, seeing the seal over and over in his mind. They were no longer the hunters. Henry and his sister were the prey and their bones would be picked when all else of them was gone.

They edged backward, reached the other side of the

container, then turned to run. They heard the clang as the bairn landed on the roof behind them, but they didn't look back as they zigzagged through the maze of half-buried and long-forgotten containers sprinkled around the transport. The sun blinded them as they climbed the run to the deck of the ship, but Henry spotted the second leopard racing across the deck to head them off.

"Slingshot!" Henry yelled to his sister. She snapped the tip of a large icicle from the side of the ship as she reached the deck and loaded it into her catapult. Her shot was wide and wild. Henry hurriedly brushed snow from the superstructure in search of a doorway within. The second shot hit the nearing snow leopard on the loin. The creature twisted in pain and skidded toward them. A stain of red appeared on its smoky gray-colored coat where the shard of ice had opened the skin.

The animal steadied itself, then growled before resuming its chase of the young humans. Behind them, the bairn had reached the bottom of the run and it dashed toward them instinctively at the sight of its mother being injured in pursuit.

"Where's the other one!?" Mary screamed. "You said there were three!" She fired a third shot that hit the mother on the front leg and the chip of ice splintered through fur and skin, into the bone. The animal wailed on the deck of the ship and its bairn mewled in distress and anger behind them. It had them cornered, but it wasn't as confident as it would've been if fully grown. It appeared to hesitate as Mary turned toward it, as if it were waiting for something.

"I found it!" Henry yelled as he revealed the doorway and a circular wheel to open it. He tried to turn the wheel but it was immovable. He pulled on it with all his strength. Nothing happened. He wasn't sure which way it should turn and he threw his weight behind it as he yanked the wheel erratically from side to side. Still it did not shift.

Mary reached for another icicle and broke a piece from it for her ammunition. The mother snow leopard had returned to its feet once more, but it could not stand properly. Mary diverted her attention again to the bairn, but it did not move. Then behind it appeared a much larger creature, ferocious-looking and twice the size of the bairn. The adult male.

"Get it open!" Mary screamed over her shoulder.

Henry heaved and finally felt the wheel begin to give way as he pulled upon it.

The large snow leopard leaped at Mary as she let fly her catapult.

Henry glanced around and watched the shot scrape meaninglessly past the creature vaulting toward his sister.

Mary fell rearward, yet it wasn't from the anticipated collision with the beast. The door had finally yielded and the girl was hauled from the waist from behind. Mary fell back through the doorway where the floor was hard and cold and the air stale and dank.

Henry slammed the door in the creature's face and the din echoed off into the dark, uncharted passageways of the ship. No reply came from within, but outside, the creature pounded and scratched at the door that obstructed it. Finally, after minutes that seemed like eons, it ceased. Henry wasn't convinced that the creature had gone away and there was no way he was going to open the door to check.

Silence engulfed them.

They lay on the floor for some time, catching their breath, the same way they had after hauling the seal onto the ice. Light filtered in through the porthole and formed an arch in the hallway. Thin luminescent strips that had once marked the floor and trailed the handrails of the corridor had been long covered by dust and frost. Their guiding light was masked and only hinted at in places by an eerie green radiance at irregular intervals.

Henry stood finally and produced the LED torch from his pocket. He wound it ten, then twenty times until the wondrous light presented itself and illuminated the bulk of the immediate darkness that had swallowed them.

"What a crafty thing, this torch. It's like a titchy sun,"

marveled Henry. Mary sat with her legs folded and her knees under her chin.

"Shame it can't make us warm, Hen. Feels colder in here than outside. I don't like it," Mary said, shivering as she spoke. Her hand bled where she'd caught it on the side of the doorway as she'd fallen backward through it. Henry pointed the wound out and Mary shrugged, then licked the blood away.

Henry patted the inside of the hull. "Ain't no wood. It's tin or something. You'd prefer it outside?" He looked at the porthole, expecting one of the snow leopards to appear within the frame.

"Let's just stay by the door for a while. No need to go off snooping. We're all right just here."

"I didn't…" Henry began.

"I know you, Henry-brother. You'll want to spend days here, picking it apart and bringing treasures to Father to please him. We don't need possessions. We got what we got."

Henry took some time to reply. He squinted into the darkness at the faint green glimmers that traced the unknown path ahead, away from the entrance door. The torchlight caught the tangles of frozen cobwebs which had draped themselves along the corridor unceremoniously. Henry had heard of spiders and the webs he saw reminded him of the stories he'd been told, yet he knew of course that even on the ship there were none, unless one lay perfectly frozen somewhere.

"Aren't you curious, Mare? You found this place. You spotted it. Don't you want to explore the relic?"

"I'm nosey about it. I won't lie to you. My heart banged so hard in my ribs I thought I'd drop dead there an' then when I saw this place. But I think I just want to stay here. I'm scared. Even the smell of it in here, it's not right. The air ain't *normal*."

"It's just anteek. This place will have everything we need. We could bring the family here. Big Whites couldn't get inside to bother us none. Wouldn't need no wire. Ginger Lanner won't find us here and even if he did, we'd make him sweat to breach this tin."

It was then, most likely from the ordeal they'd just gone through, that Mary confessed to her guilt about Ginger Lanner.

"It was me that put you all at risk. I thought he seemed nice. I dropped my guard and let him into our lives. It's my fault we had to move and we nearly died in a snow storm trying to put distance from everything. It's all me. But if we can see this place from way off, so can others. So, could he. Sometimes, it's best to be small and unseen. I know you," Mary pointed into the darkness ahead, "you'll walk down there and want us all to follow with sleds and skins packed up."

"It wasn't your fault. He might've killed you if you'd gone for the sling. Maybe, he trekked Father and me back to the homestead and it was us that brought him into our lives. Not you, Mare. We can't know it and it ain't worth spit."

"I thought you all..."

"No. He was just this bad thing that appeared and went away. None think bad of you."

"Really?"

"Yes. Done and dust."

"Thank you, Hen. I mean it. I've dreamt it over and over," Mary replied.

"As for this place here? It'll be Father who decides. Maybe it's just dark and empty through and through. But I don't fancy loading up those sleds for a long time. That last trip nearly killed us all and I know it."

Mary kept quiet.

Henry saw her indecision and started to walk away from the entrance door, taking the light from the torch with him.

"Come, sister," he said, knowing she wouldn't stay on her own, nor let him explore and face dangers without her.

Mary looked back toward the porthole where the beasts remained outside. She stood slowly, then came toward him, weapon drawn once more.

The first body was slumped in the corridor, not thirty steps from the entrance. It looked to Henry like it had not been long dead; it wasn't skull and bones. It was a woman, with skin still upon her face and most of her hair remaining upon her head, scraped back from her forehead and tied with a simple band.

She wore a once-red boiler suit with epaulets on the shoulders, and had not decomposed beneath the clothing she wore, as her body still had a shape to it. A tear announced itself unexpectedly and snaked a path down Mary's cheek until she swiped it away.

"*Min Gud*! Poor girl. And not much older than us," she said under her breath.

"She's a Great-Great." Henry studied the corpse. The woman's eyes had lost their color. Her skin was cerulean and it shimmered in places from the ice. "Cold came quick and froze her solid. She's been like this ever since."

"Looks like she died yesteryear, not a hundred ago," Mary said solemnly.

"It means no one has been here all this time. None have messed with her, or eaten her. It's a good sign. She's near perfect."

In the woman's left hand was a claret-colored drinking cup bearing an emblem that once meant something. The cup was stained brown within from the contents.

"They'd not foreseen it. They weren't as lucky as yours and mine," Mary said, tapping the cup with the tip of her boot, but not daring to touch the corpse.

"They might have known it was coming, but were too far out to do anything. I doubt something this big moved faster than a human on foot."

"I bet it could have gone fast. Mother said the water moved quicker before it got stuck under the ice. Called them, waves. The Great-Greats could have shifted this for sure. They knew everything," Mary replied.

They came to a series of doorways which were the cabins and there they found more bodies of the crew, all well preserved from the sudden freeze that had captured a moment in time; a final moment for the people on board the MV Greyhound.

The floors were angled where the ship wasn't level and it took a while to get used to, but they made their way slowly through the rooms on the two floors above the deck with the directing light of the torch.

They admired the signs and safety posters on the walls, and the furnishings; the beds with their pressed linen, the metal lockers that held the personal effects of those that lay wherever they fell when the ice came; packets of cigarettes, ID badges, keys, combs and communication devices, a holograph of a family portrait taken *at New Year's Eve on The Bund* (according to the laser inscription), two wristwatches, a deck of cards and the most exciting find for Mary, which was a book that had a butterfly upon its cover. It was called 'Papillon' and Mary held it as if it were the most precious thing on Earth.

There were ornate desks made of wood from a time when it was in abundance, and chairs with cushioned seats and armrests. Henry and his sister stayed at the top of the superstructure, never venturing down into the belly of the ship beneath the deck; much of it was below the ice, and that they feared the most. They explored offices with navigation charts, whiteboards and computers, and the canteen where a meal had been prepared and placed ready for serving. The sidewall of the canteen was missing and spears of ice hung around the gaping hole, so it looked like a mouth with razor teeth that allowed daylight to breach where once only a porthole would've given it opportunity. Half of the room was covered in snow and ice where the wind had brought it in without obstruction. If the vessel had protested once, it had been long silenced by the wind and was left defeated.

Mary and Henry didn't touch any of the food preserved on the tables or in the serving counters, but in the galley that they entered through a set of double doors, they found rows of glass jars and canned goods. Mary read some of the labels, unsure how to pronounce the words. "Green Pitted Olives. Sardines in Oil. Pineapple Rings in Natural Juice. Pickled Cucumbers. Real American Hotdogs in *Brine*... Never heard of any of this boon."

The body of the chief cook was bent over the stove, frozen in his chef whites with a thermometer in his hand that showed them how cold it always was in the galley, the small dial pointed at minus eight, They took no notice of his corpse – it was the tenth they'd come across within the hour – and they rifled through the drawers and cupboards about him as if he weren't there, the torch providing light in what was the darkest place they'd ventured so far.

"Let's try it," Henry said, plunging a kitchen knife into the top of one of the tins before holding it to his nose to sniff the contents within. He pulled a face as he did so. He shook it and it made a sloshing sound, but the bulk of it rattled within. "Mainly frozen," he added. "The chill out here, farther from landside, is enough to give a walrus frostbite!"

He poured some of the dark brown juice from the tin onto the palm of his hand. He put his hand to his nose tentatively.

"It's been here forever. It'll probably make you sick," said Mary.

"Ain't going outside until those creatures have found themselves a meal that ain't us. We'll stay here tonight, sleep in one of those beds. Head back tomorrow. Right now, I'm hungry, so I'm trying whatever grub these Great-Greats have to offer," Henry replied.

"Mother and Father will be worrisome, Hen."

"They'd prefer us alive and late, over dead and on the nose of it. When they hear our tale, they'll forget their anger soon enough. We should find something to take back, to prove it right away." Henry studied the knife in his hand which was unlike anything he'd ever seen. It was perfectly sharp. On the handle it read 'Sheffield Steel,' which meant nothing to Henry, but it brought up all possibilities of the significance of Sheffield. *Was it the name of a legendary hunter, or soldier? Was it a place? Was it the name of a man who was good at making knives? Was it the name of a man who was known for gutting fish and other things? Was it the place where all knives came from, or all steel? Was Sheffield the name of the man who made these particular knives, but not all knives? Was Sheffield just a word that sounded nice and meant nothing to no one?* Every object they beheld threw up so many questions they would never know the true answers to.

They looked at the body of the chief cook. His hair had been jet-black under a net and his leather skin much darker than theirs, or even Lanner's. Henry couldn't tell the man's age, but he'd been clean-shaven when he'd died. He wasn't a child and appeared to have been much older than Henry was. This confused him as both Lanner and Father had beards and he assumed that every male above a certain age would wear one. The idea of not wearing a beard (and appearing younger) was absurd.

"Do you think those people that lived on this yot-boat had families?" Mary asked her brother without taking her eyes from the chief cook.

"Some of them must've."

"How sad to die out here, so far from them. I wonder if any of their families survived."

"Maybe they did. Maybe this lot were linked with our lot. Don't matter none. They're still dead." Henry didn't mean it to sound as harsh as it came out and regretted it as soon as he'd said it.

"I'd like to think some of them did. Life isn't that cruel, is it?" Mary said.

"I'm only ten and four, or six. I ain't been here long enough to answer that."

"Go on, then. Eat the anteek food. If you don't drop, I might try some." Mary picked up a tin of Peeled Whole Tomatoes and studied it.

"You will?" said Henry.

"I swear on your dead body," Mary replied.

Henry licked the palm of his hand, then tipped his head back and poured the juice from the can into his open mouth. It was the worst thing he had ever tasted and the texture of the bronze-colored juice made him heave; specks of frozen brine, tiny fragments of meat that had broken down and mixed with flakes of corroded metal. He couldn't fool his sister. She laughed at his plight and finally Henry spat it out onto the galley floor, then wiped his mouth his sleeve.

"Maybe we should try another one. That tasted like puke."

FIVE

# A Duesenberg

There was no sight nor sign of the snow leopards when they left the next day.

The sky was clear, and they could see for half a league in every direction about them. It felt like a good day and Henry felt triumphant as they strode away from the container vessel, like he had when they'd placed the seal in the sled and started dragging it home.

Henry had insisted on walking around the exterior of the vessel before they left, so he could see the hole where the wall should have been in the canteen from the outside. It did indeed look like a mouth.

"I wouldn't have been as keen on going in if I'd seen that face from the outside. It's like a shark!" Henry had said, and Mary agreed.

Henry felt refreshed. They'd slept in one of the cabins within the protective radiance of the torch. The bed had been equipped with a spongy mattress and Henry had felt like he'd been floating from the second his head touched the pillow. Henry was used to lying just inches above the cold, hard floor of the igloo, with little of anything to separate him from the ice itself.

In contrast, Henry began to suspect his sister had lain awake for most of the night. She looked beyond tired as they walked, although her mood was okay. She seemed unaware of Henry's scrutiny, staring at the fur wraps around her feet as she trudged onward. Henry knew that to him, the ship was a wonder that had enabled them to step into the past, but he remembered Mary's fear when they first entered the ship. To her, it was a tomb that showed them what had been lost to humankind.

As they took a final glance back at the ship, Henry caught his sister's morose expression. He felt sad that something so amazing and promising could unsettle her the way it had. There was nothing he could do to change the way she thought, or felt. Henry knew it was Mary's way and they were just different.

They'd taken a few things with them as proof of their find. Mary had taken the new book and a glass jar of pickles. She'd tried one and found it disgusting, but wanted to give the others the opportunity to come to the same conclusion. The jar itself was precious, as it could be used for holding water or extra blubber oil for the lamp. She'd also taken the cup that the girl in the hallway – the first corpse they'd found – had been drinking from. Henry had wanted to take the holograph portrait, but it felt like a trespass and Mary told him not to.

Henry found a bottle of bourbon whiskey in a drawer in the chief engineer's quarters. He'd tasted that also, not knowing what it was, and although it had made him cough for some time, he found it warming afterward. He supposed it might benefit the boy-bairn if they needed to keep him warm again through the coldest times.

Henry also took a pearl hairbrush for Mother, a trouser-belt with a silver buckle that read 'California State Bull Roper Champion 2027' on it for Father, and one of the chief cook's knives for Hilde for the gutting. He hadn't originally intended on taking one of the dolls from the container for Iris, but he changed his mind as they passed it. He took a toothbrush from one of the cabins and some *Toothpaste*, which is what the Great-Greats used before people had to grind cuttlefish bone with blubber oil. They'd put everything into a rucksack they found in one of the lockers, and Henry thought they could give that to Martin. It would be a good heirloom and it was a practical gift.

Henry felt nervous as they neared the homestead; he knew

too well what Father's temper could be like. But it was Mother who unleashed her anger upon her children as they reached the igloo, striking her two eldest with the palm of her hand several times before hugging them. Father stood back, surprisingly calm. Henry thought he glimpsed a smile from Father, but it was hard to tell behind the thick beard that cloaked the lower half of his face, and he remained quiet.

Henry's stomach churned, partly from the nerves, but mostly from the anteek food. He hadn't been sick, but he felt *off*. He had wind, but daren't fart in case he followed through, which Mary would've remembered until the end of her days and punished him for it whenever the opportunity arose to make his cheeks turn pink.

Hilde seemed pleased to see Henry and Mary face Mother's wrath when they first arrived back. Henry heard his sister mutter, *"I told you they were just breaking yourn rules!"* in a sly way, but Mother shot her a look of disapproval and Hilde went off in a sulk with her words not having the desired effect.

Iris was holding the bairn, and Henry and Mary kissed each of them on the forehead once Mother let them go. Martin hung back as usual but fidgeted with excitement at seeing his siblings return home safely. Henry tussled the boy's fair hair playfully and Martin mouthed the word *'Hello'* in response, although no sound came out.

They all followed Hilde into the igloo. Once seated, Henry and Mary told the story of their adventure and handed over their gifts. Iris asked many questions, mainly about the snow leopards. Hilde tried to appear disinterested, but she couldn't help listening to the tale.

"We can't keep these possessions here," Father interrupted without warning, "Be asking for trub." He didn't raise his voice, or sound angry. He was calm and spoke with conviction. Everyone knew what he meant. Although they had trekked for leagues to find their new home, further on Lantic than any had ever been, there was still a possibility that someone (if not the same someone) would again find them and the anteeks they possessed.

"But we moved all the way out here because you said so! Ain't we safe here, Father? Even now?" cried Hilde, to everyone's shock.

"Hilde!" Mother Exclaimed, "Father knows what is best. So, do I. Hold your tongue."

"I like our new home," Iris added innocently.

Father seemed embarrassed by Hilde's outburst. An awkward silence followed, until Father insisted that he go to see the yotboat the very next day, which none argued.

There was a tension in the air for the remainder of the day. Everyone avoided conversation, because that was the best way to avoid further conflict. After dinner, however, Father made an announcement.

"Usually, when the young reach a certain age, it is decided when the time is right for them to take on the Ritual.

"As Father, I get to choose when that day is, and I say that for Henry and Mare, what they did last night – what they discovered – well, I think they've completed their Rituals. Any test now would only rob them."

Henry and Mary exchanged shocked glances. What Father had just done was unheard of. The Ritual had always been determined in advance of the event. However, when Henry thought of his and Mary's recent adventures, he felt that they deserved Father's accolade. Father wasn't sparing them, or going easy on them; Henry and Mary were lucky to be alive and they'd come back with treasures none had discovered before them. It was the rarest thing and the rarest feeling.

"Mary-daughter. Henry-son. You are no longer children. You have survived the cold like our Great-Greats before us. I am proud you are of mine and your mother's blood." For once, Father beamed. It was a smile Henry would never forget. Father wrapped his giant arms around his eldest children and their faces were lost in the fur of his coat. It was the best feeling Henry had ever had, and the only time he could remember being praised by Father in front of the whole family.

"Hilde," Father said turning toward her, "you must step up now an' help protect the homestead with Mother when we are over the wire. Martin will learn to fish an' gut now, an' Iris can handle the bairn."

Hilde looked like she was going to be sick, although she'd not yet tasted the pickles. Henry knew she wanted to do more than catch and clean fish, but to receive the news as a result of something her siblings did left her conflicted and so she took her news badly. In contrast, Mother looked overjoyed.

Iris spoke up earnestly. "Henry doesn't have his face beard yet. How can he be a man?" Henry was embarrassed, but smiled kindly at his sister. If Hilde or Martin had said it, no doubt Henry would've fired back some smart words, but Iris was at an age where she said what was on her mind, or asked whatever she needed to know. It was straightforward and true.

Father laughed, his shoulders bouncing.

"*Min kara*, your brother is what he is, an' that's no longer a chook." Father grabbed his beard with two hands. "I ne'er got this fuzz betwixt one daylight an' next. Hen will be grizzly before long!"

"Not before Mare!" Henry added. She punched him hard on the arm.

Father opened the bourbon whiskey and held the bottle to his children to drink from first. They both coughed as the whiskey hit their throats and then it was passed around the igloo and everyone else did the same. Henry hoped there was another bottle somewhere on the yot-boat.

Henry could tell that Father was awestruck by the sight of the container ship, when they finally found their way back to it. He was half expecting to see the snow leopards once more, but they never appeared.

The first corpse Henry and Mary had found was just where they'd left her in the corridor, and Father marveled at the sight of her and the museum she was part of.

"These boots are good. Not worn out. Best man-mades I ever seen," Father said.

"Should we take the corpses out?" Henry asked.

"I don't see a reason. They're not harming none and it's their yot-boat," Father replied, studying the boiler suit adorning the body. "She won't miss the boots, mind. Wrap some fur around an' they'll be fine."

"But aren't we going to live here?"

Father fell silent. Finally, he said, "No, Henry-son. Mary spoke to me about this and I have to hark my agreement with her. It doesn't feel right. This whole place is asking to be found by the next lot. But we should go through the yot-boat and work out what is what, and what is of use to us. Some of it might suit another purpose one day." Father paused. "Maybe we could relocate near it someday, but not just yet. Mother is still angry I made her up sticks with the bairn still on't tit."

It perplexed Henry that Father didn't want possessions in the igloo, didn't want the family to live on the yot-boat, yet wanted to itemize what they found. He was also slightly annoyed that Mary had told her fears to Father on the quiet and that he'd sided with her. Henry wondered what other purposes the new items could serve – or had Father merely changed his mind about keeping possessions in the igloo? He felt it would be stupid to ask such questions, but now he'd passed the Ritual, he had the right to. He was no longer a boy. But adulthood puzzled him, and he decided to keep quiet and try to work it all out for himself, starting with Father and his ever-changing mind.

After Father had seen the inside of the vessel, they started with one of the containers. They spent a week traveling back and forth to the ship, gradually digging it out. They took their meals in the captain's office when the temperatures dipped too low and started using the room to store the most useful items they found, or those they perceived to be of interest, until they could decipher the use and purpose of each. These things included a lighter, two handheld radios that still held charge (though they couldn't fathom how to operate them), fall arrest rope and harnesses, thermal gloves, a fire axe, a cube with colored squares upon it, cutlery and cooking ware, four more bottles of whiskey and three of something else called *vodka*, a pair of sunglasses, a box of matches, toothbrushes, sleeping bags, a bucket, and countless other items.

Mary claimed one of the cabins as her own and would often read her new book in there by the light of one of the torches they'd found. Father wouldn't lie on the beds, but he did seem to like swiveling in the captain's chair. Henry himself liked the control room where there were rows upon rows of buttons and dials on the main console. He decided he would push every button, but would wait until Father wasn't about; it proved a long wait, as Father insisted on going to the ship every day. Henry was slightly annoyed; the ship was his and Mary's discovery, but Father had taken it over and was making all of the decisions. However, he didn't say anything about it.

On the seventh day, they cleared the last foot of snow from in front of the container and opened the heavy, frozen doors without ceremony. Inside were more boxes of dolls which made them laugh, but annoyed them equally. Each of them had found the dolls to be creepy. Identical, motionless copies of tiny humans. Father proclaimed that he knew the struggle in raising a real child to an age where it would survive and the dolls were like *dead'uns*.

They spent another three days trying to open a second container, and this time they had better luck. Inside was a pristine motor vehicle with a long bonnet and imposing curves. It had spoked wheels surrounded by white tires and although it was cloaked in a thin layer of dust, a brilliant red color shone through. To Henry, it looked like a whale of some kind, encased in some unknown material and out of the water. He was unsure what it was, but he was struck with awe at its magnificence.

Mary removed her hood. Father and Henry did the same.

"Never seen such color on anything, nor so much of it," Mary said, then added, "except blood."

"It's a pretty thing," Henry agreed.

Father traced his fingers – which trembled with excitement – along the surface of the bodywork, then wiped the dust from the windscreen to peer inside, discovering it was of a different material to the rest. Mary kicked one of the front tires, and Henry found a badge that revealed the name of the car by rubbing it with his glove. *Duesenberg*.

The Duesenberg had been built for a niche, trillion-dollar retro futurist car market. It was a beautiful machine, based on a primitive vehicle from the first half of the twentieth century.

"It's a *car*!" Father exclaimed, becoming animated as he spoke. "There was a kindly old 'un in the Favela when I was a boy and he had a toy car you could fit in the palm of your hand. Was meant for young 'uns but he'd had it his whole life long. The car had bits that opened at the side and he said that's where you'd get in and make it move."

Henry and Mary squeezed down one side of the container to see if they could find a way to enter the vehicle. Father took the opposite side. The space was dark and they each felt along the panels. Mary wiped dust from the roof of the vehicle, uncovering a grid of solar cells, not knowing what they were.

After a few moments, Father called them around to his side of the vehicle to show them what he'd found: a dent in the shape of a hand in the chassis on his side. Father took off his glove, placed his fingers within the recess and the bodywork illuminated underneath his skin. He pulled his hand away and the glow disappeared. More courageous the second time, he placed his hand once again on the bodywork and kept it there until they heard a click from within as the door's catch released.

The smell of leather hit them as they entered the vehicle. It was the same sort of scent as the captain's swivel chair, but it clung in the air and filled the car. There was no steering wheel or control panel inside the car. Father sat on one seat and Henry and Mary shared the other. As the door closed, they stared out of the windscreen at the outside of the container; an all-blue sky above an all-white terrain.

"What now?" Henry asked.

A face appeared in front of them, a smiling woman with lips as red as the body of the car they sat in. They all jumped as the projection flickered in the air before them and remained even when Mary passed her hand through the image. When it spoke, the words came from the car itself.

'*Congratulations on purchasing your new Duesenberg SJ LaGrande Dual-Cowl Phaeton vehicle. I am here to help.*'

The trio sat in stunned silence, gripping the seats and each other. Henry couldn't take his eyes off the holograph. She was both beautiful and plain, remarkable yet not. Henry wondered if she were real, living somewhere on the ship in the rooms he'd not yet ventured to beneath the deck.

'*Calculating location and searching for roads. No roads found. Your location is unknown. Switching to VADM. Vicinity Analysis Driving Mode. I am helping you.*'

A grid of lines and circles appeared on the windscreen as the car scanned the terrain outside the container.

'*Adjusting tire pressure...*'

The car raised slightly as a hissing sound came from below.

Father laughed and slapped Henry on the shoulder.

"What's it doing?" Mary asked.

"Hello, lady," Father greeted the holograph, who smiled back but said nothing. The engines roared to life, and once again, the passengers leaped in fear. From over their shoulders came restraints that secured them to their seats. Henry and Mary sat tight together; the seatbelt had wrapped around both of them. The holograph spoke once more.

'*Seatbelts activated. Location unknown. What is your destination?*'

"Merika," Father said.

The holographic lady looked puzzled, then smiled broadly.

'*That destination is not recognized.*'

"Home," Mary said.

'*You have not yet set your home address. Would you like to do that now?*'

"Move," Henry said and the car instantly lurched forward and accelerated out of the container at speed.

'*Your vehicle is moving. Speed limits are not detected at this location.*'

"*Vamos morrer!*" Father exclaimed and Henry knew it to mean '*We're going to die*' in the tongue of the Favela.

They sped in a straight line faster than Henry had ever traveled in his life. They clung to each other once more and the holograph smiled warmly at them. Ahead, a container blocked their path. Henry screamed as they neared it, but the car calculated the obstacle and swerved by it just seconds before impact.

"Stop," Mary yelled, and the vehicle abruptly halted. She looked like she was going to be sick but seemed able to compose herself now the vehicle had stopped.

Henry let out a sigh of relief. So did Father. Then all three of them burst into fits of laughter.

The holograph was calm as it asked, *"Would you like to try Manual Driving Mode?"* as a steering wheel emerged from the console in front of Father. Slowly, he reached for it with both hands, then gripped the steering wheel after some hesitation.

"I'm the captain of it," Father said, turning the wheel slowly.

"Go," Henry yelled and the car sped forward again with a roar of the mighty engines. This time, the line of direction wasn't as straight and Henry realized the car was reacting to Father's hands. "You're drivin' a car."

Father grinned jubilantly. "Yeah. I am!"

They drove in a wide circle back toward the ship, then left weaving tracks in figures of eight and loops upon loops in the snow. Mary had a go at driving next and she was a natural at it, like most things she did, and she sped faster than Father by ordering the holograph to *Go Fast*.

After some time, it was Henry's turn. He wanted to outdo his sister, so he drove the car hard and fast and tried to scare Mary by steering close to the containers and the ship. The projected lady looked on approvingly. This gave Henry all the encouragement he needed to push it even further, and they found themselves heading for the stern of the ship at lightning speed.

Where the spilled containers met the ramp to the ship, a creature leaped from one of the rectangular cuboids and sprinted up the ramp toward the sloped deck.

"Look! A snow leopard. They're back!" Mary pointed at the creature just as it met the deck and disappeared from sight.

Henry had been distracted by the sight of a snow leopard and took his eyes from the ship for a few seconds, but it was all that was needed to lose control. Panicking, he pulled the car into a skid, then into another. Mary screamed as they clipped the side of one of the half-buried containers then careered into the side of the next one, smashing the corner of it with their rear wheel.

The impact jolted the ice beneath them, but luckily it did not crack through. As Father and Mary scrambled for the steering wheel, the car flipped once on the ice and up became down. The restraints held the passengers tight in their seats and a very strange thing had happened to the air; a mist had sprayed into the car on the first impact, and it had formed a transparent foam cushion around them all. Henry and Mary should've butted heads as they were sharing a seat together, yet the air between them was a buffer that prevented them from doing damage to each other. The car slid on its roof and finally stopped moving.

He tried to turn his head to see if Mary and Father were all right, but he was held fast. Then he realized he couldn't breathe. The foam had covered his face and mouth. His eyes met Mary's and he could tell that she'd realized the same thing and was going through the same silent ordeal as he.

Then the protective foam around him shifted; it seemed to deteriorate until they could move once more and breathe again. It left them covered in a film of gray dust as they welcomed the air back into their lungs. Henry had a strange taste in his mouth from the dust. He spat onto the roof of the car, which was now the floor.

Henry made a strange noise and heard Father groan, but all of them were safe and unhurt. Mary had vomited this time and was clearly in a rage at her brother.

"Idiot!" was all she could manage, which was the same word in English and the language of her mother's Great-Greats.

The holograph tried to flicker to life, but it was gone and remained the only true casualty, other than the car itself. The restraints would not release them, so Father used his knife to set them free and they fell in a heap to the roof of the car, which had become its floor. They crawled through the space where one of the doors had been ripped off and surveyed the wreckage of the Duesenberg SJ LaGrande Dual-Cowl Phaeton vehicle.

"You killed it," Mary said as she backed away from the pile of twisted metal. Her braids had come unfurled and she looked wild and comical, with fresh vomit stains on her clothing to finish the look.

"And you puked in it," Henry argued back.

"You're a prong, Hen. A stupid, stinking prong."

"You're the one who yelled about the snow leopard! I took my eyes away just for a... Do you think there's another car in one of them other boxes?" Henry looked around at the litter of containers still strewn and half buried around the ship.

The wheels of the car still spun, apart from the rear passenger side, where the wheel had been forced into the body-work at a right angle and the white tire had blown.

"If there is, you ain't drivin' it. You could've killed us all, Mother would blame my ghost for it I'm sure," Father said, walking away from the scene. Henry thought he saw him smiling, but couldn't be certain.

Guilt twisted Henry's stomach about wrecking the anteek car. It had been such a beautiful thing and he supposed it had taken years to build, by hundreds of people no longer of the Earth. Mary punched him on the arm but didn't say anything more. Henry shot her an apologetic smile, knowing he'd already been forgiven.

Eiderdown snowflakes fell lazily upon the wreckage and Henry wondered how long it would take for the car to be forgotten once more. It really was a shame he'd wrecked it. They could've got back to the igloo in double quick time and he was sure Mother would've liked a go at driving. He felt guilty about that part especially.

"I should've gone slow. We could've rode it to China, or Canada. Might'n be trees there that can out-do the snow. Imagine!" Henry sighed, full of regret.

"Hilde's never going to get over this! She'll spit!" Mary laughed, following Father to the ship. Henry took a final glance at the car, silently mourned the passing of the holograph, then took off after his father and sister.

He'd been scared. He'd felt terrible afterward. But for those precious minutes, traveling at great speed in the Duesenberg, it was the most fun that Henry had ever had.

He didn't need to ask Father, or Mary, but he knew from the looks on their faces in the vehicle, in the moment before the car had flipped onto its roof, that they also felt the same.

# SIX

## Skills

---

Another snowstorm had confined the family to the igloo for a couple of days. Hilde sat reading the new book Mary had brought from the wrecked ship. She'd barely spoken to her family in weeks, furious that she'd been excluded from the great excavation of the cargo and that she only got to hear about the trove second-hand.

Taken from their original homestead, the mirrored shard turned slowly as it always did. It was the family's dreamcatcher and warder of evil, another constant in their lives. The doll Henry had given Iris also looked over the family in silence, with a seemingly bemused look upon its face.

"How's the book?" Father asked. Hilde ignored him and turned the page defiantly, keeping her eyes on the printed text. Mother shook her head as she worked at patching a hole in one of the sleeping bags. Henry knew that Mother knew her daughter's stubbornness well, for she'd commented on it often.

Mother had always noticed more than anyone else about the changes in her children as they grew. Henry had heard her say that Mary was looking more like a woman each day and Hilde was on the cusp of it all (although he didn't know quite what that meant). Henry had once heard Mother tell Father that Hilde had a harshness to her that not many men or womenfolk would ever suffer.

Iris lay beside Henry as he rested from the day's work, digging the container free of the ice. The bairn crawled over them both, flapping his tiny hands at them with excitement, screeching with delight at the discovery he could move around on his own. Henry studied the boy-bairn.

He'd become interesting; no longer a thing that just lay there, demanding food and attention. The bairn had grown a single quiff of blond hair that looked like an upside-down question mark. He recognized his siblings. He smiled and pulled surprised expressions whenever he discovered something new, often things that the others took for granted. He had confidence and character already, which reminded Henry of Iris and a little of himself.

"I thought it'd be like the other book, but the world inside it is another," Mary finally answered for her sister, as she'd read from its pages already. "It's like starting over as you read it."

"What's this'n about?" Mother asked.

"There's a man who gets sent on a yot-boat because people thought he was a bad 'un. They send him to a place where the Devil lives, although you don't see the Devil, an' he keeps trying to get out and they keep finding him an' punishing him, but he keeps trying an' trying to be free."

"Not all gods are devils. Ours was neither one nor the other," Mother commented, referring to the fable of how they'd come to the icescape.

"Is he from Derry?" asked Henry, fascinated. The bairn cooed and blew a raspberry, which Iris returned.

"No. He's from a place that were beknownst to them as *France*," Mary said quite seriously, oblivious to her sister's renewed annoyance.

"Does he get away?" Father asked, seeming genuinely interested in the tale.

"He does," Mary replied as Hilde let out a maddened groan, threw her book down on the floor and turned to face the ice wall of their home.

"Sorry," Mary said to no effect and picked up the book,

placing it carefully in the plastic bag where it joined its distant cousin.

Later, as the family was distracted with preparing the evening meal, Henry watched his younger brother, Martin, slip away from the igloo, trudge his way to the wire and wriggle his tiny frame through it with ease, but absent stealth. One of the only rules in the homestead was that no child should cross the wire alone. Martin wasn't meant to stray far from the igloo, but even with a large brood of siblings, they couldn't keep an eye on him all the time.

Henry was surprised at his brother's newly acquired boldness, but then, he'd not paid much attention to Martin of late. He knew Hilde was angry and jealous about being excluded from the excavation, but Martin was often the invisible one. Henry felt a pang of guilt that he'd neglected his brother in all the excitement that the yot-boat afforded.

He caught up with Martin, careful not to be seen departing from the homestead himself.

"Where do you think you're sneaking off to, nipper?" Henry inquired, grabbing him by the scruff when he reached him beyond the wire. "You're too young yet for crossing the wire, but not too young for a hiding. Mother'd kill you if she knew you'd trekked out in this cold, boy." Henry wouldn't have hit Martin, but the boy winced anyway.

"Don't tell none of 'em, Henry. You promise, or I won't show you." His eyes betrayed him, and Henry looked over his brother's shoulder, seeing nothing at first.

"You show me now, or I'll kick your rump," Henry said.

Martin's shoulders slumped in defeat and he pointed in the direction he'd been heading. Henry blinked, but saw nothing through the haze of snowdrift.

"It's over there. I'll take you to it, but don't tell the girls. It's no devilry, *jag lovar*. I promise." Martin led the way from the wire in silence, and Henry saw the boy's worry in the way he was stooped and the way his boots dragged in the snow.

After fifty yards, Henry fancied that he could make out something ahead of them, and he smiled at the memory of the day

Mary had seen the yot-boat in the distance before he had. This was different, though: a blur, not so distant, bleached and camouflaged against the all-white backdrop. As they neared it Henry could make out an irregular mound, with an opening that faced them. It wasn't made of ice bricks like the igloo; the shape had clearly been made naturally during one of the recent snow-storms, where the cold air had frozen the snow during the blizzard.

Henry recalled the way their igloo had been buried so many weeks before, but he

couldn't believe that only Martin had discovered the anomaly in the weeks that they'd been there, unless it had been made recently. He recalled Mary talking to him in the yot-boat about being small and unseen. There was an absurdity to the situation, but the family simply wasn't looking for a new formation, especially so close to the wire and the homestead.

Martin crouched into the discreet opening and Henry followed on all fours.

Inside, Henry was met by a sight so beautiful he knew he'd always remember it. Henry had always respected and feared the ice equally. It had nearly wiped the human race from the Earth. Everything about it was unceasing and dangerous. It was death. On that day, for the first time, he saw it anew; the ice could be majestic. More than the stalactite teeth that made a face out of the side of the container ship, the sight that met Henry was something else.

The tiny opening broadened into a room the same size as their igloo, although its shape had been created at random. Unlike the igloo, the structure wasn't a dome within. The very walls of it were crystals that shimmered in confused flakes and spikes in shades of blues and frosted greens not seen from the outside. The ceiling was translucent in places, letting in light through a handful of rime clouds frozen above them. Henry's heart raced as he took it all in. In that moment, he was glad he'd found the corpse in the snow all those months ago, for it had triggered the events that had led him to explore the yot-boat with Mary and discover Martin's cave.

Martin sat on the floor next to a tool that neither Henry nor Father had realized was gone. The boy had been at work, sculpting a block of ice the size of a kettle-pot. The sculpture was starting to resemble the shape of a face, and the features hewn on one side already hinted at a woman. *Mother.*

"I didn't mean any harm. I just wanted a secret, and a place that was…just for me. I found this place and I thought you all would too, except you never did. You're always out with Mary, or Father. The bairn isn't any fun yet, Mother just scolds me for this an' that and the girls get on my nerves." It was the most that Martin had ever spoken all at once.

Henry studied his brother. Martin too had changed in recent weeks. He'd gotten taller and had lost some of the chubbiness from his cheeks. Henry had always thought of Martin as a nuisance until that moment. *Just a kid.* He'd forever let the girls sort the boy out, as they were nearer Martin's age than he was. Henry had also been distracted, learning the things he needed to become a man. He felt another crush of guilt as he stood in Martin's secret den and listened to him speak from his heart.

"The girls told me about fairies and I never believed them afore, but I think fairies might be real because this place is so bleedin' pretty," Martin said earnestly.

He was simply a young boy; playing, exploring, and believing in things that Henry had never been given the chance to believe in. He envied his little brother then, but also wanted Martin to stay the age he was, just for a while longer, before Father put a blade or spear in his little hands.

"I won't grass you up, Martin. It's very…*nice. Muito bom*," was all Henry could manage. He wished he could've found more fitting words to praise his brother's genius, but he just didn't have any that could do it justice.

Henry drew toward the sculpture and studied it. He liked that it was smooth and perfect on one side, with contrasting jagged edges on the other where it was yet to be humanized. To Henry, it didn't need finishing. He liked all that it was. All that it wasn't.

"This is good, Martin. *Bleedin' pretty*," he said and watched his brother's cheeks flush red at the compliment.

"It's Mother," Martin replied with a smile, as if Henry had never cast his eyes upon her face before and hadn't made the obvious connection.

Without thinking, Henry took off his glove, then reached out and touched the finished side of the ice being's face, leaving his hand upon its cheek for some time. The side that was complete was the perfect image of Mother. Henry remembered the holograph of a family in one of the lockers of the container ship. Although that had captured a moment in time so perfectly, his brother's artistry had captured something more. It wasn't just a likeness of Mother; Martin had captured the way he saw her and what she meant to him.

"I know. I never knew you could do anything like this."

"Nor did I. I know her face better than my own. I just started hacking the ice at first. Then I fathomed what I was doing. It makes me feel good. Like I can do something no one else can. Don't tell Father. I bet he'd wreck it or scold me some."

"I won't tell him, just as long as you promise that the next one you make will be your handsome brother, fighting a snow leopard!" They laughed together and Martin promised Henry that he would, but added that he'd heard Mary had done all the hard work defending them both.

Henry left Martin in his den and made his way back to the igloo to see if anyone had tried a pickled cucumber from the yot-boat yet.

-

In the morning, the sky was clear again and they all knew that meant another trip to the ship. The trio spent a few hours clearing the front of one of the stricken containers to try and free its doors, but to no avail. Instead, Father sorted through the trove of goods they'd relocated to the captain's office and Mary lay on one of the beds in her cabin, braiding her hair whilst apparently deep in thought.

Henry wandered the corridors. He'd been everywhere and searched all of the cupboards, shelves and places he could think to store anything of interest. He knew where all the bodies lay and in which position, and had secretly named them after characters in the family's first book. The chief cook was Mike Hanlon, the second mate was Richie Tozier and the woman in the boiler suit was Beverly Marsh. He wondered if the creature from the story, the demon, lived somewhere in the belly of the ship beneath the ice. The thought made him shudder.

He stood in the doorway of the stairwell, transfixed by the deep darkness below. His torch's light caught the shimmering surface of the ice that blocked the stairwell a few flights down and blurred the steps as they disappeared beneath it. Without thinking too much about it, Henry descended the stairwell and pushed hard at the door of the first sub-level beneath the deck until it groaned against his weight and juddered open for the first time in a hundred years.

Martin's cave had been wondrous and majestic, but the underbelly of the ship was an ugly nightmare; twisted rails and arcs of steel made crooked webs in the shadows as the torchlight found them. A disorder of rusting machinery filled the spaces between the mezzanine floors, much of it shifted or bent out of position by a tremendous force. Henry stood at the top of what had been the engine room, sharing the walkway with another corpse that he'd not yet chosen a name for. This one wore a hard hat with a green logo upon it and wore thin trousers and a casual shirt with the sleeves rolled up. It lay with its legs twisted and a bony arm dangling over the side of the walkway, still gripping a clipboard that had a pen hanging from it by a piece of string.

Just like the stairwell below, the water had frozen inside the bottom third of the engine room and Henry was amazed at the glimpse into the past it provided – the arrival of the Ever Winter. Henry shone the torch slowly in a long straight line from one end of the engine room's iced floor to the other. A blue crab scuttled across his line of light and disappeared under a fallen cabinet. Henry wished he'd had his net with him, having caught a few blue crabs when they'd swum up for bait, usually just once a year.

"How'd yous get in here?" Henry spoke quietly, not wishing to hear his voice echo in a such a place.

His torchlight caught a large moving shadow beneath the carpet of ice. Henry thought he'd imagined it at first, but caught it again a second time: the distorted yet unmistakable silhouette of a shark stalking the extremities of the ship to the keel. *The shark was swimming inside the ship*. The hull had been breached, yet the ship had not sunk.

Henry searched until he found evidence of a tear; the tip of something huge, pointed and man-made, of the same material as the ship had speared the hull. The top of it was visible above the ice and the rest obscured beneath it. Henry had no idea what the thing was, or what it had been used for, yet he did understand then that the ship's hull had both torn and frozen before the crew realized – so instantaneously, that the rushing waters which entered the hull had no time to fill it, or sink the vessel and the man with the thin trousers and rolled-up sleeves had no time to drop his clipboard and alert others.


The squall and the freeze had come so rapidly that the surface of the sea had crystallized in a single moment as the vessel was impaled. Henry recalled being confined to the igloo in the blizzard and that Father had feared breaking the ice whilst they were there, because below them, under the ice, was the deep dark waters and all the creatures within it. If the family could not escape the igloo and the floor beneath them broke apart, they would have all drowned. Maybe not all at once. Maybe not in the same minutes. But without an escape, they would have sunk to the depths below.

Henry looked around him in the engine room and knew that were the weather to ever change, or were the sun to ever return to its former brilliance and bring with it a thaw, everything on the yot-boat would be lost. Time would uncase. Both the object that had impaled the ship and the ice itself would release the vessel from their grasp and it would continue its fateful course to the seabed below, with all the prizes inside forever lost.

In Henry's mind, even without the sun bringing its warmth to the ice, he pictured the bottom of the ship just falling apart from the rest of it. He'd seen the rust on those parts exposed on the surface of the ice. Below it would be far worse.

"Shark got in. Whole time we've been here, we've been sharing it with sharks."

The stark revelation brought panic to Henry. The comparison of the buried igloo and the stricken, rotting underside of the ship.

"This rotten underbelly. It could break apart down there and the shark knows it."

Anxious and unable to stand being in the engine room anymore, Henry ran from the sub-deck to the corridor above where Beverly Marsh lay without her coffee cup. The ship was no haven for his family. The ship was death itself, waiting languidly to slide from the sword that held it and drag them all down into the darkness.

Henry wanted off the vessel, but he knew Father would mock him and Mary would enjoy his confession were he to voice it. They'd lived on Lantic their whole lives. Lantic was far from the Favela. Lantic was safe. *It was home.* The difference between the two places was that if the ice beneath the igloo cracked, the family would have time to escape. If the ship began to sink with them inside it, there would be no escape.

He composed himself and let his heartbeat return to a normal thump. Mary appeared from the door to the accommodation. Her hood was up, and she held a shovel across her shoulder. Father followed her with a crowbar, both of which had likely been found in a general stores room.

"Brother," Mary greeted him, "Let's get back to it."

"Back to it," Henry replied, acting as normal as he could, then followed her toward the door where he'd left the axe he'd been using for the job.

They toiled for another couple of hours and had almost cleared the container doors, a mere inch of ice still sealing the bottom of them shut. Henry wore his new sunglasses, and neither Mary nor Father had inquired where they'd come from, although Mary had said he looked stupid in them.

Finally, Father signaled for them to pack up and leave, but Henry refused to down his tools.

"We're nearly done. I could shift this in a bit. Let's finish." Henry smashed his axe into the ice, sending chippings of it up into the air.

"It's time to get back to the homestead, Henry-son. Night comes quick this time of it." Father rested his arm upon Henry's shoulder. Henry stopped striking the ice and looked up at the sky. Both the sun and the moon were visible at the same time, which Henry had never seen before.

"We're close. We'll get that open in no time, an' all that's inside is ours. Ain't you keen to see what's in this'n?" Henry moved his Father's arm back so he could take another strike at the ice encasing the bottom of the doors.

"It'll be more dolls, or another car for you to mash up," Mary quipped, impatient and clearly eager to be home.

"I'm staying, Father. Like you said, I'm a man now. I can choose to dwell beyond the wire." Henry struck the ice once more. "Well, I choose to. I'm staying, and I'm getting this tin open," he said, ignoring his growling stomach and his tired body's demands for warmth and rest.

"Henry, you prong!" Mary rolled her eyes and walked away in the direction of the homestead.

Henry felt Father's stare boring into him as he hit the ice again. Neither of them said anything for a while, but finally Father spoke.

"All right. You did your Ritual. I said it myself. You're no chook." Father placed his arm upon his son's shoulder once more. "You can hack that floor a while longer, but don't be too long. Mother will be worrisome. An' she'll take that out on me."

Henry laughed and went to speak but Father interrupted him. "Won't do you good missing a meal, though. You need some meat on them arms if you're ever going to wear this pelt!"

It warmed his heart to hear his father acknowledge that

Henry would one day step into his furs and lead the family, and all he could do was grin and nod a few times.

Father turned to catch up with Mary. Henry called out his thanks, and watched his father's silhouette get smaller until it joined Mary's in the distance and they both disappeared in the panorama.

# SEVEN

## Road to Ruin

It took Henry over an hour to chip away at the ice until it no longer barred the doors to the container. Still they would not open on their own, so Henry used the ax, then the crowbar to bend the doors at the bottom, then lever one side open. Pulling at the doors was no use, so Henry decided he'd be better off forcing them inward, providing no cargo had been placed directly in front of them.

He looked through the gap he'd already made, where the dwindling light had penetrated a few feet. There was no cargo there, which worried him; if the container turned out to be empty, there would be much laughter at his expense when he returned late for his meal with nothing to show for it.

The doors were hinged on the outside of the container, and when he had no luck with his assault on the center, he worked tirelessly on the hinges themselves, which was easier on one side where they had already rusted considerably. Henry was exhausted, but excited that he alone was unearthing the treasures within.

His stomach groaned under his furs, but he ignored its protests, resisted its demands for him to head back to the igloo to see what Hilde had added to the pot. His arms ached and the remaining hinges stood firm, so he threw his weight against the doors once more and barged them with his shoulders, which hurt, but caused the ingress he'd made to buckle further. There was a thud as something hit the floor; one of the rusted hinges had disintegrated entirely and the left door now hung from the bottom joint alone.

Henry focused on that side with crowbar and axe once more, then resorted to kicking it over and over, wondering to himself if his drumming of the container was being heard by Mary and Father on their way back to the homestead. He thought momentarily of the snow leopards too, not to mention the big whites.

Finally, the doors submitted to his assault, and a daydreaming Henry fell into the container and landed heavily on whatever was stacked within.

Henry ached all over, but he was exhilarated. He had done what he had said he would do, and he'd done it alone. He felt altered; broader, taller, despite what Father had said about his arms. Henry raised his face from where he lay on the cargo, then turned finally to savor his victory against the broken doors.

Outside, the shrinking sun made its curtain call sky, having dipped to make way for the pearl moon that rose in its stead. The sky was dark now, but had light from two opposing sources at the same time on different ends of the panorama. It felt eerie. Henry reached for the torch in his pocket and wound it up to see what surrounded him inside the container. Identical rectangular boxes filled the entire space, each carbon-colored and made of a plastic material, which explained why none had degraded since they were first sent overboard from the ship. The words *British Army* were stenciled on each box in an identical font and some had numbers upon them, which were all meaningless to Henry.

Henry barely noticed the roiling mist that descended upon the plateau as he unclipped the fastenings on the first box. The box held some kind of bodysuit. The dark gray material felt strange. Unlike anything Henry had ever touched. It was thin, like an undergarment rather than something you would wear to brave the cold, but it felt immensely durable. Henry tapped the breastplate with his knuckle and it made a din as if he was hitting man-made steel. He drew his blade and dragged it gently across the fibers of the material, then more aggressively when nothing happened. The material held, the fibers remained intact and there wasn't even a visible scratch on the bodysuit. Henry stabbed it several times, but the blade failed to penetrate the outfit.

Henry sensed something then and turned instinctively to see the thickest of fog had swept down upon him and he could barely see six feet beyond the broken doors of the container.

Henry grabbed the suit and the crowbar. Every direction was obscured by the fog. The other containers were invisible and even the ship was concealed from him despite its immense size. The fog hung all around him and above him. It encroached upon him and left Henry claustrophobic, confused at how quickly the weather had changed. The need to return home grew suddenly overwhelming.

Henry thought once more of Father telling the family many times to stay put and weather the storm when they'd built their new home as the storm arrived. He could hear Father's voice in his mind, then Mother's too. But he was scared to remain and wanted to get back to everyone.

Henry took a breath, then made off in the direction he thought was home. The air around him was thick. It seemed to penetrate his lungs, adding weight to them, threatening to make him wheeze the more he inhaled and exhaled. He walked, blind. But very quickly, he faltered, smacking into the side of a container that he didn't realize was there because his bearings were so muddled.

He punched the container in frustration and the noise of it rang out, but that too seemed to get lost in the mist. He changed direction, but after a few steps, the same thing happened and he cursed. He strained to see through the mist, but it became a gray wall. Annoyed with himself and frustrated with his situation, Henry conceded and realized all he could do was go back to the ship.

Henry sat in the captain's chair, eating one of the blue crabs he'd lured from the engine room with some of the tinned food he'd long given up on eating himself. He'd simply removed the lid of one of the cans, made a hole in the side through which he knotted a rope, and lowered it from the walkway into the pit below. He'd smashed one of the crab's claws to get to the meat, which he ate raw. It tasted like everything else from the sea; same texture, same smell. The only other new food he'd tasted was the man-meat, and though he dared not admit it, he found himself thinking about it time and again, re-imagining the taste and the way he had to chew it thoroughly before swallowing each mouthful.

Henry had no idea how many hours he slept, but when he peered out of one of the portholes he saw that the fog had lifted, the sky was clear once more and it was a new day. A light snow had fallen, but it looked like it would be a good day.

Henry set off for home after putting on the bodysuit he'd found in the container. He wore it as an undergarment, but was surprised how warm it felt, and as he trekked through the snow, he actually felt hot and loosened the top layers. The suit was unlike anything he'd ever seen and the heat it provided made it precious. Henry had marveled at himself in the captain's mirror when he put it on, knowing it had been worth the effort of digging the container free – and worth whatever punishment or harsh words awaited him when he got back to the homestead.

The journey home was similar to when he'd walked back with Mary after first discovering the ship. He had the same feeling of guilt in his stomach, the same worry. Only this time, Mary would be one of the people scolding him for being late and allowing them to think he'd come to harm alone in the fog.

Henry smiled when the homestead appeared in the distance. He picked up his pace, passing the hidden cave that screened Martin's sculptures from the world. He didn't look inside, but he could picture Martin's creations still; *ice imitations*.

It was then that Henry noticed something odd about the homestead. He broke into a run.

~

The wire was down on one side. It looked like it'd been trampled. As he neared it, Henry could tell it had been cut in several places and dragged apart. Dusky smoke billowed from the igloo, and outside there were several mounds upon the snow, which reminded Henry of the containers scattered around the vessel. A thin layer of recent snow masked them, and some instinct urged Henry not to look at them for too long. Not to focus too clearly on the shapes. Not to count their number.

His heart pounded with urgency. There were footprints in the snow, trailing in every direction. *Too many*. Still Henry couldn't grasp what he was seeing. Nothing made sense. Everything he saw was wrong: the plastic Mickey Mouse cup lay half-buried in the snow by his feet; a swathe of fabric flapped in the wire beside him; Mary's slingshot was broken in two pieces by the entrance of their home, and one side of the igloo looked like it had collapsed in on itself. The white of the snow was spoilt in places with little dots and lines and pools. *Blood*.

Henry clutched his knife. Everything was silent. Mother wasn't calling after any of the children. Hilde wasn't yelling at Mary, or Iris. Iris wasn't giggling and Martin wasn't climbing the wire to sneak into his secret cavern. Father's voice did not boom, or curse. The baby didn't… *the baby*.

One of the mounds arched in an S shape a few strides away. Henry saw it out of the corner of his eye, but ignored it. He called out, too scared to go straight to the igloo itself. No answer came. No warmth, or scolding. Just silence.

Finally, something inside of him dared him to look at the mound. A wicked voice inside his head, barely audible, goaded him on.

*You know what it is. Take a closer look. Fathom it, you prong. You know what it is.*

Henry found he was approaching the stack. A gust of wind swept through the homestead and brushed some of the fresh snow, unmasking a face beneath it. Henry was startled, yet relieved that it wasn't any of his family. The face belonged to a young man, not much older than Henry but with a full beard of yellow hair. Henry called out once more and went toward another mound, finding an older man stretched out on his back with his arms laid above his head as if he'd been dragged by them. The snow around the body was pink, and as Henry's boots breached the surface of it, a darker color hemorrhaged the top layer and Henry could tell this man had lost a lot of blood as he lay dying. Henry rolled the body to one side and found a whalebone sticking out of the man's kidney area.

"Mother! Father!" Henry screamed, frightened and unsure exactly what he should do.

Among the footprints and bodies were traces of sled tracks and paw prints. There had been more than one sled, by the look of it, each one much bigger than that which the family owned, each one pulled by five or six animals of some kind.

Henry's mind raced. He tried to put his thoughts together. His family had been attacked. They were nowhere to be seen. Who might have done this?

*Lanner!*

The dead he'd seen weren't his kin, and that meant his family had fought back. He pictured a battle, with Father charging into the melee head-on. Father was strong. Father had killed a Big White. The two men Henry had seen had not survived.

It was a good sign, but he'd not checked all of the mounds. He was scared to. *In case.* There was still a chance that his family wasn't among the fallen. They might have chased off the attackers, or gone looking for Henry to warn him, or join him within the safety of the yot-boat. Henry hadn't checked Martin's cave. They could even have been hiding there! As long as Henry didn't see any of his family amongst the mounds, there was still a chance.

He looked instead at the entrance of the igloo, from which smoke still escaped.

*Go to it. You know what's inside. Prong. You know what happened here, and it's your burden.*

Henry found himself walking to the igloo once more, tasting the smoke as he neared it. Before he reached the entrance, something caught his eye: a figure was laid across the ice hole, partly submerged in the ice. Father was sprawled in a star shape, with his arms and legs wide open, in a position almost as laughable as it was tragic. His torso was bare and it was covered in wounds from blades and blunt instruments. His skin was pale and his eyes were closed.

Henry fell to his knees, broken at the sight of Father. A thousand remembered images of the man he loved with every fiber of him came to Henry in quick succession. All smiling and reassuring, nothing like the pitiful sight before him.

Henry tried to gather his thoughts but he couldn't. He was tormented and pushed his hands over his eyes to shield them for what he saw, hoping it would be a different scene when he let his hands fall away. He was confused as to why Father had not sunk into the water without a trace, then he saw the anchor looped around his waist and embedded in the ice next to the hole, which alone kept him from slipping under. They'd wanted him to die slowly. They'd tossed him into the waters after they'd beat him and tortured him. They'd wanted him to be found and wanted Henry to see it and forever drown in that vision, with no chance of shaking it from his mind. *Lanner!* Henry saw then that the net strung from the anchor was also tangled around Father's legs beneath the knees, knotted in an imprisoning web. *Catch of the day!* he thought, somewhat hysterically. Father would not have approved of the assailants leaving the anchor that they'd used to catch fish behind. *It was wasteful and stupid.*

Henry leaned forward, wiping the tears from his face before pulling his father from the ice by the waist. He failed at the first attempt, but found the strength to lift him the second time. As he hauled his father's body up, he was repulsed to find small fish attached to Father's back, nibbling from the open wounds. All but one of them fell back into the water, and Henry pulled the last one from his father's skin in disgust and threw it across the ice.

Nausea engulfed him. He sank to his knees again and thought about how everything was linked. The walks back to the homestead, the death-stares of strangers, the mounds scattered like the containers, and now lifting Father's corpse from the ice hole just as he'd dragged a seal from the waters just weeks previous. His family fed on fish. The fish fed on Father. *A tin can to bait the blue crab and the old man to bait the fish.* The world was a cruel place.

In Henry's head, the voice continued to mock him.

*This is yours. On you, boy. Look at the bear killer!*

He wasn't sure then if the voice was his, or if it belonged to Lanner.

Henry tried to untangle the mess of net around Father's feet but quickly gave up, looking around instead for Father's coat to cover his body. It was nowhere in sight and he assumed it would be inside the igloo somewhere. He closed his eyes, not wanting to venture further. Henry knew the path ahead would only lead to sadness. *Heartache.* He called for his mother and no reply came, which he'd expected by now. *So many mounds. A cemetery of snow dunes.*

An agonized groan came from the corpse beside him.

"Don't. Go in. Don't go inside." Father's rasping voice frightened him so much that Henry scrambled away from him. Then he crawled back just as quickly, realizing Father was still alive, or still clinging on to life at least.

"Father!" Henry took off his own coat and placed it over his father's bare chest. He rubbed the shoulders to try and bring warmth, but Father grimaced, from the pain of his wounds, which were everywhere. "I'm sorry, Father! I should've come back. I should've come back with you and—"

"No. Don't go," Father managed. He gripped Henry's wrist feebly.

"What happened? Where are yours and mine?" Henry asked desperately, hot tears sliding down his cold cheeks.

"Lanner. Fa...favela," Father whispered. His lips were blue and his body shook uncontrollably. Tear tracks lined his face, a thing that Henry had never seen before. Rage built inside him.

"Don't go inside the igloo," the dying man pleaded and Henry could tell his beloved Father was summoning all his will to bring the words together.

"I'll kill him. And whoever else did this." Henry said this

plainly, as if it was a matter of fact. A done deal. He turned toward the igloo. When he looked back, Father was smiling.

"Love you, Henry-son," he muttered, before the last of the life left him.

Henry clutched the knife as he entered the igloo. The smell of the smoke almost overwhelmed him and it made the scene that unfolded seem dreamlike. The family's few possessions which had not been taken had been smashed or overturned. Part of the ceiling and wall had indeed caved in; the outside world had breached the inside, in more ways than one. His home was now a ruin that would eventually bury itself.

Mother's body was slumped in the corner where the igloo had collapsed. She stared at the entrance, sightless yet defiant, her hair and clothes in bloody disarray. She'd killed four of her attackers. There were two bodies to each side of her, and her right hand still gripped the hair of one of them. She held the shard of mirrored glass in the other, which she'd used to kill the men with, before she'd died herself from her wounds. The pot and the blubber lamp were on the floor, cracked and broken. In the center of the room, something smoldered. Something in a blackened blanket.

Henry looked at the shard of mirror. The dreamcatcher that had failed them. His mother's blood was upon it, mixed with the blood of the men she'd killed. That thought disgusted him also; the mixing of the blood. The pure cordial of Mother's, diluted with the filth spilled from the new enemy.

*All on you, Henry-boy. Yourn doing.*

Henry forced himself to go to the small pile that smoldered in the space between him and his mother's corpse. He moved slowly, still gripping the knife. He touched the blackened blanket. It still showed the pattern on one side, which he recognized well. Tears streamed down his face as he unraveled the coverlet.

*Fathom it!*

Henry screamed and screamed until all strength left him and

his voice broke. He hoped that his scream would be carried across the ice to the ears of Ginger Lanner. His scream was despair at first, but in the end, the sound changed and it became a warning. His scream was madness. It became a promise. He hoped Lanner could hear him.

The cruel voice in his head disappeared. He'd set it free and now he was altered. The Ritual was one thing. That had made him a man. But this had made him something more than that. Something else. He had not been watchful, but he would be ruthless.

Martin, Mary, Hilde and Iris weren't amongst the bodies scattered around the homestead. After all that time thinking they were safe, forgetting the danger, Lanner had found the family and he'd taken Henry's siblings. All except the baby, whose tiny body was swaddled, but whose head had been replaced with that of a plastic doll.

# EIGHT

# A Bedtime
# Story

## THE GIRLS.

"This one's mine," said the woman warrior, grabbing Mary by the scruff of her collar as she knelt. Mary hugged herself, her chin tucked into her body protectively. She barely acknowledged what was going on, rocking herself in a vaguely comforting rhythm. She was confused, distant. She could feel the mark of a purple bruise which spoiled her cheek and the eye above it had puffed beyond its usual size.

An improvised shelter had been hastily thrown together in case the weather turned, but no snow fell that night and the sky was clear. The pack dogs lay in a sleeping, stinking huddle by the opening. They were unlike the dogs of the Great-Greats as they'd been bred over and over from the same bloodline for over a hundred years. Mother had told the girls this. *Mother.*

The animals' teeth protruded painfully at all angles. Their manes were thick and their muscles strong. The dogs resembled wolves, ancient family pets, fighting dogs. All of these. Mostly, they resembled monsters.

Mary, in her daze, thought about the stars. She wished she was outside so she could look at them all. Only the stars. *Nothing else. Never anything else.* She closed her eyes and imagined that her mind could wander from the shelter and view the stars from outside. Outside, where it was safer, away from the people around her and the beastly animals so unlike the snow leopards she'd once feared.

Like a hawk in flight, her mind soared around the icescape and flew up to the sky until she was amongst the stars. Mary was so far from Earth and everything upon it that she could no longer see Lantic and all the terrible things that happened there. She lingered, drawing warmth from a single thought: that clouds would form again soon and shroud the surface of Earth from her completely. Only then could she forget everything.

Hilde hugged Iris and Martin closer to her, as they huddled like the pack dogs that guarded the entrance. They'd given up trying to engage their sister. They hoped she'd come back at some point and go back to being Mary, but the longer she was estranged, the more they worried, and it seemed less likely they'd ever see the old Mary again. None of them spoke. They'd learned not to in the days since Lanner had announced himself once more at the wire.

"Pare." *Stop.*

Ginger Lanner stretched his arms and then tilted his head from side to side to stretch his neck muscles. He yawned, displaying his gapped teeth to all, taking his time to reply to the woman who wanted to claim Mary as hers. He wore the Big White pelt that he'd taken from the children's father. Although he was a tall man, the coat was too big and hung awkwardly upon his frame. The fur was no longer one color. It was two; white and red.

"Comrade, *amigo.* The king determines the spoils." His voice was soft. He wasn't as animated as he'd been when he first met the children some months previous. He no longer needed the mask he had worn for them. "Erasmus, I'm promised the little one. I'll put in a word about this 'un, *si,* but the king may want all of them, for some time at least. Or he may put them all into the ice. Either way, we deliver the subjects as seen. The witch will check them over. None got permission to ruin."

Erasmus grunted a response and sat back down. She was as old as Mother had been, absent Mother's softer features and warm smile. She was sporting a fresh wound to her own face where she'd been struck on the bridge of her nose during the assault, but it had clearly been bent many times before. Hilde thought she may have been beautiful once, before she had been spoiled by the violence upon her. Yet Hilde could not feel sorry for Erasmus, who'd been one of the butchers that wrapped an anchor around Father and left him spread across the ice-hole to perish.

Erasmus kept her eyes upon Mary, who was oblivious. Erasmus bit her bottom lip as if she were suppressing words, or thoughts. It drew blood and she let it run down her chin. Her teeth looked orange. Hilde in turn kept her eyes upon her, uncertain how she could intervene and protect the younger ones at the same time. Though she hated Erasmus and her companions, she was also angry with Mary. She needed her help. She needed her strength and guidance. Yet she understood. What they'd all gone through, what they'd seen, had been unthinkable. It would stay with each of them forever.

There were four other raiders in the shelter, two men and two women. One couple was sleeping close together, with the woman's arm draped around the man's form as they snored in unison. The man's beard, like his hair, was mottled into unruly knots. It held morsels of food and other things and gave off a stale stench, which the children could smell from the other side of the shelter along with the pack dogs. They'd heard the others call him Jared, but he himself rarely spoke, and his eyes were mostly hidden under the peak of his *Hooters* trucker cap. The lady tucked next to him was Ula and she was bigger than all of the men in height and heft. She'd not been cruel to the children and hadn't been directly involved in the deaths of Mother or Father, but she was present and had helped drag the children to the sleds. That made her just as guilty as everyone else. Hilde would never forget her name, or the names of her cohorts.

The other pair were keeping guard reluctantly, looking like they needed to sleep themselves. One was a short, walrus-looking fellow with ashen hair and a thick mustache. He called himself Needol. Needol blinked continuously to try and keep his eyes open. He wore the belt that Henry had given Father when he'd first discovered the yot-boat. The girl, Dookie, had her jet-black hair cut short, which made her look like a young boy. She had a slim frame and none of the usual curves of a woman. Just a few years older than Henry, she glowered at the children hatefully. One of the raiders Father had killed had meant something to her and she blamed the children for it. At least when Ula was on guard, Hilde could relax slightly.

Lanner sidled up to Iris and she slunk away from him, nestling under Hilde's protective arm, which Lanner ignored. He held his hands up and grinned. The gesture wasn't surrender, but it was hard to interpret exactly what it was. Lanner was the clown. *The demon.*

"I'd like to tell you a story. It's an old story that was told to me by one of the old 'uns at the Favela. Are you listening? Good."

Lanner hadn't waited to see if anyone was listening to his tale, but the heavy-eyed guards eavesdropped, interested, even if the children weren't.

"There was once a little girl who thought that the moon was the most beautiful thing in the world. One day, she asked her papa to get it for her. Her papa, he made something called a ladder and it stretched up and up and up. He climbed that thing until he came face to face with the moon. '*Hey, amigo,*' he said, thinking them lifelong buds, because he'd gazed at that moon his whole life long. Then he reached out and he took it. The moon! That's right. He went back down with the moon in his hand and he gave it to his little girl. *The moon!* The girl was so pleased that, do you know what she did? You've no idea. She took the moon and she *danced* with it! She danced with the moon. *Si?*" Lanner moved his arms then like he was dancing. He looked insane.

"But as she danced, she jumped up and up and the moon

went up and up with her. Except it kept going. Zooming. Up and up! It grew tiny as it got further away, until none ever saw it again and the world was in darkness forever. Ever and ever, amen. All because – let me tell you why – all because the papa thought he could just take the moon and keep it for him and his! That's the moon!"

Lanner had become agitated as he told the story and laughed his childlike laugh in all the places he thought were funny. His arms moved wildly as he told it, until he came to a final stop. He shook his head as if he were trying to work it all out, closing his eyes as if he were viewing the story inside his head and replaying it to himself. He smiled sardonically, then continued, "Now, *your* papa, he thought he could take you all and keep you to himself out here in the mid of nowhere. Keep the rest of us in darkness. Whilst he danced with you all. That's not right. It's mercenary! It's wrong 'un! I found you. Me. I found you. I *found* you! The king has promised you to me. I accept his gift. Whole-heart. It's my turn to dance. It's my *turn*. Up and up and up. Until none can see you anymore."

It was clear finally how frayed Lanner's mind was. He was more dangerous than any of them could have imagined when they first met him back in the homestead. Then Hilde remembered; Father had known. Father had wanted to stick him. *If only he had*.

Before Hilde realized it, Martin, who hadn't spoken in days, sprang up.

"Leave her alone!" he said bravely, throwing a shard of ice at Lanner, which missed pathetically, and wouldn't have caused any bother if it hadn't. It was the first time Martin had ever had an outburst of any sort and the first time Hilde had heard him raise his tiny voice. Lanner looked furious and went to strike Martin, but Hilde grabbed his arm with both hands, screaming for him not to touch her brother, who looked so small compared to the man that towered above him. Dookie had readied her weapon, eager to step in and cause harm to the children, but Lanner shoved her backward, keen to handle things without her. Ula and Jared leaped up from where they lay, but Lanner changed tact and let Hilde go. He laughed hard before regaining his usual sinister expression.

"Hark at you, girl! There are *spikes* upon you. I have noticed. The king will see it, of course, but just in case he don't, I shall help him fathom it! There'll be a few choices for you. None great, *si*? Bite your tongue, serpent bitch. And you, boy, unless you want me to not treat you as well as I have been. I can adapt my behavior."

"Why wait?" Hilde blurted out. "Why don't you just kill us like you did our mother and father? And our—"

"You ain't mine to kill," Lanner interrupted, red in the face. "I ain't sorry about taking any of you, or doing them in. That man who raised you out here had no respect. *Sem respeito!* You don't make treasures and keep them all to yourself. From your king!"

Lanner closed his eyes and took a deep breath.

"*Dorme* and dream sweet. Don't make me switch on you right here. Soon you'll wish we butchered you with your family. They goners now. Like the Great-Greats. Yourn misery is just starting. *Compreendo?*"

He turned to Iris, who cowered behind Hilde, but still formed a barrier to Martin. He scratched at his patchy beard and softened his voice.

"Night, my little dear. Won't be long and we'll be home, you and I."

Iris shuddered and sobbed into her sister's arm. Lanner gave them all the creeps, but after what she'd witnessed at the homestead, Iris clearly thought he might just be the devil himself. Hilde held her tighter than she ever had, even after Lanner retreated to the other side of the shelter. It was Henry or Mary who usually comforted the youngest siblings. It was Henry or Mary who played with them. Mary was absent even though she sat just an arm's length away, and Henry was gone. If the fog didn't lose him forever, there'd be other predators on the ice that he couldn't match alone. Hilde realized she was now sister and mother in one. She looked down, twisting her sister's hair in her fingers the way that Henry often did, and at some point, Iris and Martin both fell asleep.

Hilde could not sleep. Not until she was sure that Lanner was comatose. She lay in silence, listening to strangers and pack dogs breathing around her, worried about all that awaited them at the Favela. She knew she had to think of a plan to keep them together and to escape the clutches of their captors before it was too late. Killing Lanner in the process would be a bonus, but right then, all she wanted was to get away. Mary was the hindrance. Mary wasn't herself and Hilde wasn't sure if she could rely on her when the time came, or whether she'd have to make the choice of taking Martin and Iris and leaving Mary behind.

Only when she was sure everyone apart from the guards were asleep did she let her tears come.

# NINE

## Salvagers

---

Father had once said you shouldn't name a bairn until it was old enough, because it was harder to lose something with a given name. Henry thought it ironic how in the nights before Lanner had attacked, the family had finally named the bairn, only for the bairn to be taken from the world in such a grotesque way.

He'd spoken the name just a single time that night, but Henry would never speak it again. The pain and the horror of what he'd seen was still indescribable and would never leave him.

Henry had trekked for twenty-two days, covering over a hundred leagues. He'd found what might have been footprints in places, but never caught sight of anyone. No clues had been left behind, intentionally or otherwise. He'd guessed they were hours ahead of him, but he could never be certain as he didn't know how fast the animals that pulled their sleds were, or for how long they rested.

Never before had he experienced such solitude. His mind endlessly replayed the horrors he had seen, causing him at times to scream to the heavens with demands of explanation, or retribution, until his throat was hoarse and his head dizzy from the exertion. He'd sobbed, often without realizing it; then, upon coming to his senses, he'd tried to pick up his pace and close the gap between him and those he sought. He thought of every key decision he'd made that past month, and in his thoughts, he altered each of the decisions, trying to grasp what course his new action would've taken. It was torture. In his mind, he put himself at the homestead when Lanner and his men had attacked. He defended his family. He died with them. He slaughtered Lanner. He won, he lost, negotiated and begged, he threatened and tricked and was tricked in return. Nothing mattered. Because what had happened, had happened. Yet his anguish and loneliness remained.

Henry tried to limit his sleep, so he could make some of the distance up between him and whatever was left of Lanner's raiding party each day. He didn't have to hunt; he'd taken the flesh with him from the dead raiders and packed it in a sealskin. Not from Mother. That he couldn't do.

*"Meat is meat,"* Father had once said to him.

He hoped Lanner's men would have to find their food beneath the ice, which would give Henry time to close the gap on them. Then he worried that, being from the Favela, they would not be well accustomed to catching fish in the middle of Lantic and would instead turn to their captives when hunger took hold. *The Favela is evil.*

Like the scenarios Henry had imagined playing out when Lanner had attacked the homestead, he also found his mind conjuring what had been happening to his siblings ever since they were taken. It plagued him even more than the events at the homestead, because unlike the decisions he'd made in the past, the things he imagined happening to his siblings could actually be unfolding somewhere on the distant ice.

Henry kept moving, because every time he sat still, he felt the urge to remain where he was and give up. He pictured himself just lying on the ice and doing nothing. Letting the snow cover him and dying upon the ice like his father had. Yet love kept him going – and, in equal amount, hatred.

When he slept, he saw blood upon the ice and Father lying across the ice-hole, speaking dying words of accusation through blue lips. When he slept, he saw Mother with the failed dreamcatcher shard in her hand. When he slept, he saw a doll's head in a swaddled blanket.

From above, the place where the salvagers worked looked like a sieve. Ice-holes dotted the terrain to give them access to different parts of what had once been a city, and that city had been built on the edge of a vast hill. The underbelly of the ice still divulged the grid of roads that lined the metropolis. No longer inhabited by their makers, the skeletons of buildings beneath the ice were home to the creatures of the sea; those with shimmering scales that flashed wherever the light breached; tentacles that skulked and felt their way around the coral and corroding man-made things; armored shells that offered protection within the sand-sealed homes that had once afforded the same to Henry's ancestors.

The salvagers stood in a circle around two of their number. One was a girl, who had come up from the ice and was rubbing her limbs urgently under a foil blanket to prevent hypothermia. The second was a boy no older than ten, who was unconscious and had been dragged from the freezing waters by the girl. The salvagers ignored the female and focused on the boy whose lips had turned the same blue as Henry's father's had been as he died. Two of the salvagers were bent over him, trying to revive him in a way that appeared almost calm, as though they'd successfully done this hundreds of times before.

Nearby was a pile of goods brought up from the citadel below in the days previous: oyster shells; plates and bottles of different sizes and shapes; silver, stainless steel and plastic cutlery; a rusted oxygen cylinder; a plastic toy dog; a misshapen funnel; a box with 'Tupperware' written on it; a reel of cabling; a window-pane with the glass still intact; a handful of colored child's building bricks; a broken radio; a bicycle; a dented and twisted brass instrument, and a small brass statuette of a child reading a book.

Henry had been told that the salvagers were adults. To see

children being hauled from the ice, surprised him and he realized there would be other things that Lanner, or even his own parents had told him, which might not be true in the Favela today.

Henry was able to get fairly close to the children before he was seen. His arrival coincided with the exact moment that the boy shuddered to life and coughed seawater over the two that had saved him. Immediately, the salvagers lost interest in the boy. He was alive. That was it. It was so casual and swift, the return to normal.

Revealed all of a sudden, one of the salvagers pointed at Henry and one of them said something, although Henry wasn't close enough to hear it. He doubted himself and his purpose then and part of him wanted to break into a run back to his homestead. It would be so easy; his sisters wouldn't know that he'd been a coward. Martin wouldn't know he'd failed them. They'd likely assume him dead like their parents. Perhaps they wouldn't blame him at all for running. But Henry had passed his Ritual. He was the son of the Bearkiller. He thought of Mother's smiling face, which morphed into her death stare. The same thing happened when he thought of Father. He couldn't bear to conjure up the image of the bairn, but that too came to him, as it did whenever he slept.

The group below turned to face Henry and shuffled into a formation around the tallest boy, a hard-looking child with his hair pulled up in a knot. The boy – whom Henry figured to be the leader – held a broom handle, which he'd been using to etch a crude map on the floor by his feet.

Henry guessed there were at least twenty salvagers, including the two recovering on the floor. He'd heard that they were hardy men and he'd expected to find Lanner amongst them, since he'd claimed to be one, but to Henry's surprise, every one of the salvagers was a child, the eldest looking no more than ten and three.

The children had blankets and furs about their shoulders, which they wore like capes, and under them they were bare-chested – even the girls, who looked as tough and unwelcoming as the boys did. Some of them had pelt headscarves protecting their ears and noses. Each of them looked underfed; their bones poked out wherever their flesh was on show, so they appeared like carcasses of children, malnourished beings from a terrible dream. Henry couldn't take his eyes from their bodies, which shimmered with the layers of blubber they'd coated themselves with to help protect them from the cold in the water. They glowered at Henry with hateful eyes, which unnerved him. Never before had anyone looked at him in that way. Until recent weeks, Henry had only experienced a life full of kindness, even though he'd never thought of it in that way before.

As Henry studied the rabble, he noticed that a few of the children bore the signs of having survived frostbite, and had parts of – or whole – fingers missing from their hands. One boy only had a finger and thumb on each hand, which reminded Henry of the pincers from one of the crabs he'd seen in the engine room of the ship.

A bird flew high above them and for a moment Henry imagined Mary knocking it out of the sky with her sling, until he remembered that she wasn't with him and that she didn't have her sling upon her and that he didn't know if she was still alive.

The leader of the group stepped forward. His long curly hair was held from his face in a top knot and he bore raised scars upon his chest in ornate patterns, hewn intentionally upon him as decoration. Henry noted that others had the same upon their arms or hands, and one upon the cheeks of his face, like lightning bolts, which took Henry back again to his homestead and the shard of mirrored glass that hung in the center of the igloo, and of Mother holding it in a death grip.

Henry walked toward the group and they held their ground, apart from the leader, who'd taken another step forward. None of them held weapons apart from the leader with his broom handle, but everyone – including Henry – knew there were enough of them to disarm and kill him, so he kept his knife strapped to his belt for the time being. He stood separated from them by one of the circles cut through the ice, half expecting a seal to emerge from the center at any moment.

"Who's this whale's prong?" sniped a brunette with pigtails when Henry was in earshot. She wore the bruise of a love-bite on her neck proudly. The children laughed menacingly, apart from the leader.

"Meat," said another girl at the end of the formation. She had an overbite, and a large red scar that followed the shape of her brow. Her scar didn't look intentional and Henry imagined she'd not been compliant in its creation.

"Looks like a cunk," replied one of the boys – Henry couldn't tell which one with so many eyes upon him – and the laughter returned.

"To beat down, or not beat down? That is the question. *Maluco!*" added one of the youngest boys.

"Dayum," one added.

"Dayum," echoed another.

Henry raised his hands in the air. *"Tenha calma,"* he said quietly, using words Father had taught him. The children all creased up, which embarrassed and angered him at the same time.

*"Acalmar esta!" Calm this.* One of the boys dropped his trousers and presented his bare ass cheeks, which the girl with the overbite slapped hard to another roar of laughter.

"Kill the cunk!" yelled half a dozen in unison across the ring of water as the group became more animated.

"We don't kill the cunk till we know what the cunk wants," said an ebony-skinned girl who'd been standing at the back of the group warming her skin under a foil blanket. She was pretty, with her hair in cornrows, still dripping from the water that she'd not long been out of. The girl lowered the foil blanket. Her arms were muscular and both her poise and posture suggested a sureness he'd only ever seen in Mother. "What's your bit, cunk?"

The girl unfolded her arms, displaying her bare chest beneath furs draped across her shoulder. Henry found himself staring at her flesh. The girl's boldness left him perturbed, as this was the first time he'd looked upon the body of a girl outside his family.

He looked away and took the time to regard each of the ragged children that might've done him harm. He tried to assess who the strong ones were and the weaklings, but he found he couldn't focus on any of them. They were a unit; a mass of unfamiliar faces that scrutinized him as one.

Two of the boys draped their arms around one another in a close, protective embrace. Everything was alien. Everything unfamiliar.

Henry tried to compose himself. "I'm looking for the salvager, Ginger Lanner." He stared at the leader. The boy stared back, then looked at the girl with the cornrows. He shrugged and took a step backward.

"What you looking at him for? I'm the boss man," the girl with the cornrows said firmly.

"You're all *kids*," Henry replied, disbelieving.

"And you a poo poo cunk!" heckled a smiling child from the end of the line who had a huge, lumbering frame, but spoke like a child of four. Laughter returned from the ranks and the smiling child stepped forward as if he were going to walk around the ice circle and greet Henry, but the others held him back subtly.

"No, Boo." The real leader gestured, smiling at the large child with something close to kindness before fixing her stare on Henry once more, all gentleness gone from her.

"Adultos ain't done this for years. It's all down to the Orfins now," spoke a child with his hair cut in a jagged fringe that hung over his eyes. He looked a year or so older than Martin. His expression remained serious, but the fact that he spoke made Henry feel he was making progress with the gang of children.

"Orfins?" Henry had not heard the word before.

"*Tranquilo*! Shut it, Bart!" cried the leader furiously.

"Boo. My name's Boo. You poo poo," said the smiling boy, who'd edged a few meters around the circle toward Henry. His friends pulled him back once more into their number.

Henry smiled at Boo politely and the boy nodded and repeated his name a few times in delight. The girl with bunches shoved the boy to the back of the group once more, out of sight.

"Us. We're the Orfins," Bart, the boy with the jagged fringe, continued. "Salvaging got hard. All the good stuff is taken. Adultos made the Orfins do it. We ain't got mothers or fathers to feed us, so we salvage for a feed. Lanner ain't no salvager. He's a—"

"Shut your beaks!" screamed the real leader. Silence engulfed them all. She moved her hands to her hips where a belt held a truncheon of some kind. She didn't reach for it, but the threat was implied. When she was sure she wouldn't be interrupted she turned and scowled at Henry. "You're not from here, so you don't know our ways. If you toss your sticks or cutters this way nice enough, I'll see to it that your death is done mercifully and proper. If not, your end will have a sting to it, no doubt. *Eu promito.*" A couple of the children sniggered, but the leader gave them a scornful look and they ceased their laughing. One of them bowed his head apologetically. The other, a dark boy with dreadlocks and the start of a beard – nearer the age of the leader – glowered resentfully.

Henry thought about why he'd traveled all those leagues across the ice on his own, and remembered his anger at finding Father beside the igloo. He summoned it then so it was still with him and took his time to answer. He tried to imagine how his father would approach the group. How he'd convince them of his strength. How his body language would fill the space between them and show them that taking him down wouldn't be the easiest of tasks, despite their number. Henry had to look them all in the eyes one at a time so they saw no weakness in him. He needed to sow an element of doubt in their minds. Sow some fear. Sow a little bit of crazy. He was older than the salvagers and although the leader and the boy with the broom handle were just two or three years younger than him, he'd passed his Ritual already, and that meant something. He doubted that any of these had ventured far on their own, although he didn't fancy daring it under the ice like they did.

When he was ready, only then did he speak.

"I've come a long way and I brought this sealskin with me," Henry slipped the sealskin from his shoulder that had contained the flesh of one of the raiders and held it aloft so all could see that it was unremarkable.

"The man called Lanner is wearing a pelt that belonged to my father and I want that pelt, because it is mine. Then I want Lanner's head, because it is mine to take. I shall take it back to my homestead in this sealskin that my father once made and look upon it whenever I fancy. If I have to fight each and every one of you to get to that man, I will. You might think you can stop me because of your number, but you won't without suffering a big loss. I've come a long way and I will be ruthless. No doubt."

The Orfins looked at their leader, uncertain how to react and waiting for her to do so.

Henry continued,

"Lanner killed my mother an' father, an' our bairn. He took my sisters an' brother to this place an' it's my job to bring them back home. He made us all Orfins like you. He needs to die for that, and I need his head."

"He's the brother," declared one of the salvagers.

"Martin!" yelled Boo gleefully from his exile at the back of the troop.

"Shit," said another and before Henry could question it, he felt the crack as a broom handle came crashing down on his head from behind and his legs collapsed beneath him. A static of stars appeared in Henry's field of vision and he lost consciousness.

Henry hadn't seen the boy he'd originally thought the leader swim beneath the ice and emerge from it like a seal pup to get at him. The boy looked embarrassed as Henry focused on him when he came to, drawing the connection as the boy was now shivering from having dove into the freezing waters.

Henry found his wrists crudely tied with twine made from old shoelaces and other things that had survived a hundred years in some form or another. His head was throbbing and he instinctively raised his hands to check the wound, finding a crust of dried blood that had streamed into his ear and down his neck. The broken broom handle lay in two pieces on the floor and a circle of salvagers sat around him, whispering amongst themselves until the leader spoke again.

"I ain't going to hurt you none, but I do have to report you. Otherwise we're done for, and I can't have that for me or my crew," she said. "I'm Sissel. You met Yaxley," she added, motioning toward the boy who'd hit Henry with the broom handle. "This is Cuba, Florrie, Paala, Beany Bobs, Jeezus, Bethlen, Keni, Bart, Dibber, Felipe, Leaf and Q-Tip. Over there we got Big L and his brother Little L, Cola, Moon, Gethen, Miley, Japan, Skindred and Boo." Each of the children nodded awkwardly at the sound of their names. Some of them smiled. Most didn't, especially one of the eldest boys with dreadlocks who'd grunted in answer to the name *Skindred*. Henry felt uneasy about Skindred. He had the same look in his eyes that he'd seen in Lanner's. He made a mental note not to trust Skindred and to put him down at the first opportunity.

"Martin. Where is he?" Henry said drowsily.

"They brought him to us yesterday. Lanner and a couple of his. They normally stay for the first dive, to make sure they go under. To make sure we enforce it. We took Martin down an' old Lanner went back to the Birdcage to take drink. Ain't seen Lanner since and ain't seen no girls yet. They might end up here, eventually," Sissel replied.

Henry fought the urge to cry in front of the strange children gathered around him. The thought of Martin's body floating in the frozen water for the sea creatures to devour was too much. Over at the ice hole, Boo was on his belly, pulling faces at the fish idling near the surface, sharing none of Henry's worry.

"He's only a little boy. He can barely swim. He's just a—"

"Look at us. You think we didn't go through the same?" Sissel took the hand of a child beside her – the one she'd introduced as *Little L* – and held it so Henry could see clearly where the fingers stood at irregular heights and a thumb was barely a stump. To Henry's horror, the boy's face featured a black hole where the nose should've been. "Each of us done this from being nippers," said Sissel. "I seen tens of kids stiff up and die under there, and double that frostbitten. It ain't on us. Like my boy said, we're Orfins."

"You killed him!" Henry wailed. Whispers erupted amongst the rabble before him, until one of the Orfins spoke up finally.

"We didn't kill him. He's still alive. He's still under the ice. But he lives," said Yaxley.

Henry turned to the leader, who nodded.

"We'll get a dram of alkehole each for dobbing this 'un in to Lanner right now," Skindred hollered, "and more favors to come, no doubt." The boy eyeballed Sissel, who stared back. Yaxley moved himself between them, clearly loyal to his leader, but Skindred was already backing down, moving his eyes to the floor.

"Sissel decides it, Skin. Calm your bit," said Florrie, the girl with the overbite. Sissel let it go and carried on addressing Henry. Skindred shoved and cursed a path through Florrie and the kids around her to the back of the crowd and sat on his own, reminding Henry of his sister, Hilde.

"He's in one of the caverns in a *high rise*. He's above the water, but under the ice. Ain't no way of getting him from the top as he's a few floors down. One way in an' out, an' that's under," Sissel informed him. Her hands were no longer at her belt. Her face seemed kinder than it had been before.

"Why is he still under there, all alone?" Henry probed, trying not to sound accusing.

Sissel spoke softly as she explained it.

"He's scared and he's been there a while. We've been taking turns, trying to fetch him back up. He won't budge. We don't know him, but he's one of us now and we do what we can."

It seemed Henry had been wrong about the salvagers in more ways than one. He got to his feet, used his teeth to undo the twine about his wrists, and took off his coat. No one helped him, but none hindered him either. The bodysuit he'd found in the container beside the ship was completely warm still and he kept that on, feeling it'd offer him better protection than the blubber oil, as its material was unlike anything he'd ever seen and he'd not once felt the cold in it. The snow had not penetrated the fabric of it and it had remained warm and dry throughout his trek. The children marveled at it, clearly having never seen anything like it either. Sissel studied it too, her eyes lingering a bit too long on Henry's body. Yaxley noticed it and looked away, frowning.

"I need to see him. My little brother. Show me. Show me now," Henry said, and Yaxley used what was left of the broom handle to draw a map on the ice.

"We'll take you and see if you can make him come back up. You and yourn brother can beat it after, but then we dob it to the king. I do this because you're an Orfin. I wish I could do more, but I got to look after mine." Sissel lowered her voice. "The king ain't well and you need to know it. Once, I saw him jump on a man's chest until it was a whole mess and lie down in the ruin of him, splashing blood over his self like he was just bathing. Sang *Row-A-Boat*, like it was the sweetest bit. You don't want to be about him. He's sick."

"I already know why my parents left this place. Knew it the second I laid eyes on the clown in the patchwork clothes. Knew it again when I found my lot dead. What they do to you and yourn ain't right. This whole place you're from, it's all sick and I ain't even seen it yet," Henry said.

"True. Take a whole lot to cure it."

"Maybe killing one man is enough. Or just them that did what they did."

Henry wondered if Sissel was curious about him and whether deep down she wondered what he had seen, further out on the ice so far from her home and skills Henry had acquired to survive. Henry knew, in another circumstance, there would be lessons they could teach each other which they would all benefit from.

Skindred disappeared.

~

Under the ice was a glimpse into the past unlike that of stepping into the preserved ship. Vast structures lined the roads: the ghosts of homes and office buildings, shops and other places of work or recreation. Most were still standing, but a number had collapsed, whether in time, from age and corrosion, or during the rising of the waters, when the world changed and the new age had begun.

The daylight penetrated where the ice-holes had been cut above, which put eerie spotlights onto the city below and kept a cover of darkness in between, where things might lurk, until nightfall pitched all into uniform black.

There was a pulley system under the water, for bringing up relics in baskets. There was one near the entrance of the tower where Martin was residing and it had been agreed that he'd be placed in one of the baskets and hauled to the surface, if he had no energy to make the swim himself.

A carpet of sand covered the floor at different depths, but on some of the streets, lines of cars could still be seen; an eternal wait at the traffic lights that still hung above. A shoal of fish blocked Henry's way, then darted in unison around him in a hurried commute to the next junction.

Henry had taken the deepest of breaths as he'd entered the water. He was capable and knew there were pockets of air awaiting that had been well described to him, but the realization came that he was at the point where the air in his lungs was enough to go forward only and turning back had less chance of survival. He put it to the back of his mind and kicked harder with his legs.

Two of the Orfins accompanied Henry; Florrie and Q-Tip. Sissel would've joined them, but she had not been long out of the water herself and the temperatures could be fatal. Henry thought of her as he swam close to the building he knew Martin to be in thanks to Yaxley's map.

Florrie signaled to an opening where a window had once been and Henry followed his companions through it, finding himself in what had been a dining area and kitchenette. A useless television still hung on the wall and a skull rested on an imposing sofa that faced it. Other human bones lay scattered about a marble table-top and the mire that had taken shape in the spaces between over more than a century.

An eel swam from an open kitchen cupboard into another, startling Henry – to the amusement of Q-Tip, who signaled with a thumbs up. They swam through an open doorway into a hallway which no radiance ever reached, then up a flight of stairs where the water stopped two-thirds of the way up.

The three of them caught their breath on the concrete landing in near darkness. The ice above hinted at subtle light in irregular spots that made it possible for their eyes to adjust enough to see each other's silhouettes, which was something. Henry had never held his breath underwater for so long before and had panicked near the end as the gloom engulfed him by the stairwell.

Florrie spoke first. "Cunk did good. I thought he'd drown. You didn't drown, did you, Henry?"

Henry shook his head, sucking air into his lungs whilst adjusting to his surroundings. His hands and ears were especially cold, but the rest of him was perfectly warm. The suit from the ship's cargo seemed to regulate heat somehow. In contrast, he could hear his cohorts shivering from their efforts to guide him to his younger brother.

"Told you he had something in him, didn't I?" Q-Tip replied, "The eel nearly made him shit though."

"Where's Martin?" Henry managed, still gasping.

"There's a hole in the floor a way down there," Florrie said. "The ice is about four feet above us, so we need to be careful when we get up. Don't want you knocking yourself out under here. We crawl until we get to the hole, then plunge in. It's a short swim through a void in the wall. *Si*? Then you head straight up through the ice after us. You ready?"

The thought of the ice being just above them sent a shiver down Henry's spine. He felt claustrophobic all of a sudden, aware that it wouldn't be impossible for the ice to break and crush them, or the building to shift and fall into the abyss below like others had, or the waters to rise and drown them. He never would have attempted the feat they were undertaking had Martin not been part of the equation. The fear he had felt in the engine room of the container ship now seemed minuscule when weighed against the dangers he'd cast himself into. He was in the realm of the sea creatures; the sharks and other nameless, unspeakable things. He was the bait in the bucket, lowered to attract the predators of the deep. He was fodder, and they would catch his scent in the currents.

Henry had no choice now. Either way, he needed to get back into the sea that surrounded him. He had to be brave, and lend some of that bravery to his little brother. This was his real Ritual. His real test and judgment. The incident with the snow leopards was now a pleasant memory, partly because it included Mary.

Henry followed along the corridor, guided by the sounds of Florrie and Q-Tip shuffling away from him. He heard the water ebbing gently in the pool ahead of them before he saw it. It was the ceiling of another desolate part of the building, and it had caved in at some point on the room underneath.

"Here we go." Florrie whooped and leaped in first.

"Be careful, cunk. Don't snag your ass on the rubble at the bottom. *Adeus!*" Q-Tip said before he dived in after Florrie.

Henry took a breath and willed himself to follow, feeling marginally safer with the Orfins in the water than forlorn in the corridor without them. He entered the water carefully. Q-Tip was just inches away, but barely visible in the murky spectrum of browns, grays and greens, disturbing silt and sand as he went. Henry followed him through the fissure in the wall, where the water looked clearer and outlines more perceptible.

The next accommodation had a bar area, defunct and forsaken, with glass bottles strung upside-down, lining the opposite wall. In the center of the space stood what was left of a pool table and a mangled spiral staircase leading to what had been a mezzanine. The pool table was covered in a blanket of mussels and other shelled creatures; a mass protest against any new game being played upon it. Fish swam in and out of the side pockets, some fleetingly curious, but most uninterested.

Henry saw light above them that Florrie had already reached, where the ceiling vaulted. She disappeared through it and Q-Tip followed. As Henry approached, their hands reached down and the Orfins hauled him from the water into the glow of a new room.

# TEN

## Grotto

---

"Is he dead?" It was Q-Tip who asked the question, and the echo ricocheted around them.

The original ceiling was invisible. A thick seam of ice obscured it like it had in the darkened hallway, and stalactite thorns dangled imposingly from it. Henry instantly thought of Martin's cave, and although this place held less light within, it still had the same stark beauty.

"I don't think so," answered Florrie. This time the children weren't talking about Henry, who hauled himself from the water and scanned the hollow. He couldn't see him at first, but as his eyes adjusted once more and he followed the Orfins' gaze, he saw Martin laid out in the corner of the room with his hands crossed protectively over his chest.

Henry rushed over, sliding on the ice into position next to his brother. Florrie remained where she was, rubbing her arms and legs to bring warmth to them, while Q-Tip, ever the salvager, returned to the water to search the area below the mezzanine.

Martin looked like a ghost. He wore undershorts and nothing else. His flesh, colorless and indeterminate with the ice on which he lay, was covered in a mass of goosebumps. It still shimmered from the fat he'd been covered with for his initiation plunge. The boy stared at the ceiling, as if he could see through the ice into the penthouse above. Only his cracked lips moved, though no sound came from them, and Henry saw that they had a blue tint. Henry was troubled at how ill his brother looked, somehow appearing worse than a corpse, with less color in his skin. Henry thought of the backgammon pieces carved from bone. Even the memory of those held more color. Only his hair remained the same flaxen hue it always was.

"Henry?" croaked Martin feebly. Barely a whisper. It seemed the effort to speak Henry's name had caused the young boy pain. Henry was upset at this, though he tried not to show it. Martin was in a worse state than he'd anticipated.

"Hello, nipper," Henry replied, smiling.

"Are you real?" said Martin, turning his face slightly and meeting Henry's eyes for the first time.

"Yes. I've come to take you home."

"Mother's looking for the bairn. I can hear him crying, but she doesn't see. I do. He's nearly walking proper. He likes me, because I'm his big brother. He's around here somewhere. I just can't fathom…" Henry wondered if Martin had witnessed what had happened to the baby.

"Martin, we need to get you out of here. It's very cold."

"I'm tired, Henry." Martin smiled. Even the smile appeared to cause him discomfort.

"Let's get you up into the warm. You can rest when you're safe and dry." Henry wiped the first of his tears away.

"I was supposed to fetch something. It's how the salvagers get their food. Mother knows…"

"Come on, nipper." Henry tried to scoop his brother into his arms, but the boy flinched in pain. Henry wondered if Lanner had struck him at the homestead, or whether it was just the cold, or the hunger, or whether he'd hurt himself getting into the cave, "You need to come back with me, Martin. You can't stay here."

"I like it here. It's my cave. I finished my carving of Mother. I've done the whole family. Look!" Henry looked at the space behind him. It was bare, but Martin's transfixed gaze showed that he believed the faces of their family smiled upon him as he had re-imagined each of their likenesses. He was delirious. Henry had no idea what to do.

Q-Tip appeared from the water with a bottle from the bar and several mussels prized from the surface of the pool table. It gave Florrie and Q-Tip something to do and they worked at opening the mussels and removing the cork of the bottle with their bone blades.

"You can wear my anteek clobber. It will keep you dry and warm. I will hold your hand all the way and we'll get you out of here."

"I'm sleepy. I need to rest my eyes. *Behaga*." *Please.*

"Please, Martin-brother. Come with me. I need you," Henry pleaded, but he knew deep down that Martin wouldn't survive the swim back to the surface.

He thought about death then. What was the crueler death of the two? Giving the boy hope, then watching him drown? Or staying with him in his cave, holding the boy until the time came? Henry recounted his own panic from his swim, believing at one point that he himself was going to drown. Drowning was a horrible death.

He knew the answer before Martin responded, and had already resigned himself to that fact that he would remain for as long as it took. Martin seemed to grasp the change in Henry's thoughts and lifted his head slowly.

"Will you tell me a story? So, I can sleep?" Martin squeezed his brother's wrist weakly. Henry nodded and helped his brother get comfortable. He felt a lump in his throat and thought he'd be sick, but he wanted to keep calm for Martin; to lead him gently into the light in the kindest way. "*Tak*," Martin added. *Thank you.*

Henry lay next to his brother and draped an arm across him. He thought of the igloo where they slept beside each other for so many years, and of their late-night talks, mainly questions that Martin had had about the world. Henry remembered picturing the boy's expressions while they spoke, even though they often slept with their backs to each other. He knew his brother's face so well, he could've sculpted it into the ice himself if he'd had the mind to.

Martin's body still felt cold, but he'd stopped shivering at least. The goosebumps remained on his skin, but the boy appeared comfortable, breathing gently, smiling as he stared seemingly through the ice above once more, as if the sky was inches above him. Henry kissed his brother on the forehead, then began.

"There once was a world of light. The sun in that place was warm and the ice was no match for it. The land was green all over and trees grew wherever they felt like it. As many trees as there were stars. Trees that had food on their wings, so none had to hunt, or harm any seal pups. People wore man-mades that they had no need to kill for and the world was good. The animals lived with the people. There were so many animals that you couldn't name them all. People were kind and they all lived together. Families and families. More children to play with than you could ever imagine."

Henry paused, feeling a pang of guilt. How often had he played with Martin of late? He had not given him his attention or time for a while. Especially since the discovery of the yot-boat.

"There was nothing to fear in the world of light, because everyone had what they needed. All had possessions and wanted for nothing."

Martin smiled as he listened intently, no doubt picturing everything his brother was describing.

"People say the world of light disappeared. But it never did. It's still out there, you just need to find it. There, the ice never came. There, the ice stayed away, because it was no match for the sun. The people still live with good hearts in great numbers. The sun is still kind and it blesses all. All you need to do to get to the land of light is picture it in your head. Close your eyes tightly and see it in the darkness. Once you see a speck of light, let it get bigger and bigger and pour all over the dark. When you see the light, run toward it. Run as fast as you can and don't stop until the light is all around you and you find yourself standing with the sun warm on your face and the wind at your back." The little boy lay smiling. "That's all you need to do, Martin. Find the light and run toward it. There you will find Mother and Father and the bairn, and I will meet you there. We will have adventures and we will sing and laugh under the sun. Never cold again. Never hungry. Never frightened."

There was silence in the cavern, and the boy lay still. Henry did the same and waited to see if Martin's chest still heaved. He waited a while. All was still. Martin had found the light and run toward it.

≈

Henry sat and mourned, then released his brother from his arms and got to his feet.

"*God natt*, Martin." *Good night.*

Florrie and Q-Tip had been listening to the story.

Henry kissed Martin one final time and closed his eyelids with his hand. "Goodbye, Martin, *min lillebror.*" *My little brother.*

"*Sono, garotinho,*" said Q-Tip softly. *Sleep, little boy.*

As Henry approached the two Orfins, they looked at each other awkwardly, seemingly unsure what to say to him. They bowed their heads, then Florrie took the lead and clumsily put her arms around Henry. Q-Tip did the same and the friends embraced him together, comforting him as if he was one of their own.

Before Henry leaped into the flooded chamber below him, he took a final look at his brother and his majestic grotto. He looked peaceful and beautiful in his catacomb, the oil spread on his porcelain skin twinkling in the penthouse light.

## ELEVEN

## The End of the Beginning

As Henry hauled himself from the water, still numb with grief, he was grabbed by the hair and pulled onto the ice. Henry saw only the man's boots at first, but then he glimpsed white fur stained red and recognized it immediately as his father's coat. *The demon clown.*

Henry stood, swinging his arms wildly until Lanner, laughing, let go of his hair and pushed him effortlessly away with one arm. Lanner had brought five of his cohorts with him, who were enjoying the spectacle whilst brandishing their weapons. Several carried bone blades, and one even had a cleaver. One held the leash of a horrifically disfigured pack-dog and another held a makeshift snowboard upon her shoulder.

The dog snarled, a string of drool abseiling to the ice floor. The children inched away from it.

"I take it the little one won't be surfacing any time soon?" Lanner sneered, looking to the other adults. "And I imagine you found what we left for you back home?" Henry leaped forward and charged Lanner before the man had a chance to repel the assault. Lanner grabbed Henry's arms, but Henry head-butted him. It hurt him probably as much as it hurt his opponent, but Henry was still on the attack with his fists despite the pain.

Face flushed with outrage, Lanner kicked out viciously at Henry, who landed more punches about his face before two of the adults – Jared and Ula, the one with the snowboard – pulled him off. Lanner, wiping blood from his lip, kicked Henry in the ribs. Henry doubled over in pain, spitting and cursing at his nemesis as his rage swelled to no avail.

He was back at the water's edge. He considered diving back into the water to escape the adults, but knew, like a seal pup, he'd only have a few places to come up for air (and they would wait for him and haul him up once more), or alternatively club him on sight.

"There, there, boy. Calm your bit. You're done." Lanner grinned spitefully. Beside him was Skindred, who held a shot of dark liquid in his hand triumphantly. The glass was made of ice itself, as were many of the things in the Favela. The other salvagers regarded Skindred with loathing and he raised the draught before them and drank it down. Sissel looked like she wanted to murder him, but daren't do anything in the presence of Ginger Lanner and his comrades. Henry didn't have the same reservations.

"I'm going to gut you!" he bellowed. Lanner and his friends jeered, unfazed. The Orfins eyeballed each other uneasily, but kept their heads bowed. There was no fight in the rest of them. They feared the adults too much and only watched as Florrie and Q-Tip struggled to get free from their captors: Needol, and the woman Erasmus, the murderess.

Henry noticed his father's belt buckle hung about Needol's waist and repeated his threat to the rest of Lanner's mercenaries. None reacted to it.

"*Louco!* You ain't doing no killing this day. Besides, I have your cutter right here. *Vejo?*" *See?* Lanner held Henry's knife in his hand, which Henry had left with the outer layers of clothing he'd removed before diving into the waters in his military suit. Lanner held it to Henry's cheek and turned the blade slowly. A sharp pain preceded a trickle of blood that met the canvas and spilled into the seawater. Henry thought of sharks catching his scent and wondered if it would carry to the waters lapping the mezzanine where his brother's body lay. There was no way he would've gotten into the water willingly now his blood was in there.

Lanner wiped the blade on his trouser and returned it to the back of his belt; just one more trophy. Henry caught Sissel's face in the crowd and could see she was opposed to everything that was unfolding. This was Skindred's doing, and Skindred's alone, and Henry was angry with himself for leaving his knife with his clothing. It was stupid. He'd trekked for nearly a month to seek his revenge, and the great confrontation he'd rehearsed in his head and imagined over and over had turned into the simplest of victories for Lanner. The reality that Henry might die that very day hit home and he struggled to get free from the arms that held him. Jared sniggered, and Henry was sickened by the stench of the man.

It seemed he would be joining Martin sooner than he'd hoped. No great ending. No victory to take from all that had been. Henry would sprint toward the light and never look back when his own time came, and hoped he would at least get to see his sisters one last time. The world, with its unceasing Ever Winter, really wasn't worth living in.

"I'm taking you to the king to request to put you down there and then, by mine own grabbers. He already made me General Manager of the World for what I done already. Doing you'll be fun. *Grande resultado!* These are the simple things that I take comfort in. Skindred, *bem feito!" Well done.* "Anything you need, you come to me. I make you a big man!"

"Traitor!" said Q-Tip, before he was slapped down by Erasmus.

"Fight me, you cowards!" Henry yelled at both Skindred and Lanner, only to be met with mirth once more from the grown-ups and the dreadlocked teenage defector.

"Cowards live. Cowards end up with treasure in their pockets." Lanner wiped blood from his nose and mouth, took a deep sniff, and told his comrades to drag Henry to the Favela.

"Why don't you just join the adultos, Skindred?" Leaf, one of the young 'uns, spoke up, flouting the risk.

"Maybe I will, pup," he quipped.

"Maybe he will," agreed Lanner, then, turning to Sissel, he declared, "I'm disappointed in you, Sissel. Skin said you've gone soft. Didn't kill the boy straight off and didn't bring him straight to me. Makes me wonder if you're the right one to lead these little cunks. Makes me want to see what the king thinks about that. Get it in the open. *Boa ideia?*"

Henry could see Sissel had had enough. Lanner had basically marked her for death, to all in earshot. Henry watched her glance at the pile of relics brought up from the water, most likely to see if any of it could be used as a weapon. Then she looked at Lanner's troop to see if she could grab a weapon from any of them. Yaxley also understood her ambitions well and he squeezed her wrist, warning her to take no action.

Lanner noticed all this too and bore his sadistic, knowing smile once more. Henry knew he was top of Lanner's execution list, and he'd come to accept that. But he felt responsible for Sissel being drawn into it all and knew her name would be etched in Lanner's mind also. If Sissel had reported Henry to the adults immediately, or allowed her crew to end his life at first sight, she would've remained in favor. But her own kindness had given Henry precious time with his brother Martin, and Henry could never repay her. He truly hoped she had not sacrificed more than her position, all for a stranger she owed nothing to.

Lanner and his crew left with Henry. Skindred followed, seemingly more comfortable with the senseless grown-ups than in the company of the children he'd betrayed.

The Orfins gathered around Sissel for guidance and reassurance. For once, she could give neither. She didn't know how to help Henry now he was in the clutches of the king. She had not helped Martin. Now Lanner would come for her anyway.

Yaxley ordered everyone to gather the relics and head back to their digs. There was no more to salvage that day, but plenty had been lost.

Lanner led Henry triumphantly up the hillside trail toward the Favela. Sunken faces emerged from their dwellings to see what was going on and just as quickly withdrew, as if they were never witness. Those that did linger were abused by Lanner's soldiers. The people Henry caught sight of looked frightened. Many appeared infirm and sickly, or frostbitten. All were filthy and underfed. Some had fewer clothes than others, which Henry ascertained was the main indicator of status in the Favela. With such a large populace, clothing must have been scarce.

The homes were the second indicator of which echelon folk belonged to; closer to the ice, the shelters were primitive igloos exposed to the harsh winds, put together with abandon, some not much more than casket-shaped holes to fit a single person as a sleeping chamber. These were the true slums.

Other shelters were larger and used salvaged materials as supporting walls or roofing; upturned boats, fiberglass and steel car doors, tarpaulin and other plastics for paneling. A few had tried to recreate what a house may have looked like and had fitted windowpanes and impractical doorways from the underwater citadel as best they could. Henry knew these homes would not be as warm as the primitive shelters below. He looked upon the people that lived in those follies as idiots, though he had spoken to none of them. He tried to picture Mother and Father living in the Favela and could not imagine them living in the follies. They must've lived near the bottom of the hill, by the ice. They had more sense than to live in something that wasn't fit for purpose. He had learned that from them. *Survival.*

They wound through lanes until they neared the crest of the hill, the highest point on which Henry had ever stood, higher still than the deck of the container ship. Henry caught a glimpse of the view behind him and saw the sieve of circles where the salvagers worked in the bay further down to reach the lost citadel. Beyond that was Lantic.

Without warning, Lanner smacked him across the back of the head and ushered him further through the winding lanes. The traitor, Skindred, laughed, walking beside them with his chest puffed out, clearly training to be Lanner's new pet and completely in awe of the man. Henry opened his mouth to speak, but changed his mind. Every step led him closer to his fate and he felt its pull. *Run to the light.*

Animal skulls, deformed and wolf-like, were the ornaments adorning the Favela. They were placed in the ice here and there to serve as decoration, or perhaps as a warning to anyone climbing the hill.

As the group reached the last of the folly dwellings, they came across the body of an old man who'd been tied to a pole in the middle of the path. He was the oldest Henry had seen yet, with long wisps of hair that barely covered his scalp and a long wiry beard. The man's face was incised with deep wrinkles and the skin on his body sagged in places, although there was no fat upon the man at all to speak of. Before him, three small ragged children in identical trapper hats, too young even to be salvagers, fought for scraps of the old man's flesh, which they'd been filleting from his chest with rudimentary tools of bone.

Erasmus seemed to find the scene particularly amusing and took a machete to the man's arm, hacking it until she could pull it free from his body. She threw it on the floor by the children, who looked shocked at first, before proceeding to squabble over the new cut. It was a strange kindness in a world that seemed warped in every way.

"Long pig," Erasmus said. "String, carve and feast. It's the old way to do with the *louco* old 'uns and feed the wild chooks."

*Meat is meat.*

The dwellings near the palace were quite different; they were made entirely of ice and were astounding, sturdy structures that had to have been made by scores of people, given the size of the blocks that had been lifted into place.

The outsides of those buildings had been intricately carved with patterns, logos, emblems and symbols. Some were religious symbols, some memories of corporations and rock bands that had changed the world before the winter came. Others were signs that meant peace, love, man, or woman. There were animals of varying accuracy, as most of the creatures depicted were extinct and had been forgotten, and there were scenes of yot-boats and other vessels arriving to the shores with people finding solace in a volcano that featured predominantly on the many facades. The workmanship was exceptional, and Henry thought of Martin then and wished he had got the chance to see what he now beheld.

One of the buildings was in need of repair. As they passed it, an artisan, with help from her companion, carefully removed a small section of a damaged block of ice, which had melted and cracked from the elements. They replaced it with a new piece, cut from the ice of Lantic below. Henry had no time to observe as he was pushed onward, up the hillside.

The lane opened into a square, where a crowd had gathered outside the grandest of all the ice buildings. It was sublime to look at; every inch of the ice had detail upon it, all of it geometric and thought out with great care.

The building's wide arch doorway revealed a vast room inside with pews and tables shaped from ice. At the far end of it, in the very center of the back wall, stood a beautiful cage that was also made of ice. It glistened, twelve feet high and half that across. Scores of people were taking drink in the hall and the vicinity outside, most from glasses also made of ice, some from ancient plastic vessels, and one from a hollowed-out animal horn. Men and women cavorted at the tables, some of which were relics salvaged from the citadel, the rest hewn from the same material as everything else.

Vulgarities and merriment rang out from the hall to the square outside, and under it, a song emerged from amongst the ranks of elderly men. Henry thought it might once have been a happy song that they sung, but from what he had seen, he sensed that the ice and the Favela would've changed any melody over the years. The key was minor and somber. The words, no longer full of promise, hung heavily in the air, aching with sorrow and melancholy. The song had a certain dark beauty to it, but to Henry, as he was led past the hall toward a fate unknown, the song was unloved by him.

"The Birdcage," Lanner said with pride, "where we wet our whistles and get laid upon!"

An elder man, almost the age of the long pig being devoured by children down the lane, stumbled into Henry's path, drunk.

"Have you seen the Canary? I heard her sing. 'Twas an old 'un song," he slurred. Ula booted him from their path. The man disappeared into the crowd without protest and was replaced by a swirl of people falling about and dancing giddily. The ocean of faces had the same effect on Henry as when he'd lain in the corridor beneath the ice in the citadel. He felt entombed and faint, like he'd been swallowed by them all. The aching song whirred about his head and filled his ears. He tried to focus on something other than people. Something still and unthreatening. He looked at the tips of the buildings and the spaces in between. An alleyway ran alongside the pub, and it was then that Henry saw the source of the drinks being served. Blue and green plastic drums were piled in a pyramid. One was open, and a child of five or six was ladling thick red liquid from it into glasses of ice. Next to the boy hung a large seal, twice his size, and its blood was draining into one of the drums whilst its guts were removed and added to a cooking pot by the boy's father.

Needol rubbed the bristles of his mustache with both hands.

"We have to leave it for a long time, then when it's ready, it gives a kick like you wouldn't fathom in a hundy mill. Strong grog, but bangs the head next daylight like a mother kisser! *Nenhuma mentira.*" *No lie.*

A woman vomited beside them to the cheers of others, and the swarm redeployed to another corner of the square where two men were taking it in turns to punch a large man-sized block of ice with their hands, presumably to see who would make the final blow and send it crashing to the floor. Their knuckles were wrapped in pelt, yet blood snaked down their arms to their elbows. Across from them, a man was held down by his friends as one of his compatriots removed one of his rotting teeth with rusting pliers.

This place had always been a myth to Henry; a list of questions, a feeling. But in reality, it was sick and decrepit. Like the morose song, the futile work of the Orfins and the children squabbling over the meat of a corpse, this was the true nature of the Favela. Vile and evil. Cruel and malicious. Henry pitied every soul here, and he thought it possible that the ones that had seen him being escorted toward the palace might've pitied him right back.

# TWELVE

## Moonbird

The palace was Moonbird.

Moonbird was a yot-boat wedged on what appeared to be the crescendo of two crashing waves, frozen into a perfect arc around it. It sat just over the crest of the hill, with a narrow ledge of rock bridging it to the rest of the Favela. Only its top deck could be seen from the plateau of the square, but there was too much going on around the Birdcage to ever notice it through the dwellings which led to it. Defiantly, the yot-boat did not face Lantic.

Like MV Greyhound, it must have been there in a past life and sailed across it from lands unknown. Someone had named it Moonbird, in a faraway place for reasons only the namer of the boat could ever know. Henry speculated in silence, whether Moonbird had pointed itself toward the rising and falling scape of a forgotten country as it froze in place on the crest of the hill, or whether a God had just put it there. Did it face the frozen landside, as if suggesting that that was where the threat came from henceforth and the perils of the sea at its stern could be entirely forgotten?

At present, Moonbird was the home of a self-proclaimed king and his followers, who had taken control of the Favela when Father and Mother had still lived there. Henry marveled at the sleek lines of the hull. Unlike the container ship in almost every way, the yacht had once been painted in regal colors intended to accentuate the natural shape and design of it. Moonbird was a celebration of a vessel, absent the serious, functional appearance of MV Greyhound. Moonbird was the biggest folly of them all.

Needol continued his guided tour of the Favela as they neared Moonbird.

"Crew of this yot-boat got to the warm pocket late. There was no shelter for them from the cold and they all died within it. The Great-Greats outed the dead and moved in when they emerged from the Cano. We reckoned it the ship of a Presi-King, which is why this, Moonbird, is our palace. Our casa."

Just a single guard was placed upon each deck, each armed with a rifle or handgun as well as a club or knife. The two who were awake were indifferent to Henry's arrival. The rest snored in harmony, oblivious to the visitors who crossed the gangway.

Henry saw that Skindred looked upon the palace with the same awe as he, and the young salvager tied his dreads back so he could take in every detail of it. Henry assumed that Skindred had never stood upon its deck before and that the ruler of the Favela that stood before them, did not open his home to the populace. (Especially orphans, or those residing at the foot of the hill).

Curved, sliding doors granted them entrance to the interior of the vessel where a grand stairwell awaited, designed to suggest the shape of a conch shell. It was indeed a palace and could have housed many more souls from the Favela than it did under the current rule.

They ascended the stairs, with Lanner taking the lead, eager to deliver his bounty. A roof lantern rained light down upon them as they reached the final doors, where two guards granted them entry. Before them was a grand lounge and bar area, surrounded by a panorama of circular glass that gave them a view out of one side into one of the frozen waves, part of the bustling square through the lanes, then the endless landscape to the other, where snow covered the plains, rises and foothills, rivers and lakes and all that had existed before the winter came; cities and highways. All of it hidden, but somewhere beneath the white, it was all there waiting to be uncovered once more.

The highest form in view was the volcano which Father, and more recently Needol, had spoken of: a sleeping giant that had spared mankind within its valley basin and secret tunnels that mined and wound into its subsurface.

On a raised stage above the auditorium, the king reclined in a red leather chair. He was a tough, stern-looking man, a few years older than Father had been, and he wore tailored trousers with a snakeskin belt. Only a thatch of chest-hair kept him warm on top, yet he showed no sign of feeling the draught which had crept in with his guests. He had a muscular frame, but a bulging belly that suggested he fed more than most. The king had a most peculiar brown mustache, shaped to an almost perfect square, no wider than his nose. It was distinctive, but ludicrous. None had time or need to groom themselves in such a way. Father had been grizzly, as were most. This man was at best an oddity. He had no hair upon the top of his head and a short young man was going about shaving the back and sides with an old barber's knife, running it back and forth. He'd already done the same to the king's eyebrows, and their absence made him look inhuman – an unsettling, and no doubt intentional, effect.

The king sat still, his eyes rolling in his head. Blood streamed down his face where the barber's knife had nicked his scalp in places; the absence of brows meant the tide of blood had no barrier to break upon and prevent it from streaming into his eyes. Like the men punching the ice outside, the king didn't flinch, nor attempt to wipe away any of the blood, and it dripped onto the red leather he sat upon and the wooden flooring.

Henry gazed at the wood, finding the material fascinating.

The barber continued running the blade back and forth, occasionally wiping the blade upon his gown, originally a woman's nightshirt.

Henry noted a gray old woman sat near to the door, wrapped in furs, reading a brown, faded sheet of paper with words printed all over it, much like the books that Henry had read, but larger. Like most things in the Favela, this scene appeared to Henry nothing less than insanity, like something out of the book he had read so many times as a child. He hoped it would soon end. He could think of no way out, save a miracle.

Lanner coughed to signal his arrival and the king opened his eyes wide, as if he'd just woken from a dream. His eyes fell on Henry and remained there. The king became a statue, then finally, after a minute or so, the statue spoke. His voice carried around the room, the acoustics of which had been designed for it.

"There is a circle of hair upon my head that chooses not to grow. So, I have enlisted the use of a barber to cut it tight." The king spoke in a deep monotone and the only word he accentuated was *barber*, which he pronounced in a childlike way. *Ba-ba.* The blood continued to trickle down his face and neck. Slowly, he raised a hand to his lip and stroked the mustache that adorned it. "This is the fashion of a tyrant, which I am. Because I choose to be."

Just like when he'd first started conversing with the Orfins, Henry had no idea what the king meant, but it was unnerving. The king had an imposing presence, already captivating his audience.

He rose from his chair and wiped the blood from his head and face with a piece of old fabric, already stained crimson from previous use. The barber sat on a sofa and crossed one leg over the other as the king took center stage behind him. The frozen vista made for an imposing backdrop. The gray old woman was yet to look up from her newspaper. Only a spider, creeping across the table, distracted her. She grabbed it with long, curled nails and ate it. *Delicacy.*

"A full house, Mister Lanner? Uncle Tom Cobley and all," the king remarked in an accent just as odd as his appearance. His face remained still, as if it were incapable of expression.

"Was no task. Just fished him from the drink. Cunk practically pulled his own cueca down and left his cutters on the ice. Ain't much of a warrior, this 'un—"

"Still managed to knock you down, coward," Henry muttered.

"Skindred here gave him up. Gave him a dram as *recompensa*. Sissel needs a word with," Lanner added, ignoring Henry's comment entirely.

The king regarded the traitor Orfin and Skindred flushed red, unable to return the steely gaze of his sovereign. The king seemed to enjoy that. From his pocket he withdrew a set of brass knuckles and tossed them to Skindred, who caught them clumsily.

"Brass knucks for yourn grassing. Put them to good use, mine little spittle," the king said before focusing his attention once more on Henry, who'd been pushed forward into the light. The king's eyes widened.

"You come here with quarrel? With blazing eyes and tense shoulders? *Olhe* those veins! I see you balling your fists like you would hammer at the very doors of hell and punch whoever opened them. What if I opened those doors?" The king adjusted his posture. "I see someone vengeful and unforgiving in strange attire. Why are you before me, boy? *Diga-me*." The king dropped the bloodied fabric to the floor and looked out the window as Henry's words spilled from his mouth without thought. They were his truth.

"Your people killed my mother and father. They killed our bairn and they took my sisters and little brother here against their will. My brother died in a room below the ice today. I have not seen my sisters. I came here because I want them back. And I want revenge. I want to kill him." Henry pointed at Ginger Lanner, who raised his hands in the air, smirking through his gapped teeth.

The king turned toward Henry once more and let out a deep barrage of laughter. The sound bounced from the vessel's walls and ceiling.

"The great and reckless idiocy of youth!" replied the king, still laughing. "This is *my* planetarium. The whole shabooley. What I say goes. What goes I say."

"You ordered it?"

"That I did. That's my lot. My doing. I'm a magnificent rascal!"

"What kind of king does such a thing? What kind of man allows this?" demanded Henry.

"Mister Lanner told me about a family living alone on the ice. He had been looking for a friend of mine." The king leaned forward then as if he was a conspirator and placed his hand over his own mouth momentarily, indicating Lanner. "He thinks you might have eaten the meat of him. Little pincers. Tut, tut. That was my property. My protein. And I didn't even get to pick his bones! I have no trophy. Nothing to commemorate the death of a dear subject. But I am open-minded and I forgive you, *Henry*. Yet you would do me harm, given the chance. Am I right?"

Henry glowered at the king and said nothing. He hadn't spoken his own name since his arrival and nothing had been announced by Lanner, yet the king knew it well. A familiar backgammon board lay upon a glass table, missing most of the carved pieces. Inside, Henry's heart was thumping hard as the king continued, his bald head bleeding anew from his barber's cuts.

"My men are loyal and follow orders. Let me demonstrate this very thing so you understand a little more about the situation. Omeed!" One of the guards at the door left his position and strode casually past Henry to the raised area where the king performed. Omeed was an ugly man with thick black curls, just years past his Ritual. He walked as if his frame was larger than it actually was and bowed slightly when he reached his liege.

Henry observed Skindred looking at the young guard with envy, no doubt wishing he held the same rank and favor.

"Omeed is like a son to me." The king stroked the guard's face tenderly, then rested his hand on the young man's shoulder. "Omeed, open your mouth." Omeed obeyed without question. The king held the back of Omeed's head with one hand, then forced his other hand into Omeed's wide-open mouth, pushing it in as far as it would go. Omeed began to gag, but did nothing to defend himself. The noises from his throat were muffled and muted, but the sound of bile rising and his stomach churning as he heaved were audible to all in the room. The king held his fist in the man's mouth, and Henry fought down his own urge to gag. Even Lanner looked disturbed as tears rolled down the guard's face, which was slowly changing color. None dared to speak or go to his aid, just as the salvager children had remained silent when Henry had been hauled from the ice by the adults.

"Omeed did what I asked him, knowing that failing to do so would encourage me to punish him considerably. What horror! At this moment, Omeed knows that I might leave my hand in his mouth, blocking his airway, until he chokes and dies. You can see he is not resisting me, just reacting to his ordeal. Omeed does not question my ways of thinking or my orders. He accepts whatever I decide. Omeed is like a son to me."

Finally, the king removed his fist from the guard's mouth. With it came a curvature of ejected vomit which the barber in the nightgown began to mop up with the old bloodied fabric. Henry wanted to be sick as well.

The guard fell to his knees and the king patted him on the shoulder dotingly before wiping his hand on his tailored trousers. Omeed's lips were cracked and torn, his lips painted red with his own blood. He held his jaw protectively. Erasmus and Needol helped him back to his post by the oak doors. After wiping his eyes and regaining some composure, he stood straight like he had when they'd first entered the room. The king came down from his stage and circled Henry then, like an animal closing in on its prey.

"Mister Lanner followed my orders, just like Omeed did just now. And he trekked all the way out on that dangerous ice, to extend an invitation to you all to join us here at the Favela—"

"He killed them! Why couldn't you leave us be?" Henry cried.

"I know he did, chap. We'll get to that in a moment. But what you need to grasp, wholly, is that I can't have people just *being*. If I allowed people to go off and *be*, then others might get the same idea and think that rules can be ignored. People talk in whispers. You can hear them at night, scratching around their hovels like crabs. Tearing the meat off each other. They would skulk off and diminish our number, even regroup and challenge. No king would tolerate that. We are all that is left of a civilized world. Our rules ensure we all continue to be. This is where we be. Here. Gathered. Strong. I am the king of it all. The entire world. This planetarium." The king held his arms open wide with the vista behind him.

"There is nothing out there. You are the king of nothing," Henry remarked, before Lanner slapped him about the side of his head.

"*Esta bem*, Ginge. We're getting to the end of it. Henry, you would have had a good life here." The king's face changed then and he leaned close to Henry. "But your mother killed two of my peacekeepers, and your father killed three. Five human beings, I had. *Cinco humanos*. They were subtracted from me. Each of them mine property. Your family owed me a debt just then. I took four. The chook made five. The fact is, a bairn can't contribute. It does nothing but consume food. Maybe my lot were *faminto*. Either way, we're all square, see?"

"You…" Henry struggled to find the words to express his anger. "You're no king! You're the devil! Where are my sisters?" Henry yelled.

The king remained calm. Henry looked at the others and could see the excitement on Lanner's face. Skindred seemed enthralled, his fist enrapt in the brass knuckles that the king had given him. He looked so eager to try them out.

"They're here in the palace, of course. I'm going to wed one of the elder ones. Haven't chosen which yet. The prettier one is some kind of mute and the other one, the sour face, has spikes upon her. She can learn to smile. I'm in a quandary, Henry, but I see it as a luxury problem, like I'm standing in the middle of a rainbow! The little one is promised to Mister Lanner here. Catharin, what say you?"

The gray old lady placed her newspaper neatly on the table before her, then croaked her reply from a black mouth that held just a couple of teeth within it.

"Not yet a woman. Not for him to ruin. Give her a year and she'll ripen for wedlock," she said.

"But *rei*?" Lanner begged.

"Mister Lanner, calm your bit. She will serve as our Canary

126

until she comes of age. We do things proper. Do you dispute Catharin's assessment? Do you *dispute*?" The king stroked Lanner's pock-marked face as tenderly as he had the guard's, tracing his fingers over the man's lips, touching his bottom teeth momentarily before withdrawing.

"I—I don't," Lanner replied in a soft, broken voice.

"Back to you, Henry." The king ran his hands down his scalp and face as if he were clearing his mind with the gesture. "If I kill you now, which I might, would it make me a terrible person? Would it make me a better king? I would certainly enjoy it, as I do most things which are appalling. But you and I are to become family, like it or not."

"I want to see my sisters."

"You shall not. You shall listen. Now, where were we? Your death. If I kill the brother of *meu amor*, I would look *unreasonable*. Hey presto! My mercy upon you would serve me better with the chosen sister, no doubt, whichever one that shall be! I can be decent and lenient when I choose, and a tyrant otherwise. I am decisive nonetheless."

"I am going to—"

"You, Henry, are going to leave the Favela. I did not bring you here and I do not want you here to make your noise. You're not taking mine property with you, and if I see you here again, I will lift the skin from your flesh and make one of your sisters a wedding gown out of it. That's not a threat. It's a promise." The king waited for a response. When none came, he continued. "You lost before you even knew it had started. Same with your pa. I can't just let you walk away, untouched by me. *Unmarked*. I've been trying to think of what I can do to you. It has to be something big and brilliant, that you would not forget. If you remain here, you would try to kill me eventually. I know this. This I know! I can see it in your eyes. The way you look at me is beyond hatred. It's beyond defiance. That is the look of someone who would have his revenge if the opportunity was extended, not just upon Mister Lanner here. To all that have wronged you and yours, of which I am at the very summit of the kill list, in large, bold lettering. Top rascal. Hold him."

Lanner and Skindred grabbed Henry by the arms. The king went to a cabinet in the corner of the room and came back holding a sleek wooden box which he placed on one of the tables. He opened the box and took out a corkscrew, the kind once used to open bottles of wine.

He returned to the cabinet once more and this time he fetched a glass jar with a screw-top lid. The jar was filled with remains; some black and rotten, others more recent, although it was hard to tell what each of the pieces were. He placed the jar on the table and turned it slowly until Henry saw a human ear. His heart raced painfully.

"Don't get upset. This is the deal. Our treaty! I'm going to take one of your eyes and add it to my jar, so I will never forget that glare and the threat you pose. Whether you die in the cold hereafter is not my concern, nor fault. I admit survival is most definitely unlikely. But I am not killing you here and now, and for that you should be grateful. If you come back, I will make that wedding gown out of you so you can be close to a sister one last time, as I do my bit."

"Not my eye! Please!" pleaded Henry, all bravery gone from him and replaced entirely by fear. Fear for himself. Horror for what lay in store for him alone. He no longer felt like the son of the Bearkiller. He trembled as the king approached with the implement in his hand. Skindred laughed; Henry could feel his breath in his ear.

"Hush, Henry! Shut your row! The decision has been made and it – is – done," said the king, and he drove the corkscrew into Henry's eye as if it was nothing, pulling it out just as quick, ripping the eyeball from his face and freeing it from the tendons that rooted it.

The first sound was like the seal's brain matter absconding when Henry had struck it with the pick. This time, Henry's blood sprayed so far, even he could see it. The second sound was piercing and continuous; a surreal animal cry, high-pitched and shrill.

All Henry could hear at first was the unavoidable sound of his blood rushing and pumping in his ears and out from the void in his eye. His head was both fire and ice. The air entering the void in his head caused a sharp pain; a most nauseating sensation. But, the rest of his skull felt like someone had poured the contents of a blubber lamp all over him and set it alight.

Lanner let Henry fall to the floor, where he writhed on his back.

He vaguely made out the silhouette of the old woman, Catharin, approaching with a handkerchief. She straddled him and forced his arm away from the socket, pushing the cloth deep into the wound in an attempt to stop the bleeding.

"Can't have you dying in his favorite room," she sniggered.

Behind her, the king casually took Henry's eye from the end of the corkscrew and held it to the light. It had split but remained in one piece.

"See how it came off! It looks delicious. Such waste to let it go," the king said and he popped the eye into his mouth, holding it between his teeth, so the ruined pupil faced out. The king bit down on it, chewed fervently and swallowed the eyeball.

"Now you can see what's inside of me, Henry," he tormented, then to his men, "such bravado! He came here with the will of a man, but look at him. He's just a *menino*; a little one-eyed boy, my brother to be." The king handed a new rag from his pocket to one of the guards,. "Walk him back to Lantic, beyond the Bone Yard - *where I will shit his eye* - and point him in the direction of home. He can lie with his parents until the end of time, if he doesn't cross any Big Whites! Give him no pelt nor coat. The boy can knock at the devil's door in his undergarments." To Henry, he said, "I could have really liked you, Henry, but you scream too much. *Boa sorte. Despedida."* Good luck. Farewell.

Henry was dragged from the palace in agony, and as he met the cold wind outside, it brought him new pain as the sub-zero air blew into the open wound, seemingly boring into his skull and mind itself.

The songs had fallen silent. The people of the Favela looked on as Henry was led bleeding through the snow, leaving a dark red trail behind him. They ceased drinking. They ceased cavorting. The artisans had stopped working and the prizefighters no longer pounded at the ice with their fists while the procession of Lanner's men guided Henry to the edge of the Favela and through the maze of circles on the salvager's bay.

Henry had been certain he would die. He was done for, but was surprised it hadn't happened already. The pain was so much that it brought only madness, and lucid thoughts were kept at bay. Yet he knew with certainty that death awaited him, lurking in his shadow, ready to usher him from the body that encased his soul. It frightened him more than he ever could have imagined. He wanted the pain to stop, but part of him did not want to let go.

It was unjust. He was too young. He had not seen enough. The world was so big that Henry could not believe there wasn't a pocket somewhere that held goodness, compassion and hope. He blacked out then and woke intermittently to realize he was being dragged roughly by his arms. The reprieve from consciousness was welcome, although the pain roused him continually and all he could see was the memory of his ruined eyeball being held before him.

The snow covered his blood trails much quicker than his screams would be forgotten by all that heard him that day. The guards spoke as they carried him and Henry understood some of their words, but could not concentrate on them, or form his own to plead with them to help him ease his pain.

Finally, they came to a stop and Henry was laid in the fresh snow, with the bloodied rag covering his terrible wound. He felt the slightest reprieve as the guards left him as the king had instructed. Alone to face the elements. A chance, no matter how small.

But, even as delirious as Henry was, he sensed something was wrong as he heard the sounds of a pair of boots in the snow, returning toward him.

Then Lanner spoke, close to his face, so he could feel the man's breath on his skin and smell it.

"The king might take a risk and leave you out here. But not me."

Still, Henry swam in and out of consciousness, with the pain and loss of blood seemingly having taken all of his energy. He couldn't think of words.

"You might not see this knife. But you'll feel it. Just like your Mother did. And your Father. And your baby brother. I come to your homestead and you look at me like I'm nothing. *Me!* Who do you think you are? You think you're special? Go, and join your family of ghosts. I'll see the girls follow you, soon enough."

The snow fell upon Henry and the man knelt over him. Henry let go of that last hope he'd had, but his body and mind were already letting go and accepting it. Henry remembered the homestead, the smiling faces of his family. He pictured Mother holding the baby and Father embracing him after the Ritual. He pictured Martin sculpting the ice in his secret cavern beyond the wire. He thought of his sisters and how he had failed them.

Henry didn't fight it anymore. He welcomed it.

Henry felt the blade on his chest. Another sharp pain. Then all went black. The last, final, long sleep.

# THIRTEEN

## Chore-up

———————————

Boo's thoughts were often jumbled, but in the moments where he could fuse them together perfectly, things became so clear, as if a picture had been drawn in his mind. When he saw Henry dragged through the lanes of the Favela, bleeding and wearing just his strange bodysuit, one of those pictures had been drawn for him. He didn't know much, but he knew what was right and what was wrong. Henry had had a whale-load of wrong poured all over him and no one had tried to help him.

No one had seen Boo slip away from Sissel and Florrie, cutting through the back-doubles and winding passages of the lanes, stopping only once at the salvagers' digs to steal Skindred's blanket. He knew that was kind of wrong, but it wasn't bad-wrong, mostly because the blanket belonged to Skindred.

A few bays over, a safe distance from the Favela, was the Bone Yard; a place where carcasses were piled after they had been butchered, allowing the very young or very old to scavenge along with the bird and roving predators for morsels. Boo waited there amongst the rotting cadavers for the adults who had taken Henry to return to the Favela. When they did, and he was sure it was safe to leave his hiding place, Boo headed in the direction they'd come from. A blizzard was sweeping in, but Boo wasn't scared of blizzards. He was only scared of the adults, and of the dark.

Boo kept going, holding the folded blanket as a shield to aid his visibility, which had little effect. His mind grew confused and he began to wonder why he had a blanket in his hands that didn't belong to him and why he was alone in the blizzard. Then he fell upon a body, partially covered by the snow. On seeing Henry's face, the clarity returned to him, but Henry looked dead already.

"Henry?" No reply came.

The snow was relentless and unwavering. The wind whirled about them and Boo lifted the bloodied rag from Henry's face. He didn't want to look at it, but had to check how bad it was. He didn't know how to mend people, but he could at least try something.

The wound was worse than he could have imagined. The absence of the eye, a void curtained off by a flap of eyelid, was grotesque. Boo thought of the things that lay in the Bone Yard and shuddered. Though the flow of blood from the eye socket had ceased, the void would allow frostbite to settle within and ruin Henry's head from the inside out. This ground was Henry's Bone Yard, with Henry the very first occupant.

Boo replaced the rag and lay beside Henry, pulling the blanket about them, hoping his body heat would bring life back to the outsider he'd met just that same day. Henry had been angry when he'd first appeared on the bay, then had fallen into sadness. Henry was Martin's brother, another outsider and newcomer to the salvagers. Boo had decided Martin would be his best friend in the whole of the Favela. Martin wasn't like anyone else. He was quiet and gentle. He was kind and sincere. No one would let Boo help Martin, but they couldn't stop him helping Henry. It was just a shame it was all too late.

"Wake up, Henry," Boo said hopelessly. "Come on, poo poo. Wakey up!"

Henry didn't respond and Boo lay with him for a while, until dusk began to fall and the threat of darkness lingered. Only then did Boo get to his feet, pulling the blanket over Henry's face so he could rest in peace.

"Na-night. Hallo be the name, Henry," were his parting

words. Words he knew to have meant something important, especially when people were no longer living, or were about to cop it.

Boo ran as fast as he could, not looking back.

## FOURTEEN

# Hello, Darkness, My Old Friend

Leagues away was the stricken container vessel MV Greyhound. In one of the containers, stuck in ice and buried in snow, was a Red Cross consignment destined to support the Fighting 52nd Recce (Lowland Division) of a Great British Army that had been losing a war they would never get to finish. The cargo didn't include drones, ballistic missiles, or Laser cannons (for they would have been on a defense vessel), but it did include surplus lifesaving equipment and apparel, much of which hadn't been tested in the field.

As Henry lay on the icescape beyond the Favela, the anteek battle-suit he was wearing beamed a distress signal as his life-signs began to dwindle and plummet with the temperature.

Dormant for over a hundred years, a single electronic pulse announced the initiation sequence for Kraftwerk PanaSony Industries' Nightingale Medical Droid, *Hepburn 8,* to synchronize and collect the data it needed to deploy.

One of four medical droids assigned to a battalion, the Nightingale Hepburn 8 was a robust unit, built to withstand heavy gunfire whilst operating on any wounded combatants it had been assigned to in the unit.

The remaining three Nightingales (Hepburn 9, Gable 5 and Lennon 2) remained in idle, cold silence as Hepburn 8 disengaged from the station on which it had been docked, then liberated itself from the container by blasting a hole in the side of it with its cannon. The speed in which it rocketed from the fissure in the container was beyond that of the Duesenberg that had been crashed nearby, mostly because Hepburn 8 was flying, but also because the technology used for war was more akin to that used in space exploration than that of the motor industry.

The droid sped just six feet from the ground, horizontal, but rotating rapidly in a circular motion, as if it had been fired from a gun. It was shaped like a classic humanoid, but had been designed not to appear too life-like; the intention being that soldiers would not risk their own lives to protect or retrieve it in battle, yet would still trust its ability to perform operations unaided upon human casualties. As such, its face was flat, with all features digitized on a pixelated screen to simulate basic expressions. Its armor was covered in the same angular splotches of green, tan and dark blue from the M90 Splinter temperate woodland camouflage that the regiment adopted in the warzone it was destined for. The Union flag was sprayed onto the droid's shoulder and a red cross was emblazoned across its chest, as well as the name *Hepburn 8* and unique I.D. code NGMD-HEP-8.1a. On the back-plate was a series of corporate sponsorship logos, with their usual colors changed to match the camouflage.

Several miles ahead, a lone caribou ate lichens growing on satellite parts that had fallen from the sky a decade previous. The animal pricked its ears and ceased what it was doing. It raised its head, scanned the horizon, appearing confused, then seemed to shake the thought off and return its attention once more to its meager meal.

A sonic boom made the creature leap into the air, hind legs first, as Hepburn 8 avoided a collision with the animal and the debris it took meal from. No sooner had the sound and the robot disappeared than the caribou went about its business once more.

The robot reduced speed as it neared the location of *Critical Condition Patient #1; Unknown Soldier* and it performed a procedural running stop, until it was able to touch down precisely next to Henry's body in a perfectly upright standing position.

As the droid scanned the patient, one of the leg plates opened, revealing a coffer of medical paraphernalia. Hepburn 8 reached inside and took out a silver box made from Carbon Nanozil, which it twisted, then shook once above its head. The box itself opened then and shifted into a new shape, which he cast on the floor about them. The material seemed to come alive, as if it were made of a million digital insects. The insects multiplied and piled on top of each other continuously in a ring, until they had morphed themselves into a perfect tent structure. When it was over, the material hardened and all life went out of it. A hint of charcoal-like dust fell from it to the floor and both the droid and Henry were inside a domed shelter that would withstand any storm on the planet.

All sound had disappeared once the dome closed around them. The air temperature moderated to a comfortable level, without risking the integrity of the ice underneath them.

The droid lifted the patient carefully from the floor and out folded a gurney under Henry's body. The droid was both the surgeon and the operating table at the same time.

It did not speak, but its digital face held an expression of calm, as it injected a cocktail of vital Adrenacol, Morphine-X and basic nutrients into Henry's bloodstream from syringes attached to transparent, snakelike cables emerging from the droid's chest.

When it had fully assessed the wounds to *Critical Condition Patient #1; Unknown Soldier,* it immediately began to operate on the abandoned and empty eye socket, using lasers to burn away the flesh that had been exposed to the cold for too long before pouring a squad of Nano-Surgeons into the void; minuscule bug-like creatures designed specifically to repair tendons and blood vessels whilst dispersing anti-bacterial agents, before harmlessly expiring within the patient host.

From outside the tent, it looked as if someone had captured a lightning storm in a snow globe, as the lasers sparked and burned in neon brilliance and an inhuman shadow danced throughout.

The droid clamped back the flapping skin of the eyelids and took out a cylindrical lens from its own spare parts attaché located in its thigh. One of the droid's fingers opened at the tip and a metal thread extended into the eye-socket and fused the lens to what was left of the optical nerve. The lens was then inserted into Henry's skull, where the Nano-Surgeons would finish the interior work. The eyelids were unclamped and bonded around the lens itself before more drugs were injected into the patient. Finally, an accelerated healing formula was sprayed around the skin now bonded to the lens, which was covered with gauze from the medical kit, not to protect the work carried out, but to stop the patient from panicking if he woke unexpectedly.

The droid ran final diagnostics on *Critical Condition Patient #1; Unknown Soldier*, then focused on the icescape outside the dome, raising its faceplate skyward as if it was trying to overhear a conversation. In mere seconds, Hepburn 8 had ascertained that there were no hostile threats in their vicinity and moved into power-saving mode, monitoring the patient's progress and the proximate terrain alone. It would be another twenty hours until Henry woke up. In that time, both the droid and human would be intertwined and motionless.

To Henry, encased somewhere in his own mind, it felt like someone had removed him from Earth. The vacuum of the dome, absent the howling wind gave him a different tune to accompany him as he sprinted into the abyss of the light; the sound of unknown tools and technology performing an opera-tion on him. The chemicals coursing through his veins took him on a journey like none he had been on before – a world of both brilliant colors and beauty, contrasted with a nightmarish place of black and white. Heaven and hell. Above the ice and below it. The past and the present.

~

When Henry awoke, it was in darkness once more.

The droid had seemingly sensed this and had already administered medicine to aid Henry's return to consciousness in the calmest way under the circumstances. The gauze still covered Henry's new eye. It had not bled and the droid was certain it would not only be fully functional, but would be an enhancement on the natural human optic design.

"Am I a dead 'un?" rasped Henry, bewildered, wondering if he was in the dream world, or one of the places he'd seen as he sprinted toward the light.

The droid fed him treated water from a flask. Henry could not see it in the darkness. He tried to remember what had happened to him, but something in his mind wouldn't allow it. He drank the water until the robot ceased pouring it.

"You are alive. You are *Non-critical Condition Patient #1; Unknown Soldier,*" said the robot plainly.

"Soul-ya?" Henry slurred. The last thing he remembered was emerging from the ice. He saw the memory three times: once, he was a seal, being hit on the head with a pick; the second, he emerged in a strange cavernous room; and the last, he was dragged by the hair. None of it made sense, but all of it was linked somehow.

"I do not appear to have been configured to your specific data. I have no further information on your rank, origin or other medical records. With the injuries you have sustained, in line with both the Primary Values and Ethics and the Occupational Health codes of the Great British Army, I declare you unfit for battle. Rehabilitation is required." The accent was outlandish and alien. Shades of it were familiar, but most of it was like speaking to a being from another world.

Henry tried to sit up, but his ribs were bruised and his vision blurred, yet it was enough to get a glimpse of his carer; metallic and cold. Something about the face. He had heard of angels and demons. He'd read of the latter in the family's book that was now lost. This thing was something else.

"You may struggle with your breath for a while. The muscles surrounding your rib cartilage have been damaged from trauma. I believe this injury is synonymous with an attempt at stabbing. But the armament did not penetrate the industrial yarn material of your battle suit," it said.

Henry was perplexed. He didn't understand much of what had been said to him, but he observed that his chest was tight as he spoke, even though he felt no pain in it at in that instant.

"You. You're not...not like me, are you? Who—no, *what* are you?" he asked the strange figure in the darkness.

The droid responded in a particularly upbeat tone.

"I am Kraftwerk PanaSony Industries' Nightingale Medical Droid, *Hepburn 8*. I am one of fifty Nightingale droids allocated to the Red Cross under Global Service Agreement KWPSI-RC-1200. I was activated after your battle suit detected and reported a significant change to your vital signs. I have changed your status from Critical to Non-Critical."

"I don't fathom it," muttered Henry, frustrated that his memory was still hiding important things that he could not bring forth. It irritated him that Hepburn 8 spoke to him in words that were confusing. "Would you come closer?"

Hepburn 8 moved its head closer to the patient and the walls of the shelter illuminated with muted, soft light. Henry lay in shock, but found himself reaching a hand to touch the robot's arm; cold and firm. Sleek and impressive like the smooth shape of the Duesenberg he'd crashed weeks before. He was mesmerized by the patterns on the droid's armor and the writing, but most of all, he could not take his eyes from the flat, unearthly and pixelated face. He reached up to touch the faceplate, but withdrew at the last moment.

"A true, talking relic. Do I dream?" he asked, feeling dizzy.

Hepburn 8 blinked. Its expression signified puzzlement. "I do not understand."

Henry passed out once more, exhausted from the exchange. The robot waited patiently for its charge to wake once more.

~

*Henry dreamed he was standing alone with an axe in his hand, smashing it against the door hinges of a container stuck in the ice. A rainbow streaked the sky above and all around him were circles cut into the ice, for as far as he could see.*

*Seals bobbed their heads from the sea to watch as Henry struck the container over and over, the clash and clank of it reverberating around them.*

*Each of the seals looked like a child. An Orfin. One had a crooked fringe, one an unforgettable overbite. One had long eyelashes and corn-rows; this one looked saddest of all.*

*A snow leopard stalked the deck of the ship and it wore a barbed crown upon its head. Henry's sisters lay before it on the deck, all smiling at Henry as he beat the steel with all his strength.*

*Finally, the hinges gave way and the doors blew open and were carried away on the wind.*

*Henry fell back in terror as an army of plastic dolls poured from the container, thousands upon thousands of them, enough to fill the container ten times over, and they all came for Henry, their faces similar to Henry's when he'd been a child. Henry crawled backward on the ice like a crab, and those dolls nearest to him started to grab at his feet as others climbed over them to get at the rest of him.*

*Henry screamed and kicked out at the indistinguishable dolls, but no sooner had his feet connected with them, sending assailants flying into the air, than they were each replaced just as quickly by a duplicate.*

*The Orfin seals watched helplessly from the circles cut into the ice and the snow leopard king mewled, whilst Henry's sisters stroked its mane and tail.*

*The doors of the other containers blew off all at once and went soaring into the sky with the wild winds, not quite reaching the rainbow that over-arched the vessel MV Greyhound. Out of those containers came more and more plastic dolls.*

*Henry fell back into an ice hole and down into the waters and the dolls followed him into the depths below. The water above turned red as the dolls devoured the Orfin seals, then followed their corpses down toward Henry as he sank further and further into the abyss.*

When Henry woke again, he was moving. Though he remained horizontal on the flatbed that was part of Hepburn 8, he could feel the vibrations of motion and hear the ice and snow grumble as the robot's metal feet smashed down upon the floor, unyielding and invariable. Henry was drenched in sweat. He listened to the robot's tread and gathered that the speed they were traveling at was faster than Henry could run, though he couldn't be sure from his lying-down position and without having a reference point on the terrain. A draught came in from below, but incredibly, the shelter remained around them as they moved, held in place by rods protruding from the skeleton of the medical droid.

"*Hej?* What is going on?" Henry asked the robot, which appeared to blink and change its digital expression from one of concentration to one of friendliness.

"Hello, *Non-critical Condition Patient #1; Unknown Soldier.* How are you feeling?" the robot replied.

"My head. It hurts. I can't seem to...where are we?"

"You are recovering from a surgical procedure that has concluded successfully. I am taking you to the location where I was deployed. There is additional medical equipment there to aid your recovery and rehabilitation. There is no current human activity in that area. I am unable to detect where our nearest allied forces are and in a battle scenario I am unable to determine which humans are of any threat to you, unless we are fired upon. There was human activity in the area where I located you. I have calculated that the best course of action is to return to and secure the deployment area and await information from the War Office, or a recognized authority, member or affiliate of the battalion."

Henry shook his head.

"I don't fathom any of it," he said, then realized something was wrapped across his left eye. He raised his hand to the gauze. "What is this? What happened to my face?"

The robot's expression changed once more and it stopped moving. Henry sat up.

"I will administer some more drugs to calm you, *Non-critical Condition Patient #1; Unknown Soldier.*"

"Why do you call me that? Tell me what—"

"In the absence of your basic data, I have assigned you with this name based on your—"

"Stop it! Just tell me what..." A memory flashed across Henry's mind and he saw the remains of his left eye held aloft on a corkscrew. "*Herregud!* I remember! My eye! He took my eye!" Henry grabbed the robot's arm. The robot looked at Henry's hand, but did nothing.

"Please remain calm. Your heart rate has increased, which is not helpful. The gauze can be removed. Your vision has been restored..."

Henry threw his hands to his face and unwound the gauze. Immediately he cast his hands over his eye as his brain made sense of the images from his human eye and robotic one for the first time. The natural and the unnatural. One eye had tried to naturally focus on what was in front of him, whilst the other, the one that had been operated on, reached back and forth at speed, zooming and adjusting his focus erratically, so he felt off-balance and like he was about to throw up.

"What have you done to me?" he screamed, feeling the edges of the lens and the bonded skin with his fingertips, finding it sickening to touch. He kept the altered eye covered, scared to reprise the experience he'd just had.

"In the absence of the complete eye, I was able to restore your sight by using an optic lens of the same technology as that used in my own assembly. It has significantly enhanced your daylight and nighttime vision. Your brain needs to get used to this change and interpret what is seen. You have been improved. Please remain calm."

"Let me up. I need to get out of here. I need to see it!" Henry despaired.

The medical droid cast aside the domed shelter and Henry fell from the gurney, holding his head as the sudden light overwhelmed him. As if presenting a parody of Henry's wounds, the sky above was bruised by a scattering of gray clouds. The fruitless sun did nothing to the ice, but to Henry, its assault upon him was too much to cope with. It was a kaleidoscope. It was a collage. It was black and white, then every color. Everything burned, then exploded in stars until Henry shielded his eye and lens fully once more, sending him into a churning black whirl where he dwelt until his heart rate returned to normal.

The gurney collapsed, pleated, then folded away into the robot. Hepburn 8 waited patiently for Henry to adapt to the change in him. He knelt where he'd fallen, his head bowed toward the ice beneath his feet. Scared to move. Scared to raise his face skyward. His hands still shook and his fingers probed the area around his new eye, tentatively touching the edges where skin met metal. Warmth met cold. Organic met man-made. It was grotesque, but it was already part of him. Henry was altered. It had already happened and he couldn't do a thing about it. Henry was alive. Alive and *altered*.

He allowed his other senses to return; the usual sound of the wind, mixed with the near-silent hum of things moving and processing inside Hepburn 8, the chill on the back of Henry's neck and ears. The metallic taste of blood in his mouth.

"Your vision will reset. Think of it like a computer, being rebooted and coming online once more."

"Online?"

The robot did not answer.

Henry explored the space immediately before him. He realized that he no longer had control of an eyelid on one side of his face; instead, he seemed to have a shield of some kind and could make it close when he willed it to blink. After trying this several times, Henry opened his hands an inch or so further and focused on the ice beneath one of the robot's feet. His vision blurred as the focus distorted, his robotic eye zooming ahead as if he'd thrown something into the distance and was trying to follow it. His other eye was slow and saw only the surface of the ice, whereas its new counterpart delved into the ice itself, looking at the particles that formed it and calculating the thickness and depth of it. This was both frightening and astonishing. Henry tried it numerous times until he could make one rich picture from the two images and govern the apparatus. When he looked at the robot's foot, he could see into the particles of paint, then beyond it, into the ultranium material itself and the wiring it protected within. He saw that the robot had liquid pumping around its skeleton. Not blood. Silver and dazzling. *Inhuman.*

He studied the robot and felt like he could peel back the layers before him, which, in a way, he was. It was thrilling and Henry accepted it then, understanding that he was more than he had been before. Henry was unlike anyone else on the planet, more akin to the robot, which he now saw perfectly for the first time since he'd woken on the gurney in the dome shelter.

Beyond the robot lay leagues of icescape with nothing to block the view. Henry reached out and let his eye zoom before him and collectively report the images back to his brain. A caribou meandered in the distance, sniffing the air. Henry saw a steam of breath come from its mouth and snout, then withdrew so he saw only the robot before him.

When Henry looked at his feet, he found that he could perceive the depth of the ice below and saw how it varied all about him. He thought about the MV Greyhound once more, speared by a giant propeller; a half-submerged, half-frozen mausoleum. His memory was returning to him fast, led by his fears.

Behind him was the Favela, but Henry wasn't ready to look in that direction yet. He decided he would only return and lay sight upon that place when he was truly ready to wreak his revenge. He'd been stupid. He'd been a child, ill-prepared and naïve. He'd welcomed his death in the end. It had been assured, despite the apparent mercy upon him.

But death had not come, and Henry felt then that everything that had unfolded before, all the great and wretched misery that had befallen him, along with his survival at the hands of the robot, had to have happened for a reason.

"My name is Henry," he said finally.

"Hello, Henry. I am Nightingale Medical Droid *Hepburn 8*." The robot beamed a digital smile upon its faceplate.

"Hepburn," Henry repeated. "Show me what I look like. I'm ready."

FIFTEEN

Therapy?

---

Henry had never been vain. There was no need for it in the modern world. Only the king had seen fit to preen and groom. Henry had not understood it, but then he wasn't a king, or a leader of any kind.

He realized that what the king was doing was making himself unlike the rest. Distinguishable from the citizens he had power over. It showed them that he was distinctive. Singular. It had worked with Henry. Never in a million years would he forget how the king had looked that day. The absence of hair and eyebrows and the little mustache. The man was an ogre. A tyrant. It made forgetting his ordeal all the harder, but holding onto his hate all the easier.

In contrast, Sissel had not done anything to alter her appearance. Henry hadn't recognized her as the head of the salvagers when he'd first entered the bay. Yet she had earned her place at the helm of the crew and Henry could only imagine the things she had done over the years to get there.

He thought about how Sissel had been betrayed by Skindred, then Lanner and knew that her decision to help him had endangered her. He hoped that Yaxley and the others would protect her as best they could.

Hepburn had shown Henry his reflection by buffing a sphere of satellite wreckage until it shone back at them. Henry was shocked to see the change in him. He couldn't stop looking at the lens that filled the void where his eye had been. The skin around it had healed well, but it still looked monstrous. The weirdest thing for Henry was that there were no eyelashes on that side of his face. They'd been burned during the operation to install the new tech into his socket. He marveled at the oddity. Such a simple detail with an unheralded function. Eyelashes.

He stared at his face for the longest time he had ever done so and studied all the details, uncertain when he'd next gaze upon his own face again. He let a few tears fall from his human eye and then he wiped them and his demeanor changed.

"I have to get used to the mess of it," Henry grimaced, speaking to his reflection, "I'm alive, at least. I can't undo his work."

Henry wondered if his sisters would become accustomed to it and accept the way he'd altered..? Would they see past it and recognize him again as Henry, their brother? Or would they hate what he'd become?

Henry came to the realization then that his sisters might already assume him dead. If he saw them again, there was a chance they might cast him away. *A ghost. Not Henry.*

It pained him to think of Iris especially turning her back on him, or unable to look upon him without seeing only the modified remains of an eye and the act that had led to its ruin. When they looked upon Henry, would they only and always picture the king and their tormentors?

All of it was out of Henry's control. He couldn't change the way he looked. It was like being born with different colored hair, or skin. Being born a hawk instead of a human.

There were other changes in Henry's appearance that he noted. His skin and the hair on his face weren't as smooth as they had been; Henry had more than a hint of sideburns growing and a shadow of stubble upon his top lip and chin. How long had it been since he'd seen his own reflection?

Even his eyebrows were thicker and threatened to meet in the middle. His hair had gotten much longer, too. It was shaggy, well past his shoulders, and flicked out in places where it wanted to curl. He tried to picture himself without it, or without eyebrows and then with a strange mustache, but it seemed absurd. Henry was far from grizzly, but he was equally as distant from being the child he remembered. Henry thought then that if his face had the potential to seed fear in his beloved sisters, then it might do the same with the king and his cohorts. He smiled into the makeshift mirror at the thought.

Hepburn was incomparable at catching fish. It simply smashed a perfect hole in the ice, waited a few seconds, then pulled Henry's dinner out by hand. The robot had instructed Henry that it was safer to cook fish before consuming it, so he'd gotten used to Hepburn heating their catch with a blue flame before eating it, finding it delicious and easier to chew. Henry wondered what the robot would've said about the canned food he'd found in the galley of the ship and thought it best not to know.

"You have not spoken for a long period of time," Hepburn said as they set off for their final trek before nightfall.

"I don't feel like it," Henry replied, using his new ability to stare ahead, far into the distance.

He remembered what it had been like to fish with his family.

"It is healthy to speak to another and voice any—"

"You're not proper, are you?" Henry snapped. "You're not alive and, it ain't the same. You might be here. But I'm *alone*."

The words burst out as if they'd been building inside him for weeks, lying dormant for a moment to be released. Henry assumed they'd been there since before he'd even reached the Favela. He'd spent weeks alone in shock, hunting Lanner's party. Conversing with no one. Only his urge for revenge gave him purpose; without it, he would've lost his mind completely. Grief had dragged him further and further away from the person he was; the Henry who'd whooped and yelled racing his sister across the ice. The one who had played with his sister's hair to get her to sleep. When he'd met the Orfins, he'd been scared, but even the brash, initially hostile interaction was something. Something was better than nothing at all.

"I am not fully sentient, because humans are not at ease with that. So, I have a logical and mathematical correlate to self-consciousness. I can hold conversations with you, Henry. I recommend that."

Henry stopped walking. Hepburn did the same and Henry remembered a day when he'd argued with Father whilst out from the homestead. He would've traded anything to be back in that moment.

"You can wrecker-men it all you like, but you ain't bright to fathom the things in my head. You're just an ancient tin and I can't hark even half of what you say. Prong."

"*Lone, solitary without company.* I am not human, but you are not companionless. *Destitute of sympathetic or friendly companionship.* I am not human, but I can be a sympathetic and friendly companion. *Remote from places of human habitation; desolate, bleak.* This factor can be worked upon in the rehabilitation modules I am programmed with. Isolation can be enjoyed. Isolation can be remedied at a later stage."

"You can describe loneliness, but you can't see it, or smell it. You don't know it unless it is happening to you. You can know the words for it. But you don't know how I feel."

"In the last few days, have you felt unhappy none of the time, some of the time, most of the time or all of the time?" Hepburn asked unexpectedly.

"Most of the time," Henry replied honestly, with more than a hint of spite in his voice.

"In the last few days, have you thought about harming others?"

"All of the time." His answer was immediate, but not as pointed.

"In the last few days, have you thought about ending your life?"

"No. *Yes*," Henry admitted. He felt ashamed at his admission and was surprised he'd said it. It had been such a deep thought, never voiced, not considered at length. Yet it had been there.

Like a feeling, or an idea, creeping up on him in the lonely hours.

"We do not need to talk if you do not wish it, but I *will* ask you these three questions again exactly one week from now." Henry believed it. The robot did not lie, or exaggerate. The robot was only facts, logic and truth. Henry didn't want to admit it to the robot, but saying those things out loud, letting his voice speak the words to his own ears, confessing things he never would've said to his siblings, was therapeutic. He looked at the robot again; it was a cunning thing. It was intelligent beyond his own imagining. It was more than an ancient tin. It was a companion. It was friendly and compassionate. In a way. It would have to do, until he could get his sisters back.

Henry placed his hand to his human eye and shielded the lids of it for a moment. He'd been getting headaches from where his eye was trying to keep up with its synthetic counterpart. Hepburn had warned him about it, but there was little he could do until the changes in his optic nerves settled fully in his brain. "The headaches continue?"

"Yes. Just as you said."

The robot raised its faceplate skyward like it sometimes did. Henry thought it was making some kind of record of it; silently updating information about him for later reference.

They set off then. Henry setting the pace. The boy couldn't shake off his anger. He resented his metal companion and resented his situation. He boiled inside and gritted his teeth as they moved forward.

Hailstones fell, their percussion almost comical as they met with Hepburn's ultranium armor. It eased Henry's mood and the sound distracted him. He'd have to plan his revenge on the Favela on a clear day; they'd hear Hepburn coming before they got anywhere near it.

Henry's suit seemed to warm him from within and a calm fell upon him.

"I've questions for you now," he said after some time.

"Proceed," replied the robot, as cold as always.

"What was the world like before?"

"I do not understand. Before what?"

"Before the Ever Winter?"

The hail slowed, then stopped altogether. The icescape was covered in a slush that Hepburn stamped in.

"I do not understand. Winter is seasonal and geographical. The season before winter is called autumn. 'Ever' implies endless, constant, perpetual. In what place do you refer to?" The robot's expression outlined confusion. Henry mirrored it. The Ever Winter had been named by those who escaped it and those who came after. The robot seemed not to know this. Henry thought of another question he could ask, that Hepburn might understand and that would give him a better picture of the past.

"Never mind. Tell me, who birthed you?"

"I was not born. I was designed, assembled and programmed. For legal reasons I am not permitted to reveal details of my design, schematics or location of assembly. What else would you like to know?"

Henry was frustrated at his lack of understanding and the fact that the robot's answers were always elaborate and confusing, filled with new words that Henry had never heard before. Every sentence created new puzzlement. One thing they both had, however, was time. They were still days from the container ship and a lot could be learned from Hepburn 8 before they reached their destination.

"What does that mean, on your shoulder?" Henry pointed to the flag in subdued red and blue against the camouflage. The robot ceased walking so he could study the symbol.

"That is the Union Flag; the national flag of Greater Britain, also known as the Union Jack, or Royal Union Flag in other commonwealth realms. It features the crosses of saints Andrew, Patrick and George, synonymous with the countries of England, Scotland and Ireland."

Henry had not heard of these people or places. More unknowns! More questions!

"What is a *flag*?"

"A flag is used for signaling and identification. In this case, the Union Flag identifies that I have been assigned to the

Greater British Army. Setting down and flying a flag also has the meaning of conquering something."

Henry thought about the symbols and emblems he'd seen carved in ice on many of the buildings in the Favela. If Henry could've created a flag for himself right then, it would've been a Big White, or an eye, in ice white and blood red. He would raise it on top of Moonbird and carve it on every dwelling with the blade he would use to smite Lanner and the king. Rage surged through him as he imagined the moment. Once more, the robot raised its head and Henry sensed it was secretly recording his latest reaction also.

The robot strode on and took the lead this time. Henry half-skipped behind him until he caught up with the machine's long, steady strides. Henry ran in front of the robot and waved his arms to stop him from walking further.

"Could you conquer a place? Can you fight?"

"I would be mostly ineffective in battle," the robot informed him, to Henry's disappointment.

"Why?" Henry was miffed that such an advanced machine from the time of the Great-Greats could save his life and his sight, but not help him vanquish the evil king of the Favela.

"The boundaries of enemy and ally are often changeable in a warfare scenario. Therefore, purpose-built military droids are used in a limited capacity in battle. Though less effective, humans are essential to negotiate with other humans in critical situations, due to the mistrust humans have of AI units. My weapon system only allows me to incapacitate an affirmed aggressor once I am deployed in a medical emergency. Depending on a number of variants, incapacitation is usually for a period of five to six minutes. I am not permitted to be an aggressor. This cannot be over-ridden at any rank, as my design does not allow this."

"Uh. I take it you don't have any of them fighting droids with you at the ship?"

"No. Berserker units are classified as pure military cargo and cannot be transported by non-military vessels under International Law."

Henry stood up, patted the robot on the back-plate and started to walk in the direction they'd been heading.

"Henry, I am glad that we are talking again," said the droid.

"You're a prong, Hepburn," he replied.

"That makes no sense, Henry."

"I'm glad it ain't just me that struggles to fathom stuff. I've got a lot to teach you if you're going to survive this world."

"I am willing to learn, Henry. It will be advantageous for both of us."

"You can start by talking like a person."

The robot projected contemplation in pixel form.

"I will *fathom* it."

SIXTEEN

## How to be Human

The first memory he had was of Mother. He guessed that it was from before Mary was born, because he felt that Mother was *his* in that memory, but he couldn't be sure. All the years since, Mother had had to care for the other siblings; always the youngest, the bairn. Once, Henry had been the bairn. Her only bairn.

Henry had not been designed or assembled. The only laws Henry followed were those that Mother and Father had made. The rules they all lived by. Henry had been born and nurtured. Fed and wiped down. Nursed through sickness and fever.

He remembered Mother's scent. Her hair. The feeling of being close to her skin, the warmth of it. The feeling of being safe. Loved. He knew he had been loved, for it was always in her smile, but in the earliest memories, the smile was for him alone.

How did Mother know how to raise him? Was it instinct alone that allowed her to pour affection upon the boy? Or something learned from others? Henry would never be able to ask her such things. That opportunity was gone forever.

Fate had put so many twists in the path Henry's life followed. He thought about the alternative path; if nothing had ever happened to his family and Lanner had never found their homestead, or if Mary had never spotted a stricken container vessel on the horizon. If Mother and Father had died naturally, not at the hands of others, would Henry have actually left the homestead in search of others, or would he have taken the role of Father and done all the things Father had to feed the family and guide them through the endless winter? *So many twists and turns.*

He thought of all the things he had learned in such a small space of time by seeing the Favela finally. Most of them were things he'd rather not know, or forget altogether. Most of them were poison.

He looked at Hepburn once more. Hepburn had been assembled by human hands and he knew a lot, but he could not be truly human. The word rang in Henry's ears. Human. Humanish?

Were the adults of the Favela closer to being what human was than Henry and his family? Were they, his family, the anomaly? Were they the freaks? He tried to imagine the king as a boy, enjoying the embrace of a mother, but he could not. Was a mother's love the elixir to being human, or a better one at least?

Then he thought of the Orfins, who knew no mother or father. They were wild and crude, but they were unlike the adults who ruled over them. Only Skindred had seemed akin to Lanner and those he joined.

A memory came to Henry then, of a day in his young life when Mother had taken him to the wire, where a prairie bitch had become entangled in it. The creature was ugly. More rodent than anything, he remembered. And it was in a lot of pain, thrashing its limbs in panic and becoming more and more ensnared. The creature was dying, slowly, and had been there some time.

Young Henry had clapped his hands in celebration. He understood that things needed to be caught so they could eat, whether they be under the ice, or upon it. Food was life, and to young Henry, it filled a hole in his stomach.

Mother wasn't pleased like Henry was. Mother was sad and concerned for the animal. She threw down her sealskin and knelt beside it. Henry joined her, emulating her posture.

The animal's chest heaved as it breathed in and out. Mother placed her hand upon its fur and stroked it gently, soothing it.

The animal closed its eyes as Mother's hand moved across the fur gently in a circle. The creature became calm at her touch. It didn't scratch or bite, try to fend her off, or panic. It knew it was in trouble. It knew it could not be saved and Mother's touch soothed it, as it did young Henry when he was sick.

Mother turned to young Henry and he realized she was crying. It disturbed him. Mother did not cry. Only Young Henry cried, when he was cold, or hungry, or angry about something.

"We must quicken it. Stop the pain and send it to the stars," she said. Then she turned to the animal and snapped its neck.

Young Henry was both alarmed and perplexed by what Mother had done. He'd seen her use a slingshot to bring down a bird, or bring a fish up from the ice below with the keel net and once with a spear, but this seemed different. The rules didn't make sense.

Mother untangled the animal from the wire and bagged it in the sealskin, ready to be skinned and gutted for dinner.

"It's called *mercy*, Henry. No enjoyment in it, but we didn't let him suffer longer than he had. It's a kindness, of sorts. It's what makes us human."

"Who-men?" replied the little boy.

"You and I, *min lilla manniskan*."

The years that separated the memory from the present moment and all the events in between brought Henry back to the icescape, and he thought of the kindness of snapping a creature's neck. He thought of the seal pups he'd dragged on his sled time and again, and his bone pick fracturing their skulls and ruining their brain matter within. He thought of Father taking the pups who hadn't survived the winter, but never taking too many. Leaving enough for other creatures to feast upon. The rules were blurred in Henry's mind; *Showing mercy. Hunting prey. Feeding the enemy. Killing for revenge. Mercy…*

His anger returned once more, this time at the absence of mercy shown to his kin: Father left to die slowly across the freezing waters of the ice hole; Mother slain trying to stop strangers taking the head of her baby.

The lesson from Mother had not been learned, for there was no form of mercy that Henry could ever afford his enemies. He was sure, given the chance, he would rip them to pieces and delight in their agony, eventually becoming just like them.

Henry regarded the ancient robot.

Hepburn, made by human hands and programmed by a human mind, was good.

The robot had come to his aid and had healed him, most certainly saving his life.

What could the robot teach Henry about being human? Could he keep him from someday being like Lanner and the king?

Henry decided he would learn all that he could. In the robot, Henry had an oracle. The answer to many of the questions that had concerned him in life.

What was *television*? What was a *storm drain*, or a *balloon*, or a *cola*? What was a *Batman*? What was a *1958 Red Plymouth Fury*?

## SEVENTEEN

## Under a Canopy of Stars

Henry ate caribou. Hepburn watched with disinterest, having no
need to partake in the consumption of food. Henry had decided
he would make a cloaked hood from the pelt, as his hair did little
to protect his neck and ears from the cold and his majestic bodysuit did not cover his neck or face.

As well as the caribou, Henry had also drunk a vial of liquid
Hepburn had administered, stating that Henry's body was
lacking essential nutrients. The nutrients were to become a
routine, until the robot no longer deemed them necessary.

Henry knew they would have long passed the place where
Henry and Father had found the corpse of a stranger frozen in
the ice. The man's remains would've been ravaged by beasts and
birds until they were just bone, then would've been dusted and
covered by the snow.

He also knew they'd also passed the place where Henry had
grown up; the original homestead the family had packed up in a
rush once Lanner had entered their lives. He hadn't seen
evidence of the place, but knew it would have returned to a
natural state, with no evidence of anyone ever living there.

But Henry knew when they'd found the site of the newer
homestead and Martin's cave, the remains of the wire sticking
out of the snow was enough to announce the land as his by right
of inheritance. *Snow dunes.* Henry wanted none of it.

He remained silent and they set up camp for the night, close to the sacred ground where Mother, Father and the bairn lay beneath the powder. There was nothing to do there. Nothing to retrieve. No ritual to conduct or words to say. All would be unchanged, and so he decided to keep it to himself and not to remark on it to the robot.

Knowing how close they were to the homestead meant they weren't far from the container ship either, and Henry distracted himself by thinking of the things he might need, eager to board the vessel and catalog all the things he could use in his campaign against Lanner and the king who held his sisters. *How many containers remain unopened?* He wondered what other ancient technology awaited rediscovery and how many of those things could bring about the deaths of his enemies. Every hour, every day he spent apart from his siblings was time in which all kinds of torment could be metered out to Iris, Hilde and Mary. And Sissel. *Block it out. All of it.*

In some ways, it was far worse than his solo trek to the Favela. His mind had sketched out possible truths on that journey, but now, having been there, Henry's mind had colored in all the images. He knew the names and nature of those in the Favela. He knew the crimes they permitted – and committed – and he'd seen the control the few had over the many.

The robot had no need for conversation, other than to aid Henry's mental rehabilitation. Henry used the silences between them to test the limits of his new eye, and considered how he could get through the Favela with stealth, retracing its lanes and alleys in his mind. He could see far in daylight; through objects, even; and he could comprehend the distance between things in minute detail. Snowflakes became wondrous, intricate things. Henry could also see at night. He'd discovered it when he couldn't sleep and found that his new eye gave things a green tinge beneath the moon. A moving object far in the distance caught his attention and he used the zoom in his eye to see it in the darkness. It was a Big White, over a mile away, heading in another direction. Henry marveled at this. Not such a curse now, but a power!

It enabled him to relax more around the robot, for as much as the droid displayed subtle human traits from time to time, Henry realized he was also a human exploring what it was like to be a machine. They spoke more than they had, and the silences were fewer.

The main thing he'd learned from Hepburn was that the robot had been in transit to support soldiers fighting in a battle zone, thousands of miles from where the container ship was. The robot seemed confused by certain details. It understood that they were standing on ice and that the ice was on top of what had been Lantic. The robot did not understand that the war had not concluded, or that the army it served, and the war office it spoke of, no longer existed. The robot, in some ways, seemed as childish as Martin had been. In all others, it was a font of knowledge. It knew more about the Earth than any human alive. Henry shuddered at the thought of Lanner or the king having access to the robot, for with it, they would hold even more dominion over the people they already ruled. Henry needed to think everything over, and when he was done, think it through once more.

"Can you blink or something? Every now and then? It lets me know you're awake. Otherwise it feels weird when you just sit there."

"I do not need to sleep, Henry, but I can assimilate blinking now and then if it pleases you."

"Thanks."

Digital pixels mimicked blinking.

"The best thing about my eye is seeing the stars," Henry said as they rested in the open, "and the moon. I wonder what it's like there."

"The moon is a cold, dry orb," Hepburn responded and Henry laughed, picking the bones of his meal.

"I still can't get used to the way you talk. Your voice is strange. No one talks like that." Henry's mood lifted and he forgot what lay close to them for a moment.

Hepburn didn't seem offended by Henry's response. "My voice is programmed to emulate an English accent from the South East region; male, mid-thirties, upper working-class media version 7.2. A soldier expects that a surgeon is of a certain age as to have the experience, seniority and credentials to operate, but they must also be battle-fit. The age of my voice has been amended to reflect this and meet the criteria for non-civilian activities. Additionally, the sound of my voice has been selected to appear friendly, reassuring, yet authoritative and knowledgeable. This is essential in order to build trust in my capabilities to perform critical surgeries, and to mask the fact that I am a machine and could be subject to malfunction, or could make decisions without emotion, which may not be agreeable to a soldier with different priorities and objectives to my own."

"You did a good job with me. Thank you for saving me and my sight." It was the first time Henry had said this. He felt embarrassed as soon as he realized it.

"Thank you, Henry. You are most welcome."

"You fixed me good, Hep."

"I fixed your wounds, but we have not addressed your basic physical health and mental state yet."

"My what?"

"You have been exhibiting the symptoms of battle fatigue, which could be a precursor to post-traumatic stress disorder. You have severe anxiety and are not sleeping for the recommended minimum five-point-five hours outside peacetime. I have seen evidence of sleep apnea. Your blood pressure is higher than it should be and you are suffering palpitations and shortness of breath. In terms of basic health, there is a distinct long-term lack of vitamins and sources of fiber in your diet which need highlighting. There is also the amnesia that we need to look into; you are still unaware of your full name, rank or commanding officer."

Henry had no intention of starting whatever it was that Hepburn had suggested they were going to do. It sounded odd and was certainly beyond his thinking, too otherworldly and anteek for him to comprehend.

Henry was unsure what to say about the *amnesia*. He understood the robot assumed he was one of the soldiers from the unit it was assigned to. He was scared Hepburn would leave him if he knew that he wasn't a real soldier and he'd just worn a suit found in a container. The robot studied him. Henry wondered if it could read his actual thoughts.

The robot raised his faceplate skyward, then returned its attention back to him.

"I have modules available on advanced psychodynamic, existential, cognitive and behavioral therapy, as well as hypnotherapy, mindfulness, humanistic person-centered counseling and various mind tools. We can start the program now if you like?"

"Sorry, Hepburn. No."

"You need to do this before we can progress your combat retraining. You need to want to do this, otherwise it will have no effect upon you. This is proven."

Henry considered this. He needed to learn to fight properly in order to exact his revenge. He now knew the numbers of people he'd need to get through to face the king and it would take skills he didn't yet possess.

A star flickered across the distant sky. Henry thought it a satellite, still orbiting aimlessly above the frozen planet. He noticed it and tried to zoom his eye toward it, but it was beyond even his capability.

"What combat have you, Hepburn?"

"We will use a certified combat program covering the principles of Krav Maga, Taekwondo, Combat Sambo, Jukendo, Sanshou, Defendu and Okinawan Karate. We will need to condition and strengthen your body before we begin, with particular work on balance. Overall fitness needs vast improvement from what I have assessed throughout our journey so far."

"So, I sort my nut, then we get punching?"

"We heal your mind, refine the body, then retrain for legal battle-fit status. I estimate this will take us six to twelve months."

Henry was taken aback. He remembered what the king's witch had said about Iris; that she would be married off to Lanner in a year. Henry couldn't imagine his sisters spending twelve months in the Favela alone. He thought of the long pig in the street and the people drinking grog from ice-hewn glasses in the Birdcage and men punching the ice for no reason other than to show strength. He hadn't fancied a single day in the Favela. He couldn't imagine a year.

"Twelve months? But my sisters!"

"Both science and history have proven that the consequences of deploying soldiers for battle that are not physically or mentally fit are dire. If you are not ready to have this conversation, we can postpone it."

*Twelve months.*

Henry had no alternatives. His best chances of survival and revenge lay with the robot. It was the only edge he had over the populace of the Favela.

Once more, everything fell into perspective and he committed himself to it. He would do everything he needed to do, everything the robot asked of him, in order to defeat the adults of the Favela and free his sisters. He'd promised Father he'd avenge their family and Henry had to deliver on that.

"We can start on the mind things when we get to where we're going."

"We can start in the morning. You will run the next leg of our journey and I will monitor your heart rate. Exercise releases tension and stress."

"The morrow?"

"Yes. Tomorrow is better than the day after," Hepburn replied firmly.

Henry thought for a while, enjoying the quiet still of the night. He gave no immediate answer, but had already decided to go along with Hepburn's request. It would ease the boredom, at least.

"Do you know everything?" Henry asked finally, yawning.

"I know everything that I have been programmed to know, but I also have the capability to learn new things."

Henry shuffled to get comfortable for the night, suspecting the robot would wake him earlier than usual.

"Still don't fathom half of what you spit. You're company, at least. Good night, Hepburn."

"Good night, Henry."

~

*The dream visited Henry again – the rainbow, the snow leopard, the container.*

*Again, he struck the hinges of the door with an ax, as seals watched from a sieve of ice holes dotting the terrain.*

*Once more, the hinges gave way and the doors blew open and were carried away in the wind – only this time, the army of plastic dolls which poured from the container all wore Ginger Lanner's face.*

*Henry crawled backward on the ice like a crab and the Lanner dolls nearest to him grabbed at his feet as others climbed over them to get at his legs.*

*Just like last time, the Orfin seals watched helplessly from the circles cut into the ice, and just like last time, the snow leopard king mewled whilst Henry's sisters stroked its mane and tail.*

*The doors of the other containers blew off all at once and went soaring into the sky with the wild winds, not quite reaching the rainbow that over-arched the vessel MV Greyhound. Out of those containers came more and more plastic Lanners.*

*Henry fell back into an ice hole and down into the waters until a metallic arm reached down with great speed and snatched him from the icy sea. Hepburn 8 cleared a circle around them with a ring of fire, sending Lanners into the abyss below them.*

*Henry stood his ground, ready to fight the remaining dolls, but his sisters had got to their feet and were pointing at him with hatred and revulsion in their eyes. The icescape fell silent. The Ginger Lanners stopped in their tracks and all waited for the girls to speak. No voices came from them, but Henry knew they were pointing at his robotic eye. They were fearful of Henry and the robot that saved him. Henry felt great shame. The Lanner dolls cackled nervously, waiting for the snow leopard king to pass judgment.*

*The girls lay back down next to the beast.*

~

"Do you dream about your parents, Henry?"

"No, I do not."

EIGHTEEN

## Some Distance to Olympian

The robot ran beside Henry with ease, quickening the pace, never breaking stride. The perfect rhythm of Hepburn's legs stamping the ice was a metronome; a steady drum that helped Henry onward.

After a couple of hours, something did change. Every outward breath took some of his fear with it; his worries and anxiety. He found that he enjoyed running, but it was obvious that he was unfit and had to stop to catch his breath at regular intervals and, on a couple of occasions, to throw up. For the first time, Hepburn appeared unpleased, or disappointed, even. This annoyed Henry, but equally made him want to prove that he could do better. Their conversations lessened as they focused on the marathon, but this time, Henry found comfort in the silence.

Finally, they reached their destination. The MV Greyhound looked as regal as it had the first time and Henry was glad to see it again, but sad that Mary was not at his side as she had been when they'd discovered it. Nothing had changed in the weeks he'd been away. Snow had fallen. Some of it had melted. More snow had fallen and the wind had blown some of that away. A little of it had melted and more snow fell. The pointless sun never, ever melted enough to change the as-is. To breach the ice that covered the seas and once green or concreted lands.

The hole in the side of the ship still looked menacing, still a shark. Henry commented on it to Hepburn, who seemed to have no idea what he meant. The hole in the side of the ancient vessel did not look like a shark to the robot.

Standing next to the ship, Hepburn, although painted in dull camouflage, looked like he too could last over a hundred years exposed to the elements. In a way, the ship, man-made in a yard somewhere, was like a distant relative to the machine that had saved Henry's life. Like the MV Greyhound, Hepburn too was a testament to all that had been, and all that had been lost.

Hepburn scanned for data and looked puzzled when no signals came. It blinked several times on his digital screen.

"What's the plan then, grandpa?" Henry quipped, scratching the skin around the lens in his eye.

"We continue your rehabilitation. That is always the plan, until it is achieved."

"What warring you teaching me, then? Grappling? Slingshot?"

"It has been one week," replied the robot. "In the last few days, have you felt unhappy none of the time, some of the time, most of the time or all of the time?"

Henry frowned at the sudden change of topic. Then realization dawned. Hepburn was the embodiment of all that was precise. *One week.*

"Most of the time," Henry replied honestly, with more than a hint of spite in his voice.

"In the last few days, have you thought about harming others?"

"Most of the time." His answer was immediate and matter-of-fact, not too dissimilar in tone from an answer the robot might have given.

"In the last few days, have you thought about ending your life?" asked the robot.

"No." It was truth. The deaths of his loved ones had broken him, but time itself had found a way to mute some of the pain signals in Henry's mind. Knowing his sisters were still at the Favela kept him going and after finally accepting the darkness from losing his eye, he saw the new light offered by the digital replacement. Henry exhaled. So much change had befallen his world in such a short space of time. He wondered if it would ever settle. If he would ever find peace. If he would ever find something to resemble normality. He hoped he would and it was hope that let him wake each new day and live it.

"Thank you, Henry. I will ask you these questions again three weeks from now." The robot moved then and banged the side of a container, causing ice and snow to fall from its roof and reveal part of a forgotten company emblem. "As I have assessed your basic fitness, Henry, we will begin your first physical training module. I want you to open the doors of the container behind me and reveal the contents."

It was Henry's turn to blink. Thick ice covered the entire area where the doors were.

"What's inside? Warring stuff? Weapons?"

"We will see," said the robot, handing Henry a tool that had been left under the ice many weeks before.

"Aren't you going to blast it open or something?" Henry replied. He zoomed the lens in his eye toward the container. His sight breached the container, but could make nothing of the boxed contents within.

"No. This is going to build your strength." Hepburn turned his back on Henry and leaped onto the roof of another container in a single movement. More snow and ice fell from the sides of the container and the robot stood in silence with a fixed digital expression upon its visor.

"You're jesting me, right?" asked Henry resentfully, already knowing the answer. The word *jesting* brought the image of the demon clown to the forefront of his mind. He pushed it back, and the blood boiled inside of him as it morphed into Lanner.

"Come on, soldier!" yelled Hepburn in a brash military voice. "Get your whiney ass moving and get those biceps pumping. Your very presence here is depriving a village somewhere of its idiot!"

Henry stood up straight, amazed at the change in Hepburn's voice.

"Are you deaf? Or are you waiting for me to take a photograph, boy?" yelled the robot, adding to Henry's confusion.

"No, I—"

"Then get to it, soldier, before I stick that tool through your ears and ride you around like a shagging motorbike. Pick it up now and free that container. When you're done, you can celebrate by running five circles of this ship."

Henry picked up the tool he'd last held when fog had descended upon the icescape, hindering his return to the homestead.

"Hit that damned box, soldier!" Hepburn screamed with all the emotion of a human. Its digital face looked furious. Its eyebrows were angry triangles with frown lines added to the effect.

The gong sound as Henry struck the container for the first time echoed off in the distance. Henry laughed at the scene he was playing in. Hepburn – factual, mild and boring to begin with – was proving far pushier than Father had ever been.

It felt good to laugh and it felt good to strike the container as hard as he could.

Henry had finally stopped vomiting and Hepburn seemed content with the end result. It assessed Henry's vitals, ran a scan, then moved his attention to the contents of the container that Henry had freed before he'd started his laps of the ship.

"What's in them?" Henry asked. He wiped his mouth with his sleeve and grabbed the box nearest to him.

Hepburn said nothing and Henry ripped the box open with ease. Then he swore.

Henry sat in the captain's chair, comforted by the strange smell of leather. Everything was connected. The past, present and future. He didn't know if he tuned in to those things; if he saw them coming. Or if everyone saw the patterns like he did. It drove him spare and made him feel exhausted. Yet the thoughts swam through his brain at speed. Unceasing. He tried to block out the noise and find something new to focus on.

As Henry surrounded himself with all the familiar objects he'd cataloged the last time he was there, he studied one of the new things he'd obtained from the container outside. With every strike of the metal, he'd imagined what might've been waiting for him inside. Swords. Dynamite. A harpoon. It was none of those things. Not even half as useful. What Henry held in his hand was another doll, except this one had brown skin, like someone had played an almighty joke upon him. One container full of sinister plastic white dolls and another full of dolls with bronzed skin. Ebony and ivory. Iris dolls. Mary dolls. Hilde dolls. And now Sissel ones.

Sissel. Henry had never been able to picture a girl before that wasn't one of his sisters. Now Sissel haunted him, with her beauty and her strength. Sissel, who had been tough with him, but fair. Extending kindness to the limits of what she was allowed. He wished he could've spent more time with her. Alone. Asking her questions about where she'd come from and how she'd become the leader of the Orfins. Henry wondered what she did that she enjoyed, and if there was ever any room for enjoyment in the Favela and its slum dwellings. Had Sissel truly smiled at any point? He couldn't remember. But when he pictured her, his mind painted a smile upon her that was meant for him.

He hadn't spoken to Hepburn since the first doll had fallen from the first box he'd opened. Instead, he drank whiskey as night fell around them. Hepburn had informed him that alcohol would not aid his mood, nor recovery, neither physical nor mental. But Henry continued to drink. It warmed his chest from the inside and took the edge off the churning thoughts in his mind. It numbed the thoughts of Sissel and the concerns he had for her and his sisters.

The light of the LED torch went out. Henry wound it several times and the room was once again aglow.

Henry placed the doll on the desk and picked up a genuine treasure he'd overlooked the last time he was aboard the MV Greyhound. It was another book. The cover held neither clown, nor butterfly. This one held the face of a man. Not a photograph, for it was not an exact image. This had been painted a long time before the book had even been printed. The man wore a dress-shirt and overcoat. He neither smiled, nor frowned in the picture, but held a look that seemed to Henry like the man knew of many things. Secrets.

"The Count of Monte Cristo," Henry read aloud, turning to look at the back of the book. "Injustice. Intrigue. Revenge." Henry opened the cover, flicked to the first page and began to read. Therapy, it seemed, came in all shapes and sizes.

Henry read until the whiskey bottle was empty. Then he slept in the captain's chair, only to be woken far earlier than he had ever imagined. The next day of rehabilitation was upon him, and it seemed Hepburn was keen to keep to his as-yet-unannounced schedule. Henry ran circles of the ship as instructed, but the whiskey he'd drunk meant that his time was slower than the day before and he'd had to stop for longer, in order to bring up much of the alcohol he'd consumed the night before.

Hepburn wasn't pleased and punished him with more laps of the ship, then press-ups and sit-ups and pull-ups on the side of one of the containers. The next two weeks continued in much the same way, except Henry couldn't find any of the whiskey or vodka in the ship and Hepburn wouldn't reveal where he'd put it, citing medical concern and his obligations to get Henry battle-fit. Still, Henry took his nutrients, as he did feel better after taking them. He also found himself catching and eating more fish than ever before, as his training became more intense and rigorous, causing him to burn off calories at an ever-increasing rate.

At night, with aching muscles, Henry read more of the book, until he reached the end of it. Then he read it once more.

∿

*In the realm of dreams, Henry watched as a version of Sissel walked far across the plains of endless ice, to a ship that she had never seen before. Though the shark's face had been torn into the side of it to warn her off, he saw as she regarded it, then, unfazed, made her way to the sloping deck. Henry had watched her travel from miles away, for his eye was all-seeing and he knew she was out there. She was no seal. She was no apparition. She was a girl in this dream. Made of flesh and bone.*

*Though it was cold outside, Sissel was dressed as she'd been when he'd met her on the sieve of holes in the ice; a bare chest, covered by a fur cape about her shoulders. He heard the echo of the steel door as it slammed shut and her footsteps as she made her way toward the accommodation area.*

*Henry left the control room, and as he neared his cabin, dream Sissel strode into the hallway. They smiled together and then stepped toward each other, enjoying a close embrace.*

*No words passed between them; just the warmth they shared, and then a kiss.*

*Sissel moved away then and led Henry into his cabin toward the bed he'd claimed as his own. Her cape fell to the floor and Henry stepped into her open arms once more, where the warmth engulfed their bodies until it became a fire.*

*When the flames went out, all was darkness. And Henry lay alone.*

*"I don't know you, Henry," she said.*

∿

"Do you dream about your parents, Henry?"

"No. I do not."

## NINETEEN

## Beast Mode

Henry had lost what little excess fat he'd had. For weeks, he had been subjected to a routine of waking up when the meager sun graced the Earth, then commencing two hours of cardio, two hours of strength, a break for lunch and then much of the same again. Henry's body had taken a new shape. Muscles appeared where he'd previously had none. Even his back took on a new shape; a rock-face with new ledges cut from the shoulders to the lower back. His chest was the same, but his stomach was a grid of squares and rectangles where it been soft and uniform before.

To vary his training a bit, Hepburn had also insisted on Henry digging three other containers free from the snow and ice, to reveal their treasures. One container was piled with things labeled as *rattan garden furniture* and *American retro-style fridge-freezers* and boxes of electrical components.

The second container had been home to a number of black and gold painted statues of a man sitting cross-legged and the third contained a sleek, dark green and silver Duesenberg Model J Coupe, part of the same consignment that Henry had crashed and destroyed months before.

After some persuasion, Henry had got the robot to agree that driving the car would be good for his spirits. He got enjoyment from it and it took his mind from the demons that lurked in his brain matter, waiting to be summoned.

Hepburn had explained about the technology of the car. It knew much of its design and was able to recognize its materials, systems and controls. Like the previous Duesenberg, the Model J Coupe had a female hologram that congratulated Henry on being the new owner of the vehicle. The hologram wasn't the apparition she had been before. Henry had seen other people, like Sissel, since and he'd seen other examples of old technology, like Hepburn.

If the car Henry had crashed had been beautiful, this was its meaner, bigger brother. The new car had blacked-out windows and a veneer of opaque panels akin to cockroach wings upon the roof, rendering a brooding appearance as it rolled across the ice. It reminded Henry of a dark storm cloud. Remembering another car in the family book he once cherished, he secretly named it. *Fury;* a word that summed up the mood of the car, and something Henry still felt whenever his mind wandered too far from the ship.

Not quite fitting into the vehicle himself, Hepburn was able to sync his own systems with the car's and as Henry drove the vehicle, Hepburn's voice crackled from the speakers within.

"Henry."

"What is it, Hep?" he replied, happy to be taking the vehicle further across Lantic, further from the landside.

"Sir, I have detected a life-form in the vicinity. Two-point-seven miles from your location."

"Lanner!"

"No. I believe it to be no threat. It is singular and does not carry weaponry. The creature, not human, has a faint heat signature. It is unconscious and its vital signs are dwindling. It may be a source of fresh food for you."

"Take me to it. Meat is meat," Henry replied, smiling, thinking about Father for the hundredth time that day.

"It will appear on your console now," Hepburn advised and the screen before Henry guided him to a distant flag, where a creature lay, almost camouflaged by the snow.

Henry got out of the car and heard the mighty footsteps of Hepburn as it appeared next to him.

"*Panthera Uncia*. A snow leopard, if I'm not wrong," announced Hepburn.

Henry had seen it once before. He recalled the day he and Mary had first discovered the ship. The beast had been much smaller then, just a bairn, but it had grown since, like Henry had. Up close, its fur was matted and unkempt, with buds of white snow upon it and a bloom of frozen reds where Henry supposed it had been injured.

The creature was conscious. It tried to raise its head at the sound of the robot and the human approaching, but it was weak and its head dropped. Henry took a few steps toward the animal, then knelt beside it, finally sure he wasn't in any danger. He placed his hand on the creature's belly to comfort it, where the fallen snow was only white. The leopard didn't resist, accepting its fate. Henry thought of Martin, solidified in an underwater cavern, just as weak and exposed as this animal was. There were so many memories that would never leave Henry's mind, and now here was another to add to a list of sadness.

"What's wrong with it?" he said, stroking the animal tenderly.

"A stabbing wound from a blunt implement. It's close to death." The robot was absent emotion and did not conceal the fact.

"Lanner, I bet!" Henry was roused once more at the thought of his nemesis and recalled what Hepburn had said about his own injuries when he'd found him. If it wasn't for the material of the battle suit, Lanner's blade would have taken his life for sure.

"Shall I end its plight?" Hepburn leaned forward and extended its metallic arm, as if it would either smash or snap the life out of the snow leopard. The creature opened its eyes, as if it understood what was being discussed. Then it closed them once more, accepting whatever was to come, or perhaps not wishing to witness the final blow.

Henry remembered being escorted across the icescape, in and out of consciousness, taunted by Lanner and unable to do anything to oppose his tormentors. He pictured one of the Orfins standing above him; the one they had called *Boo*.

"What do you mean, *plight*?" Henry asked, concerned for the creature. He no longer felt the way he had when he'd driven toward its location. He thought once more of the words Mother had spoken to him as a child. He had a choice. He had an opportunity. He was human.

"Shall I kill it? The creature will most likely expire very soon."

"No, don't. Can you not save it?" Henry replied.

"It is not impossible if I act now. However, this creature, once healed, could pose a substantial threat to you. I recommend aiding its death. You need protein and this is an excellent source, in the absence of alternatives."

Henry looked at the creature and saw how fragile it was, diminishing before his eyes.

*Martin.*

*Father.*

*Mother.*

"Save it."

"This is not recommended, Henry."

Henry moved his hand to the creature's face and ran his fingers across its fur, tracing a line from its brow to its triangular ear. Up close, it was a beautiful animal. And it was dying.

"Save it, Hep. Or I go back to the Favela now and start my warring."

"That is unwise. You are not battle-fit."

"I know. And they would end me the daylight I arrive."

The robot paused as it calculated the situation. This was unusual, as Hepburn was usually swift and decisive in his responses. Digital frown lines appeared on Hepburn's faceplate.

"You are an effective negotiator," it said finally.

"Save it. Like you did me," Henry affirmed.

The creature lay on the tilted floor of the cabin. Its chest heaved as it slept after the ordeal of its operation. Henry felt like he was witnessing his own return to the land of the living, as if he'd watched the robot repair himself, so many months before. The only recollection Henry had of that was of lightning in a dome of some kind, so bright that he saw it through his eyelids. The same drugs pumped through the creature's veins as they had his. Did the creature also dream of its mother and father? Were they scouring the icescape somewhere, looking for it? Or had Lanner killed them too?

The creature stirred, as if it was amidst a dream. Henry nodded. He understood so well. They were akin, somehow. Brought together again, by the sun, or the moon.

He went outside, leaving Hepburn to reluctantly monitor the creature. The robot cited a waste of resources and vital medicine as Henry left the room. Henry did not care. Part of him wondered if the robot was jealous of the new arrival. Something that lived and breathed. Something not of the same species as Henry, but still, closer to him than an assembled and pragmatic machine.

He thought about someone finding one of his siblings in the snow and hoping the same mercy would be afforded to them. Life over death. Life over meat. It was not unthinkable that they might escape and find their way on the ice. He had, kind of.

And then the thought came to him: what if they no longer lived at all? He had not seen the girls in the Favela. What if they had all been killed, or worse? He could not trust the king, nor Lanner. A cold thought entered his mind. Could he even trust Sissel? He'd known her for mere hours, and spent just moments in her company. In his dreams, she was good. He was sure of it. She was his. But was it all a trick? Was she wicked, like the others? Henry tried to remember how she had actually behaved toward him. Had he missed something? He had not seen Skindred slip away to tell Lanner of his arrival that day. Had Sissel sent Skindred to squeal? Henry thought he could trust his own mind. But it had been so long.

Then his sisters came into his thoughts once more, as they so often did. Were they too now in other rooms beneath the ice? Preserved as they once were? Statuettes in ice, like Martin had carved of them.

Henry had no proof of anything. He had nothing but what was left of his hope. Hope that had been kept alive, because he had been. Henry had to care for the bairn creature. It was a welcome distraction. Another one to busy his mind.

He smashed a hole in the ice and finally caught some fish, taking far longer than Hepburn would have. When he returned to the cabin, the beast was awake. It paid no attention to Hepburn, but when Henry entered the room, it changed its posture and prepared to leap into battle mode. The creature bared its maxillaries like it had done when Henry had first faced it as a bairn on the deck of the ship. It extended its claws, digging them into the carpet of the cabin.

"Hey, no need for a war. I'm a friend," Henry spoke softly.

Gone were its injuries. The only hint was a gap in its fur, where Hepburn had operated. Not even a scar was visible. Henry thought of his eye and the crude tear around it where the skin had reformed around the lens attached within.

"The creature is perfectly fine. A little disorientated. He doesn't seem to like you, but you are, after all, human," said Hepburn.

Henry put down his sealskin and placed his spear onto the floor. Slowly, he removed his fur coat, sending flakes of snow onto the once royal-blue carpet of the cabin.

"It's all right. I'm not going to hurt you," he said and the snow leopard gripped the carpet harder with its claws, ripping a jagged shred of the flooring. It mewed, seeming to remember Henry, perhaps fending off its own mother and father that day on the ship.

"It is likely to attack you, Henry. You should have allowed it to expire. You've significantly increased the chances of injury to your person."

"It's just scared and hungry," he replied, taking a fish out from his sealskin sack. "Have this sea-fodder, little 'un." He tossed the fish across the floor toward it. The scent of the fish reached the snow leopard and it changed its posture slightly. Although still in an attack position, it used its paw to bring the fish closer. Not taking its eyes from Henry, it sniffed at the offering where it had shredded the carpet, but kept its eyes fixed upon Henry.

Henry took a step back to demonstrate he was no threat. The creature regarded him still, then flashed its eyes at the fish. It licked its lips. Henry moved back further still, until he reached the wall of the cabin and slunk down so he was in a sitting position. If the snow leopard wanted to, it could've leaped onto Henry and he wouldn't have been able to shift out of the way quick enough. The creature clearly knew this and tilted its head, trying to work out why Henry would be so stupid. But it seemed the smell of the fish was intoxicating to the starving animal, and it drew back under the safety of the writing desk, using its paw to bring its intended meal with it, and there it ate the fish, biting its head off first, still watching Henry the whole time.

Henry felt happy for the first time in an age. He had done something good and he had provided food for a creature that would have died without his help. A creature most others would have killed out of fear, hunger, or sport. Henry had made a choice of his own. He wasn't entirely sure why, but he felt good about it. The fact the creature ate his gift was all the trophy that Henry needed. He wondered what Mother and Father would have thought. *Meat is meat.*

"Hey, Hep. What did you call the beast? When you first saw it?"

The robot raised its faceplate skyward, then answered.

"Panthera uncia. It is the science name of this creature."

"Panthera," Henry repeated.

～

Every day, Henry brought the creature food. He never let it out of the cabin and the creature never tried to leave. A few times, when he'd gotten too close, the creature mewled at him, or lashed out with a paw, although Henry felt the swipe was more of a warning than anything intended to draw his blood.

Henry ascertained that Hepburn was uneasy the whole time, often reciting the sum of drugs and ointments it had used on the snow leopard, stating they were best saved for Henry's own need. Henry ignored it, proud of his own compassion.

Eventually, the creature came to realize Henry was never going to harm it. He had, after all, brought it in from the cold and spoiled it with offerings that would have been otherwise harder to come by. The creature regarded Henry as a kind of slave. Someone beneath it; loyal and stupid. At the same time, it began to become fond of its slave. It missed the companionship and warmth of its parents. Using their body heat to stay warm in a huddle. Nestled in a pile against the elements. One evening it decided the slave could keep it warm and it crept over to Henry one night as he slept and moved into position next to him.

Henry woke briefly, then tried to go back to sleep, smiling. It was the first triumph he'd had in a long time.

Yet he knew Hepburn was still concerned that the creature might attack him in his sleep should it become hungry, or simply forget where it was and why. Henry was aware that Hepburn kept a very close watch and had even changed the times he went into rest mode. He liked that the robot did that, even it if was out of some duty, he couldn't fully understand and not out of the kind of bond of love that Henry and his family had.

He went back to sleep happier than he'd been in a long while.

Some days later, Henry allowed the creature to join him outside as he trained. He was fearful that the snow leopard might run off, but it never did. Sometimes it watched him, but other times it hung around the containers, biting the heads of the many doll carcasses scattered in the snow.

Then, after watching Henry run laps of the ship from the sloping deck, it began to run alongside him, keeping a good pace with him and aiding its own recovery. The two became friends then. Real companions, and somehow, still to Hepburn's concern, inseparable.

Training got more difficult. Hepburn introduced new exercises and routines, ever increasing the distances and repetitions, but reducing the rests between each part of the program. Then it used the vessel and the terrain itself for Henry to jump upon, climb and scale. In a short space of time, Henry was climbing the sides of the vessel and leaping from containers. To make it more difficult, Hepburn started to project assailants around the vessel, which would fire upon Henry with unknown weapons. Still Henry had not been trained to fight, but he was ever quicker on his heels to avoid the various enemies targeting him. Henry began to enjoy his training and thrive under the supervision of Hepburn. Slowly, every target that had been set for him, he exceeded. Every time, or speed he had set, then reached, he improved upon and every weight he lifted became easier as he trained.

In the evenings, Hepburn would project training modules onto the wall of the captain's office, so Henry could understand the best ways to move toward opponents without being detected and how to use the terrain to his advantage. Then Henry advanced onto modules of human anatomy, so he could understand more about the human body and its weaknesses.

He continually asked Hepburn to start the fighting modules, but Hepburn refused, focusing purely on Henry's superior fitness, strength and agility. Father had never been as strong. Father had never been as fast. Henry was stronger and his body broadened as he progressed with his training.

Henry had taken to showering most days, using the cubicle and shower head in his cabin, rigged up to a plastic water tank he'd been able to heat with solar cells. Hepburn had showed him some new practical skills also which would be invaluable should he ever start a homestead of his own one day. A warm shower was, so far, his defining moment.

When the coldest nights came, Henry read the few books he had and the snow leopard listened, as did Hepburn. Henry's reading had improved and even the way he spoke was more in line with the sentences of the books. Without him realizing, he spoke words he had never known before and put them in an order he would not have used in his past life. Sometimes he had questions for Hepburn about the meaning of the words and although Hepburn was a font of all knowledge, the android didn't know what a 1958 Red Plymouth Fury was.

## TWENTY

## Lessons in Absolute Violence

When Henry took the car that he had named *Fury* for a drive one afternoon, the snow leopard leaped into the seat beside him and went along for the ride, unfazed by the radical speeds they were driving at.

"Now we're getting along, I suppose I'd better give you a name as well," Henry said to the snow leopard, "I don't know many names, so let's see what ones you like."

The snow leopard stared at Henry, then looked out the window. The sky was cloudless as they sped under it.

"What about Ragnar?" Henry said, recalling a name from a story once told to him by Mother. The creature remained unimpressed and Henry changed course, so the ship was once more in sight. He thought of characters in the books he'd read and spoke the names of those. "Georgie? Caderousse? Dega? Eddie? Jacopo?"

The animal yawned, seemingly bored by the car journey now too. Henry turned the car sharply and the creature looked at him, seeming annoyed as it sank its claws into the seat to steady itself.

Henry thought of the names of the Orfins. Boo, Leaf, Q-Tip, Dibber, Yaxley... They meant nothing, those words, but they suited the people they belonged to.

Henry couldn't use the names of Father, or Martin. It didn't seem right. It would be different if Henry had a bairn. He knew that John would be a good name for a bairn. But not for a snow leopard.

He scrutinized the creature. It wasn't a naïve Georgie, a meek Dega, or a coward like Caderousse. The snow leopard was none of these. The snow leopard was a strong, dangerous creature. A wild, primitive killer. A beast. Then he recollected the day they'd found the big cat injured and that Hepburn had spoken the creature's name.

"What was that which Hepburn called you? Your science name, Panthera something?" Henry asked the creature, who of course said nothing in reply.

"Panthera. Do you like it? I believe I do. Panthera?" Henry spoke and this time the creature reacted, with a loud mewl and a tilt of the head which the movement of the car almost turned into a nod. "Panthera," Henry affirmed. "You're no cunk. You're true grit, with spikes upon." He sounded like Father, when he spoke those words. Deeper, somehow.

Back at the ship, Hepburn awaited, ready to start the next module. The car door opened and the animal leaped from the leather seat within, skidding to a stop on the ice before setting off on its own adventure around the containers.

"From now on, we call the animal *Panthera*. It's from his science name and I think he likes it."

Hepburn acknowledged it in silence, unmoved and uninspired, then Henry asked sheepishly, "Hepburn, what's a science name?"

Panthera started to join in with the training modules. Rather than just run beside Henry as he exercised, when Hepburn projected assailants onto the terrain, the creature would attack those that posed any immediate threat. He no longer ran next to Henry, but rather aligned with him; taking strategic positions, understanding the hunt as if it were the most natural thing in the world. They became a unit and Hepburn acknowledged it, amending the training modules to include Panthera as an attack dog.

"I'm fast. We're both fast. Me and Panthera. Now I want to fight. It's time, Hep."

It wasn't what Henry expected. At all. Firstly, he thought Hepburn would reject his idea and say he wasn't up to optimum fitness, physically or mentally. When he got the nod from the robot to begin the combat modules, he assumed he would be starting with an elaborate move of some kind. Something that would get the best of Lanner or any of his men. Something not even Father could have done.

Instead, Hepburn showed him how to stand in a defensive position, and they spent several hours focusing on balance as the robot struck at him with his arm, elbow, or leg. The snow leopard watched intently, unsure at first if Henry was in genuine danger, or if it was a game of some kind.

Henry begged Hepburn to stop several times as he could no longer raise his arms to the blocking position, or even worse, use his shin to block kicks. This was a new level of grueling fitness training, and after the first day, Henry was frustrated with his lack of progress.

Henry limped to the cabin that evening and used the abundance of ice to bring down the swelling in his legs. Panthera gave him the warmth he needed, sensing he was in pain, and not in the best of moods.

The next day was a repeat of the last and the routine was identical, yet the bruises on his limbs had bloomed and continually blocking the unceasing strikes from the robot grew ever more painful as the day went on. Panthera lost interest and went exploring on his own, coming back only when the day drew to a close.

That night was subject to something remarkable and glorious, however. Hepburn had not been present at mealtime and had been otherwise distracted in the control room. As Henry massaged his legs in the cabin in the dim light of the wind-up torch, the ship came to life and a strobe of lights flickered throughout the hallways and cabins, finally remaining on.

"Hepburn!" Henry screamed, forgetting his aches and running up the sloping corridors toward the stairwell. "The ship is alive again! It's woken up! Look how it glows! Everywhere!"

The snow leopard followed him, equally as startled and excited by the illuminations. The innards of the ship looked totally different in the brilliance of light. Colors presented themselves and dank corners became unhidden.

Hepburn stood in the control room, triumphant, if ever such a word could be said about a robot.

"What did you do? It's amazing!" Henry yelled, marveling at their surroundings.

"I've made a breakthrough. I had to replace much of the wiring, solder and re-route some of the circuitry, but we have very limited power, sufficient for lighting and, I hope, communications. It's generated mainly from solar cells today, but it is a start."

Panthera hopped onto a chair and sniffed at the flashing buttons on the console.

"What does all of this do, then?" Henry asked.

"It used to control every aspect of this vessel, which is no longer seaworthy. Most of it is just these lights."

"It looks real pretty, though. I've never seen anything like it afore! Like you've plucked stars and put them on that table," Henry replied.

There was a hum in the control room as the electricity surged through the wires and circuits of the computers that adorned the room. It was barely audible, yet Henry was aware of a presence. Something inhuman. He'd never heard anything like it before, but he realized that the things that made Hepburn walk and talk, the things that made him what he was, they were all of this.

"So, can you communicate now, Hep? With others?"

"Not at this moment, but I can look at the vessel's log whilst you sleep, which might tell us more about things. Go to sleep,

Henry. Tomorrow you will learn how to punch, and once you do, you will throw punches until you can no longer raise your arms. This is conditioning."

Henry huffed, but complied. He clicked his fingers and Panthera followed him to his cabin bed.

# TWENTY-ONE

## Canary, Caged

She'd heard the screams. They all had. And she knew – although she'd never heard such a sound come from his lips – that the screams belonged to her brother, Henry.

Yet there was nothing she could do. Bound and gagged in a bedroom suite somewhere in the belly of Moonbird, the stench of her own urine on the clothes she wore. Iris was embarrassed by the fact, but knew, like everything else, it was not her fault.

Hilde, also bound with her arms behind her back, leaned into Iris' body, to comfort her by being as close to her as she could, unable to put an arm protectively around her little sister. Their tears met and they shared a look of terror, uncertain what was to befall each of them. Only able to imagine what was being done to the brother they'd thought lost until that moment.

The screams, unceasing and inhuman, seemed to last for an age. Not just carried from the scene immediately as their brother was dragged from the vessel, or heard as he was led into the square, through silenced crowds. Distant, even in the Bone Yard, Henry's agonizing screams could still be heard.

Mary was unmoved. Sitting upright on the edge of the bed beside them, distrait, as if she were listening to an entirely different sound to everyone else in the favela.

Iris looked at her, amazed how she could remain so calm and unaffected. Mary had not been the same since the attack on the homestead and hadn't spoken to any of them in weeks; she had somehow drawn deep inward where none could reach her, or perhaps even projected miles outward, eons from them all. Iris envied her ability to close out the noise and hide away from all that had happened to them. Iris couldn't escape any of it and she realized, although her own mouth was gagged with a filthy rag, that she was screaming just as her brother was, sharing his pain and hoping he could hear her, though it all seemed caged inside her. The inward screams of a captive.

Mary shook her head, as if remembering something, half-smiling to herself despite the gag in her mouth. Iris wondered if Mary would run if she'd not been bound like her sisters, or if she'd remain upright on the edge of the bed taking in her surroundings. Docile.

Finally, the noises ceased. As if the screams never were. Iris thought she had imagined them and that Henry had not found his way to the Favela and had not met the king. But she knew the truth of it and her only puzzle was whether he had died already, or suffered still beyond the winds that carried his cries. Part of her hoped he'd died and that the pain was over for him. That Henry was with Mother, Father and—

Footsteps. The witch, Catharin, came for her then, an elderly lady as crazy as the king himself. Catharin spat on the carpeted floor, punctuating her entrance. She went straight for Iris and took her by the arm, kicking Hilde out of the way, cackling at Mary, who acknowledged nothing. Iris tried to escape the woman's grip, but Catharin was rough with her and spiteful, pinching the skin of Iris' inside arm which made her scream out once more.

One of the accompanying guards closed the door behind them and Iris saw her sisters for the last time.

Iris traced her fingers over the figures carved in ice on the bars of the birdcage. Her nails, though bitten, had been painted burgundy, with glitter nail polish. Her eyes were jet black where ash and volcanic rock had been smeared from lids to temples, to make her look otherworldly. To show it off, her hair had been scraped up in a bun and she wore what Catharin had called a *lemon chiffon lace bridesmaid dress* that had been kept in near perfect condition. Iris had at first wondered if the dress had once belonged to Catharin, who could have been over a hundred years old, but she thought it more likely that it had been taken from someone, as were most things. Iris shivered from the cold, wishing she had a pelt of some kind around her instead.

At least her feet were warm. There were no shoes to match such a dress in the Favela and Iris was permitted to keep her boots on.

The great hall stank of blood and sweat. It was dark inside and every space was occupied. Those who had sat in the pews had to stand, because others had blocked their view. All eyes were upon her and there was an atmosphere in the room; a great expectation.

Toward the back of the room where Iris stood, a hole cut into the ceiling allowed light into the room and the steam and heat from the scores of bodies to escape and prevent the building from melting from within. Snowfall entered the room with the light from above and separated the birdcage from the crowd. The effect was beautiful.

Iris was nervous. But she'd been well prepared. From the moment the witch, Catharin, had taken her, she'd been held in a great house made of ice and the lessons had begun with much ceremony.

She recalled a female guard sat on a chaise, flicking through the faded and worn pages of a brochure of some kind. Iris' bonds had been untied some days previous and the marks caused by them had faded from her wrists and ankles. At the time, Iris had deliberated how much she could hurt Catharin, or whether she could kill her before the guard could pry her off. That thought was broken by the sound of music, which came from a small white cube the size of a thumbnail that the old lady had placed before them.

Catharin had closed her eyes and nodded her head to the

music, which filled the room to Iris' alarm. The only percussion she had known was the clap of hands, or the sound boots made in the snow. The only strings she had heard had been the wire that whistled in the winds about the homestead. The only vocals she had heard came from her family, from songs remembered and passed down, but never in such perfection; notes sung like they were played by hand somehow. Iris had never heard this song. It was new – which meant it was extremely old. The words sung were beautiful and crafted in a way so unlike the speech of the modern world. Iris felt her heart race and realized that her right foot had been tapping along to the beat of the music and her fingers danced against her thighs. She felt so much through the music. Joy and great sadness, peace and so much excitement. The song finished and Catharin, opened her eyes finally.

"Once upon a time, old 'un folk would venture underground with a yellow bird they called Canary. When its wings flapped, it meant the air was bad. The canary was their light. They held it dear. But it was also their slave. Their fodder. You, my little bird, are our fodder, and you shall sing for your sup. Sing songs like that' un."

"I can't. I can't do that. I've never—"

"You will. I will teach you, and beat you if you can't. Lots more music where that came from, hidden in that little box. Only you and me get to unlock it. It's a priceless treasure, this 'un, powered by the very sun itself. More anteek in years than even I, if you could ever believe it."

Iris had asked where it had come from and all she'd learned was that it was found in Moonbird and could be charged by the sun. It held many songs, of many different voices and sounds. Fast ones and slow ones. Uplifting tales and heart-breaking ones. Iris was intrigued and touched by it all. It was like her forebears were speaking to her. Showing her a world that had died off.

"Dunno who put the music in there. But I wondered over whether this was all the music from the old world, or whether there was more of it. Did this one Great-Great leave us music that all thought the best of the lot, or was it noise to most?" Before leaving Iris alone for the rest of the day, Catharin said,

"Pick a song. Learn it. If I like what you sing, you get a chowder in the morn. Otherwise you go hunger some."

"But—"

"It's this, or salvaging in the ruins of the underbelly. A girl your age and size? It'd make a nice graveyard for you in no time. Let them sisters of yourn go visit them pretty bones. Singing for sup? This is the charmed life up here. This is what you will do."

Catharin and the guard left Iris alone then, to listen to the tiny sound box.

The first song she played became the song she would fall in love with for the rest of her existence. It took weeks fed on morsels to earn a proper chowder and she'd been prodded, poked and – once – bitten by Catharin, the witch. She'd thought about hurting Catharin on most days, but she had become frightened of losing access to the music in the little box, which kept her spirits high and made her want to get up in the mornings.

Catharin, surprisingly, had a wonderful voice. After many lessons, she had told Iris the full tale of her ancestor, a famous actress loved by all in the world. When the Ever Winter came, she had been stripped of her riches and imprisoned in a cage, where she was to sing for all. She belonged to all. Catharin had been born into her status and her slavery. The girl hated and pitied Catharin equally. If Iris closed her eyes, she couldn't believe that the notes sung to her came from the old lady. Yet the old lady was just that; her voice did tire and her breath was short partway through a difficult song. Was that the very thing that made Catharin so bitter and twisted?

Finally, Iris was ready for her moment. The big reveal of the debutante. The long-awaited new Canary of the Favela.

She looked over at the old woman, Catharin. She felt that somehow, for Catharin, it was a bittersweet moment. The old lady had done her duty and found her successor. She had trained Iris how to sing and perform. She had guaranteed the music for years to come, and Iris understood then that her only reward would be to fade from people's memories; to become invisible like the elders that had come to age before her.

Iris was nervous, but she was ready to command the audience. For endless hours she'd practiced, scolded by Catharin every time a note was wrong, or even a phrasing or gesture slightly off. In the end, she found that she could sing. She could pour her heart into the music and sometimes, the words would bring images to her as she sang; the faces of those she loved that she would never see in this world again.

Music had become a drug to Iris. She needed to hear the sounds from the little cube every day. Sometimes she just played the same song, over and over. Other times she would skip tracks until she found what she was after; what she needed for that day, or that hour.

Catharin screamed for quiet in her shrill voice. Near silence filled the room. Lanner stood by the doorway, Iris could see his silhouette. The room was a single, breathing creature. A great beast, made of many.

Iris steadied herself, holding onto the bars of the cage in which she had been placed. The cage was beautiful and it was hers. It was the barrier between Iris and all that filled the darkened room. The snow that fell beyond its intricately carved bars was another.

She took a deep breath as all waited. Iris hadn't started, but she already had command over them.

Sitting beside the cage was her band; an old blind man with a cigar box instrument devised out of junk that had a single string to it and a younger fellow with his hair in a mess of tangled curls, holding a sealskin drum upon his knee.

They waited, as the crowd did, for the Canary to sing.

She took her time, feeling an invisible energy build in the room. Still the snow crept into the room from the breach above.

*"We passed upon the stair, we spoke of was and when…"*

# TWENTY-TWO

# Changeling

The vessel log had shown nothing new. A captain's recorded diary had shown insight into the individual who had commanded the ship more than a century before, but it revealed no secrets and was of no interest to Hepburn, or even Henry, who had by now seen a number of holographic images of the past since finding the stricken vessel.

The only good to come from the robot's maintenance of the vessel was the achievement of getting lights working in most of the accessible areas of the ship. Pushing darkness away had lifted Henry's mood, and from a practical standpoint it meant he no longer had to take his torch everywhere with him and tended to bump into things less inside the vessel.

What Henry had enjoyed, however, were the tactical streams that the robot had played in the evenings as he nursed his aching muscles and joints. Hepburn had actual footage of battles which had been turned into aids for military training; drone and helmet camera footage of assaults on encampments and fortifications, as well as examples of defense against armies of various strength and number.

The projections also showed one-on-one combat, some of it taken from staged fights in rings and cages, or tournaments with many people watching, unlicensed brawls and purpose-made military footage.

To counterbalance this was the peace that came from the teachings and the philosophy that came from the martial arts; the history of them, and the beliefs that they were more than fighting. They were a way of life. A way of training the mind as well the body. A way of committing to something that was unselfish, that taught respect in a battle arena and in a person's day-to-day life.

Henry realized that much of the footage showed men fighting with weapons he had never seen or heard of. Guns of all types, hand grenades and missiles; things that seemed simple to use, yet caused so much damage and destruction. Henry was glad they were absent and alien in the new world. These things, these implements were the opposite of the martial arts he was being taught by the robot and so Henry focused on the modules with hand-to-hand combat, or rudimental weapons that Lanner's men and others in the modern world might use.

He'd scoured the ship and the containers, and the most dangerous items of weaponry on board were the fire axe, an arsenal of chef's knives in the galley of the ship, and some of the tools that the chief engineer had been responsible for. Henry decided to fashion his own weapon and assemble it with Hepburn's help.

Joining metal to metal was no easy task and Henry would not have been able to generate enough heat from a simple fire to melt and bond what he needed to make something new. Surprisingly, Hepburn supported this also. The robot stated that it was good for Henry to have such a project and the outcome would also be effective in the planned battle itself.

Henry began sketching his idea in the dust of the office wall, until he uncovered a whiteboard and pen. He spent some days drawing different weapons based on the items he had available. He thought of different ways to join the items and different materials they might use. He had experienced a blow from a wooden broom handle when Yaxley had crept up on him on the icescape a few months prior. It had knocked him unconscious, but the broom had snapped with the impact of that single blow.

He needed a weapon that would survive as many blows that were aimed at or rained down upon him.

After much scavenging through the vessel, Henry assembled his materials and gave Hepburn his instructions on how to bond the items using the robot's lasers to cut and melt the pieces into one. The crowbar was melted down with the remains of spanners, drill-bits, hammer ends, shackles, bolts and other items from the engine room and deck store. The new mass was stretched and rolled into a new shape, then fused and set with other items.

The final result, after it had cooled in the snow outside, was a deadly-looking staff, spiked at both ends with knife blades and axe heads below each spike. It could be used to spear an enemy, but also to swing at them and slice them with. It was light enough to wield, but strong enough not to shatter, or bend. The staff itself could be released in the middle, so it became two shorter weapons; a surprise in battle for an unsuspecting assailant.

Henry practiced with his new weapon, getting used to the weight, the basic handling and how he could manipulate it if he held it at different positions on the shaft.

Henry smashed the ice with it to fish the waters beneath, and used it to hunt, though he found nothing big enough to kill with it. He hadn't seen one in some time, but Henry even reckoned his new weapon would help him bring down a Big White if he ever had to. The staff would be more than up to the task of killing a human, but as Hepburn had stated more than once, killing another human in battle was the real test; more than physical, it was an emotional, mental thing.

Hepburn thought Henry a soldier. But he was barely a hunter. He had the anger to kill, and he'd wanted to, every step he took toward the Favela. And he was learning quickly how to defend himself. How to cause pain to another. How to render someone useless. He'd killed things for food, but he'd never hurt another human. He remembered the childlike eyes of the seal and wondered if he could've killed it if it'd been able to speak. If it could plead for its life.

~

Henry took scissors from a drawer in the galley, stood in front of the mirror and began to cut his hair.

Watching the training footage each night, he'd observed that no matter what era or what army was shown, none of the fighters depicted had long hair. He thought of the way Lanner had dragged him from the frozen waters and of the way the king had used a blade to remove every hair from his scalp. Long hair was good to keep the ears and neck warm, but in battle, it was a hindrance.

As his hair fell to the floor, he tried to recognize himself as the boy that had lived happily in an igloo with his family, all the while wishing he could leave and find others in the world.

When Henry was done cutting his hair, he chucked the scissors into the sink before him. The image in the mirror looked strange. It stared back and moved slightly as he did. The very shape of his face seemed totally different to how it had always been. He felt a chill on his neck as a draught crept into the cabin from elsewhere in the ship. No longer could Henry hide the lens protruding from his eye-socket. He examined the scarring. He compared it to his perfect, unchanged eye. He covered the lens with one of his hands, to imagine that behind it, his other eye was also perfect and unchanged. Then he let his hand fall to his side. He supposed he looked frightening, and that in itself might help him in battle. No longer a boy. But something inhuman. Raw and cold, like the robot.

## TWENTY-THREE

## Time Travelers

---

*Henry was back in the homestead, lying warm in his old sleeping bag. He could smell something in the pot. A stew. So familiar.*

*Nothing was broken. All was as it had been. The backgammon board and its pieces set mid-game. A book carefully placed in a plastic bag. Henry knew the page would be folded carefully to mark where the reader was up to.*

*There was another scent in the igloo. It was always there. The scent of his family. Their hair and their bodies. Something he'd never noticed before, but in this dream, it was so distinct.*

*Above Henry, a lightning bolt of glass turned slowly in the center of the room, and he watched it as it captured the reflections of each of his siblings and his parents, sleeping peacefully.*

*Henry allowed himself to smile as he watched his family in the glass as it turned, then he dared to grin, unable to contain his happiness, yet he remained silent, not wanting to wake them. They were alive and they had been alive all along. Henry had been mistaken!*

*A thought tried to connect in his mind and it made no sense, so he pushed it away.*

*And still they slept and the shard of mirrored glass showed him Martin and Iris. Mother, Father and the bairn. Hilde, then Mary.*

*For a split second, Henry looked away from the glass and saw that he was alone in the room. None of his family was there. Yet when he looked at the turning glass once more, there they were! Sleeping!*

*He checked again, looking at the places in the room where they would each have slept, yet his family was gone from the real world and slept imprisoned in the glass.*

*Henry tried to make a sound, to call out to them, but it would not come. It was as if someone was sitting on his chest and he couldn't let the air in or out. But something knew! Something knew he'd seen them and spotted the trick of it! And the glass stopped moving, then turned the other way, faster than it had been. And they all slept peacefully as the glass spun faster still, whirling their images into one; a kaleidoscope of his family, then a blurred, whirling mess, broken when the glass shattered and its pieces splintered the room.*

❧

Henry woke with a start, sweating profusely, finally able to relax his chest and let the air out of his lungs before taking a fresh sip.

Hepburn knelt beside him in the cabin, its digital faceplate illuminated green in the dark of the room.

"You are still having bad dreams, Henry."

"No. I'm not," he lied, placing his hand on his neck, feeling the cold sweat upon it.

"Do you dream about your parents, Henry?"

"No. I do not."

"I believe that is untrue," said Hepburn, with its pixel eyes somehow projecting concern. "There is no expiry date for grief. It will creep up on you and surprise you just when you thought you were over the worst of it. You should not feel ashamed, Henry."

The words wounded him and took the air out of his lungs. Their images came back to him. The dream just seconds before had brought them all to him, as if they'd traveled through time, or he had.

"I loved them all so much," Henry said, then threw his arms around the machine and cried hard upon his armored shoulder, with his face pressed next to the painted flag of Greater Britain.

"Let it out, Henry," Hepburn instructed. And Henry did.

"I could smell them. My family. And I could see them in the

glass. I was there with them all around me and it felt so real, Hep. It was so real. But they're gone. I know they are. But for a second, I had them all back! And I didn't want to wake. Because I knew...what I know now. All the things that...I wanted to stay there. I wanted to just be with them and not wake up..."

The robot listened and held Henry in his manufactured arms.

Henry could sense that the robot was assessing him still, probably silently referring to old modules available to him, to determine if he was satisfied that Henry had reached the next stage in the process. 'The process was progress', he had once informed Henry.

This time, Hepburn 8 stayed silent and matched no words with ones that Henry had spoken.

Unembarrassed and unashamed, Henry stayed in the cold embrace of the droid.

Panthera watched the whole thing, but was too comfortable to move from where he lay. He found humans and now robots beyond stupid. And long as he was fed, he would stay.

## TWENTY-FOUR

# Husk

Mary had imagined that she could pinch the air between her index finger and thumb to feel the very fabric of reality, then peel back the layers of it, kind of like skinning an animal. These things were visible only to her, and she chose to believe that she alone could pull back one of those layers and slip inside, to a safe place. Each layer was a world where she wasn't being harmed; a place where bad things didn't happen to those she loved. Each layer was further away from the real world, and for Mary to get furthest away, she pinched and pulled as many layers apart as she could, which took many days. Only now and then could she hear whispers from the real world. Echoes of ghosts. Yet they sounded so far away it was like a dream. In the place where Mary resided, her parents still lived, although she hadn't seen them yet. The deepest layer.

Mary had been aware when her youngest sister, Iris, had been taken away. But it felt like a trick, to get her back from the deepest layer – to make her leave her sanctuary and go back to the house of pain. Mary let it go, not trusting the ghosts that called out for her, and she stayed, in case Mother or Father appeared. She sensed they were both looking for her in the safe place.

Her other sister, Hilde, had tried to speak to her often, but Mary couldn't make out the words from so far away; most of them got lost in the layers that separated them. She didn't wish Hilde any ill and wished she could pass a message back to her sister, but of course the words would be lost, and the husk of Mary, sitting in a bedroom in the real world, wouldn't receive anything. That Mary was mostly useless now.

Catharin, *the witch*, as Iris had named her, visited Hilde and the Mary husk regularly to push food into their mouths and make sure it was swallowed. Mary sensed this from an almost aerial view. The Mary husk ate and so she was sustained in the other place. It was important for the Mary husk to eat, for the time at least. Mary checked on her just as often as the witch did, but spent most of her time in the deepest layer, where it was safe for her.

She did not know how it had happened, but when the safe Mary returned to the bedroom to check on the Mary husk, she found that Hilde was alone, sobbing. The Mary husk, her mortal carrion, had gone.

Mary searched for her, haunting the corridors and suites of Moonbird in panic, finding no trace of the body that had belonged to her. She'd had no warning of this and was unsure how long she'd been in the deepest layer, or if time moved differently there.

Outside it was twilight and the sun and moon shared different ends of the sky. The Favela was silent. Even the guards slept at their posts and Mary could see no place where the Mary husk could be, although two sets of fresh footprints trailed from the super-yacht to higher ground away from the Favela.

She followed the prints at speed, soaring like a wraith through the winding lanes of the Favela until she passed the last hovel. Up ahead, she could see her husk being led gently up the side of the volcano, then disappear as it descended over the horizon, into the basin.

There were no guards. None with weapons. As Mary caught up, she saw that the Mary husk was seated dutifully on a rock, looking up at the stars that dwindled as the sun rose.

The king, wearing a pale blue snowsuit, a helmet with Quiksilver written on it and reflective goggles, was crouched twenty feet from the scene, talking to a creature unlike anything Mary had imagined. A truly demonic entity, scorched and wretched; a travesty of a being that any would be loath to behold.

"You come to me in the sweet light. The blue hour," the demonic god said. His voice was low and hoarse.

The king kept low, stooped in a way that he would allow none in the Favela to witness.

"I do. With an offering to you, my god. A sacrifice."

The god was mostly naked save for a pelt strung about his waist. Yet he did not flinch in the cold, though the basin offered some protection from the wintry squall. The king's layers of man-mades were a stark contrast.

The god looked at the Mary husk, who hadn't moved from the rock on which she sat.

"This? Why do you bring this to me?" he demanded. His skin was unlike anything Mary had seen. It was a lava crust; a map of the world, with deep-cut rivers and ranges of mountains upon it.

"She is untouched by all men. My entire citadel would have her, but I bring her to you, to do as *you* wish. She is my gift so that you look upon me with favor, like you did with those who stood here afore me." The king raised his gaze, then dropped it at the sight of the god, who was truly grotesque.

"Look upon *you* with favor? Not you and your people?" The king paled at this and chose to remain quiet. The god did not question the man further. "I will accept this offering. Bring her to me, then go."

The king turned, keeping his eyes averted from the god, then motioned toward Mary, who hadn't moved from the rock. He raised her to her feet and looked her in the eyes.

"You do me a great service, Mary. Thank you," he said to the mute girl, adding, "yours will be a grand death."

"Bother me no more, king. This is my sacred place, the gateway to whence I came. Disturb me none. Or I might come knocking at your house – and you might not like that." The god looked at the husk of the girl and pointed to the entrance of a cave below them in the basin.

"Go," the god instructed and the girl walked toward it as if drawn by unseen forces.

The king bowed once more, then climbed up toward the edge of the basin, leaving the volcano swiftly for the safety of the Favela

Mary caught up with her husk as she reached the mouth of the cavern, uncertain what the god would do next. She pinched her finger and thumb and peeled back some of the imaginary layers between them, so she could be closer to the surface of the real world. She wondered if the god held the secrets to the deepest layers; if he was the one who could find Mother and Father, or Henry, who the king had said had been banished into the wilds alone. She realized that if her husk were to be killed, she would find her parents soon enough.

A half-buried human skull bit the ground at Mary's feet. There were other bones too, all human, scattered and by the entrance itself, an assemblage of hollow craniums piled deftly on top of each other.

She had heard of gods from Mother. She knew of Thor and Odin. She knew of the Christ-God and of Mohammed who had hated him. As she peered into the darkness of the cavern that wound deep into the volcano, she thought of only one god, that now ruled the Mary husk. This was the demon god. *Destruction. Accuser. Deceiver. Father of Lies. Blood orange skipper. Murderer. Lucifer. Son of Perdition. Tempter. Thief. Angel of the Bottomless Pit.* And that is where they went.

# Part Two

# TWENTY-FIVE

## Pickings

It had been a year, more or less, since Henry had been saved upon the icescape by a Nightingale android. Henry could back-flip. He could run for an hour solid without feeling tired and roll through the air into a somersault when he willed it. He could flip to a standing position from lying flat on his back. With the improved strength in his arms and legs, Henry could climb up the sides of the vessel and use his momentum to swing across awkward crevices to aid his ascent.

Hepburn had told him he wasn't just battle-fit; he had the strength, dexterity and fitness levels that would legally permit him to fight in the harshest environments on Earth. Hepburn had named places that Henry had never heard of, but in the end, Henry supposed the only environment that mattered was the one they all lived in.

Henry could throw kicks and punches continuously without tiring. He could block and parry blows dealt to him under a continuous assault, without needing to drop his guard at any time. Henry had balance and movement. He could read the terrain and the environment about him. In the training sessions, whenever Hepburn projected assailants, Henry knew instinctively where to take cover and how to get close to them without being an open target. He understood the anatomy of a human body; the areas to strike that would disable someone, or render them unconscious. He knew where and how to kill someone in theory, and in theory, he could do it.

Panthera had also become a master on the projected battlefield and a true partner to Henry in training. They understood each other and had developed signals between them – originally designed for military attack dogs – for different commands and maneuvers.

Henry got up early as usual. He no longer needed Hepburn to summon him for training. He desired to be better, and he was. Father had never been as fast, or as strong, or as skilled in combat. Henry knew this just by what he had learned from the robot and his arsenal of training projections.

When he reached the slanting deck of the MV Greyhound, he was surprised to find Hepburn at the bow, staring into the distance. He called to the robot, but no response came and so Henry made his way to where his companion and teacher stood.

Hepburn wore a digital frown, more serious than usual, yet when it spoke it was monotone and absent of fear or concern.

"There was a fire in the night, not far from here. An encampment, set by humans, who are now mobile and heading this way."

"An encampment?"

"Six adult humans, five male, one female. Primitive weaponry bar one handgun; right-handed Browning 9mm Hi-Power MOD 1935. Take a look."

The robot pointed into the distance. Henry followed its arm with his gaze but could see nothing, not even on the horizon. Then he allowed his vision to travel forth, his lens taking the lead to bore the distance between the vessel and those who were heading toward them.

"Three kilometers," Henry said, seeing what Hepburn had been looking at already.

Six from the Favela laughed and joked as they packed their belongings into an otherwise empty sled, pulled by a pack of disfigured animals. Henry could not see a gun upon any of them straight away, but recognized two of the group immediately. Erasmus, the woman from Lanner's group who had been there when he'd been hauled from the ice. She who'd tossed a limb from the long pig to the paupers in the lanes. She who'd been there when Father and Mother died. Now she wore a black leather coat that flapped in the wind like a black flag. And there was Skindred, the betrayer, wearing a fur tunic Henry hadn't remembered him wearing before.

"It's as if they're right in front of me. They don't know I can see them," Henry mused. "They're so far away, but still..."

"By installing your new optics, you were improved."

Henry paused and focused in on Skindred, feeling annoyed that he'd imagined him so many times as he was on the day Martin died. Seeing the boy in a fur tunic, different from his memory, made Henry feel like his mind had betrayed him. What else had changed?

"Skindred. He's a big part of it. If he hadn't told them – if Lanner hadn't been waiting for me by the ice – how different might that day have been?"

Henry turned from the robot and walked toward the funnel ramp, holding his weapon upon his shoulder.

"Where are you going, Henry?" the robot asked.

"My morning training. They won't be here for a couple of hours," he replied, realizing that he was about to have his first real test. Nothing would be projected. Every blow would be dealt with intent to kill him. And he would respond in kind to each of them.

The first sign was a black vulture, soaring high above the terrain. It followed the humans, no doubt hoping they would leave some pickings, or that at least one of them would expire and become the very morsels the great bird craved.

Henry stood before the ship, practicing the kata he had mastered already. Panthera watched from the roof of the Duesenberg, parked neatly between two containers.

Henry felt both calm and exhilarated at the same time. He was excited about what was to come. The fear was there, but it was muted by his surety in what he could do. As one of the training projections had said, Henry had become a weapon.

As the vulture neared, six dots on the horizon appeared with the rolling mist as pack dogs dragged their sleigh toward the vessel. Henry paid them no heed and continued training, ready for what was to come. He noted a shift in the dots that approached. No longer a rabble, they had collected themselves all of a sudden, walking an equal distance from each other, with tighter grips upon their weapons and more purpose in each stride. Henry allowed his eye to take him to them once more. He saw how their expressions too had altered. First, they had seen only the ship, but then they had spotting a human figure casting shapes and movements in the snow, along with the imposing figure of Hepburn, still watching from the deck of the vessel. The invaders proceeded with caution, clearly uncertain how many people awaited them inside the superstructure, or how many lay in wait around the containers, ready to ambush.

The pack dogs were secured and the sled left with them. Only the humans proceeded. The vulture flew higher, perhaps sensing that blood was about to be spilled.

Henry ceased his training, for that time was now over, and he knelt on the powder snow with his weapon laid at an angle before him. He waited for the invaders to get closer. He waited for recognition, for he was no doubt assumed by all to be long dead.

"What is your strategy?" the robot asked.

"Skindred's gun. He was probably given it for doing some bad chub, or took it from someone."

Hepburn scanned the approaching group once more in silence. It focused on the weapon that Skindred had armed himself with, the Browning pistol he'd already identified. But this time he looked closer, beyond the outer casing, through the metals it was constructed of, studying the firing mechanism up close and the chamber where the bullets would be held.

"It is unloaded," ascertained the robot.

"I know. You did a good job on my eye. I peeped it up close. Through and through. He brandishes that thing like a tool. I think, even if he had bullets, he couldn't ever fire it like a Great-Great. That took more skill than he could get."

"What is your strategy?" the robot asked once more.

"You said six. Six with primitive weapons. Six that won't have any idea that I've trained for so long to outfight them. To outlast them." Henry nodded, agreeing with his words as he spoke them out loud. "My strategy is to let them think of me as the boy they dragged to his fate. The boy that screamed for life, then death. When they see him, their confidence will grow and they will expect nothing that follows."

"You plan to fight them in the open, all at once?"

"No. I'm going to use the ship. I know it well. It's ours. They can't all attack me at once in the hallways."

"From a military perspective, that is your best option. Henry, you are a well-trained soldier. I wish you great stealth and victory."

"Thanks, Hep. Those are not the Great-Greats. If I can't deal with six here today, then going to the Favela is nothing but folly. I need this test," Henry said.

The group drew closer, having left their pack dogs tethered together on the ice behind them.

Hepburn remained silent and became a spectator and it looked to Henry that it was simply waiting for the battle, waiting for a call to provide medical aid to his unit of one serving soldier.

He wondered, had Hepburn been a human, whether he might've shown signs of fear, expectation, or even excitement. Yet, the robot was perfectly still and his pixel smile matched it effortlessly.

It was Skindred who recognized Henry first and announced with relief that an unseen army wasn't waiting in the wings to resist them.

"It's the boy. The brother. Henry!" he exclaimed, waving the gun in his hand like a club. His dreadlocks hung over his face and he tried to blow them out of his eyes. "Done him once. Get to do it all over again!"

"The dead brother lives? Let us do him proper this time!" Erasmus held her claw hammer aloft and quickened her pace.

Her leather overcoat trailed behind her, whipped up by the wind like a black flag.

"What about that thing up there?" one of the invaders asked, looking to Hepburn. None of them had seen the snow leopard on the Duesenberg.

"It moves, use your cutters. We got enough to sort all here. Then we look for the loot the sister promised."

*The sister.*

The invaders approached in an arc, no doubt intending to close a circle around Henry. Panthera sat up on the roof of the car and mewled, but Henry spoke to the creature and he too relaxed his stance and waited for the invaders to move in. On seeing the car finally, the invaders halted and stared in awe, reminding Henry of the time he'd first seen the original Duesenberg with Father and Mary. Yet it was just something else for the invaders to take in, a prop alongside the majestic form of an ancient container ship. It was all new to them. All promised treasure.

"Ain't ever spoken to the dead before. Can you hear me, dead boy?" Erasmus spoke when they were close enough for Henry to hear. She spun the hammer in her hand continuously, clearly eager to use it. Henry raised his head slowly, displaying his shorn hair and altered face.

"Cunk! What done to him? Dayum!" said one of the invaders, a tall yellow-haired man with a plaited beard.

"Looks like some diablo," added another, looking as uneasy as Skindred, who seemed unable to meet Henry's gaze. Still Henry remained silent, calculating the moves he would make to deal with the imposing threat closing about him.

"Leave me alone," Henry spoke finally, his voice fragile, cracking, to the delight of those that faced him.

"Don't see a devil. This just a scared, dead boy we gonna put under. Done and dust. Slim, go an' fetch him so we can make him double-dead," Erasmus ordered the yellow-haired man, who nodded and approached Henry.

The man held a weapon that had been fashioned from antlers; an impressive fork with a handle that furled around his lower arm. He took several steps toward the boy, who remained perfectly still, a statue of himself. Henry felt his heart race in his chest, knowing his months of training would either get him through the moments that were to follow, or not. Outwardly, he gave nothing away. It was all part of the wider plan. *Stealth and victory.*

Henry let out a whistle – a command they'd rehearsed during the many training modules – and Panthera sprang up from the roof of the car and fled the scene. The group facing Henry smirked and sniggered, assuming the creature had deserted the boy and further reduced the threat toward them.

"Seems it knows when it's time to roll over. *Vergonha.* Shame you don't, boy. We'll teach you," one of Erasmus' men, a short man with a flat face, his nose stubbed short from frostbite, spoke for the first time.

"Please. Don't hurt me again," said Henry with sincerity. Then, without waiting for a response, he ran, turning the corner of the first open container, where he was out of sight.

"Oh, that pup gon' get hunted. Slim, Skindred, bring him back here," Erasmus ordered and the boy and the man set off after Henry, each taking a different route around the first container, into the maze of rectangular prisms.

"Here, cunk," called Skindred as he searched for Henry, his gun held as a truncheon.

Slim joined in from several containers away. "Come out, pup."

Then there was the sound of clawed feet sprinting on the ice and Panthera appeared in front of Slim. The man raised his arm and readied the antlers, unaware that Henry was behind him, having quietly lowered himself from the roof of a container. Panthera stood unmoved, obedient to his unseen master.

Henry smashed Slim hard on the back of the head with a blunt end of his weapon, sending the man crashing into the side of a container. The noise echoed around the metal maze and it was unclear exactly where it had originated from. Henry tried to imagine what was going through Slim's mind. Surprise at the suddenly changed odds? An idea of what might follow? A fleeting sense of helplessness, like when a boy had an eye taken from him in a room full of adults?

*Kill.* "*Matar.* Double-dead, Slim," Erasmus bellowed from where she waited with the rest of her crew, clearly imagining an outcome only in her favor.

Slim had time to turn and see the effigy of the boy before him as Henry, in a single arachnid movement, flipped his body back on the ground and used his legs to kick the yellow-haired man's knees at the same time, sending him head-first onto the ice, flat out before Henry.

Henry was in a new position then, crouched over the bewildered invader with a speed that none would have expected from him. He took hold of Slim's arm and smashed him over and over in the face in quick succession with the man's own antlers, reducing it to a pulpy mess that only the vulture would appreciate. It was a horror to behold, but Henry did not intend to wait for the others to arrive and marvel at his creation.

Looking at the snow leopard, it was clear to Henry that the smell of blood was intoxicating to the animal and it pressed a paw on the man's chest and another on his skull before burying his head in the meat of him. Yellow hair was then strawberry blond with crimson streaks.

Skindred turned the corner and Henry enjoyed that the boy was met suddenly with the view of the animal wrecking his companion and Henry covered in much of the man's blood. Their eyes found each other. The smile faded fast from Skindred's face and he was rooted to the spot, transfixed. To Henry, he looked like he was wishing he was somewhere else.

"Over here! Quick!" Skindred yelled the alarm to Erasmus and her crew, seemingly not able to take his eyes from Henry.

Panthera continued to feast on the remains of Slim, but kept a watchful eye on the dreadlocked boy.

"You look frightened," Henry smirked, but rather than attack Skindred, he picked up his weapon, whistled to the snow leopard, who ceased his meal, then fled the scene with the beast, side by side at equal pace. They zig-zagged the maze, with Henry letting Skindred catch eyes on them every now and then through the gaps in the containers. Then Henry and his cat scaled the funnel that led to the deck of the vessel beyond.

## TWENTY-SIX

## Underbelly of a Dead Dog

Erasmus swore when she arrived at the scene where the remains of Slim were opened up for an intimate view.

"I just got here," Skindred lied, pointing at the ramp that led to the deck of the ship. "Think he went up there, with the beast."

Erasmus screamed and ordered her crew to follow her, charging out of the labyrinth of containers, up to the superstructure of the MV Greyhound, where the dimples of portholes could just be made out in the rime.

The deck was silent apart from the wind. The gratings they all stood on were a frozen grid of squares, no longer giving any grip to those that trod the deck. In front of them, the door hatch was wide open, inviting them into the dark unknown. Traces of Slim's blood dotted the walkway in between.

"Skindred, you wait for us here. If he comes out before we do, kill him. You fail to do that, *you* get my cutters." Erasmus spoke with authority, clear with her intentions, yet she added, "*Entender?*" *Understand?*

The boy nodded, relieved to be left outside with a view of the panorama. Then a shiver went up his back. "*Esperar.*" *Wait.* "Where's that thing that was up here? The metal creech?"

"Must be in there with the boy and the animal. We'll get it. We'll get them all, and no quick death either." Erasmus didn't wait for a reply this time and she led the way through the open hatch, into the narrow corridor where the corpse of a Great-Great lay under a tangle of frozen cobwebs thirty feet from the entranceway.

The corpse, a female, was clothed in a once-red all in one suit and had her hair scraped back from her face. Her face was illuminated by the faint green glow from strips that lined the corridor. Her skin was taut, glistening with a sheen of ice, and only the eyes – gray and congealed where they should have been white – really gave it away that this wasn't a person that had just fallen asleep. As they looked on, a tiny spider emerged from the corpse's mouth and disappeared around the side of her neck, looking for something it hadn't yet found.

"Dead girl in man-mades. Is she a—"

"A Great-Great. *Si*," Erasmus interrupted her cohort.

"*Escute*." Listen. "This place gives me the creeps."

"This relic makes Moonbird look like a speck."

The four of them moved carefully past the well-preserved body, each of them off-balance and unsure of their footing, as the vessel had listed at an angle before it had frozen so long ago. Each struggled to see in front of them as they went deeper into the ship, where no portholes dragged light into the superstructure. The corridor opened into a stairwell and gave them a few choices: go up, go down, or proceed straight on where the tilted walkway was flanked by door hatches leading to unknown rooms.

Erasmus signaled for them to stop. They listened to the silence of the ship. Nothing moved, or creaked.

She knew that somewhere, Henry waited, finding comfort in the familiar darkness to him.

Erasmus called to him loudly, letting her voice travel the corridors of the ship ahead of her, "Pup. Come out and it will be done quick." When so response came, she carried on, "*Bem*, we come then. For Slim. We will take your other eye, then the rest of you. Cut by cut."

Henry waited still. He could hear the noises the strangers brought into the ship with them. Tripping over things they would not have known were there. Using hands to guide them along where even the faint glow of old safety strips had failed in time, or been covered by dust and webs. He heard them cursing to themselves and he heard them call out to each other, their fear starting to creep in and get the better of them.

He took the first one in a corridor in utter silence; placing a hand over the man's mouth, cutting him precisely and holding him until his life had gone, before letting him slip to the floor in a puddle of his own making.

A while had passed. Twenty minutes, or more. The body of the man had not been discovered by anyone, for no one had shouted in anger, or threatened for all to hear. The ship stirred, as if it knew those inside it didn't belong.

A second intruder wandered into the engine room. A walkway stretched around the vast auxiliary and main engines, high above a floor of solid ice where spider crabs dwelt in the pit having found a way into the ship through one of the rusted fissures and breaches at some point in time. Below them, shadows moved where the saltwater sea had found a way into the bottom of the ship, eroding the hull beneath the ice from within. They were predators, stalking, perhaps sensing the humans above them. *Meat is meat.* Or perhaps that part of the underbelly had simply become their home.

A body lay on the walkway clutching a clipboard, a pen dangling from it on the end of a piece of string. A draught caught the pen and swung it lightly like a pendulum, as a shard of glass once turned in an igloo home.

The intruder looked ahead at the walkway beyond the corpse. The darkness there was impenetrable. There, Henry could have been hiding, but the intruder made a decision then not to go further, scared that the darkness could swallow him and anxious that something else, something more terrible than a human, might dwell beyond the walkway in front of him. The man, if asked by Erasmus, would lie and pretend that he'd looked everywhere he'd been.

He went to turn back to the stairwell then and noticed another body in the pit below, being eaten by the spider crabs that scuttled and abided there. They feasted upon it with such frenzy that it felt strange to the man; there was something odd about it that he couldn't place at first, to do with their fervor. *A new dish? A recent addition to their menu.*

He looked back to the body on the walkway, but it was no longer clutching the clipboard and it was instead animated, already striking him with a blade, once, then twice, then a third and final time before he was launched over the handrails into the pit below to make the feast a banquet.

The weight of his body cracked the ice and stirred the predators below it so they also smacked it hard with their powerful fins and heads. The noise escaped the engine room and traveled up the stairwell, but Henry was already gone and was on his way to another part of the stricken relic.

Only the clipboard remained on the walkway in the engine room. Henry had written his name upon it, in large, uneven letters, claiming ownership of his latest work.

A body had been discovered. Henry didn't know if it was the man in the engine room or the one he'd cut in the corridor, but he'd heard a shout of frustration, which trailed off before the silent hunt had resumed.

More time passed. Henry had sensed another intruder moving toward the galley. In there, where the dead chief cook still lay upon the hob rings he'd cooked his meals on, Henry hid amongst the racks of dry and tinned food and gave a signal for Panthera to leap onto a third man, the short man with the stubbed nose, sending him tumbling over the seats where a crew would have once eaten dinner. The intruder dropped his weapon in the tumble and had no chance to defend himself. This time, the man's screams were heard throughout the ship and they were sustained as the animal bit chunks out of him.

As the mauling continued, Henry listened at the galley door

for approaching footsteps and tried to envisage where they were in the ship, knowing that the short man's tormented screams would have great effect on Erasmus, who remained alone somewhere in the vessel.

Henry signaled for Panthera to stop and the creature did. The man, bleeding heavily from his neck, was still breathing, although no medic, not even Hepburn, would have been able to save him. The man with the flat face knew he was done for, no longer trying to stem the blood from his wounds with his hands, but staring at Henry with accusation. Henry thought back to the first body he'd ever encountered; the frozen man he'd found with Father. He remembered the death stare of the corpse and how it had affected him, even later when he'd lain awake next to his brother Martin. After all that had happened since that day out with Father, looking into the eyes of a dying man no longer had any effect on him.

Henry took hold of the hood on the man's coat and dragged him across the space to the jagged breach in the side of the wall, which looked like a shark's mouth from the outside. A rubicund trail ruined the snow-covered carpet of the chamber that had been exposed to the elements. Henry hoisted the man to his feet at the edge, where the floor came to an abrupt stop, and cast him through the void, out and onto the ice below, leaving only the blood to tell the man's story.

Skindred had waited for what felt like an hour as a vulture circled in the sky high above him. He'd heard the terrible screams from within the ship, then seen the body of one of his companions, plummet from the jagged hole in the side of the superstructure. He didn't look over the side of the deck, because the sound of the body hitting the icescape, bones snapping on impact, told him that another adult from the Favela was dead.

He looked in the distance and saw the pack dogs, still tethered where they'd left them. He thought about what Erasmus had said; if Henry came out alone, Skindred should end him, or face his own death at her hands. Though the screams from within the ship had stopped, they still rang in Skindred's ears.

He didn't want to face Henry. Henry was reformed and there was something dangerous about him that was not there before. It came down to the odds of his own survival and who he feared the most in that very moment. Skindred looked one last time at the open door-hatch through which his companions had headed. He descended the funnel ramp from the deck of the vessel to the maze of rectangular prism containers. Then he ran for his life.

## TWENTY-SEVEN

## Ungodly

There had been no thunder of drums in the deep on the volcano. No hidden army under the mountainous rock, nor undead beings and creatures waiting in the fissures and tunnels, embracing the dark.

No sacrifice on that first day, or any since. No danger, although she expected to witness it upon her mortal body that rarely moved or shifted where it sat in the pit.

In the volcano, time had confused both Mary and her mortal husk. The absence of daylight and any routine fleeced her of when in the day – or night – it was. Here, there were no guards patrolling the deck of a prison, opening the door to place a meal tray upon the bed. No noise from brawling men and women, or crying children. No shouted orders from the king himself. No stinking, wretched pack dogs.

The darkness enveloped the two Marys and the husk decided she would stay, for a while at least. For she was curious. Her god was no Odin. Although he had looked wretched when she had laid eyes upon him, to her, his voice was soft.

As her eyes adjusted to her surroundings, she sensed the things that slithered and crawled on the surfaces around her. She heard the scrape and scuff of unseen insect creatures and something small and beetle-like dropped from the ceiling onto her lap before scuttling off. In another life, Mary would have cried out and been scared. But here, the two Marys felt a distinct calm in the otherwise silence and became one again for brief, fleeting moments.

The god brought her food, warmed from the deeper chambers where the very air became steam from the boiling lava rivers below. That food was, most likely, the things that slithered and scuttled in abundance. Yet she ate it and found herself savoring the taste, finding the texture similar to that of raw fish.

The voice, though it spoke of all sorts of things, offered no threat to Mary. Subconsciously, Mary pinched her index finger and thumb together. She felt them peeling back those invisible layers of reality to find her way back to the real world; to return to her mortal carrion and reclaim it.

She started to tune in to the pitch and tone of the god's voice and she decided he was an un-god. She listened as he spoke of the old Great-Greats and the old world, like her Father and Mother had. Once, he brushed her arm with his hand and she could feel the ruin of his skin; so rough and uneven. Leather, older than the volcano itself. The un-god apologized.

For the first time, listening to the soft voice of the un-god, she was able to dare remember what her life had been like before.

She pictured a girl that was her. Younger. Fair hair, blue eyes and a nose tipped up slightly at the end, just like Mother's. Smiling back from the surface of an ice hole. Her reflection rippling gently in the saltwater. Her skin had been unblemished by the sun. Never struck by a violent hand. Kissed by pursed lips if ever she had fallen, or grazed it.

She pictured a slingshot. Hers. She imagined a voice telling her to aim for a bird in the sky and remembered how she felt on doing it the first time.

Faces assembled in her mind and she was now able to cling on to those images, where for so long they had only withered in her mind into gray and bent corpses, or caused such pain that she could not dare to summon them. They lingered, as did she. She wondered if they were the apparition, or if it was she, Mary, who was the ghost, having hovered in and out of her shell for so long.

Feelings accompanied all these things, yet the pain was dull. Barely there. For how long had the velvet voice of the un-god spoken to her?

For the first time, her father appeared to her. His beard was as thick as his hair was long. His frame was huge, equaled only by his vast, warming smile that preluded the formation of creased lines around his eyes. Then the family was all there. It was so many, many nights before, when Father had for the first time in her life praised her in front of them all at once, when he spoke of her and Henry's Ritual; finding the great ship in the ice and surviving a brush with the snow leopards.

*"What they did last night, what they discovered…well, I think they've completed their Rituals. Any test now would only mug them,"* Father had said. He'd said so many things. Some more poignant. Yet this was what came to her first, after so long.

In the utter dark of the volcano, where things slithered and crawled, where an un-god spoke in the gentlest of voices, Mary, for the first time in over a year, just in secret, smiled.

## TWENTY-EIGHT

# A Ripped Black Flag

Henry walked the incline to the bow of the ship, accompanied by Panthera and Hepburn, who had stayed well out of sight during the battle but had been monitoring Henry's activities and vitals throughout. The midday sun shone bright, though nothing melted.

"He's getting away," the android announced, motioning toward Skindred, who was running as fast as he could from the ship toward the pack dogs.

A pinging noise came from the Duesenberg below them, where the passenger door was wide open.

"Must've tried to steal the car. What a cunk." Henry shook his head, then called out to Skindred across the ice that separated them. "Coward!" The word carried with the wind. "You got a head start, Skindred. But I'm coming for you."

Skindred stopped mid-stride at the sound of Henry's voice, but he never turned around. Instead, he quickened his pace and closed the distance between himself and the pack dogs.

A clang heralded the arrival of Erasmus as she appeared in the doorway and hit the steel hull with her claw hammer. She could obviously see Skindred retreating in the distance and a vinegar look appeared on her face.

Henry faced her and signaled for Panthera to sit. The animal relaxed by the bow, licking blood from its own fur. Henry

225

reached for his weapon; the war lance he'd wrought with a mélange of blades. Slowly, he made his way toward his opponent.

Erasmus nodded appreciatively. One warrior to another. Yet her hatred for him was clear.

"To your ruin, boy," she spoke, moving closer to him.

Henry said nothing.

The Duesenberg pinged to remind everyone that the passenger door remained open.

They met in the middle of the deck. Seconds passed and the silence remained. Momentarily, the vast wings of the black vulture obscured the wavering sun and it became the signal for all that was to follow.

"*Parabens*! You killed my lot, like a thief creeping up in the dark. A little devil child. But out here, I'll double-dead you mine self, boy," Erasmus threatened, no longer twirling the claw hammer in her hands but brandishing it like she meant business. "If only you knew what's become of your sisters! They're damned. Each and every one." They *are* damned. They *are*. Henry clasped onto Erasmus' choice of words, which meant *the present*. His sisters were still alive. Finally, he knew something of them.

Henry and Erasmus. One versus another. Henry smiled, thinking about the odds, unfazed by his opponent's words. They circled each other. Henry, so confident in his new abilities, was sure of the outcome. If only he'd gone to the Favela so well-prepared before!

Henry's weapon was superior. He had forged it and designed it. Its reach was far greater than Erasmus with the hammer. But he knew the murderess was strong. One hit with her weapon would end him and so he had to keep his advantage over her.

Now just the two of them, when she had arrived no more than an hour before, with her greater numbers, Henry saw the odds were fifty/fifty. Him or her.

They circled each other and Henry felt strangely confident in his new abilities. He was still unsure of the outcome as he studied his opponent, yet there was no going back.

Before he spoke, he realized that Erasmus too must have

been thinking about the same odds. How she'd expected a quick slaughter of him, and how she'd already been so wrong.

"It's you what's damned. Whether I let that black vulture come down and pick at you, once my beast over there has had his belly full. Or whether I strip your flesh with a whalebone and cook it up with a flame. You saw what I did in there. Thief? Maybe I am. Or maybe I *am* a devil. Maybe I have been dead afore. It doesn't matter, cause this next bit just has you lying on the crust, bleeding out into the snow. This is not a fair match. It never was. I know that now."

Henry was the first to swing his weapon, but Erasmus reacted and took her moment to dodge the assault and charge before it could be wielded at her again. She was close to Henry now, but once more, her coat became a black flag that signaled her intent as she moved. She swung the hammer toward him and Henry stepped aside with ease. She aimed a second swing at him, but Erasmus was so off-balance that Henry barely had to brush her arm to send her slipping onto the ice ungracefully.

"You think you'll go back there with that freak face of yours and get your sisters back?" she taunted, catching her breath.

"I know now that they're alive. After I'm done with you, when you're a carcass, I will go to the foot of the hill of the Favela and I will cut down every cunk that stands in my way. This time, I'm all for it. I have the teachings of the Great-Greats in me, and it's yours who are done for. Not I."

Erasmus, the murderess, swung the hammer twice more. Henry avoided the first swing and blocked the second, but wasn't ready for the headbutt that sent him sprawling backward. Henry's vision swirled as his enhanced optics tried to correct the vision from his human eye and moved in and out of focus.

Henry dodged another swing of the hammer. He kept moving, keeping a distance between him and Erasmus' hammer whilst his vision adjusted. He appreciated how training with projected images or with Hepburn himself was different to fighting a real person, especially one as unpredictable as Erasmus and she pronounced it, by taunting him with, "That shut you, boy."

She moved toward him, screaming like a wild creature, but Henry's vision had restored and his blade caught her shoulder, making an epaulet in her coat from a flap of torn leather. Erasmus cursed and her face registered pain. Henry didn't wait for her to recuperate and smashed the blunt shaft of his weapon on the bridge of her nose, which split on impact and spouted blood. Erasmus lurched backward, gasping for breath, clearly growing exhausted. The liquid from her nose and shoulder made a red slush in the frozen gratings.

"I'm ready to talk again," Henry provoked.

The woman took out a knife from under her black overcoat, now wielding a weapon in each of her hands. The weapons were mismatched and of different size. Henry knew this gave her no advantage; she looked awkward and off-balance. She had no fear, but he saw a desperation about her. Erasmus swung the hammer at him as she had many times, then followed with a knife lunge. Henry blocked each of these with ease and countered them with kicks to the legs, causing Erasmus to stumble as her knee gave way.

Henry gave the center of his war lance a twist and it separated at the middle into two shorter weapons. He changed his stance and crossed the weapons over each other so they formed an $X$.

They both knew Erasmus had been bettered. She was done for. Still she came at him, off-balance and barely able to stand, making it easy for Henry to parry her feeble lunges.

A swish of one of Henry's blades sent three of Erasmus' fingertips flying free of her hand. Her hammer dropped to the deck along with her fingertips. She regarded them, confounded. Then the rage returned to her face.

With a final thunderous scream, the warrior threw herself at Henry, her knife blade flashing in the sun. But it was already over. Henry tossed one of his weapons toward her chest, and before it had even connected, he raised his other armament high above his head in a two-handed grip and brought it down on top of Erasmus' skull. The momentum and power took her to her knees as the executioner's blade stuck fast where her neck met her breastplate.

A shattered face had parted into two near-identical pieces that unfurled before Henry, showing splinters of teeth and bone protruding from places they shouldn't.

Erasmus' knife was still held tight in a perpetual death-grip at her side. The two sides of her face had a carmine gulf between them. The black flag of her coat was at low mast and Erasmus was no more.

After the adrenaline passed, Henry felt no real triumph, nor release, nor regret at what he had done. He had survived his first test. A minor victory witnessed by a disinterested android and a preoccupied snow leopard. He was simply still alive.

Henry caught his breath, leaving his weapons protruding from his enemy for the time being. He scanned the horizon for the fleeing Skindred and laughed when his robotic eye found him still running from the scene in the distance, stopping only to untether the pack dogs and the sled, which were free for the taking. Henry would let the coward be consumed by his fear, then hunt him down. Henry had the Duesenberg.

Panthera mewled approval. Hepburn was silent and the vulture dared to descend upon the plain; Erasmus' blood had decanted itself from her skull, tapped from her ears, nose and mouth. It appeared to have crawled and reached out in the powder snow. Henry and Erasmus had danced across the deck of the MV Greyhound, spilling and spraying blood in what might have been a ritual, and from above, it would have looked like someone had painted a swastika on the icescape.

Looking at the drying blood on his hands, Henry decided to take a shower and try to formulate his final plan to dispatch Skindred and bring his war to the Favela. The time had truly and finally come.

## TWENTY-NINE

## The Girl Who Would be Queen

Hilde awoke with a start to find Iris standing at the foot of her bed with a young boy she'd never seen before. Iris signaled for her to keep quiet and Hilde sat up, pulling the duvet around her as a shawl.

Iris was much changed. Her hair was cut about her ears, with a fringe that met her eyebrows. She had smoky eyes and burgundy nail polish. She was self-assured, no longer a playful little girl. Iris was strangely beautiful; otherworldly, her very appearance hinting of danger. *A mini-Mother*.

"This is Boo. He's my friend. He won't tell," whispered Iris, embracing her sister for the first time in months. The two girls both looked far healthier than they had been upon arriving at the home of their captors. Both had since been given preferential treatment. Good food. Alcohol.

Hilde wore a silk nightgown that came to her ankles and thick thermal socks on her feet. A wardrobe held clothes for all seasons, neatly hung in order of color.

The boy, Boo, smiled a broad grin at Hilde. Unlike everyone else Hilde had encountered here, kindness poured from Boo and she took an instant liking to him. Some people were just like that. Hilde was not one of those people.

"How did you get in?" Hilde asked, reminding herself they were deep in the belly of *Moonbird*.

"Boo is super sneaky. He's everywhere, but no one really takes any notice of him. We get out a lot, but this is the first time we got in here. The guards sleep the whole night long. Oh, Hilde, how are you?" Iris hugged her sister once more, taking in the room around her which she'd shared for several days when she'd arrived at the Favela. Hilde had been there alone ever since.

Hilde ignored the question and settled into the embrace. "We never hugged much afore, did we, Iris? I was never a good sister." The room was not as stark as it had once been; the king had had it furnished with paintings and prints, gilded mirrors, porcelain trinkets and diamond-encrusted picture frames that held images of happy people that no longer lived. A glass case filled with murky water rested on a sideboard and inside it was a lobster, alive and ready for the pot. It seemed a strange gesture of romance, if that was what it had been.

"We've only got each other now. Boo was with Henry when he died and I heard that Mary—"

"He took her while I slept. He gave her to...at least she wouldn't have known what was happening. Her mind was gone. I like to think of Mary how she was. When we didn't get on so well. I did love her though. That whole time. We just..."

"Hilde, how are you?" Iris repeated the question again, gently stroking Hilde's face. Hilde marveled at her sister's painted nails and dared to touch them. They were an anomaly, like books had once been. Like silk gowns and diamond-encrusted picture frames.

"Once I read a book with a butterfly on the cover. I wish I had it still. Mary said that in the end, the man was freed." Hilde shook the memory away and straightened her posture. "I told him about the ship. I told the king. I shouldn't have. He'll just use it to make himself stronger. But I hoped he'd go and there would be a chance something would happen. Like a Big White. Only he didn't. He never leaves. And I'm to marry him."

"*Jag vet.* He told of it in the Birdcage. Hilde, we could kill him! Boo can help us. I will do it, for Mother and Father."

"For Henry and Mary..."

"For Martin and the bairn."

For a second, Hilde had seemed invigorated by the idea. Then, she looked behind Iris' charcoal-daubed eyes. She thought of Henry twiddling the girl's curls in his fingers whilst she lay her head upon his lap. Iris was not the same girl anymore.

"I will not let you, Iris. When I am his bride, I can do it when he sleeps, or I can do it as he takes his meal. I will be the one they accuse and make suffer. Not you, Iris. Behind this paint they have you in, you're my little sister. I will seek vengeance for both of us."

Iris's face transformed with the fiery expression that Mother had perfected when any of them needed scolding for bad behavior. She left her sister's embrace.

"And is your grief more than mine? Your pain and your loss? More than my own?"

"Iris!"

"Well? Have you seen more than I? We were not beside each other as they wrapped an anchor around Father's body and cast him below? When they murdered Mother in the igloo?"

"Iris, please…" Hilde was desperate and wounded.

"Do you remember how the bairn burned in his swaddle on the fire of the blubber lamp? Have you forgotten? I wake up every night with that smell in my nose. On my clothes!"

Boo looked confused and smiled politely. He distracted himself with the lobster in the glass tank, tapping the sides to get its attention.

"Don't talk about it. Not that. Ever."

Hilde shuffled back to the where her pillow rested on the far end of the bed. She wore the duvet protectively then and pulled it tightly about her.

"I will. Because I see it over and over, every daylight. If I don't speak of it, it will send me madder than the old witch, or Mary."

"I will end him, the king. In my own time. I promise you."

Hilde spoke calmly and measured, but her sister's response took her back.

"You will not, Hilde. We both know you will be his queen

and it will suit you. You will forget all about the family, that you never really loved and you will live here, with all these silly dresses that never keep you warm."

"I did love them. Each and every! Not that they ever favored me! Always the boys. Always Mary and you. But, still, I loved them, I won't allow what you would do. I will put a stop to it!" Hilde warned, realizing she'd raised her voice all of a sudden, a little too loudly.

"You would? You would stop me?" Iris studied Hilde.

"Don't you see? I will be his queen. And I will be your queen too. When the time is right. *I* will do it. Just me. Then, I can look after you as they would have wanted."

"Too late, Hilde. We've got to look after ourselves now. We've been failed. The king said it himself." Iris hesitated, "It's a race, then Between two sisters. His throat and his head are the end-game. Until then, play princess, or queen. I will play the Canary."

She made for the door, and Boo followed, leaving the lobster in peace in the murky water.

"Iris!" Hilde pleaded, leaping from the bed and taking her sister's hand in her own forcefully. She was angry and desperate and she was also petrified of the king and what he would do to them. To her.

"Let go, Hilde. I see you now. What you are. They were all right,." Iris tore herself from her sister's grip.

Hilde felt her temper boil and she took her hand away from Iris'.

"I won't let you do it, *little sister*. It is for me. My place!"

"Your place? This?" Iris gestured at the room around them and laughed, angering her sister.

"You don't understand. How could you? You're a child," Hilde pushed her face closer to Iris', "But I have

warned you now. Don't come back here. You would regret it." Her finger was pointed at her sister like it was a gun. Boo copied the gesture and fired an imaginary bullet at the lobster in the glass case. It was the kind of thing the salvagers would've laughed at.

Hilde regarded her sister then and felt a mix of love and hate inside her. It churned, over and over so Hilde could not work out if there was more love than hate, or if all things were equal. Then she wondered if their connection as sisters had permitted Iris to read her very mind, as the younger sibling spoke. "Remember their love, Hilde. We had so much of it." And Iris slipped from the cabin.

"Bye, bye, Hildey." Boo waved, careful to close the door silently behind them.

Hilde did not go back to sleep that night. Surrounded by ancient trinkets and obscure ornaments in the moonlight that breached her porthole, Hilde pondered her future and the decisions she would make. Hilde the invisible. Middle daughter. The least-favored sister. The obstinate. The unlikeable. She had tried and there was a moment when, in Mary's absence, she had become the trusted and the dependable. And so quickly had that eroded in front of Iris. She hated the way her sister had looked at her with such disgust. Her youngest sister, painted in the colors of death and speaking to her as if she were an idiot of some kind! She was done with Iris. She did not care what the dead thought of her.

Wrapped in the comfort of her duvet, Hilde looked at the cabin that was her cell and pictured the souls huddled in the frozen lanes at the foot of the hill. She invoked their sunken faces, their sallow cheeks and hollow eyes. She imagined their hunger.

Of all of the Favela, of all who feared the king, Hilde was the one who would get the closest to him. Out of her cell. Closest to the malevolent tyrant. Could she do it? Could she paint a smile upon her face the way Mother had once done when Lanner first arrived in the homestead? If she could, would it outweigh the alternatives? In his orbit, Hilde would be in her own position of power. A diluted version of it, but still something beyond her current status. None would dare cause her harm or speak to her with anything but respect. The king would not allow it. The king would punish all and sundry. And once the king's trust was secured, she, the obstinate girl, would become queen. Would they fear her as she did him? Would they respect the power she also commanded at his side? Out of her cell. Into his orbit.

She pondered the marriage that had been proposed and what she might become. She thought of the hideous man that would be at her side, and then she had a strange thought that did something in her brain. *Click.* One that had not occurred to her before. *Click.* If she became queen and the king was no more, would she have ultimate power over the populace? Would she be accepted in his stead? To rule. To lead above all. To have all she might desire. Such things she had yet to discover! She had come a long way and the king had chosen her, of all her sisters. What if she could choose any from the Favela to rule at *her* side? *Fear is the key.*

*Click.* Hilde remembered the love of her family and how it suffocated her. She remembered the resentment she felt every day at the homestead. But the homestead was no more and neither was that mundane existence which had been her life. It was time to forget and to move on. To elevate. It was time to write her own chapter. She had such potential! And cruelty was surely within her.

*Fear is the key.*

## THIRTY

## The Inhuman Condition

Night had fallen, and it was beautiful.

Henry gazed at the constellation he loved the most; *Canis Minor*, 'The Little Dog'. It wasn't the brightest, or the most spectacular, and that was why it was special to Henry. He had chosen it as his favorite amongst all others.

He wondered if Mary, Hilde and Iris ever looked at the same sky; if they caught the flicker of the stars he had chosen and recognized their shape. And if they thought of him. If they lived still. Henry would soon know their fate, as he met his own. He'd determined that scalping Lanner and the king at the very least would be worth his death.

Panthera lay beside him on the deck. His head was laid upon Henry's lap, and Hepburn, the miracle that had saved Henry from certain death and given him so much, sat opposite. They mirrored each other exactly. *Man and machine.*

Hepburn projected a moving image on the control tower of the vessel. There was no sound, or color. It was a man sitting at a table, sporting the same kind of mustache that the king had fashioned for himself. The man had his hands tied and he was being fed food from a machine that didn't work very well. He was trying to eat a corn on the cob, but the corn kept moving as he tried to take a bite. Henry stopped looking at the stars and marveled at the old film.

"Moodlift. It looks good on the outside of the hull, I believe."

"It does. Did people eat like that? Looks lazy," Henry replied.

"No. This is entertainment. It was considered very funny."

Henry studied his hands. He'd scrubbed the blood and there was no trace of it left, but in a way, Henry felt it would always be there.

"Did you see me out there? Hep, I didn't get hurt, but I gave 'em some. Those people who did what they did to my lot and took my eye. They're all corpses. Except the coward. I did that. Mine self." Henry watched the man in the old film slurp soup from the bowl before the next course appeared.

The robot blinked and turned his face to Henry, studying him.

"Beyond your stealth, which was impressive, you fought for barely two minutes. You did not tire. You did not face anyone of skill, or any weaponry that posed a sizable threat. If you are surrounded by an army and have to fight for even ten minutes, the outcome will be different. You're a proficient fighter, Henry, but you remain one man."

"One man, with a pet Panthera and an old robot!" Henry joked, glancing at the moodlift.

"I can only heal you if you're not quickly put to death. I am most ineffective in battle. The creature has bonded with you and I believe it will instinctively protect you where it can, as it did on the container ship, but still the odds of further victory are minuscule."

*"Minuscule,"* Henry repeated the word, deciding it was one he didn't like.

The realization was always there. Henry knew he was only alive by the mightiest of luck and that revenge was only the tiniest flicker of possibility because of Hepburn and his modules. Yet even the smallest of hopes seemed a worthwhile venture. Any existence entirely alone on the icescape, knowing that the Favela existed and that his sisters were in it amongst the Lanners, Needols and kings of the world, was no existence at all. Henry had always accepted that he would most likely die.

As he considered it then, it became the most likely truth. The reality over any dream he may have once had. Yet he accepted that over any other existence and knew there and then that he would not spend any more time sparring with his android companion or the projections he put out on the icescape. He'd no longer run circles around the MV Greyhound, treading ever deeper tracks into the ice that encased the ship. He would meet his fate, his final Ritual, and then he would join his parents and brothers in the Afterworld; the next life. He accepted everything. And it was fine.

"I know about my chances, Hep. I've been up against it since it started."

"It is good you recognize this."

"I just...I'd like to see my sisters again. It's been so long. I miss them, and sometimes, their faces don't come too easy to me. I have to think hard to remember their faces up close."

"I recall when you first spoke of the crimes committed against you and your family. I have it recorded for reference. Your voice has since changed and the words you use to express it. You have recuperated your mental wellbeing. This is a positive feat. You should be proud of the journey and your achievement, Henry."

Henry smiled. His mind had repaired in time. He felt strong, in every way, although he'd never imagined that he ever would again.

"I never told you everything. But I'd like to tell you this now," Henry cleared his throat, "Mother had lost bairns before. The cold, or sickness and both. So, they never named any of us, until they were sure we would survive. The night before I left for this place here, we named him. Our bairn. We made him real. We named him after a great being who had made it possible for us to exist as a family on the ice. The whole family was there, for the last time. It was the happiest moment. Perfect. It felt like the start of something good. New homestead. Boon of the yot-boat. Naming our brother. But I've never said his name. I couldn't. Because of what I saw when I came home. I was a coward and he deserved more. He deserved that I remember him and say his name aloud. His name, *my baby brother*, his name was Penhaligon."

"It is a fine name, Henry," Hepburn looked skyward for a moment, then elaborated, "Penhaligon means having a power of expression in speaking, or writing. Being clever and clear-sighted. Those called Penhaligon have led eventful lives. You're no coward. You're a brave soldier."

The robot placed a hand on Henry's shoulder; a learned gesture of friendship and empathy.

"You know, though you're a man-made thing, sometimes, the way you act is like a person."

"I was designed to—"

"I know what you're going to say. You've said that so many times. But you've changed since I met you. You learn, don't you?"

The robot blinked, which was something Henry had once asked it to do.

"I have learned many things, and adapted."

Panthera stirred, but did not wake. His warmth was making Henry sweat.

The man in the old film ate cubes of food that were pushed into his mouth at speed by a mechanical arm. It *was* funny. Henry laughed at the projection, feeling such relief at speaking his brother's name out loud. It had set him free in that moment, of so much guilt and pain.

"Hey, Hep. Do you think there are any other people scattered out there, like the ones in the Favela? If the Great-Greats survived in a Cano, then maybe in other parts of the world, some others did too."

Hepburn leaned in close. A human-like gesture.

"I have a purpose which is closely aligned to healing, rehabil-itating and, to some extent, protecting humans. It is why I exist. If humans do not survive, I shall still remain for a long time. I will not deteriorate as quickly as you would imagine. And so, I believe a human would call it, *fear*. I fear to exist with no purpose, knowing that I will simply *be*. I too would like to answer your question. To truly answer it."

"You're afraid. To be alone. Just like me."

"It was never calculated when I was built, for there were so many humans. So many wars. I am to accept being outdated by more enhanced versions of myself. That is logical. In that event, I would be decommissioned. I would no longer be, and my purpose would have been served. But I cannot compute being dormant, simply idle, with no rationale, rusting and crumbling into dysfunction. It is a waste of my technology. Therefore, I cannot accept, *to just exist* with no possibility of humans. I am dedicated to humans. So, your question is my question. Even through my design and limited sentience, this is true. We both *fear*. We both fear endless isolation. We both need people. I have learned this, since I learned that an event happened on this planet which diminished man and womankind to near extinction. When your battle has concluded, if you would permit it, I would seek the answer to this question, because I cannot leave the question unanswered."

Henry thought about it some more before offering a response. "That's the most you've ever said in one hit. You know, I've been harking about being alone for so long, but really, I haven't been alone at all. If I'd truly been alone, I would've lost my mind. You have been there for me. You've been my friend."

"Thank you, Henry. I have taught you much. But you have also educated an android."

"I mean it. When the battle is done, you can go and find the answer, and if I survive, I might come with."

The man in the film was unable to keep up with the food being served to him, and the machine in the projection had malfunctioned. Two men in suits were trying to fix it; smoke billowed from it and the man was struggling with the corn on the cob that was assaulting his face.

"I do hope you survive, Henry. It is an unlikely outcome, but one I prefer. For you, the battalion, Greater Britain, and also for myself. May you not die. But if you do, may it be instantaneous."

"Now that is moodlift!!" Henry quipped.

Hepburn's pixelated eyebrows raised in puzzlement.

"I am glad that I was assigned to your unit, Henry. I believe there is indeed a friendship between us."

"There is, Hepburn, there surely is."

It began to snow. Panthera raised his head from Henry's lap, annoyed at being woken. The snow penetrated the projected film and the man on the side of the hull was also being snowed upon. Henry didn't want to cut the night short, assuming it would be his last, but he needed to sleep to have the sharpest mind he could prime as the bullets started flying.

The projection ceased, but Canis Minor remained in the sky.

# THIRTY-ONE

# The Rambling Man

"I realize," he said, "that I have done all the gabbing."

Mary had gotten so used to the deprivation of her sight that her other senses had intensified. Although the un-god had crept into the far corner of the chamber and not spoken for some time, she'd smelled him; his body soiled and foul from all the living and dead things that filled their world. Traces of earth and the strange mosses that grew, fed by moisture in the air and rare beads of water that breached cracks in the rock. The un-god was unwashed and unashamedly so. She supposed it had been over-whelming when she had first been confined in his volcanic lair, but she hadn't been of sound mind for hundreds of daylights and all the many uncountable ones that had followed underground. Somehow, she'd found a peace in the quiet of the caves. She'd become whole again. *One Mary.* Still and silent, but present.

She knew that her own body was smelling worse each day and that smell would, in time, meld with her companion's, if it hadn't already. She couldn't remember the last time she'd bathed, or even washed in haste by hand. It was both puzzling and bemusing, because the realization came that she didn't care. Who would judge her?

She noticed the un-god's breath. She heard him respire when he'd first entered the chamber and sensed that he'd tried to keep as silent as possible. Somehow, she could tell, from the other side of the dank space, that he'd eaten something just before entering the room, or brought it in with him. It wasn't snake, centipede, or bat, which she'd eaten whilst barely alive. *It was from the sea,* or the waters that met it.

"Maybe yourn absent manners. For I've fed you and you must've fathomed that I've no intention of plumping yourn ass to eat, by way of butchery or sacrifice." The un-god paused for Mary's reply and when none came, he continued. "I prefer the company. But alas, my girl, your company is shit."

She laughed. The first sound she had made in the longest of times. She placed her hands over her mouth in the darkness and took them away again. The un-god shuffled closer. *Ten feet away. Five feet away. Closer still…*

"She squeaks, that shit girl." He spoke as if he were addressing the insects in the cavern and not her. Somehow, in the dark, Mary could tell from the un-god's voice that he was smiling as he spoke his words. She wondered then, as she had often, if he had a name.

"I've sensed yourn battles. Sometimes you listen. Sometimes you don't. And I've said over that you're safe here. Maybe you heard that?" The nameless un-god shuffled closer. "I may look like a dead 'un from the state of me, but I'm not your nightmare. Far from, *si.* And I'm no god, as you can tell. I'm just a man."

*A comfortable silence.*

Mary took a short breath and readied her dry mouth. The un-god gave her all the time she needed to work up the courage to speak. "Why do you hide in the dark and let them think you a devil?" she asked finally. Her voice, unused for so long, sounded alien and frail.

A droplet of water somewhere in the chamber fell from a height and made a din as it landed.

"This is where the Great-Greats came to survive the start of this cold," said the un-god. "My pa was one of them. Just a bairn, from no place he ever did recall. He lived here. Then *out there* for some time, then he came home, to the dark."

"Your father?" Mary replied, keen to grasp her proprietor's

story. Her voice was louder this time and sounded more like she remembered.

"Maybe. I'm a hundred years old. I don't know. But we lived here, quite happy in the heart and hearth of the volcano. Warm. Fed. Fishing deep rivers that flow underneath all of this. Boiling them fishes in the channels we made where the magma ran. We made light into this place from the fires of that magma. A few families, a couple of orphans and some friends."

"Families? Here?"

Another droplet of water dropped peacefully from the ceiling to the floor behind Mary. A tranquil, inaudible suicide.

"Come, follow," he said, and crept away from Mary to the place where he'd entered the room.

Mary abided and crossed the room on all fours, sensing the un-god's movements ahead. There, a narrow course took them away from the chamber and Mary, still sensing her confidante's movements ahead of her, used her hands to guide her, at times catching webs in her hair and fingers and brushing insects off the sides of the passageway. The route twisted and turned. In places it felt like it had been dug out by tools. In others, it was the natural course of the inner caverns beneath the volcano. A draught swept a different kind of air into her nostrils, fresher than the stale, acrid stench of the chamber where she'd remained since her arrival. It was hard to keep up with the un-god, for he clearly knew the track well, yet he didn't slow for the girl, who knocked and grazed her elbows, arms and feet regularly trying to keep up, losing her footing altogether on a couple of occasions. It seemed they'd trekked for half an hour and Mary tired, realizing she hadn't moved much in her chamber since the un-god had first brought her there.

Then there was a faint glow ahead. A tiny dot. *A titchy sun.*

Mary pressed forward, and at the last turn, the passageway opened into a vast room adorned with pillars and columns of stalagmites. Here, she could see, for orange light fed the room from an entranceway on the far side. She shielded her eyes at first, finding it hard to look at.

"The light comes from a deeper chamber where the magma

swells. I never come here. Haven't set foot down this part for an age. It's a sorrowful place, but it was… Well, you should have seen it." The un-god waved his arms in the air ardently. "We carved rooms and painted walls. We performed marvelous scraps of plays on the steps of our amphitheater and recited poems! Aeschylus, Ayckbourn, Euripides, Shakespeare, Du Bartas, Agbaje, Faber, Wilde, Wagner and Gupta! Artisans and teachers dwelt here, descendants of doctors and writers!" The un-god spoke passionately, then stopped to take a breath, changing his tone to a grave one. "All gone now. Cruel how that lot can be. Always the way. And I'm still here. Where it all began. And it serves a purpose."

Steps had been hewn into the rock. On one surface, the alphabet had been written in dye or ink of some kind. Beside it was written the phonic sounds for each letter, then basic sentences. One read *'I started on time, but I arrived late.'*

There were drawings of yachts and vessels with people standing up on their decks, and of the volcano itself; a story told upon the rock. A backdrop of winter, illustrated by eloquently drawn snowflakes, followed them from sea to land. The waves themselves were portrayed to roll, then ice over. Dead creatures were depicted and a city of people, which Mary thought was to represent all of humankind, metamorphosed into a giant catacomb. She wondered if all that had been daubed and captured was the truest account of the apocalypse.

"What does it serve? To stay here, or in the chambers, all alone in the dark?" Mary asked, a hint of challenge in her voice. She looked upon the un-god then; scaly skin. Skinny limbs. A potbelly hanging over a loincloth. There were a few singular strands of hair on his head, that had been miraculously untouched (from whatever had ruined him), or regrown. The un-god looked grotesque. Only he wasn't.

"One day, the king of the Favela at the time decided to end us. He could not stand the thought of people thriving outside of his control. Thought that in time we might rise up and overthrow him, or some nonsense. It was his fear. Not ours. It always is with tyrants."

Mary was intrigued. "Go on," she said, still marveling at the cave around her.

"I was deep in the volcano when all that was below me started to growl and rumble. It shook the rocks all around us and I thought the devil himself was going to rise up from the floor as it budged. But it was the magma that breached, and the scorching heat from it bubbled my skin and I reckoned it would cook me alive. It fizzed. Seemed to liquify. I screamed like nothing you've ever heard and I tore through the tunnels, rolling and bouncing off the walls aflame, until I reached the top where the bastards were cutting the last of our people. They had already heard my screams of course, echoing out to them with the very shifting and quaking of the volcano itself, but the fear in them when they beheld what had become of me was something else. Their eyes!"

Mary spoke with kindness and empathy, saying simply, "You, poor man."

"I was a young man, and none from that Favela had seen fire beyond a blubber lamp."

"And they ran."

"They ran. Because I was their devil. Born on that day from such agony that most could not endure. My screams as I lay somewhere betwixt life and death kept them away for days, weeks. I'd rolled myself in the snow to quell the flames and numb my body, but it was no drug, or dram! Somehow, I crawled back into the guts of this place, tormented, damned; a Dante, for the new age!"

Mary recalled the piled human skulls in the basin of the volcano. "But they came back." Mary had moved closer to the un-god and found that she had taken his hand in hers. Unafraid.

"Eventually. A few times, them early years. I would pick them off and make a mess of the bodies. I howled like a madman to keep them away from this place. I became a creature to scare the children with, not that they needed that out there." The un-god squeezed Mary's hand. His voice seemed to tremble at the touch of soft skin upon his malformed flesh.. "But I also became something else. A helper, in the dead hours, to those who needed it.

This place is a sanctuary that none but the desolate and forlorn would dare enter. Those who have nothing more to fear than the Favela itself. Not many. Not many brave enough, or desperate enough. But, over the many years, a tiny few."

His eyes were bloodshot. Mary wondered if they could ever form tears, or if the heat of the magma had taken it from him.

Mary looked at the painted figures on the walls and wondered if the un-god had been the one to help Mother and Father leave the Favela. She pondered the question, but it was the un-god that spoke first.

"You said 'What does it serve? To stay here alone in the dark?' Well, I say that you, despite eating all the morsels I bring and succumbing to the nocturnal brilliance of this place and not trying to leave that chamber back there even once, I say that you still hold on to something in the world out there that you would feast your eyes upon. Something you're not ready to give up for this place. The stars that dot the sky. The sun that would crisp my skin twice over. You just need to find your place in that light, or find it again."

*Stars.*

"My place in the light? It's not the Favela. It never was and never could be."

"But you have woken to yourn senses, *shit girl*. You have been all right for some time in here, I know. Just silent, making me do all the talking, like a rambling old man in a devil suit," the un-god said. "But I should kick you out now, topside onto the icescape. Ain't no company to me, anyhow."

Mary thought about sprinting across the icescape with a whalebone pick in her hand and the wind on her face. She remembered diving into the freezing waters and the shock that hit her when her body registered the freezing temperatures. The slingshot, the Ritual, the homestead. She thought of the exhilaration of being around other people. Of love, in all the forms that she knew of it.

"I would go and see the stars. And find a place to live that I could call a home. And eat better food. But I would not do that knowing there is an ancient, rambling old devil slinking away in the tunnels of this hole. Now I know you exist and all that you have done for me in my grief that you know not about, I would wrap you in furs, so you do not crisp under the sun like fodder, and I would talk to you in the light until you finally shut up."

It was the un-god's turn then to go quiet and think about what he might say next and all that had been said before.

"But this is—"

"This was. No, this *is* your home, but if you don't want to leave it, there are orfins out there who would fill it with light and listen to you *gabbing* all day and night long. Why wait years for them to stumble down here to speak to a demon? Go to them and be a good god. Save them from that place. Teach them all these things you know. All them Shakesheers, Guptees and Fables, whatever you harked. All they got out there is the knowing, that they could go under that ice and never return.

"I know who you are. Who you *really* are," Mary added, "Let's go and see them Orfins. *Now.* I know of two that I would like to bring here."

The light that trickled into the room shifted and made the figures painted on the cavern walls come to life.

"I liked it more when you were mostly shit and silent. You talk too much, mute girl," the un-god replied.

# THIRTY-TWO

## Dream

Henry found himself in the cavern where Martin had died. It was a perfect recreation of the room where the body of the young boy still lay under the ice. Yet in the dream, Martin wasn't there. In his place, lay Father, wearing a pelt that Henry knew had been taken from him in his final hours and was being worn by another in the real world.

Father opened his eyes and sat up, unfazed by the cold of the room in the dream, whereas Martin's lips had once turned blue and his skin a porcelain color.

There was brilliant light in this version of the cavern and it cast Henry's shadow upon the wall. He looked behind him, but there was no torch, flame, nor fire. An orb of light simply hung in the room. An orb, that never was. Henry's mind accepted it; a dream anomaly.

"Henry-son," spoke Father, pulling himself up into a sitting position. He looked healthy, with color on his cheeks and no signs of anything that had befallen him.

"I miss you," Henry replied. He felt how much he meant those words and he wanted to throw his arms around Father, but he knew it wasn't really the man he had loved so deeply. He let the dream play out, seeing no point in challenging the journey his mind had set out.

"You're all right now. You know it."

"I wish things could go back to the way they were. But I know they can't"

"Then don't wish it. Move forward. Release the last of your anger."

"I will Father. In the morrow, I will avenge you."

Father shifted where he sat. His shadow mimicked the movement.

"The dead don't care for vengeance. I just came to tell you what comes."

"What comes?"

"What comes after the winter. What follows, Henry?"

"I don't know."

"Think."

"I don't know."

"What comes after the ice and snow? Think."

"I don't know."

"Is the Winter forever? Think. What comes? Think. What is next?"

"I can't. I'm not sure what you mean."

"Think!"

"The thaw."

Father disappeared in an instant, as if he were never there. Henry knew that neither of them had been. It was a dream and as he pondered it, he started to forget the details of it all. He knew he'd wake and that his mind would hold just the feeling of what he'd experienced, but the details would be lost to him.

The thaw.

## THIRTY-THREE

## To Catch a Royal Snitch

There wasn't much to load into the car. No need for provisions, or tools of any kind. Henry took the weapon he'd forged with Hepburn and every knife he could find, strapping them around his torso and limbs so he could easily get at them. Henry had been determined at one point to fashion armor for himself after seeing it worn by soldiers in the old projections he'd watched, but once Hepburn explained the qualities of Henry's bodysuit – which had been made for the battlefield – he settled instead for a tactical helmet which formed part of the same battle kit.

Henry took a final look at the ship that had been his home in these dark times. The ship that he had rehabilitated himself in and trained hard for what was about to begin.

The shark face of the vessel no longer appeared scary. It was just a hole that had rusted in time, filled with icicles that may have looked like teeth to some, especially the man with the flat face who had been pushed through the mouth of it to the icescape below.

Panthera didn't appear to care about the vessel and hopped straight into the Duesenberg. Henry had seen how the animal had grown accustomed to traveling in it with Henry and enjoyed the warmth within once the engines came to life.

And, so they set off. The journey was morose. They spoke little, for much of it had already been said and Henry knew that

Hepburn could recall every conversation they'd had for reference at any time. It was the inhuman condition.

Fury brought them on their way at great speed. The car looked like a giant cockroach, insectoid in shape and color, reflecting the sun from its panels. It was enthralling to be traveling at such speeds across the icescape. They passed each of the places that Henry had known in his life on Lantic. A jet stream of ice and snow followed them as they made their way across the vast plains; a superstorm was coming and the people of the Favela would soon see it.

Panthera sat up at the windscreen, watching the panorama, distracted now and then by the hologram.

"Thing just won't die, will it, Pan?" Henry had said, to no avail.

An hour into the drive and they found the whalebone sled that the invaders had brought with them. The car rode over it, but there was no sign of Skindred or the pack dogs. They kept their eyes on the terrain after that, looking for the boy coward. The royal snitch.

Two more hours passed, and Henry slowed the vehicle when he saw a Big White feasting on something fallen. More successful than Panthera with the hologram, the Big White had pinned its cadaver by the head, crushing the skull flat, so it was unrecognizable. Henry pulled up alongside the Big White to take a closer look and the animal stood on two legs and roared at the car that had disturbed its meal. The meat had been butchered. Bones stuck out in places and the shape of it looked more like a butterfly than an individual; opened flat. A meat envelope.

"It's hard to determine how long this body has been here whilst the polar bear confronts us. Shall I scare the creature away?"

Henry peered at the corpse. He couldn't be sure because it was in such a mess, but he thought it might've been wearing a fur tunic. He looked at what was left of the face; flat matter spread out on the snow. A piece of hair remained. A dreadlock. Then, just meters from the body, he saw the unloaded gun.

The Big White roared again at the vehicle, challenging the inhabitants.

"It's Skindred. Didn't get far and not a good end for him. But I s'pose that pleases me a lot," said Henry as the Big White charged toward the Duesenberg. "Don't worry, big fella. We don't want any of that coward meat." Henry steered the vehicle away just as the bear was upon them.

With Skindred gone, it made things simpler. He figured he only had forty, perhaps fifty enemy fighters left to kill.

Henry accelerated and the car traveled faster than it had before. It was exhilarating. There wasn't a creature alive or a bird that could keep up with them. Even the android seemed to be enjoying himself.

"Let's get this done. I want to see my sisters."

The car soared across the ice. A land rocket, delivering war to the adults of the Favela, finally.

# THIRTY-FOUR

## Tattoos

Sissel looked at the meager finds from below. She knew every room in every building that was close enough to swim to from the holes already cut into the icescape. The salvagers had started going back over things previously discarded and had brought them up top to see if they might satisfy Ginger Lanner, the spiteful brute whose clothes were a patchwork of garments that had once belonged to others. Lanner had given himself the role of foreman to the salvagers, mainly to hold power over Sissel, who he'd come to hate since she chose to help the boy, Henry, find his weakling brother, rather than report him to Lanner as instructed.

Yet Sissel had to hold it together and keep in line for her crew, the Orfins. Lanner would too easily find cause to lash out at the children, or worse still, make examples of them. She'd lost two under the ice in less than six months. At least she had Yaxley, who always had her back. Dependable Yaxley, who was now more than her right-hand boy. Yaxley had become her lover.

Sissel had chosen him and instigated it all. It had been for comfort at first, after feeling a strange loss at the death of the brave, stupid boy that had come looking for his siblings so long ago. And somehow, beyond comfort and company, she had developed feelings for Yaxley (though she'd never tell him), and he knew her well enough not to embarrass her by sharing how he felt about her (which she knew was a lot). The Orfins knew, but she'd never let Lanner find out, as he would make it his mission to hurt her through Yaxley, maybe cut him down in front of her, or drown him by the foot of the hill so all would see. So their love was a closely guarded secret. They understood each other more than anyone else could, and it worked. It was the nearest to happiness that Sissel had found in her life, and that troubled her. In the Favela, happiness was not permitted and deep down, she felt it would be short-lived.

"This stuff has come up time and again. I'm sure we even put some of this crap back down there. They ain't ever going to swallow it," Yaxley said, holding an unopened tin of paint and a wall clock.

Sissel looked about her to see if Lanner was on the icescape, and when she was sure he wasn't, she leaned forward and kissed Yaxley on the lips. She withdrew from him, but he placed his hand on her waist and pulled her closer. His chest was a decoration of raised scars. Upon it were a skull, a bird, and a whale surfacing on an etched ocean. Sissel ran her fingers across them admiringly, then showed him a fresh tattoo on her own forearm; a bird that matched his. Carved out of something close to love. A growing feeling, yet a pup. The skin was sore and the scab had cracked and bled.

"Same, same. When did you do that?" Yaxley asked her, blushing.

"Two days ago, but you notice nothing," she said in response. "The Orfins, we can't send them lower, or further. You know that. This game is up, like that kid said."

"That kid? Henry. Always him." Yaxley looked hurt, withdrawing from Sissel slightly.

"Don't look at me like that, Yax. He was right. What we do and why we do. We could explore instead. Spread out and go landside. We might even find something to help us."

"Like weapons?"

Sissel lowered her voice as two salvager kids surfaced from the circle of water beside them. "Yes, like weapons. If we found guns that worked, we could take them." She balled her fist, then relaxed it.

Yaxley took her hand and kissed it gently. "Lanner will sniff it a mile off, you know it."

The salvagers helped each other out of the water with a collective groan and spooned their bodies close on the ice, rubbing each other to generate heat.

Sissel bit her lip in frustration. "*E Para.*" *I do.* "You're right."

A call came from up on the hill. It was Little L, one of the smallest of the crew, returning to the sieve. They couldn't hear what she was saying, but she was gesturing with her arms frantically about something behind them, something in the distance. Sissel assumed it was a Big White and turned with alarm. The Orfins all ceased work and shielded their eyes from the sun, trying to see what the girl on the hill was looking at.

Yaxley saw it first. He took Sissel's arm and pointed.

A low storm, a churning mist, an object traveling at such speed that none of them had ever witnessed before.

"What is it?" Sissel asked. The salvager kids appeared from their makeshift shelters and out of the waters. An excitement spread across the children who started calling out what they thought they were seeing. *A sea-monster, a rocket machine, Santa...*

"Ain't no storm. Ain't a sled either. Looks like trouble," Yaxley said, not taking his eyes from the horizon. He squinted, yet Sissel knew it was pointless trying to bridge the distance and see what was rolling toward the Favela.

"Maybe we don't have to go searching for anything. Let's get the children off the ice and up the hill."

"Do we report?"

They exchanged a look that said it all. Whether that was hope, or opportunity, or just a perverse desire to watch the kingdom crumble up close, neither expressed it aloud, but they wanted to be there and witness what was to come.

"No. Whatever happens, we didn't see anything coming. Let us leave this shit here and tell the crew to shut it up tight."

"Yes, boss man." Yaxley gave an overwrought mock salute.

"I'm your warrior and I'm your leader. Call me boss man

again and I'll break your arm." Sissel smiled, then punched Yaxley hard on the shoulder. "You're still my bitchboy, Yax."

"Always, *meu amor*," he submitted. *My love*. It was the first time he'd said it out loud.

"I hope it," affirmed Sissel, before she signaled for everyone to return to the Favela. None questioned it and they moved in unison, dragging their eyes from the unidentified object that sped ever closer in a plume of mist.

## THIRTY-FIVE

## Dead Dogs

Skindred had never felt as much fear in his whole life. There were beatings he'd had as a small child and always the threat of death in some elaborate form in the Favela. He'd also done his share of salvaging and had his heart and lungs pumped on more than one occasion after running out of breath in the underbelly of the old citadel. But Henry, much altered and inhuman, had alone given him a new level of fear that he couldn't shake. Skindred remembered the look on Henry's disfigured face after he'd smashed Slim's antlers into his skull, over and over with such speed and ferocity and lack of remorse that petrified the betrayer.

He hated the feeling. It was Skindred that put the fear into the little ones. It was him who made them wet their strides and fill their furs. He made them suffer in silence, never daring to tell any of the older salvagers, who would get word back to Sissel in a heartbeat. It was fun. The best game.

But Skindred felt bullied. He'd been made to run. To do someone else's bidding. To feel worthless and small. His confidence had melted away on the ice by MV Greyhound and he had to keep reminding himself who he was. *Skindred.* Skindred! Skin...

When the sun fell, Skindred became too anxious to sleep. Worried that Henry would appear before him, or in his nightmares. He'd seen the car that was parked beside the ship and had tried to take control of it, but he'd been too flustered, worried about Henry, his snow leopard or the metal monster appearing at any moment. He'd deserted the vehicle. He'd heard about them and knew they were quicker than pack dogs, but he had no idea how close Henry would ever be to him, or if he'd see or hear him coming. He wondered whether his nemesis would ride up on the back of the snow leopard, or on the shoulders of the tin being and kill him with few words. His neck hurt from looking over his shoulder constantly.

Skindred reached a place where a corpse lay untouched in the snow. A peacekeeper. One of six other comrades he'd set out with from the Favela. Henry had been met with six, including Skindred, yet there had been seven comrades when they set out, until one was ended by his own lot. It had been trivial, but the result was that Erasmus had killed one of their own in an argument on the way to the yot-boat.

Only Skindred knew, and it was the biggest stroke of luck. He thanked the stars that a few choice words and raised voices had escalated into this man's death so close to the final encampment. He thanked Odin and he thanked the main God that people harked about. Had the argument taken place a day or two earlier in their journey, it would have been too far for Skindred to reach and Henry would've caught up with him and cut him down. He thanked Mohammed and Neptune. He thanked Erasmus and her quick temper.

And the plan lay there in the corpse. The only one he had, which had come to him in the seconds between being asleep and lying awake following the briefest of naps.

Skindred took out a knife and hacked at his dreadlocks with it, cutting four of them free of his scalp. Then he wove them into the hair of the dead peacekeeper, before he brought out his unloaded gun and used it to smash the dead man's skull beyond all recognition. Such trickery! Skindred delighted that Henry might think him dead in the snow. Skindred was slippery, like an eel, and that was how he liked it.

Skindred took off his fur tunic and swapped it with the dead man's old fleece jacket. It wasn't nearly as warm, but Skindred needed his plan to work. He tossed his gun next to the body and surveyed his crime scene.

With the addition of his hair to the mess, he thought it looked convincing and could buy him time, or allow him to truly disappear. That thought too had come to him, of course; the idea that he could try his own luck on Lantic and live alone as a free person, far from the king, Ginger Lanner and the Orfins who all wanted him dead. Yet Skindred knew he would not last. He would go insane in his own company and he would not know how to survive. He'd seen girls catching fish, unfurling the bloodied rags from inside them and putting them into the water to attract a catch. As a youngster, Skindred had only scavenged from the Bone Yard. Always going for the easy option. As he grew older, he bullied others for dog meat, fish or seal blubber, or traded for things he had salvaged or stolen. His only course of action was to tell his tales. Yet the journey back to the Favela, unarmed, would be an impossible one.

After setting the scene of his own death for Henry to discover, Skindred headed in a new direction and trod a wide circle away from any path that Henry would take. Skindred was going to take a long route back to the yot-boat, several days further on the ice. Skindred had a notion to steal its treasures and find whatever weapons he could to get him back to the Favela as a returning hero.

To increase his chances of survival, he'd kicked two of the pack dogs to death and slung them in a sealskin. His stomach was empty and he'd started salivating about the meat in his sack, but he'd been too scared to stop.

A distant rumble and a continuous spray of snow showed him the car, driving at great speed toward the Favela. Henry had not seen him and had likely taken the bait with the ruined corpse of the secret peacekeeper.

Skindred fell in the snow, laughing hysterically to himself. By the time he reached the Favela, it would be over, one way or another. He would prepare his stories for every eventuality, for that was where his strength lay. Deceit and treachery and self-preservation. Never a warrior, Skindred was and always had been a true survivor.

Skindred opened the sealskin, reached in and took out the hind quarter of one of the deformed pack dogs. He felt triumphant. And safe.

# THIRTY-SIX

## King of Hearts

Hilde took the stairs which were shaped like a conch shell and took a deep breath before she entered the room. Ginger Lanner had his arm linked with hers, and as beautiful as she looked in her white, sleeveless lace panel wedding gown, Lanner was the perfect contrast, in his patchwork outfit that he'd only smartened by adding a ladies' brooch to his breast pocket; a single red flower that caught the light as he moved. He'd hung the bearskin, stolen from Hilde's father, by the gangway entrance of Moonbird. In a way, he was being respectful.

The loyal guard, Omeed, stood at the doors to the grand room, dressed in a dinner jacket that was too small for him and holding a machine gun. He greeted the pair and turned to open the doors and grant them entrance.

"Didn't I say you would be happy here?" Lanner bared his gap-toothed smile at the girl about to walk down the aisle to meet her waiting groom.

"You're a man of your word. Long may you live, Mister Lanner," Hilde replied, with more than a hint of spite in her voice. Lanner smiled nervously this time, aware that Hilde was no longer someone he could mess with. She was about to surpass him in the pecking order of the Favela.

The room was filled with peacekeepers and those who were high in the king's favor or debt. All were sat on chairs of different shapes and sizes. The room had been decorated with ice sculptures and fairy lights, some of which worked. The floor had been polished. Hilde was glad it no longer showed any sign of Henry's blood upon it, which the king had left there for some time after he'd taken her brother's eye.

Iris was nowhere to be seen; Hilde had insisted on banning her from attending, and she was relieved that the king had kept his word. She couldn't have Iris interfering, or spoiling things for her. This was her day, after all.

Before walking in, Hilde raised a hand to check her hair was in place in the chignon style one of her new servants had set it in. She wore pearls about her neck and ears and on one of her wrists. She truly felt like a queen, as though her very appearance gave her power over all others in the room. And how they looked at her!

The king sat in his red barber's chair at the far end of the room, elevated in front of the vista which was shielded only by the curved glass. Frozen waves, the square, and the endless white landscape lay beyond it. Nothing in the frame changed, unless there was a blizzard, or fog. Beside him stood the witch, Catharin, who jittered and shuffled nervously in her furs, awaiting the arrival of the bride.

Catharin had started referring to Hilde's sister, Iris, as her daughter. Hilde thought of their argument in her cabin and the spiteful words exchanged between the two of them.

In the absence of the Canary, the music began with a simple drum and all fell to silence as Hilde took her first steps toward her future husband, who stood to greet his bride where an altar might have been placed.

Unconventionally, he looked handsome. His mustache had been shaped into something new; waxed with blubber oil and twisted into a carnie. He wore a pure white cotton three-piece suit with a pale pink paisley shirt and matching bow tie, plus a handkerchief protruding from the jacket pocket. Today, the king was more eccentric than lunatic. More relaxed than unsettling. He was one of a kind. All power. Soon to be hers.

The people in the auditorium were dressed in their usual

affairs. Furs and skins. Pelts and ancient factory-made rags and garments. It made the scene even stranger as Hilde reached the king and Catharin on the elevated stage and felt everyone staring at her bare shoulders from behind. Did they envy her?

"James," greeted the king, taking Hilde's hand from Lanner's. Lanner nodded, smiled nervously at Hilde and backed off into the crowd. The king told Hilde how beautiful she looked and she responded in kind.

The drum ceased and Catharin took center stage between the couple. She opened a leather-bound book she'd been clasping and pretended to read out loud from it, although Hilde could see that the book was upside down and she was making up the words as she spoke them.

"Hear ye, blah, blah. We gather here to get these two wedded. 'Til death do either of. And we shall have a new queen, for our king. Yee haw." The crowd soaked up Catharin's words as if they were fine words, poetry even. Hilde had been made aware that weddings didn't happen often, although children were born frequently by mothers and sometimes daughters.

"Do you, the king, take Hilde as yours to have, hold and handle for this and that and that and this? Infinity, mighty universe, to the moon and back, always?"

"I take her," the king replied, not taking his eyes from Hilde. The crowd made a collective *ah* noise at this, which seemed to annoy Catharin, as if it was not part of the ceremony. Still pretending to read from her upside-down book, she continued.

"Now you, young girl, known by Hilde. Will you have, hold and handle the king for this and that and that and this? Eternity, forever, many years ahead beyond the Ever Winter?"

"I take him," Hilde said with confidence and leaned forward to kiss the king, who had to bend to meet her lips, despite the lofty heels on her shoes. To a stranger entering the room, the scene would have looked like a couple hopelessly in love, being joined in matrimony. It was what Hilde wanted. *The façade.*

"Then with that kiss there shared, you're king and queen. Of the Favela and the entire planetarium. May the sun warm your faces, blah, blah. Hark the wind at the backs of the angels.

So, it is done! Hip, hip, amen." Catharin slammed the book shut and told everyone to go home whilst they were still cheering. The crowd silenced themselves and filed out of the room as one. There were drams in the square waiting for all and none needed encouragement to exit the palace and commence drinking. The whole thing took minutes from start to finish and Hilde had become queen. Iris would hear about it soon enough.

Only the king, Lanner, Catharin, Hilde and Omeed remained in the vast room. Catharin sat at a table that had already been set, and the rest followed. The king waited until Hilde was seated before he took his own place at the table. In the center was a platter of oysters, sardines, seal and dog meat, a swordfish and the lobster that had been sharing Hilde's cabin with her for many weeks. It had been a gesture of affection from the king, to the girl whose family he had ordered the killing of and whose brother he had sent to his end, long ago.

Omeed used a silver lighter to light the candles that adorned the table and the king raised a crystal glass full of the red grog produced in plastic drums in an alley beside the Birdcage.

"Before we eat our wedding feast, I would like to raise a toast to my beautiful bride. Queen of this world and now mother to Omeed here, who I consider my son, until we make one of our'n. A good queen can get anything she wants in a place like this. I trust you will be a most excellent queen. I do not wish to replace you soonest," said the king to his bride, who smiled and held his gaze throughout. Omeed kept his eyes upon his dinner plate, clearly uncomfortable at being sat with the king for a meal and at having a girl younger than him referred to as his mother.

"I will be mother to Omeed, your son," Hilde replied, placing her hand on her husband's as she spoke, "and I will be a strong queen. I would ask for one gift from you on the day of our wedding."

"You don't waste time. I like that. A 'get to it and cut through all the gristle' kind of girl. What do you desire?"

"I thank you, my husband, for bringing me to this place. You've made me your queen and I am ever grateful. But Mister

Lanner's presence upsets me. I want his head. Serve it on this table with the lobster if you will."

The king laughed long and hard. Lanner let out a series of panicked noises and stuttered words, which made the king laugh even more, joined by Catharin, who cackled and clapped her hands, excited at the prospect of seeing another death up close.

Omeed remained quiet. He almost seemed disappointed with Hilde and looked upon her curiously, trying to understand who she was.

"We are well-matched! Mister Lanner! What's your view on this? Why should you keep your head this day? Is it a good head?" the king asked, finishing the last of his blood drink. But Lanner did not respond. Something had distracted him and he looked out of the glass window in the same way Omeed had stared at Hilde when he was trying to understand her.

One by one, they all turned to the glass vista. What they saw was a fast-moving, rolling mist, spoiling the scene that never changed apart from whether it was day or night, or presenting blizzard or fog.

The king stood and walked toward the glass. Hilde followed and stood at his side next to the red barber's chair, as they had just moments before during their wedding. Together they faced it. What was heading their way.

"Did you lie to me?" the king spoke softly.

"My king?"

He raised his voice then, so suddenly that Hilde was startled.

"Did you lie? You told me of a yot-boat. You told me of a car. You told me your darling brother had killed that car dead and ruined it, did you not?"

"I did. Tell you about the car. And he did…" It was Hilde's turn to stutter now, aware she had quickly fallen from grace and that her husband was a very dangerous man.

The king grabbed Hilde by her cheeks and squeezed his hand tight around her chin and jaw, causing her pain. Tears followed quickly.

"Then did you lie?" he spat.

"No. I never did lie," Hilde cried. But it was all too late. Their masks had dropped and it was clear what they were and were not to each other.

"Lanner. Every weapon in the gunroom; cutter, rifle, spear, gun, grenade launcher. All we got. Find every bullet, every blade. Each man, woman and orfin there is. Arm them up to the hilt of it. War has come. Something ancient this way comes and we will send it back to the olden days with fuck'n wings upon it! Omeed, come with."

Omeed did as he was commanded, shooting Hilde a look of pity this time. The king took off his bow tie and jacket and threw them to the floor. He rolled up his sleeves, went to the cabinet and took a set of metal nunchaku from the top drawer. Hilde watched as Lanner ran from the room, triumphant over her once again.

Before he left, the king turned to Hilde once more.

"I fear ours will be a short marriage. I wouldn't blame you if you took your own life this day, for what will happen to you on my return will never be wiped from your memory. I have perfected the art of making others suffer. I will set such an example with you that poetry shall be written for the generations to come, with tales of how you screamed. After hearing your brother's cries, the very notes that came from him, I'm expecting grand things from yourn."

Hilde trembled and felt her legs turn to jelly beneath her. She steadied herself on the headrest of the red barber's chair and caught a glimpse of herself in the curved glass window. The fallen queen of the Favela.

*Fear is the key.*

# THIRTY-SEVEN

# Fury Delivers Landside

The Duesenberg came to a halt at the foot of the hill, having skirted and weaved through the sieve of holes that dotted the icescape before it. Its engines purred, but otherwise there was a silence about it. The doors did not open. No one spoke from within and no shots were fired at the first adults that had made their way to the foot of the hill. Those closest tried to see inside and make out how many were in the car, but the windows were black and only permitted a view from within.

Henry had thought about stealth. *Stealth and victory*. About creeping in the middle of the night. He wished he'd had a rifle that he could've learned to shoot from a distance. In the training modules, he'd seen snipers doing damage far from the vicinity of their enemy target. They judged the wind, the distance and the power of their weapons. Every plan that Henry had thought of still ended up with him fighting forty or fifty adults. So, in the end, it made sense to him that the vehicle, his Trojan horse, simply drove straight up to the foot of the Favela to herald the start of a war.

His temperament must've been heeded by someone, as the skies bruised over and *rain*, not snow, dropped thick and fast, stirred by a sub-zero wind. When had it ever rained that he could recall? *What follows the winter? Think! The thaw.*

Bodies filed down the hill toward the purring car that waited with all the patience in the world. Those who hadn't already loaded their weapons did, and then at a given signal all fired at the Duesenberg, peppering its insect-like shell and the ice around it with slingshot shrapnel and bullets, sending shards of solar panels and blistered bodywork into the air around it. Men and women cursed and re-loaded, slowly, without any skill. Still the engine purred defiantly as it waited for them to ready their weapons once more.

"Go get!" shouted one of the women.

The first to reach it was Jared, one of those who had taken the girls from the homestead. He adjusted the peak of his trucker cap so he could see more clearly. Then he readied the large bone club he'd armed himself with, holding it like a baseball bat, ready to take a swing the second a door opened. Several feet behind him stood his partner, Ula, a hefty tank of a woman with an impressive death toll to her name. She held a chainsaw in both hands; a relic that had been oiled and cleaned regularly, but had not been used in many years. It was a simple enough weapon. Lift and point. Swing. Cut and slice. Butcher.

"Give me some blood, sugar," Ula shouted at Jared as she pulled the cord on the chainsaw, which started with a splutter and a thick cloud of acrid smoke. The blades spun and the noise, a different tone to the engine of the car, became the loudest sound in the Favela.

The faces of pauper children peeped out from the hovels lining the lower lanes of the hill; frightened, but excited by the sounds and the arrival of the car. None of the adults told them to hide, or move to safety. None cared for the weak underlings.

Jared turned toward Ula for the briefest of moments. "*Sim*, I got this down," he replied, just as the car window lowered and Panthera leaped out, going straight for the thorax, protected only by the man's tangled beard that proved no obstacle for the snow leopard's maxillaries.

Ula screamed and ran forward as Jared fell, but withdrew as her comrades began firing their slings and guns toward the beast and the car once more. She screamed at her own people to cease so she could have her revenge.

Henry clung to the face of the cliff, hauling himself over a ledge onto a flat roof halfway between the Duesenberg on the icescape and the square of the Favela above. He had swum the sieve of ice, coming up for air in each hole, just as the seals and their pups did. All had been distracted by the arrival of the car which Hepburn had piloted from within.

Henry had climbed, finding it easier in some ways than the containers and the hull of the ship. All of the pull-ups and press-ups he had done to condition his arms had paid off. His upper-body strength was notable and he scaled his precipice in no time.

The first to meet him on the hill was a child, no more than six years of age. The child held a bone that had been sharpened into a blade and stood brave and defiant.

"Ain't here to pain you, lad," Henry spoke quietly. "Adultos only."

Without a word, the boy ran back into his shelter and Henry stood alone once more, half-expecting the boy to betray him and come running out with adults.

The tight lanes of the Favela served as a funnel for the crowd heading for the Duesenberg. Those at the back had lesser weapons, or none at all, but it was their voices that would raise alarm and their numbers that would be his undoing if he were seen.

Henry climbed onto the roof of a shelter and lay still as bodies passed just inches away from him. There were far more adults than Henry had envisioned and for the shortest time, he felt like a little boy again, like the one he'd just sent into the safety of his shelter. But Henry wasn't a boy anymore. He'd stood up and fought Erasmus and her warriors, and he'd defeated them. How many strides now stood between him and his sisters? Where was the king? Cowering? Waiting? Plotting?

He hauled himself up to the roof of another shelter, then used it to scale a little further up the hill before dropping into a deserted lane. A man rushed out of a doorway beside him, eager to join the fracas below, not expecting to be confronted by anyone in the lane. Henry dropped his weapon, not wishing to spill blood just yet and give himself away, but was quick to take the man by the head and snap his neck. The man had no time to register anything, or call for alarm; he just stood with a puzzled look upon his face, staring at the tactical helmet that Henry wore. Henry dragged the body back into the man's shelter, which was empty, and put a sleeping bag over the body, so it might look at a glance like he was resting. Henry picked up his weapon and continued up the hill. In the next lane, he dispatched two in succession, quickly and quietly, without spilling any blood on the all-white ground. Then he choked a younger, unarmed man until he lost consciousness and dropped at Henry's feet.

Henry realized that the firing below had ceased, before it picked up again just as quickly; no order to it at all, just panicked and random. Sporadic. The roof on which he knelt gave him a view of the sieve below and it was then that he saw Hepburn from the driver's side of the vehicle, walking casually into a hail-storm of shrapnel and a few of the priceless bullets meant to put him down. The pixels on the android's faceplate showed confusion and annoyance, but nothing more. His armor had small indents from the shots he had taken, but he was mostly undamaged, having been designed to give aid on the battlefield.

Ula wielded her chainsaw once more and charged the robot. Hepburn sensed the danger and let fly a low-voltage charge to unarm her. Despite the defensive intent of Hepburn's parry, the large warrior skidded backward on the ice - more out of alarm than anything else - and impaled herself on the rotating blades of the chainsaw. The saw bored her insides and spun freely within her torso, making a minced carnage of Ula.

Shouts rang up the hill as many of the men and women that had come to greet the automobile began their hurried retreat back to the square.

~

The lanes were winding and narrow, which worked to Henry's gain. Just as he had used the layout of the MV Greyhound to his advantage when Erasmus and her men had discovered the vessel, this had been his plan in the Favela. Fighting unceasing numbers would tire him and he would certainly fall. With stealth, taking advantage of the terrain around him, he would only ever fight as many enemies as could fit immediately in his path, although he'd need to check that none were hiding in the houses and hovels as he passed.

All he wanted was to reach Lanner and the king, then to hurt and humiliate them in front of the populace. There would be no mercy afforded to Henry, nor his enemy. It was night, or it was day. And nothing else.

Like when he'd climbed and jumped from container to container around the stricken ship, Henry used the buildings and walls around him to scale the hill by every means, until he found himself at the very top. He dropped down from the side of a building he had hidden in whilst people with weapons marched both up and down the hill in confusion. *To and from danger*.

The Birdcage was empty. None drank grog or punched blocks of ice until they cracked and tumbled to the ground. It was eerily silent and in the distance was *Moonbird*, the palace, reached by a narrow bridge.

The sounds of the mob drew closer. Dark clouds wrung themselves of all the rain they held and pendants of water carpet-bombed the Favela, finding percussion upon the tactical helmet adorning Henry's head.

Atop the vast hill, there was nowhere for Henry to hide. No camouflage to be made, or shelter to be had. No crowds to blend with. It was as sparse as the Lantic itself.

Henry crept to the side of the square furthest from the Birdcage.

## THIRTY-EIGHT

## Shaming Shadows

A sallow-faced old man with a cemetery of wonky teeth not unlike the Bone Yard bent himself doubled on the floor of the Birdcage and raised his hands to the sculptured ceiling in praise. Shapes around him shifted between the rimy pews.

"Praise him! Here he comes. That old saint Nick," he cackled.

"Shut up, old man," spoke a hushed voice in the darkness, "you'll get us murdey'd!"

The old man laughed and gave the shadows a better view inside his mouth. His teeth were grays and browns, with some black tar.

"He comes to take each an' every oneya up that hill and into the pit, *si*? I seen um do! Nonaya ever believe. But now? Praise him, out there in the driving rain like I ain't seen in a hundy!" The man's arms shook from old age and excitement. They shook like he was possessed by an unseen spirit and the shadows around him cursed and told him to keep his voice down, *or else*.

"In here, oh Lord! We all in here!" the old man announced, then just as quickly found his voice stifled as one of the shadows reached out with a blade from one of the pews. The man fell sideways, twitched a couple of times, then fixed his final stare upon the arched entrance to the hall.

Sporadic shots rang out in the distance, presumed by some to be thunder and muted to some extent by the rain that beat down outside.

Silence fell in the Birdcage, and from the rear of the room, she came. The Canary. Wild and beautiful. A little fractured. Somehow delicate and dangerous at the same time. The girl with the healing voice. The starlet of the gilded ice cage.

Each of the shadows became still in her presence. It was always her room. Her audience. She commanded it. None of those in the room had known her how she once was; a deliriously happy little girl living on the ice with her family. They saw and heard what they wanted to see, never imagining joy beyond the Favela. Nothing like that was ever permitted. Those who had left were always hunted. Those who challenged the as-is were made examples of. To the punters and regulars of the Birdcage, the Canary was Favela-born. The very best of them.

"I was sleeping. What's out there?" she asked all and no one. Iris rubbed her eyes, smearing the ashen paint around them. Iris noted the man lying sideward on the floor. "Why you all on your knees? And what's been done to him?"

"A demon! I see it!" came the answer finally. Other voices spoke up in hushed tones.

"*Diablo!*"

"Ain't no devil. It's a *spirit!*"

"I see it. It's a child, but something wicked about it."

"Old serpent, that's what he is."

"No child. Thissa man. Watched him creep like I've never seen, then snap another man's neck!"

"*Verdade.*" *Truth.*

"A man can't do that. It's a spirit of one of the Great-Greats!" whispered another.

Iris knelt beside the old man and followed his stare toward the entranceway. She used the palm of her hand to close his eyelids, as if that was the thing needed to let him take his final nap. *The long sleep.* She would go back and check his pockets for a weapon of any kind, but only when the shadows were distracted.

"You all scared of an old man?" Iris asked the shadows. "Well, are you?"

"He was yelling. Was gonna give us all away!" said the one who'd sent the old man sideways, still in the shadows.

"Whatever is out there, it ain't a devil. I spent my life on the icescape, out on Lantic. And the only devil I ever saw wore a coat of sewn-up patches and you all know him very well. He who wears a Big White pelt like he skinned it himself." She paused at the thought of Father's coat. "If something comes for us all and it's out there, I'd rather you all go out there and show me what you got. This is my place. My hall. And cowards aren't welcome in here. No songs ever for the unworthy. No drams either."

The command she held, something taught by the old lady, Catharin, went out in the room like two mighty hands that picked out the men in the shadows and lifted them onto their feet. None wanted the Canary to think lowly of them. The Birdcage was their light, and in it, the Canary was the governess of it all.

The adults moved toward the entranceway and left the old man to his quiet slumber.

Iris pilfered the man's pockets and smiled to herself, feeling the handle of a tool sharpened for only one purpose.

It was a test. *Loyalty*. Command. As she watched them leave the grand hall of the Birdcage, she supposed the power of her songs might just one day lift the rabble to turn Ginger Lanner inside out before her. Her songs were power. In her own way, she was ascending the Favela.

## THIRTY-NINE

# Man, Made Flesh

Henry was finally discovered.

No longer a phantom or wraith, he was made flesh in his gray battle-suit and recognized by Dookie, the woman with short, jet-black hair who had been part of the original raiding party. She was accompanied by three disheveled men armed with makeshift clubs, a whalebone blade and an ornate sword. The tallest of the group, a man wearing a knitted hat made sodden by the rain, held a pistol in his hand and seemed to wait for approval from Dookie, his superior, to fire its precious bullets.

"This is what all the noise has been about?" she laughed, then nodded to her companion with the gun.

Realizing he was a sitting target, Henry started moving his body so he became harder to hit and zig-zagged a route toward them.

"Eat this, cunk!" The man in the knitted hat fired the first shot and it missed Henry by several feet. He corrected his aim and prepared to fire a second shot, but Henry tossed a blade across the space between them and watched it embed in the man's heart, yanking his body to one side and sending his second, final shot skyward, toward the clouds that still wrung their contents out.

Without hesitation, the man's companions confronted Henry with their weapons drawn, but he used his war-lance well and cut ribbons and bows into them, his blades splitting the falling rain into smaller droplets. Henry put his training into practice; Krav Maga, Jukendo, Okinawan Karate. Every move had a rhythm to it. It seemed automatic and he did not tire yet.

"He's a warlord," declared one of the companions before he died. The man almost looked impressed with Henry as he took his final breath.

Then a familiar face appeared in Henry's field of vision, a figure that leaped out from the crowd. Unmistakable. More than deja vu. Memories flickered in Henry's thoughts, like the projected moodlift on the side of the container ship; laughter, made-up games, play-fights, arguments, cuddles, the bonds of love. He'd expected her and had hoped he'd see her first. If he could choose to see only one of his sisters, it would be his youngest, who he doted on.

Though he'd expected he might see her, Henry was mesmerized. A second passed. Then two. She'd changed so much, but there in the flesh, across the square in the doorway of the Birdcage, there she was. *Iris.*

Henry, distracted, failed to see Dookie pick up her comrade's gun and take aim at him. It was a grave mistake and in losing concentration, Henry had invited his enemy to take a fatal shot.

The warrior squeezed the trigger and sent a bullet forth impatiently, hitting Henry on the upper arm, rejoicing as it made contact. Henry dropped his war-lance as he instinctively went to grab the place where the bullet had struck him. He looked down at it, confused. Feeling stupid. Forgetting everything he'd rehearsed in a second and letting his enemy take the cheapest shot. Yet there was no blood from the wound. His battle-suit, the garment he'd found so long ago in a military container, had not allowed the bullet to penetrate its mesh of material. But the force of the bullet alone had been enough to render his arm useless and cause damage to the muscle. His arm throbbed and hung at his side uselessly.

On the other side of the hilltop, beyond the rocky bridge, on the gangway of Moonbird, stood the two men Henry wanted to end the most. Ginger Lanner and the king himself. He had their attention finally. He saw, with his enhanced eye, that they smirked in admiration as Dookie closed in on the injured boy, with an arm stretched out before her ready to take the next shot.

It was over, then. The king and Lanner were already making their way to the square to defile Henry's carcass and celebrate his failed revenge. Henry raised his uninjured arm in a feeble attempt to block the next bullet. It was pointless and he knew it.

The gun blast sounded and Henry felt his head explode as the bullet hit the side of his tactical helmet and ricocheted. The sound erupted in his eardrums and shook his skull and all that was in it. Henry found himself lying on the ground, with all about him just a whirling mess as his vision faltered. Blood trickled down his face where the helmet had been crushed inward above his temple and Henry spent an age working out where he was and what had happened to him.

Dookie stood above him then and took a final aim with her companion's gun. He closed his eyes, waiting for the shot that would end him and take him to see Mother and Father on angel's wings.

The shot never came. Henry opened his eyes to find Dookie lying next to him, staring back at him. She was dead. Henry couldn't see an obvious wound, but he was still in a daze. He had no idea who had saved him. The icescape swirled around him and the thought came to Henry that the two of them, lying next to each other in the middle of the square, looked quite absurd. He tried to lift his head, but he couldn't raise it. His legs felt like blubber beneath him. He thought of the bairn, trying to walk, and then much younger, lying on his back, kicking his tiny legs out.

Henry could taste bile, along with the blood that seemed to cover him. All around him, the square had erupted into battle, and from where he lay, Henry could see faces of those whose names he couldn't instantly recall; a girl with an overbite, an orfin boy with frostbitten fingers, two siblings, someone who had been with him when Martin died, a strange boy who talked to fishes and a girl so beautiful that his heart almost stopped right there. He'd dreamt of her and imagined scenes and futures over and over again. Then she was lost in the crowd as blows were exchanged between the adults of the Favela and the children they'd treated as outcasts and made into lowly urchins.

Henry saw a giant of a man trying to shake two of the children off his back and saw the gleam of a shiny silver belt buckle about his waist that stated 'California State Bull Roper Champion 2027' upon it. Henry's gift to Father. The children clung on, scratching and clawing at Needol, biting and tearing at him, until his knees went from under him and he sank under the trampling feet around him.

Yet the brief triumph was short-lived and replaced by immediate sorrow; a young 'un that Henry did remember, Little L, was held high above a woman's shoulders and thrown to the floor with a sickening crack. Henry could only catch a glimpse of the child through the carnage unfolding and realized in an instant that he was already dead, his back and neck broken.

Henry tried to stand once more. He cried out in rage at the death of Little L, but his voice was defeated by all the other sounds around him. Then, Henry caught a glimpse of the dead boy's elder brother, distressed and afflicted by the violent end of his kin.

All of the hurt around him, was of Henry's doing. He'd bought his war to the favela. Yet, from where he slumped, he could see the orfins rising up against the adults, fighting with all the strength and courage they could muster.

An electric glow crept toward Henry, until brilliant light engulfed him and a dome encased him safe from the outside world. Hepburn was with him and had encased him in his healing dome, built by what seemed like a million digital insects. Henry, unsure if he was dreaming, realized that this had happened before. Yet, the last time the robot had encased him in a healing dome, he'd been unconscious as it was happening.

The robot was dented and scratched. Its faceplate cracked on one side so a digital-smile leaked pixels into the real world as a shiny, metallic liquid.

"Hep…" Henry tried to speak, but he was enervated, breaking out in a cold sweat.

Mimicking the ricochet from when Dookie's bullet hit the tactical helmet, a sound echoed in the tent and a dent the size of a mouth appeared in the side of it. Hepburn regarded it, his expression puzzled, then annoyed. Another dent appeared a meter from the first.

"Bullets," the robot announced. Seemingly satisfied that the dome would hold, he continued his work. Henry cried out once more, the image of a broken Little L transfixed in his mind.

"You have a concussion, Henry. I'm administering a cocktail of medicines to help you to continue to fight," the robot inserted a line into Henry's skin, "and a shot of Aexacylin to bring sensation to your injured arm, minus some of the pain. I'm obliged to tell you this could cause long-term damage to your limb…"

Several more dents appeared. The dome remained intact.

"Pan?" Henry managed.

"It's all right, Henry. I'm your friend and I am looking after you." The robot smiled, even as more liquid sprayed out from its faceplate.

Another dent appeared on the side of the tent where Hepburn was operating, then another.

Sparks flew inside the tent as Henry's head-wound was sealed by a laser. The lightning ceased as quickly as it had begun and no mark of it remained on Henry's skin.

"It going to be fine. I'm just bringing you around now, Henry. You've done very well. You could say that I am quite proud of—"

Hepburn was unable to continue his commentary as a sudden boom shook the dome. Flames engulfed the air around them and the sky opened up above, letting the rain back in. Hepburn took the full force of the explosion and his final expression was one of dismay, that some of his own body parts were strewn across the square, beyond the dome that had sheltered them.

FORTY

## Falling Dominoes

The king, still in his wedding attire, hurried impatiently to the battlefield with a grenade launcher in his hands that had never been fired before. He bent to one knee, as if he was proposing, and he fired the rocket at the dome that had been erected over the boy who wanted to kill him more than any other in the Favela. He didn't care if he hit his own people. The boy was a nuisance who had somehow returned to challenge his very being, and he couldn't tolerate it.

The king was furious. He tried to recall how he'd instructed his guards to leave the boy. The boy, Henry, was never meant to survive. He'd taken his eye and they'd left him in a blizzard in his undergarments to freeze. Yet there he was; reborn. Fierce.

Never had the king been challenged in such a way. His rule over the people was robust and immaculate, his word distinct and final. Yet in front of him was an uprising. He saw Orfins lashing out and stabbing their elders, and elders challenging the well-armed peacekeepers loyal to the king. If ever he had imagined a worst-case scenario, this was it.

The grenade propelled backward in the direction of Moonbird, instead of in its intended direction. Had he cared it would have caused the king great embarrassment. The grenade hit the top deck of the palace in the backdrop of the battle and sent two guards hurtling in the air to their deaths off the far side of the cliff, pedaling their legs and flapping their arms as if to encourage unnatural flight. Lanner grimaced and the king swore at him and ordered him to kill anyone who defied him. The great usurpers.

The king spun the rocket launcher so it faced the correct way, reloaded it, aimed and fired at the dome. This time, the shell turned in the air and homed in on its target perfectly, striking the dome where several bullets had failed to penetrate. This time was different. One second the dome was there and then it was gone.

Flames licked the air, then diminished at the taste of rain. Bodies dropped, some voluntarily, others because the rocket had brought their death swiftly unto them. For brief seconds, it was impossible to tell which was which.

Lanner, for the first time, did what he was told and already stood within the smoke and the confusion, searching for Henry's body, to ensure he'd perished, or help him on his way before the gathered populace. The lesson needed to be learned, a second time.

The machine, some kind of relic from the time of the Great-Greats, was no more. It bled nickel gray and seeped a translucent gel substance onto the ice, which fizzed in the pools it created. The pieces of the robot were scattered amongst the human forms that lay at all angles. It sparked, but none of the pieces jolted to life. None of it re-assembled as it once was. It was like the cadavers and skeletons in the Bone Yard. Something that was no more.

It seemed like only Lanner was on his feet then, continuing the fight, because even those far from what had been the dome had ceased their battles, as if shell-shock had fallen across the square and the brutality of what the rocket had caused, such swift destruction, had taken the fight out of everyone. Full circle; once more, everything as futile as it ever was.

Then Lanner, the man in the patchwork cloak, a technicolor nightmare, found his prey lain down on the ice, beneath the torso of the machine. Henry was unarmed, but even then, Lanner didn't take the risk and loaded his shotgun.

Part of him admired Henry. He remembered the defiant looks Henry had sent him in the igloo his family had called home. He remembered feeling a pang of jealousy at the life that boy had, which was completely unlike his own childhood and certainly unlike everything he'd experienced as an adult. The way the boy had made him feel was the very reason Lanner needed to end him once and for all.

He saw Henry's eye; once ruined, but since replaced by something ancient he could not comprehend. He remembered stabbing the boy in a parting gesture, to speed up his demise. He had no time to wonder at all the things that had happened to Henry, or all the changes his body had been through, but there would be no parting gift this time for Henry. No wounding. Just something fatal and ultimate.

Lanner, without saying a word, without need for a final speech or farewell, readied his weapon for a headshot, to finish Dookie's work. To witness the uncasing of the boy. The dehumanizing of him.

The beast leaped from a rooftop into the fracas, primed for Lanner, maxillaries bared, as those around him moved out the way and created a path directly to the king's right-hand man.

Lanner moved closer to the boy, needing to see the ruin he was about to leave behind. His face wore a twisted grin, as Henry raised his head an inch from the ground and met his gaze.

Lanner was jubilant, "Stabbed you once. Now I get to blow your head off."

Lanner was the victor, already enjoying the moment. But the boy looked away from him. Not scared, or defiant. *Distracted.* Lanner went to follow his gaze, but he was languid, unsure how the scene was changing before him, not registering the shift that others had seen. Panicked, he squeezed the trigger of the shotgun, but Lanner was already tumbling, knocked off his feet by the snow leopard, taking all the wind out of his chest as he fell hard on the ice.

The cocktail of drugs that Hepburn had administered coursed through Henry's veins, doing all the things that Hepburn said they would and many things it hadn't. Fueled by his natural adrenaline and the added stimulants in his blood, Henry crashed back to life as if his heart had been restarted and his body had been given weeks to heal. He let out a scream to the heavens above with his arms outstretched.

He saw Lanner, then Panthera. Then Panthera on Lanner. Henry was unarmed, but he realized this was his final chance. Not satisfied with seeing Needol fall, or finding Skindred's corpse, or Dookie lying next to him, or Erasmus' death at his own hands. Henry was yards from Lanner and a little further from the king. Those were the scalps he wanted. No other prize would suffice.

Then, as his senses came back to him, his focus realigned and the ache in his damaged arm disappeared, he knew it was time for all the hours he had trained to come to fruition. The grand finale. Henry's final battle.

No shots rang out anywhere, although people held weapons still. The ammo was spent and all that was left were the adults versus Henry and the children who had come to his aid. He saw Felipe and Dibber. Q-Tip and Leaf. Cola and Yaxley.

Lanner was using his shotgun to keep Panthera away from his neck. It looked like he was lifting weights, bench-pressing a snow leopard. Henry rolled to his feet and whistled at Panthera, signaling the creature to fall back and leave Lanner be.

A muscular man stepped before Henry from the crowd, brave and unwittingly stupid. Months of Defendu, Sanshou, Taekwondo and Combat Sambo came back in an instant and Henry sent the man back into the crowd with a series of blows, with Panthera diving onto him to ensure he stayed down. A peacekeeper, standing close, unarmed and seemingly unwilling to attack Henry also hit the deck, beaten with ease by Henry's intricate skill.

Then to Lanner, who used his shotgun as a staff to get to his feet. He seemed amazed that Henry stood before him. There was something in his expression that Henry couldn't quite place, but later, he'd recognize that it was concession. Lanner knew his time was up.

And there were no words. No exchange. Henry descended upon him without remorse, absent mercy. Henry's assault on him was unceasing and swift. Henry bent to take up the war-lance he'd dropped and he parted it in the middle so he could wield it in both hands. Two weapons once more.

Lanner swayed. His teeth had been knocked loose and his nose bent to one side. His jaw hung at an angle and his hands, no longer holding the shotgun, dangled at his sides.

"Don't. Don't do me, boy," Lanner managed, his voice gargling on the blood in his mouth. The man in the patchwork clothes was never pitiable. But in that moment, he was sunk and lamentable and Henry was surprised by it. He'd expected much more from the demon clown. Curses, threats, tales to stall time. Anything to give him an opportunity to slit Henry's throat. Yet the man was base. A coward.

Henry crossed his blades, then, like a pair of scissors, parted them at Lanner's neck, freeing the man's head from his body. Lanner's head bounced and span until it came to a stop at Henry's feet. The clown was dead and nobody was laughing.

"For Mother," Henry whispered, then moved his attention to the king.

# FORTY-ONE

# A Fine Garment Made of Skin

The man in the knitted hat lay with Henry's knife protruding from his heart. Dookie, lying with her knees tucked up, looked like she'd found peace in death that she'd never achieved in life. Lanner had no head, and the crowd had ceased fighting and had fallen utterly silent.

Hepburn 8 had been obliterated, but Henry could not bring himself to think about it at that point.

Little L lay crumpled on the snow. Iris stood above him, sorrowful, yet unable to take her eyes from the dead child. His brother, Big L, had been knocked unconscious; his tears had ceased for a time, though they would return.

A sea of faces, what was left of the fighting Favela, surrounded Henry. Henry thought fleetingly of the shards of mirrored glass that turned in the igloo, with his family sleeping as the hours of the clock. Henry was the dial.

The king bellowed across the silent square. His white suit set him apart from everyone in the Favela. An alien in their midst, but one that had been revered for a long time and had pulled every string imaginable to stay in his position.

"*Olhe*. Has the little boy returned looking for his eyeball? He knows I ate it," the king mocked, then to Henry he added, "You know I ate it! You saw me do it."

"You know why I'm here." Henry was calm, unthreatening.

Matter-of-fact. He held his weapons as if he still meant business. He caught his breath in the interval created and tried to work out if he could finish the king from where he stood, before the crowd enveloped him. He knew nothing in battle was certain and anything could change in a single moment.

"I suppose I should congratulate you on not being dead. It's impressive. But damn your memory, lad. I recall telling you that should you return, I would make a fine garment for your sister out of your skin. The bitch will not get to wear it, but I suppose I should bury her in something new tomorrow."

Henry felt his pulse quicken. Had the king murdered one of his sisters? Had he been too late? Some of the peacekeepers in the crowd sniggered, but only Henry responded, his voice carrying across the space between them.

"I think it is yourn skin that will be parted from yourn flesh, and no other. Come and stand before me. Lanner's gone." Henry turned the blades in his hands so the king could see Lanner's blood upon them. "Now, I'll show your people what a king looks like. From the inside."

The King looked tempered. Henry suspected that no one had ever spoken to him the way Henry had before and so publicly. He knew that whatever response came from the king next, would be measured by his subjects.

The king addressed his people. "The first to bring me this boy's skull gets them and theirs a room in the palace for life and a free ride in the Favela. No work, no dues. Just sweet drams and ass. Or prong. Same deal for whoever brings me the creature with him."

Panthera bared his teeth at the king, as if the snow leopard understood the threat he'd made.

The square did not come alive. None moved. The king's words did not ignite the Favela against Henry. The crowd simply stayed as they were. Neutral. Nonchalant. Even the peacekeepers. Henry had expected claw hammers and wrenches, but the people were waiting. To see and hear more. To understand how the challenge would be dealt with by the king in person, without peacekeepers bullying everyone into submission. It was a story to be told evermore.

"You're a coward. You get everyone to do your work. But they hate you. All these people. It's just fear. You're nothing," Henry surmised.

"Kill that fucking boy!" the king commanded one and all, but still no one moved.

"Don't you sense it? How the mood has changed?" Henry said and for the first time, the king looked nervous. The crowd, no longer surrounding Henry, seemed to be with him.

The king looked at the faces of his people and must have seen their hatred, because now, so many of them, buoyant from Henry's fight and his challenge to the king, had unmasked it. Then Henry saw a real sign of weakness in the king... The man's own eyes, they too betrayed him and Henry realized the king could no longer meet the gaze of his own people.

"I command you to kill this—"

A single voice, pitched high above all others, rose and was carried by the wind. Morose, sad, beautiful. Iris, the Canary. The girl sang the first line of an old song that none would have heard in their lives.

Henry had not heard his sister sing in such a way before and felt the hairs on his arms and neck rise as she sang to the crowd and to the king. Her voice was effortless. Some notes she resonated. And it was beautiful.

She came forward, one step at a time, slowly. Still singing. All were enrapt. All were in awe of everything she was to them. The words, they were aimed at him now, the king, and they were defiant. Her dress blew in the wind so it seemed like she floated beside them. The song pierced all who listened to the melody and the king, manifesting his indignation in front of the populace, reacted in the only way he knew how.

"Child, you venture far from your cage! You dare? You die!"

Henry watched with dread, as the king grabbed a fire axee from the belt of one of his peacekeepers and before anyone could stop him, tossed it in the direction of Henry's youngest sister.

The blade missed. Iris, still singing and ever defiant, never flinched. It was all the catalyst the Favela needed at that point and the king became a target to all then. Surrounded by his people, angered, all open to betray him, for they no longer saw him as ruler and he was to be dethroned.

And it was Omeed, the obedient son, who made the first cut. Pushing a blade into the king's back, underneath his dinner jacket. The king spun and looked at Omeed with hurt in his eyes.

"Son?" he asked, disgraced and forlorn. But Omeed backed away and turned his back on the king, not fearful of retaliation.

Then Sissel came forward, her hair drenched in someone's blood. And she made a second cut, announcing to all that it was for Little L and then, looking at Henry, she added it was also for the boy, Martin.

The people of the Favela descended on their king like ravening shark catching a scent of his blood.

Henry moved forward, pushing others out of the way. The king, being spun into knives and cutters presented for him in the crowd, tumbled into Henry and he sent one of his blades deep into the king's stomach.

"For Father. For Mother. For Martin and Penhaligon. For all that you've ever done!" Henry spoke through gritted teeth to the fallen king.

Then he flung the king back into the crowd; a whirling dervish in a sodden red wedding suit. Folded and unfolded into the sea of people, who served justice upon him with a thousand cuts, each telling him who they were doing it for; whose memory they cherished and sought vengeance over. And there were so many names and so many cuts, long after the king's soul had left his body, yet the crowd each took their place to speak a name and partake in the end of the king's tale.

Henry, triumphant, could only fall to his knees finally. The emotion took hold of him. Panthera found him and nuzzled close, mewling in his embrace. Iris was there, yet they had no words in that moment. Hilde also appeared, but came no closer upon seeing her brother's scarred face and altered eye. She wasn't scared of him, but Henry could tell that she was disgusted. He'd imagined that same reaction so many times, that it didn't surprise him. Henry had no energy to call it out. To challenge his sister. He felt exhausted, like his mind had been so full up, that it had emptied itself.

The king was dead. It had been Henry's only purpose, and suddenly, it was over. He spoke it out loud. "The king's dead." He realized it had not been by his hands alone, and somehow, that made it all the greater. The people had done it. The adults and the children. The old and young.

Henry supposed it was more their right than his to end the reign of the tyrant. He could only imagine what living under the rule of the king would have been like for the people of the Favela and it was evident in the people around him; scars and broken bones that had never healed as they should have.

He saw the same triumph in the faces of those around him. And the same loss. Another, deeper wave of emotion came to him then. He thought of Mother and Father. The bairn and Martin. Hepburn 8...

Hepburn was motionless; a scattered wreckage of camouflage-covered ultranium and what had once been complex serpentine circuitry. There would be no bringing him back. No fixing him, like the robot had fixed Henry, twice.

Could he grieve for a machine like he could a human? Was it the same?

It was.

Hepburn was his friend. His only friend. The only solace he'd known in his darkest times. The only voice he'd heard in such a long time. Henry thought of watching the moodlift with Hepburn and of the robot questioning him every third week on how he was feeling.

Henry felt the loss in the pit of his stomach and the center of his heart, and he was utterly desolate.

And Henry heard himself repeating the same words, not knowing if it was the king or Hepburn he spoke of. No one knew, but it was all he could say for a time, over and over again.

*"He's dead."*

FORTY-TWO

# The Willow and the Wisp

The crowd mingled now, animated by the death of the king, each person trying to witness the truth of it and see the body for themselves. Much of him had already been severed. *Meat is meat.*

The wounded were tended to by those who knew anything of healing and by those who knew a little of being kind.

Henry and Iris remained in their embrace for some time and they became one in their sorrow.

"We did it. We killed him. We set them all free," Iris spoke, watching the populace collect itself and take stock. Henry pulled back from his sister and moved her hair out of her eyes as he often used to.

"I've missed you, Iris. More than you could ever imagine." Henry wiped his own eyes, then hers.

"And I you. Though you cut your hair, and..." Iris traced her fingers across the scar around her brother's eye socket. "You're odd enough already, but I can get used to this." She laughed, so unlike their sister Hilde in every way.

"I forget how I look most of the time. Used to it now. But you," Henry said, "your face. You've grown beautiful. You look a bit like Mother."

Iris smiled. "Feels strange to smile."

Hers was so genuine and natural. Henry knew it as the kind

of smile that comes from family. She squeezed her brother once more, as if to check that he was really there.

Sissel, limping slightly, came over to greet Henry. In her hands was the pelt of a Big White.

"Thought you'd want this back," she said, handing the fur to the altered boy, unable to take her eyes from the lens in Henry's eye socket.

"Thank you, Sissel," he said nervously, then to Iris, "you have this, Iris."

"I can't, Henry. It's yours by right."

"The cloth I wear is all mine. This fur will fit you well in time. Mother and Father would be so proud of your strength. What you did. Your song. You changed everything today." He cast the fur around his sister's tiny shoulders and let it rest there, proud. Henry turned to Sissel once more.

"Thank you, Sissel. The salvagers..." Henry began.

"I think we lost some. Bart and Keni. I can't see Bethlen." Sissel spoke softly in a changed voice, also exhausted. Henry could tell she too was fighting to keep her emotions at bay. To remain strong for her Orfins.

"I'm here. But Q-Tip. He's gone," the girl called Bethlen spoke up, but Henry did not take his eyes from Sissel.

*Q-Tip.* It had been Q-Tip and Florrie that had guided Henry through the cold waters to where Martin had lain in his cavern. Henry felt the weight of responsibility for the deaths and was truly saddened to hear of Q-Tip's passing.

"I'm so sorry. Last year, Q-Tip...he was with me, with Martin. If I hadn't..."

"You did and we did. And it was right. We did it right. No use crying. We owe it to them to make this day count. All of them. Adultos and Orfins. Sort this place and make it work for everyone." Sissel spoke like a true leader. Henry noticed the way the adults in the vicinity were watching her. Working out whether she had what it took to step in and lead in the absence of the fallen king. The children already knew she did.

"Q-Tip... He wouldn't have wanted it any other way. I know it. But it starts now. The real work."

Henry sensed Yaxley and Florrie arrive by his side.

"All them anteek weapons ain't no use now. Spent all the bullets. Guns all history," said Yaxley, pleased.

"That'll change the whole damned world," Florrie countered.

Henry noted how Sissel looked at Yaxley. Almost apologetic. It was linked to Henry somehow, and he understood when he saw how Yaxley looked upon her, for it was the same way that Henry did. He'd not seen it before. It hadn't been there by the sieve when he'd first met the salvagers. It had obviously bloomed after he'd been left for dead. And on her arm was a fresh decoration she'd cut, to match the symbol emblazoned on Yaxley's chest. A lover's gesture, that time would weather, but not erase from the skin.

It all became so clear. It was Henry's turn to feel embarrassed then. For he had spent so long imagining something between them, creating conversations, believing in scenarios and scenes and memories. None of it had been real, apart from his feelings.

Yaxley took hold of Sissel's hand and kissed her on the cheek. Henry saw that the kiss wasn't about marking his territory and warning Henry off. It was just a real thing. Something as natural as the smile Henry had extracted from Iris after so long.

He thought about it. Henry wasn't hurt. He wasn't upset. What could he do? He understood it, and as he looked at them, he was happy for them both. He knew they would have each other's back whatever lay ahead for them.

Yaxley greeted Henry. "Thought we'd never see you again. But look at you, amigo. You don't do being killed, do you?"

"Not yet. Got a big world out there to explore," Henry replied. He liked Yaxley a lot; perhaps they might become good friends, and both help Sissel in whatever she had planned, for they both had a love for her, even if she only ever saw part of it.

Some of the bodies were being dragged from the square to the Bone Yard. It was already changing. The clean-up. The new start. The rain had long stopped, but that in itself was something that would be talked about for some time. Rain. Not snow. *Rain*. That was something to take in; whether the Ever Winter had started to thaw, or if it was simply the gods that had tired of looking down on the all-white planet. *Hadn't Father warned of it in a dream?* They would find time to work out what it meant. To see if the frozen crust upon the sea was their future, or the landside.

Hilde, still in her wedding dress, had left the square and was hurrying back to the palace. Henry called after her, but she quickened her pace and scurried on, to the gangway of the Moonbird. He knew she'd heard him yell her name, but he was past caring.

"I don't know where to start," Iris said, regarding their sister.

"Thought she might say *hej*! Or curse me some," Henry said, feeling the tingling sensations come back to his damaged arm, the first sign of the pain that would follow.

"She's a cold fish. Ain't no changing her scales. She'll come around, even if it's to spit at you."

"At least I got you, little one," Henry said, happy for the first time in a long time.

The Favela felt strange to Henry. For the first time, he didn't fear it. He didn't see it as ugly. He looked at it like it was the first time he'd set foot in the place; a place with a minuscule dot of hope about it. Something to build on.

They wandered to where the wreckage of Hepburn lay scattered. Jagged pieces of ultranium protruded from the ice like tiny stalagmites. Henry recognized a faded flag on one of the camouflaged limbs and saw wires and tubes protruding that he'd never known were inside his robot friend. Hepburn's faceplate was shattered. Henry bent and picked it up, wiping debris from it with care.

"You were a good friend. The only one I ever had. I won't ever forget you and all you did," he said, before motioning to one of the orfins to hand him a sealskin. "You mind?" he asked, taking the bag and placing what was left of Hepburn's faceplate inside it.

"Can't bury him. Don't want to leave him in that Bone Yard, or under the ice. Going to keep him with me for a while," Henry explained to Iris, who had not left his side since they'd been reunited. The girl stroked Panthera, who'd seemed to instantly take a liking to her.

"I get that. You keep him forever if you want to. I have so many questions. About him. About you. Where you were."

Suddenly Henry jolted, realizing something was amiss. Something he'd overlooked entirely.

"Mary! Where's Mary, Iris? I didn't even think." Henry glanced at Moonbird, then scanned the faces of the milling crowd. He remembered something the king had said and the feeling Henry had that one of his sisters had been killed. His heart raced. He turned back to his youngest sister.

"Mary!" he called louder, but no one would make eye contact with him, like they were embarrassed or ashamed. Once more, Henry turned to Iris.

"Where is our sister, Iris?" Henry placed a hand on the side of her face and raised her chin gently so she looked into his eyes.

Iris opened her mouth, but no words came. Then, before she could reply, before she could offer any explanation or comfort, a voice spoke up from the place where the dome had been, amongst the remaining fragments and shards of Hepburn 8.

Henry's heart raced. He thought of the things Erasmus had said. His sister, telling the adults where the yot-boat was. Had she been talking about Mary? How had they got the information from her? He felt sick. He needed the answer, but he was also afraid to hear it. Mary had been his closest sibling in age. They had grown up together. Flashes of memories with his sister came flooding; running beside her chasing a seal, lying in the corridor of the container vessel after escaping the snow leopards. His earliest memories of her; Mary at four or five years old with her hair braided like mother's; chubby cheeks and a snotty nose. Games of backgammon. Nights in the igloo. Then the images were broken by the sound of a voice that wasn't Iris'.

"Mary's with the Red Man," Boo interjected, grinning his childish grin. The boy's belly hung over his trousers. He stood proud, clearly elated in how he looked and supposedly happier than all others.

"The Red Man? Who is he, Boo?" Henry asked. Boo nodded and clapped his hands.

"Mary's with the Red Man," the boy repeated.

Henry turned to Iris, but she remained quiet. "Sissel? Yaxley? The Red Man. Who is he?"

"Penhaligon. The Red Man's name is Penhaligon," spoke a man, wrapped in furs with his hood pulled low, shrouding his face in shadow, "and I am he."

A gasp resounded from those that stood nearby. Orfins and adults alike stopped clearing the debris.

Henry let the name sink in. *Penhaligon?* The fable! The one who had helped Mother and Father leave the remnants of the Great-Greats and start anew on the icescape with their unborn child. *Henry.*

Penhaligon was their benefactor, who Mother and Father had named their youngest child after, yet fear was evident on the faces of all those around him, and it was clear the people of the Favela saw him as something else. Henry noticed a few people making the sign of the cross. One man knelt and threw his arms in the air, then lay them on the ground before him.

The man wrapped in furs removed his hood, revealing a face that was a ruin of deep crags and boulders – a mountainous terrain. He appeared ancient. Older than anyone still living in the Favela. A miracle in himself.

Several of the adults readied their weapons once more. Some did the opposite and dropped theirs.

"I'm a gifted, wonderful horror, but you are quite safe," the man said to the nearest group of people that had backed away from him. They looked at each other in shared confusion and maintained their distance.

The un-god stood aside then and made way for Mary, who had been standing there all along, a wisp in his shadow, unrecognizable with so much mire and grime ensconcing her once-pale skin.

Mary cast her arms wide to show she was unharmed and that she was no apparition.

Henry beamed with relief, as he had been certain for those brief seconds that something had befallen his sister. It was Iris who bounded forward and threw her arms around her, planting a kiss firmly on her cheek.

"You're alive! We thought… the king told us you were…" Iris clung onto Mary and Mary wrapped her arms around her youngest sister tightly, locking the embrace.

Penhaligon, the un-god, looked on. The old man grinned mischievously and winked at Sissel and Yaxley, who looked at each other. Neither of them seemed to have any idea what to do, or say.

"I live and I'm well," Mary replied. "Iris, I am sorry that I left you. Not *then*. I mean, when I left you before. I was broken and I hid. In my mind somewhere. I just wanted to be safe and I did nothing for you. I…"

Henry had joined the embrace and the three siblings held on to each other. He felt sure Hilde would be watching from a distance somewhere in her wedding dress.

Mary studied the lens where Henry's eye had been. She embraced her brother tighter then.

Henry could only smile, finding himself present in a moment that he had dreamed of. It was no premonition. He had, with the help of Hepburn 8, healed his mental wounds, trained for battle, planned his revenge and made all that followed come true. The reunion, the happening, was the sweetest of moments.

Mary would not let the un-god disappear and beckoned him to step forward, taking his hand in hers.

"His tale is so sad and he has done great, kind things. He argued, but I could not leave him alone in the volcano. He can teach us so much, Henry," Mary said, then repeated it for all to hear. "He can teach us and he has shelter for anyone who doesn't want to stay out here in this hell. Don't be afraid of him! He is the best of us all!"

As Mary spoke, Henry thought of the choices he had to make, which only he knew of. A pivotal moment, where his future and the future of all others could go in one of two directions. A scratch to be made in history. Such promise of a brave, new world. Could he be anchored to the Favela, or would he forever roam the lands and frozen seas until he found the place where trees grew?

Henry studied Iris, then Mary. Penhaligon, then Boo. He soaked those images in, weighing up his options for the future. Which was the greatest choice he could make? The right choice?

Then he looked over at Sissel and Yaxley, who stood with an arm around each other. Henry knew instinctively that Sissel would make things right for the populace and do good by the people. They would survive.

Should Henry do as Hepburn had envisaged and find the other remnants of humans in the world, or just rebuild the Favela as it should've been?

Silently, Henry knew the path he would take, but there was no rush for it. He would not stay in the place responsible for so much pain in his life. He would let his sisters, the orfins and Penhaligon shape a new augmentation of the Favela, casting the darkness out and bringing in the light. He would not stand in their way, or counsel, but he would take them to the MV Greyhound and let them take all that would help them start over. The world was a vast mystery and Hepburn had shown him how minuscule the homestead and the Favela had been in comparison to everything else that waited to be uncovered and seen.

Somewhere, there were other ancestors of the Great-Greats, rebuilding pyramids near other volcanos, under the shade of trees that grew. Elsewhere, across the frozen ocean, there would be more. And Henry would find them.

Henry embraced his sisters again, to reaffirm that all was real. *Strength. Vigor.* He saw that they weren't children anymore. Looking around at the orfin salvagers that stood amongst them, he realized that his sisters didn't need him for protection, or guidance. They were astonishing and stalwart. Stayers. Leaders.

After all that had ensued, after the hideous tragedy and crushing grief that had befallen all of them, Henry knew that life could still be made beautiful again.

Martin and Hepburn had taught him that.

**THE END.**

# Acknowledgments

My brilliant, eccentric grandmother, encouraged me to write from a young age and fueled my creativity with trips to London and afternoons watching classic films. Big nan; cockney legend.

Endless thanks to my mother, Alison, who dragged me up on her own and has a knack for remembering only the good things I did, as if no windows were ever broken.

With thanks to my author friends - the instigators - Taran Matharu (who played an important role in beating this book out of me), Stephen Landry and Jason Kucharik; three amazing, genuine guys that are passionate about what they do and truly care about their craft. Onward and upward for each of you... *Bebopalula!*

Others whom I have wearied with book talk *(in order of perceived ennui)*:

Rob Ramage, Louise Ramage, Ben Backhouse, Jen Backhouse, Neil Boyle, Julie Boyle, Declan Rate, John Tarrow, Tom Purser, Liam Ash, Dean Ford, Tony Lewis, James Gallop, Paul Muscroft, Gary Nevill and Mia Ronneberg... *Damn!*

Finally, thank you to you, for reading Ever Winter. Whoever you are!

To become a full-time writer, I need your support. Glowing reviews and votes on Amazon in particular make all the difference to a writer, so please do spread the word if you liked this book and feel free to connect with me on social media if you have any questions about this, or other works.

Printed in Great Britain
by Amazon